THE SAMHANACH AND OTHER HALLOWEEN TREATS

STORIES BY
LISA MORTON

TREPIDATIO
PUBLISHING

PRAISE FOR LISA MORTON

"Morton has disinterred centuries-old folklore to breathe life into a little-known Halloween monster. *The Samhanach* goes right to the crux of our deepest fears—the abduction of our children—and pits the power of family against the terror of a shapeshifting killer bent on revenge. Deeply and darkly disturbing."
—Lesley Bannatyne, author of *Halloween: An American Holiday, an American History* and *Halloween Nation*

"Lisa has really come into her own as a writer and is in my opinion one of the best writers in dark fiction today. With *Hell Manor* she gives us a tale where she draws upon her vast knowledge of Halloween...and what a tale it is. If you have ever gone to a haunted house attraction on Halloween, and who hasn't, you will absolutely love this story."
—Peter Schwotzer, *Famous Monsters*

"In *Summer's End*, Lisa Morton has created something so strikingly unique that it stands alone in the genre. All writers pull their work from inside themselves, but Morton has literally put herself inside the work, and she has pulled it off so beautifully, so seamlessly, that it does not read like fiction—it reads like an account of actual events. Her extensive knowledge of her subject and her impeccable skills as a writer and storyteller are combined in a wicked and delightful potion that gave me *real* goosebumps,

real chills, and reminded me that horror fiction can and *should* frighten the hell out of the reader. *Summer's End* is a thin volume, but it is a formidable achievement. I'll never look at a jack-o'-lantern the same way again."
—Ray Garton, author of *Live Girls* and *Meds*

"...ambitious marriage of postmodernism and horror...occasionally poetic...terse encounters with malignant spirits evoke chills, as does the atmospheric presence of Samhain."
—*Publisher's Weekly*

"The Devil Came to Mamie's on Hallowe'en"
—Honorable Mention, Ellen Datlow, *The Year's Best Fantasy and Horror*

"Pumpkin Rex" © 2012, first appeared online at *Literary Mayhem*

"The Devil Came to Mamie's on Hallowe'en" © 2009, first appeared in *Cemetery Dance Magazine* #60

"The Samhanach" © 2010, originally published by Bad Moon Books

"Finding Ulalume" © 2015, first appeared in the anthology *nEvermore!*

"Alive-Oh" © 2013, first appeared in *The Horror Zine*

"Summer's End" © 2013, originally published by JournalStone

"Tam Lane" © 2014, first appeared in the anthology *Out of Tune*

"The Halloween Collector" © 2014, first appeared online at *Halloween Forevermore*

"The Devil's Birthday" © 2014, originally published by Bad Moon Books

"The Legend of Halloween Jack" © 2012, first appeared online at *Cemetery Dance*

"Sexy Pirate Girl" © 2014, first appeared in the anthology *October Dreams 2*

"Hell Manor" © 2012, originally published by Bad Moon Books

"The Maze" © 2015, first appeared in the anthology *Dark Hallows*

"The Enchanted Forest" © 2016, first appeared in the anthology *Dark Hallows II*

Trepidatio books may be ordered through booksellers or by contacting:

Trepidatio Publishing, an imprint of JournalStone

www.trepidatio.com

www.journalstone.com

ISBN: 978-1-947654-06-8 (sc)
ISBN: 978-1-947654-07-5 (ebook)

Trepidatio Publishing rev. date: October 20, 2017

Library of Congress Control Number: 2017956885

Printed in the United States of America

Cover Design: CirceCorp Design—Carolina Fiandri www.circecorpdesign.com
Edited by: Jess Landry

THE SAMHANACH AND OTHER HALLOWEEN TREATS

CONTENTS

TRICK OR TREATING WITH LISA MORTON

BY
NANCY HOLDER

You are about to read my friend Lisa Morton's bag of treats, flavored with that special taste of Halloween— thrills and chills of various sizes and shapes, the sweet taste of fear that will linger in your mind long after you finish this collection. Lisa wasn't always the official Queen of Halloween, but in all the years (decades?) that I've known her, she's been reigning royalty when it came to mesmerizing tales of horror and the supernatural. Lisa has absorbed the Matter of Horror through her skin, and the breadth and depth of her knowledge has allowed her to boldly (accent on boldly) go down new streets that I, as a fellow horror writer, have not gone before. Through the years I've read her wherever I could find her, but I've been aware that I've missed a lot of her work. I'm so glad that *The Samhanach and Other Hallow-een Treats* helps fill the gap on the Lisa Morton shelf of my office bookcase.

A bit of Lisa's history: She assumed the presidency of the Horror Writers Association after the untimely death of Rocky Wood, and as I feared, her output diminished—but only for a short time. Lisa's back and her work is stronger than ever, as this collection will attest. Her quirky, offbeat

11

perspective on the world—so evident in her first produced screenplay, the whacked-out *Meet the Hollowheads*—gleams like a jack-o'-lantern on every page. Her artistry as a writer—earning multiple Bram Stoker and Black Quill awards and nominations—blazes.

A bit of Hallowe'en history: By sampling these tales, you will find yourself something of a connoisseur of Samhain yourself, as Lisa offers a delectable array of lessons on the origins, developments, and departures of the beliefs and customs of All Hallows' Eve, ranging from propitiating gods to divination to apocalypse. This is an unpredictable box of chocolates all dedicated to the facets and nuances of Lisa's favorite day—which she celebrates 365 days a year.

A special treat that Lisa brings to the horror genre is a screenwriter's attention to structure. Renowned horror editor Ellen Datlow has stated repeatedly that what short horror fiction often lacks is a good ending (or an ending at all). Not so with stories by Lisa. The stories in this yummy sack of mind candy are built on intriguing openings, surprising twists and turns, and endings that shock and surprise—"Pumpkin Rex," "The Legend of Hallowe'en Jack," and *Hell Manor* come to mind.

They also empower. In "The Devil Came to Mamie's on Hallowe'en," a deal with the Devil takes a surprising and refreshing turn. In *The Samhanach*, Merran, the main character, is every bit as heroic as the mother in *Poltergeist*, as is Lisa Morton herself, in the brilliantly metatextual (fully annotated!) masterpiece, *Summer's End*.

But make no mistake. Even though these stories all feature Hallowe'en, they are as distinct from each other as black sesame gelato and black licorice, Red Hots, Red Vines, and chocolate covered cherries. From a retelling of "Tam Lane" to the Poe homage "Finding Ulalume," these tales span forms and formats, tones, and perspectives. The vicious edginess of "Sexy Pirate Girl" gives way to the kind nostalgia of "The Enchanted Forest"; the Fowlesian weirdness of "The Halloween Collector" to the slasher's delight of "The Maze."

Now it is your turn to chew on these tasty morsels of fear, delight, horror, and optimism. These treats are now all yours to unwrap and devour. In the words of *The Devil's Birthday*, you are about "to join the best Halloween party imaginable." I envy you that fateful first bite. These treats are to die for.

Nancy Holder
Seattle, Washington
August 4, 2017

PUMPKIN REX

Devin clutched the jack-o'-lantern mask in his lap as he looked out the car windows at the urban wastescape. "Is this part of town even safe?"

Maxx glanced at him from behind the driver's wheel. "Dude, it's Halloween. It's not supposed to be completely safe."

"I know, but...well, are you sure you're going the right way? These buildings all look...dead."

Devin couldn't think of any other word to describe the rundown warehouses and factories they'd passed for at least four blocks now. He was starting to wish he'd just stayed home; at fifteen, he might have been too old to trick or treat, but he could have found a party, or just watched horror movies. But he'd let Maxx talk him into his first rave ("C'mon, it's all ages, *and* it's Halloween, so you gotta love it"), and since Maxx was sixteen and could drive already, they wouldn't need a chaperone.

Maybe Devin would even meet a girl. That'd been part of Maxx's pitch.

Devin looked down at his mask and thought at least this Halloween wouldn't be a total waste. He'd saved up his allowance all summer for the mask, which was a full over-the-head, hand-painted beauty complete with light-up eyes. Halloween was

Devin's favorite day of the year, and this mask—called "Pumpkin Rex"—had a traditional, iconic look that pleased him. Devin was a Halloween fanatic—he'd read all the history websites and studied all the lore. To him, the carved pumpkin would always be the king of Halloween. He'd had the mask for a month now, sitting perched on a shelf in his bedroom, just waiting for this one night. He'd even bought a secondhand tuxedo jacket from a thrift store and a bright orange bowtie. Tonight *he* would be the King of Halloween.

Maxx, on the other hand...zombie Elvis? Devin had to admit it was a good costume—Maxx even got Elvis's little hair curl down—but everybody dressed as a zombie these days.

As if on cue, Devin spotted a pair of the undead staggering down the street ahead of them. For a moment, given the dilapidated buildings, it looked startlingly like a scene from a post-apocalyptic zombie movie...then the illusion was shattered when one of them gave the other a playful shove.

"See? We gotta be almost there." Maxx gestured at the zombies as they passed, turned a corner, and sure enough—there was a line of cars waiting to enter a parking lot. A block down, lights flashed from one of the larger buildings, and now Devin could hear a throbbing bass beat rumbling through the October night like the pulse of some ancient god.

Fifteen minutes later they'd parked, Devin had pulled his mask on, they'd bought their tickets, been searched, and entered the "First Annual All Ages Halloween Masquerave." Just inside they stopped, staring: Before them was a world of colored strobe lights, hundreds of dancers gyrating to techno music, and a DJ dressed as the Grim Reaper.

"Okay, now tell me this isn't awesome," Maxx shouted, elbowing him.

"It's all right. Sure are a lot of zombies here, though." Devin couldn't resist the dig; besides, it was true. Half of the male attendees were zombies, wearing tattered clothing, pale makeup, and gallons of fake blood; the rest were vampires, cowboys, soldiers, and various celebrities. Devin was pleased to note only one other jack-o'-lantern, a cheap plastic face mask surmounting a t-shirt and jeans. Most of the women were dressed as sexy princesses, sexy fairies, sexy pirates, sexy cartoon characters...Devin felt like he was looking at one of his older sister's Victoria's Secret catalogs. The energy in the room was a palpable thing, impacting all of Devin's senses in a way that threatened to overwhelm him.

Maxx tapped his arm. "C'mon." He began moving through the crowd ringing the dance floor; Devin followed, threading his way among the tightly-packed wallflowers. He passed a twenty-something man buying and then swallowing a pill, and he felt a thrill of rebellion. *Wow, people are just taking drugs right out in the open!*

They reached the lines for a bar, where they overpaid for Cokes. Then Maxx led the way to an empty spot near a wall.

"This is great, right?" Maxx had to lean over and yell in Devin's ear to be heard.

Devin nodded, surveying the throng. Over half of the people around them wore glow bracelets or necklaces, standing out in the darkened space like thousands of jumping phosphorescent animals. The drums rumbled through Devin's chest, and his body vibrated in synch. There was something spiritual about the sensation, as if they were part of some vast ritual on the most magical night of the year.

The DJ came to a song with nothing but a rhythm line, which he spoke over. "Three hours out now from midnight, when barriers fall and worlds collide, when transformation happens and we *become*. After a thousand years, are you ready?"

The dancers shouted approval, pumping fists into the air as a synth melody kicked in. Devin, though, was thinking about the DJ's words: *When transformation happens? A thousand years?*

"That was some weird shit," he shouted at Maxx.

Maxx shrugged. "These DJs love to spout this stuff that sounds like some freaky book or something."

Devin continued to watch the DJ, who looked up from his turntables for a second—and Devin had the uncanny sensation that the Grim Reaper was staring at him. As he watched, the DJ extended an arm, pointing, and Devin couldn't help but think the man was pointing at *him*. That wasn't possible; there was no way a DJ on a stage at least a hundred feet away had picked him out of a dark crowd, even with the light-up eyes in his mask. Finally the DJ lowered his arm, executed a bow, and returned to spinning records.

Devin shivered under his tuxedo jacket.

"Hey, are you listening? I said, check those babes out."

Devin shrugged off the chill before following Maxx's gaze to see a circle of three teenage girls standing away from the dance floor, giggling together. One was dressed as a 1960s go-go dancer, with short skirt and tall boots; another was over-spilling a skimpy genie outfit. The third, however, was the only female Devin had seen tonight who was covered head to toe: She wore a witch costume complete with tall black hat, cape, and even a puppet black cat cradled in one arm.

He knew instantly he had to talk to her. He just had no idea how to go about it.

"Okay," Maxx said, running a hand through his slicked hair and giving his jacket a little shake, "I dream of genie. Wish me luck."

Devin laughed, but watched carefully as Maxx approached the trio.

He stopped before them, struck an Elvis pose, and then did a passable hip-thrust. Two of the girls laughed. The witch rolled her eyes.

Devin liked her more by the second.

The girls conversed with Maxx, who finally looked back and waved Devin over. He came forward, suddenly realizing he'd never been this nervous on Halloween before. When he reached them, Maxx threw out a hand. "This is my friend Devin." He was even affecting Elvis's accent.

The go-go dancer frowned at Devin. "What's with the mask? Is he like deformed under there or something?" The genie snickered in embarrassment and made a half-hearted attempt to shush her friend.

"I think that mask rocks," said the witch.

Maxx exchanged more meaningless words with the genie and the go-go girl, but Devin wasn't listening. He was looking at the witch, who was unexpectedly pretty under her green greasepaint and black wig. Finally Maxx gestured at the bar. "I'm going to buy these lovely ladies something wet. We'll be right back."

Devin barely acknowledged as Maxx and the other two girls left.

"Hi, I'm Kara," the witch said, and then, as the cat puppet bowed, added, "and this is Belial."

"Hello, Kara and Belial—Devin. And I'm not deformed under here."

"I didn't think you were. I love the way the eyes light up on the mask."

"Me, too. Do you…want to dance?"

Kara shrugged. "Belial and I don't really dance." The cat made a funny little attempt at dancing and then sagged in disappointment.

Devin laughed. "I don't, either. Pretty dumb that we both ended up at a rave, isn't it?"

She nodded, said, "But maybe we could just go talk…?"

Devin felt 50,000 volts of happiness flare within him. "Uh… yeah. That'd be great. What about your friends?"

"What about yours?"

He looked behind him, but couldn't find Maxx and the girls in the dark and the bouncing crowd. He had his phone, though, and knew Maxx wouldn't leave without him.

"This way." Kara was tugging at his tuxedo; he let her lead the way through the crowd to a side room, where the noise levels were considerably lessened and conversations were happening. Conversations, and couples kissing. Kissing passionately. As he felt heat rise to his face, Devin was glad Kara couldn't see under the mask.

They found a quiet corner, where Devin took off the mask. Kara eyed his face, smiling. "No, you're not deformed."

He cursed himself for blushing again, and tried to stammer out a response when his breath caught in his throat:

The Grim Reaper stood behind Kara, watching them.

"Is that the DJ?"

Kara turned to follow his gaze. "Yeah. I recognize that skull mask. It's pretty good."

"If he's in here…who's running the music?"

Kara shrugged. "They usually have more than one DJ at these things."

Devin tried to look back at Kara, continuing the conversation as if he wasn't in a dark corner of a decrepit factory being stared at by a man dressed as Death. "Oh. So do you…you know, go to a lot of raves?"

"Not really. This is only my second one."

The attempt at casual conversation wasn't working. "Give me a minute here."

Kara watched as Devin walked to the costumed Reaper, who showed no response at his approach. "Hey," Devin said, realizing he had no idea how to handle this situation. "Do…um…I know you? I mean, I just wondered why you've been staring at us."

When the man spoke, Devin recognized the same smooth, modulated tones he'd heard over the song. "A thousand years have built to tonight."

Devin thought back over everything he knew about Halloween, but he couldn't think of anything important from the year 1017. "Why is that?"

The Reaper leaned in closer, his voice still low but bristling with excitement. "In 1017, in a small Irish village near Teamhair, where the Celts had once celebrated Samhain, the first real Halloween celebration took place. A group of peasants, overworked and exhausted from bringing in the harvest, decided to combine the new holiday of All Souls' Day with All Saints' Day and their ancient, beloved Samhain, and they drank and told fortunes and stirred up such furious energies that they invoked spirits. Certain forces were set in motion that night."

"How do you know that? I mean, I know a *lot* about Halloween, but I've never read that one."

The Reaper mask bobbed in amusement. "There's more to history than just books."

"So…what happens at midnight? You said something about 'transformation'?"

The Reaper nodded. "You'll find out. The energy is right, a thousand years have passed, and the time has almost come."

Another chill passed through Devin. "The time for what?"

The Reaper's grin widened, and Devin thought, *How did he do that? That's just a mask.* "The time for Halloween to take its dominion, for it to become more than one night a year of costumed play. Just a few minutes left now."

Devin shook his head. "No, it's just a little after nine—" He pulled out his phone, lit up the time—

And saw it was five minutes until twelve.

"But that's…this can't be right, it's…"

He looked up, puzzled—but the DJ was gone.

Devin's head started to spin. He tried to turn, to find Kara, and he nearly lost his balance. She was there, though, supporting him, guiding him to an old wooden bench against one wall. "Hey, whoa there…"

Devin's whole head felt large and light, as if he were a balloon filled with too much helium. He wondered if he'd been drugged; maybe Maxx had slipped him something with the Coke. Or Kara—what if she was a real witch and had cast a spell or something? No, that was ridiculous. He shook his head, trying to clear it.

"Should I get help?" She was leaning over him, concerned.

His vision cleared somewhat, and Kara's nearness centered him again. In fact, he was starting to feel good now. Not just good, but ecstatic.

"I'm okay," he said. "Did you know it's almost midnight?"

She smiled. "The witching hour." The puppet black cat, Belial, wiggled in her arms. Devin didn't even care that he could see both her hands, that he knew she hadn't done that.

Devin realized he still held his mask in one hand; he didn't want midnight on Halloween to come while he was bare-faced, so he tugged it back on. Out in the main room, he heard the DJ intoning over low music, "We've created and channeled the necessary amount of energy tonight, and certain forces have been invoked. Thirty seconds to lift-off, everyone. Say goodbye to your old life and hello to a new world."

From somewhere, some carefully protected part of himself—call it his conscious, his *soul*—Devin heard silent shrieks, a voice telling him something was wrong, to go NOW, to run, get to the exit and then keep going, regardless of Maxx or his ride or the neighborhood (which would be safer than HERE)...but he looked at Kara, and he knew he'd stay, because she was where he wanted to be now.

So he listened to the seconds called out: "...SEVENTEEN... SIXTEEN...FIFTEEN..." With each passing number he felt new, newer. When Kara reached for his hand, he knew she felt it, too, that whatever the transformation would be in ten, nine, eight more seconds, they'd go through it together.

"...THREE...TWO...ONE..."

Devin's consciousness flared, a mental nova. When his vision returned it took him a few minutes to realize what it was: He felt bigger, more confident—and he was no longer looking out through eye holes.

But...

Beside him stood a witch—no, stood *the* witch, the most perfect

Halloween icon he'd ever seen. Her skin was pale green, her eyes glowed with some inward crimson light, and the cat that leapt from her arms and circled her feet was black as pitch and lively as the Devil.

He heard screaming then—dozens, hundreds of screams—and other sounds, too: Moaning. Wailing. *Chomping*. He strode forward, briefly surprised by the length of his stride—he crossed yards with each step.

He saw pandemonium: Zombies—no longer boys in make-up, but real revenants, with glassy eyes and clawed fingers—were tearing apart the princesses and fairies. They ripped limbs off and raised them to dried, hungry mouths; they shoved through the crowd to reach for more flesh. Shredded glow necklaces spilled phosphorescent liquid to the floor like the ichor of a slain angel. Soldiers and cops fired guns randomly into the crowd, more often than not hitting each other; vampires soared overhead and lunged for ballerinas, while werewolves tore into politicians and movie stars. Near the bar, zombie Elvis feasted on a severed foot still clad in a blue suede shoe.

He drank in the tableau, feeling neither horror nor panic, but instead...a *naturalness*. This was *right*. This was what he was meant for.

On the stage at the front of the room stood the Grim Reaper, motioning him up.

He glanced at the witch, who cackled in glee; together, they walked to the stage and ascended. The Reaper bowed to them, and then gestured to the mad scene below.

"Behold your Halloween kingdom, come to pass at last," he said, in his mellifluous voice, then added, "Pumpkin Rex."

The King was dimly aware that he'd once had another name, but that no longer mattered. He'd arrived at last, to rule over his realm with his witch-queen at his side. Starting from tonight, time would be obsolete and useless; it would always be midnight on Halloween, and the world would always belong to the October creatures.

The King smiled down benignly. The trick was his treat, and it was good.

THE DEVIL CAME TO MAMIE'S ON HALLOWE'EN

It was Hallowe'en night, and business was slow at the whore-house.

Leona didn't put much stock in the stories that kept other folk indoors on this night. She'd laughed over stories about Jacky-Ma-Lantern, who'd once outsmarted the Bad Man and then couldn't get into Hell or Heaven, and so on Hallowe'en he wandered around lighting his way with a coal kept in a pumpkin. She'd once seen the strange blue lights in the bayou that some said led unwary travelers to their doom on this night, but she didn't really believe they were spirits. And her favorite of Miss Mamie's girls, Lizzie, had talked about going down to New Orleans once and meeting up with a real hoodoo man, who she'd watched bring a dead boy back to life on All Saints' Day. But as much as Leona loved Lizzie, she thought even decent, smart folk could sometimes be bamboozled when they found something they just plain *wanted* to believe in.

It was about midnight now ("the witching hour," Leona remembered Lizzie once calling it), and the swamp behind Miss Mamie's was dark and quiet, no flatboats poling up to the dock tonight, unloading new customers. Leona wondered again where Lizzie had gotten to; Beulah, the cook, said she'd left out the backdoor about four that afternoon, just as the sun was going down. She'd taken a big kettle with her, and said she'd be back around night. It wasn't safe to wander around the bayou any night, and Leona couldn't imagine where Lizzie had gone.

It didn't help that Mamie's scrawny old cat, Lumpy (so named because he was as black as a lump of coal), was missing, too.

So Leona sat on the back porch, waiting, hoping one or the other would show up soon. Beulah had already gone home, and the kitchen was cool but the night was unseasonably warm and humid. Usually she'd have to be in the main parlor, playing the piano for the customers, but there weren't many of them tonight.

Leona cranked the phonograph again, and settled back on the old splintered wood of the porch steps to listen to Ma Rainey. Harold, Miss Mamie's bartender and muscle, had been into town today, and Leona had given him seventy-five cents to get the record for her. It was "Traveling Blues," and Leona swayed back and forth, humming along, as the song spilled out of the phonograph's big horn.

I went to the depot, looked up and down the board,
I went to the depot, looked up and down the board,
I asked the ticket agent, "It's my time on this road?"

Leona had listened to the song enough now that she'd be able to play it on the piano when she went back in; if anyone wanted to hear, she could sing it, too.

Fact was, she thought she could sing it just as good as Ma Rainey herself.

One of the funny things about Miss Mamie was that she only wanted live music at her "establishment"; she claimed the menfolk didn't want to hear just records, although Leona knew plenty of menfolk who liked Bessie Smith and Ma Rainey and Sippie Wallace. Miss Mamie, though, said she'd paid plenty of money for that piano, and live music gave her place "a touch of class." Truthfully, Leona was glad, because it gave her a way to make herself useful around Mamie's place—she had a natural gift for the piano and for singing.

Unfortunately, even those gifts wouldn't carry her much longer.

Miss Mamie had come into the kitchen yesterday afternoon, before most of the other women had even gotten up yet, and she'd called Leona away from the washing and sat her down at the table. Mamie'd just gotten back from doing some banking in town, and she was dressed up, looking fine for a woman of forty. It was no wonder she still got customers requesting her services.

"That Jackson Smith done asked about you again last night," she'd said, while lighting a cigarette.

Leona had tried not to squirm. "That so?"

"Um-hmm." Miss Mamie took a drag from her smoke, then went on. "He'd pay extra for you, Leona, since it'd be your first time. We'd both make some mighty nice money off'n it."

"I'm not doin' nothin' with Jackson Smith," Leona had replied.

"He's not so bad," Mamie said, squinting at Leona through her tobacco haze.

"I know he's not, Miss Mamie, but I..."

At that point Mamie had actually set the cigarette down and leaned across the table, and Leona'd had to struggle not to lean back, away. "Now you listen to me, child: You sixteen years old, you a woman now. I promised your mama, God bless her, to look after you till you was growed. She was one of the finest ladies I ever had work for me, and I owed her, but I figure the time you growed is *now*. I can't keep carryin' you, Leona—"

Leona had cut her off. "But Miss Mamie, you your own self said I was the best piano player you's ever likely to hear—"

"I did, but, honey, we need somebody to play something livelier here, not those slow things you like. You put a few drinks in these boys and give 'em that slow music, and they likely to just fall asleep before we can even get 'em upstairs with a girl. Don't nobody make no money then."

Leona looked down, hurt. "That slow music's the blues, Miss Mamie. I thought the men liked it."

Mamie reached out and stroked Leona's wrist. "They do, honey, but it's not good for business. Now, I could get me somebody from town to play the piano, play them nice fast tunes; might not be so good as you, but I wouldn't have to give 'em room and board, neither."

Leona had felt a cold chill settle into her then. She'd known for a time this was coming, but she'd hoped she might have a little longer. Just long enough to save for a ticket to Chicago or Atlanta and a couple of months of room and board while she tried to get a job singing, maybe even make a record of her own...

Miss Mamie had taken a last pull off her cigarette, then stubbed it out in a china plate. "I love you like my own, Leona, you know that; I done raised you since before you could put two words together. But you need to be makin' a decision: Either you stay here and take up The Life, or you move on."

Miss Mamie had gotten up then and left.

Beulah, the cook, had worked over the stove in the corner, listening quietly. She was a kind woman who came out here, to the edge of the bayou, every day to work for Miss Mamie. She'd never minded that Leona slept in the kitchen, and kept her phonograph there; she liked the music, too, and she liked Leona.

She'd waited until Mamie had gone, then she'd come over to where Leona sat, wiping furiously at her tears. "Don't cry, honey," she'd said, in her soft, sweet voice. "You can sing just as good as any of 'em, just as good as Ma or Bessie or Victoria Spivey. You don't need this place."

Leona had looked up at Beulah gratefully. "You think so?"

"I know so," Beulah had said, giving her a hug that smelled like warm cornbread. "The only men you need to make money is the kind that'll let you sing, and you'll make a lot more money than you'd make here. You believe that."

Leona wished she could.

She tried to imagine herself saying yes, going into one of the upstairs bedrooms with Jackson Smith, who would be sweaty and smell like machine oil and liquor, and feeling his rough hands on her skin. She tried to imagine doing that every night, five or ten times a night, until she was too old and none of the men wanted her.

Leona felt something hot on her cheek, and realized she was crying again. She brushed the tears away, angry at herself. It was a simple decision.

Stay or go.

Sing the blues…or live them.

The song finished, and Leona lifted the needle off the record. She was about to play it again when she heard something out in the brush, near the edge of the swamp.

"Lumpy?" she called out, hoping to see the mangy old cat scamper up.

Instead, she spotted a light bobbing among the trees, nearing. A few seconds later the lantern rounded a big mangrove, and Leona saw it was—

"Lizzie!"

She started to smile and was about to dart forward, when she saw Lizzie stop about thirty feet away.

"That you, Leona?"

Even from this distance, Leona could see her pale smock—usually spotless—was spotty and stained, and the night breeze took on a terrible scent, something spoke of death and terror, as it passed over Lizzie.

"It's me, Lizzie. Is somethin' wrong—?"

Lizzie took a few more steps forward. "Anybody else out here?"

Leona shook her head. "No'm, just us."

"Good."

Lizzie reached her now, and Leona gasped. The older woman was covered in bloodstains, and there were long scratch marks on her hands and arms, marks that were just barely scabbed over. Her left hand was also burned, and Leona saw pink flesh and white blisters.

And the smell nearly made Leona gag.

"What that smell, Lizzie?"

"Leona, sugar, can you do me a favor? Bring some warm water, a towel, some new clothes. I can't let nobody else see me like this. Can you do that for me?"

Leona couldn't stop staring. "Should I get the doctor?"

"No, that's…that's not my blood. It's Lumpy's."

Leona placed that awful odor now: She'd smelled it once when Lumpy had lost part of an ear in a fight with a raccoon, and he'd somehow covered himself in this acrid fear scent.

"Lumpy…?"

Lizzie made a fluttering motion with her hands. "Oh sugar, we'll talk about that ol' cat later. Can you just get me those things now?"

Leona nodded and ran off.

Five minutes later she had a pail of warm water, towels, and a new dress. She stood by as Lizzie stripped out of the remains of her old clothes, and started to towel that smell off her skin.

"What happened to Lumpy?"

"I'm sorry, Leona, I know you liked that critter, but he's dead now. Just as well, anyway—cat's bad luck in a whorehouse."

"Dead?" Leona flinched from the news.

Lizzie looked at the girl carefully. "Leona, sugar, can you keep a secret?"

Leona nodded, but she was already starting to suspect this was one secret she wasn't about to much like.

"All right. Remember I told you about that hoodoo man I met in New Orleans? Well, he gave me some secrets."

"Secrets…?"

"He told me how to call the Devil."

Leona gaped for a moment, then stifled a laugh. If she didn't believe in Jacky-Ma-Lantern, she didn't see much reason to believe in the Devil, either.

"Don't laugh, child. I did it, and it worked."

Leona made an exaggerated gesture of looking around. "Where is he, Lizzie? I don't see me no Devil."

Lizzie ignored her. "Here's what that hoodoo man told me: On Hallows' Eve, he said, you needs a black cat. You boil that animal alive, then you take the bones and wash 'em in a spring, until the Devil comes to you. Then you can ask him for whatever you want."

Leona suddenly realized the meaning of the scratches, the blood and the burns on Lizzie's arms, of the kettle that Beulah had seen Lizzie leave with in the afternoon, and the knowledge staggered her. "Oh lawd, Lizzie…you boiled that poor animal alive…"

"Leona, that cat was so old he couldn't even catch him a horsefly no more."

"But that…that ain't right…"

"Right or not, sugar—it *worked*. I boiled him near that spring out in the woods, the one not far from ol' Guffey's farm, then I washed those bones in that spring, and I looked up…and sure 'nough, I seen this man walkin' up to me. He asked what I was wantin', and I tol' him."

"What'd you say?"

Lizzie finished washing, and started shrugging into the new dress. "I tol' him I wanted a rich man to come and love me and take me out of this place, far away. And he said it'd happen tonight."

Leona guffawed. "You can't believe that—"

Lizzie finished straightening out the dress. "I can believe it. It's happenin' right now." She walked up to Leona and gave her a small kiss on the cheek, and whispered, "You 'bout the only part of Mamie's I'll miss."

Then she walked past Leona, into the house.

Leona stood for a moment, shocked, unable to move.

She toed at the tattered dress Lizzie had left on the ground, trying not to imagine Lumpy being forced into a boiling kettle, screaming in agony as Lizzie held him down…

She shook the pictures out of her head, then turned and walked back into the house.

She was just leaving the kitchen and heading for the piano in the front parlor when Miss Mamie's bustled up. "There you are, child! We've got johns, and we need some music. And for lawd's sake, try to play somethin' lively!"

"Yes, Miss Mamie."

Leona hurried to the piano, and glanced towards the bar, where there stood only a single customer. He was leaning across the mahogany counter, chatting idly to Harold while his drink was fixed. He wore a spotless, expensive suit and hat in the most current style, in a pale pastel color. His hair was neatly pomaded into curls, and his posture and build shouted confidence and money. When he turned to glance back towards the piano for a moment, Leona's breath caught in her throat.

He was without question the handsomest man she'd ever seen. He grinned as he saw her, with his liquid brown eyes and perfect jawline and gleaming teeth.

Miss Mamie was fawning over this newcomer, plainly sensing the money as well, and just before she sat down to play, Leona overheard the name "Lizzie."

She was into the third bar of Sippie Wallace's "Jack of Diamond Blues" when Lizzie entered the bar and sidled up to the stranger, smiling. Leona couldn't hear their conversation, but it was only a few seconds before Lizzie cried out, ecstatic, leapt up from her bar stool, gave the stranger a brief kiss and then ran from the room.

The stranger smiled after her, and then turned that look on Leona.

And in that instant Leona's fingers failed her, because she knew who the stranger was, and she knew that Lizzie had told her the truth.

"Leona, honey, play somethin' happy," Miss Mamie called to her, still grinning at the fine-looking man. "Looks like Lizzie done gone and got herself a marriage proposal."

Leona tried to smile, but it was a weak attempt. She tried to remember one of the rags she'd heard on a trip to the music store last month, but it came out sounding melancholy.

Leona saw Miss Mamie bustle from the room, and realized it was just her, Harold the bartender, and the stranger now. She felt his eyes on her, and looked down at her hands, moving across the keys, trying to find the sprightly melody that was hidden somewhere inside the tune—

"Why don't you play something you can sing to?"

Leona started to reply, happened to glance back—and froze, her jaw hanging open like a cartoon character.

The handsome black man was gone; the man who had just spoken to her was white, mid-thirties, wearing a pinstriped suit.

"I heard you can sing pretty good," he said, resting an elbow on the top of the piano, grinning down at her.

"I…ain't so good," Leona said, not because she believed it, but because she didn't want to talk to him, no matter what color he was.

The Bad Man.

"C'mon, now, girl, you act like it's a sin to sing."

"Might be," Leona said. Her palms felt sweaty, and she could hear her heart thumping faster than a rag rhythm.

He shrugged, and took a step back. "Guess I got the wrong girl. See, I'm scouting for the Toby. You know what that is?"

"Yes, sir, I knows." Lizzie'd once had a john who played fiddle for Butterbeans and Suzie, and Lizzie had made sure he talked to Leona all about "riding the Toby," or traveling the circuit put together by the Theatre Owners' Booking Association. The fiddler had told her horror stories about being stranded in towns without hotels for coloreds, and dealing with theatre owners who charged performers three times what a meal anywhere else would cost…but he'd laughed as he told his tales, and Leona could tell he wouldn't give up that fiddle for anything.

And it was sure better than working for Miss Mamie. Leona dreamed of a day when people came to listen to *her*, not just be entertained until they could get a girl to take them upstairs.

"I'm looking for new performers. Heard through the grapevine that there was a colored girl working in some backwoods whorehouse who'd knock my socks off. But, if that's not you…"

"It's me."

What if he really was a booking agent for the Toby? Could she afford to pass up what might be her only chance? And if he wasn't—if he really was the Devil himself—then she'd sing like heaven for him, and give him a case of the blues he'd never get over.

He chuckled, amused, then said, "So sing for me."

She thought for a moment, and remembered Beulah telling her that she sang "Hard Time Blues" even better than Ida Cox. She picked out the opening notes on the piano, then let the pain and fear and humiliation and sadness explode deep inside her, until all the emotions could only be channeled up through her throat and out through her words, released into the world.

I never seen such a real hard time before,
I never seen such a real hard time before,
The wolf keeps walking all round my door.

All thoughts of where she was and who she was playing for vanished as she gave herself, body and soul, to the song. She closed her eyes and just felt and played, and when she finished she knew she'd never sung that well before. She was drained, covered in sweat and tears, weary with a bone-deep exhaustion.

The sound of slow applause drew her back.

She wiped at her eyes and turned to see the white man slowly clapping. He finished, and half-collapsed onto the piano.

"Lord, girl, they weren't just whistling Dixie. I do believe you may be even better than Bessie or Ma. You could make somebody a lot of money, you know that?"

Leona should have been pleased, but right now all she wanted was the comfort of her little pallet in the kitchen's warm pantry.

The agent stepped closer, bending over her in what he probably hoped was some sort of intimate, even fatherly, gesture. "It really takes it out of you, don't it?"

Leona just nodded.

"You're too damn good to be stuck in this place. That Miss Mamie, she's okay, but she don't realize what she's got in you. You need to be on the circuit. We can start you touring, just a few of the smaller theaters first, maybe opening for one of the bigger acts, then we move you up on the bill, get you bigger venues, start recording. How'd you like to see your name on a number-one record?"

Leona finally risked a glance up at him, and offered a shy smile. "That'd be fine, mister."

He laughed. "Atta girl. Okay, so let's make a deal, you and me."

Leona's fatigue was suddenly replaced with a numbing dread. "A…deal…?"

"Sure. Always gotta do the paperwork."

He reached into a pocket and pulled forth a few sheets of folded paper and a pen. "Standard contract. All you have to do is sign, then I'll make your arrangements. In twenty-four hours you'll be on a train to Atlanta, ready to play the 81 Theater."

Leona knew that wasn't possible; no real booking agent could get anyone into Atlanta's biggest theater in a day. At least no *human* booking agent.

"You're him, aren't you?"

"Who?"

Leona couldn't bring herself to say the usual names; she settled on the one from the Jacky-Ma-Lantern story. "The Bad Man."

She looked up now to see him squinting down at her. He didn't look like the Devil—no red skin, no horns, no pointed ears or tail. He looked like what he said he was.

And yet...there was something in his eyes, something that wasn't right. She suddenly knew this—*thing*—standing over her was ancient, and intelligent, and wanted her soul.

"C'mon, Leona, what's worse: Me giving you the life you deserve, or Miss Mamie wanting to make you part of The Life that killed your mama?"

Leona didn't answer, didn't move. She got the impression that the lights had gone down around her. In an instant of panic she looked up for Harold, but couldn't see the bar in the sudden gloom. She wasn't even sure she could find her way out of this room now.

"Look what I'm doing for Lizzie: Giving her a fine, rich, handsome husband. She's going to be happy, Leona. You could be, too."

"Lizzie called you here tonight?"

He cocked one shoulder in a half-motion of apology. "Yes, and I know you liked that old cat, so I'm sorry about that, but sometimes the rituals must be...obeyed."

"And what you want from me?"

"You know, Leona. It's the usual transaction."

Leona whispered, "My soul."

He murmured in agreement, and then just stood there, looking at her.

Leona slid just far enough away from him that she could stand to look up, into his old, old eyes. "But how would I sing?"

He looked back at her, and Leona saw the first sign of doubt on his face, a crack in his confidence. "You'll still sing just as well, your voice will still be yours—"

Leona dared to cut him off. "But the voice ain't nothin' without the soul."

"It won't matter. You'll be famous and rich anyway."

"It'll matter to me."

He seemed to gain several inches in height, and the lights grew even dimmer, until his pale white face was all Leona could see.

"So, what—you'd rather be working here, letting Jackson Smith grind into you, or worse—how about Parson Mills? He must weigh—what, three, four hundred pounds? How'd you like to have that on top of you, Leona, pounding away at you, and all so's you can make fifty cents, and get on with the next customer? Is that what you want?"

Leona's face grew hot, and her eyes filled with tears. "No, but I—"

"But you WHAT?" He was furious now, and Leona half-expected to see him start spitting brimstone sparks. "You really think you can get out of here some other way? I got news for you, honey: You're good, but you're not that good. You'd just be one more little colored girl trying to hustle up jobs until you get forced to be some white lady's maid to earn a dollar, or worse—wind up as a crib whore in some house that'll make Miss Mamie's look like the Ritz. Hell's gonna look pretty Goddamn fine after what life's got in store for you, girly."

Suddenly, something changed in Leona, something she'd kept carefully tamped down erupted out, and she let it. She was on her feet and shouting into his moon-like face:

"Let me tell you somethin', mister: I know how good I can sing, and I know there's lots of white men and colored men both who'll try to take advantage of me. But maybe I'm smarter than you give me credit for, and maybe I don't mind hard work and some heartache, because I'm already pretty used to it. So maybe the best thing you can do right now is get outta my way and let me leave here on my own two feet."

Leona walked by him, and the room was there again, and Harold was staring at her, her face still wet but determined.

"Leona...?"

She ignored him.

It took her maybe two minutes to rush to the pantry, and pack everything she owned into a burlap potato sack. If Lumpy were still alive, she would've taken him, too.

As it was, she'd leave alone. She'd managed to save up nearly ten dollars from tips over the last year, and she thought it might be enough to get her a train ticket to Atlanta, or maybe New Orleans.

She walked back through the parlor, towards the front door. Miss Mamie was there, staring at her.

"Child, what—?"

Leona silenced her with a quick kiss, and a goodbye. "I'm sorry, Miss Mamie. You been kind to me, and I 'preciate it, but I got to go."

"Tonight?"

Leona nodded, and headed for the front door—

—where the Bad Man stood, waiting.

"You sure you want to go that way? Even if you do get to the city, you know what to do when you get there?" Now his laughter was a hollow, bad sound. "You're just like a rabbit runnin' right into the coon dog's mouth."

"Get out of my way," Leona said.

He didn't move. "Last chance, Leona. I won't come to you again, no matter how bad it gets. You're liable to be wishing you could conjure me back up a month from now. If you even get that far; it's a bad night, tonight. Lots of things out there in the dark that'd find you mighty tasty."

Leona looked straight at him as she reached for the doorknob. "Can't be nothin' worse out there'n what's in here."

He let her go.

Without another word she strode out the front door, down the steps, and onto the soft dirt trail that eventually led to town, five miles on. He was right, of course; it was dangerous to walk this path at night, with everything from snakes to robbers about.

Somehow Leona didn't think they'd trouble her.

There was a railway station in town, and she thought the first train came about sunrise. She'd be on it, no matter where it was headed.

She cradled the burlap sack in her arms, and started to sing to herself as she walked into the warm Hallowe'en night, away from Miss Mamie's, never looking back.

THE SAMHANACH

MERRAN

Merran Alstead held the severed hand up to catch the light from the house, turning it slowly, admiring the blood that flecked its stump.

Too bad it's not Will's, she thought, half-smiling.

"Put it over here!"

She turned, lowering the gruesome rubber prop, and saw Jeannie on the far side of the lawn, pointing at a Styrofoam tombstone. Merran crossed to join her daughter, stepping carefully around the fake spider webs, flickering pumpkins, and ghosts made from white sheets. She reached the leaning marker, knelt, and carefully wedged the hand down into the grass until it seemed to be jutting up out of the earth, an undead thing struggling to rise.

"That's cool!"

She reached over and flicked Jeannie's witch hat, causing the six-year-old to giggle. Under the wide black brim, Jeannie's face was painted green and sported a long nose they'd glued on with spirit gum; the costume was complete with black dress and broom.

No princess for my little ghoul, Merran thought, eyeing her offspring with amusement and pride.

The girl was jittering with Halloween excitement; she flew across the yard, pretending to cackle with fiendish glee. "I'm the Halloween witch!"

Merran's attention was drawn away by a muttering coming from the sidewalk; she thought she'd heard something like "Halloween bitch," followed by teenaged snickers. Her stomach clenched as she saw Jay Saunders, Manny Posada, and Luke Ehrens slinking by. The three sophomores were at least smart enough to know they were too old for trick or treat tonight, but Merran didn't want to think about what alternative they'd come up with to act out Halloween. Manny and Jay leered at her openly, and Luke barely looked away, trudging along in his baggy, would-be gangsta clothing with his hands thrust deep into his pockets. She thought she heard someone mutter "milf" as they climbed into a parked car.

"Mommy…?"

She looked back to find Jeannie leaning down near the porch, eyeing something curiously. "Did you put these here?"

Merran joined her, then squinted in the dim light; she could only make out small white shapes.

"What are they?" Jeannie asked.

"Huh. I don't know."

Merran retrieved a lit jack-o'-lantern from the porch and carried it over to where Jeannie stood. Kneeling with the flickering orange gleam, she now saw that the pale forms were mushrooms, each the size of her fist, about twenty of them growing in a ring, enclosing a space six feet in diameter. In the center of the circle was a small book; even in the soft light Merran thought it must be bound in leather, the kind with ribbed bands on the spine. She picked the book up, and saw that it had no lettering on the covers.

"You didn't put this here?" she asked Jeannie, already suspecting a Halloween gag.

"No. What are those other things?"

"Mushrooms, or maybe toadstools. They must've just come up."

"How'd they get so big?" Jeannie asked.

"Good question. Halloween, I guess."

Jeannie started to reach for one. "I could use these for my witches' brew—"

Merran's own hand instinctively shot out and blocked her daughter's tiny fingers. "No, I don't think we should touch these. Some mushrooms are poisonous."

"Oh," Jeannie said, her eyes wide at the thought.

As Jeannie ran off into the house, Merran pocketed the book; she'd look at it later. She gazed up into the night sky and shivered once. It was completely dark now, almost time for the trick or treaters to appear. The air was slightly chilled, just right for late October, and the evening breeze carried a faint scent of smoke and decaying leaves. She loved this night, always had; in fact, her affection for Halloween had eventually led to a major in Folklore Studies…and a useless degree that had nothing to do with her secretarial job in a dull office.

She inhaled deeply, trying to fill her lungs, to chase out the thoughts of a failed marriage and lackluster career and single motherhood. She wondered if Will was off at a party somewhere, girlfriend on his arm, glass in hand, dressed as a pirate, or maybe an especially irritating cartoon character.

Stop it, she reprimanded herself. *He's gone, a thousand miles away, and it's Halloween, and you've got Jeannie and you'll both enjoy the evening.*

"Hey, Merran."

She looked up and saw her neighbor, Keesha Johnstone, waiting for her. Keesha was dressed as a cat, with one-piece jumpsuit, tail, ears, and painted nose; her five-year-old, Darren (rigged as a Transformer), peeked out from behind her striped leggings, and her seven-year-old, Marissa, a queen in crown and home-sewn robes, stood regally off to one side.

"Oh, hi, Keesha. Let me get Jeannie."

Merran leapt onto the porch, calling into the house. "Jeannie, Mrs. Johnstone's here."

From the bathroom just off the kitchen came a muted reply: "I'm fixing my nose!"

Merran bent to a large bag by the door and came up with mini candy bars, which she placed in Marissa and Darren's outstretched bags. "I'll be your first tonight. One for you, Your Highness, and for you, your…uh…truckness."

Both children shrieked out gratitude, then started off for the next house. "Don't go beyond the Lees'!" Keesha called after them, then turned her attention to Merran.

"My witchling is fixing her nose."

Keesha laughed. "Witch, huh? I thought she wanted to be a vampire."

Merran shrugged. "She did, but we couldn't find any fangs small enough."

A moment lapsed, as Keesha glanced past Merran. "Your yard is great, but…y'know, I've got Jeannie for the night, if you want to go off to Rick and Shirl's party…"

Merran wrinkled her nose. "Thanks, but…"

"What? C'mon, girl, there'll be some nice men there from Rick's dealership…"

"I'm not interested in men, Keesh. I mean…right now, I'm not. It's just…y'know, too soon."

Keesha gave a halfhearted nod. "Well, if you change your mind…I'm just saying, I'm fine with keeping Jeannie for the night."

"Thanks."

The screen door erupted, and a small cloaked figure rushed into the night. "Trick or treat!" she shouted to no one in particular.

Keesha rolled her eyes. "I can see I've got my work cut out for me, trying to corral these three."

"Go get 'em, mama cat."

Keesha set off after the three anxious children. Jeannie paused at the edge of her own lawn long enough to call back, "Bye, Mom! I'll be back with candy!"

Merran waved her daughter off, then sighed and headed back to the porch.

TRICK OR TREAT

An hour later, Merran had given out four full bags of candy and opened two more. She'd seen a dozen Disney princesses, at least ten pirates, six cartoon characters, four zombies, three ghosts, two politicians, and a lot of creations she couldn't begin to name. Plus one witch, who she'd assured herself was no equal to Jeannie.

She'd watched in satisfaction as a few very young children, urged on by their parents, had tiptoed through her yard with many sidelong glances, snatched their candy, and fled back to the relative safety of the street. She'd scowled at teenagers who offered no costume but held out pillow cases already bulging. She'd fought back both temptation and revulsion as she watched an already-drunk couple stagger to Rick and Shirl's place half-a-block down.

But it'd been five minutes now since she'd had her last masked beggar, and she was considering going into the house to warm herself up with a shot of brandy, when she felt a bulge in her pocket. She remembered the book, pulled it out, and, holding it beneath the porch light, opened the cover.

The paper inside was old, covered with small brown spots and a spidery but legible handwritten script. The first page bore an owner's name, and Merran's breath caught as she read:

CONNELL McCAFFERTY

McCafferty...her name. Before she'd married Will and become an Alstead. A name she'd considered reclaiming.

Connell...she searched her memory, but couldn't recall the name. She flipped to the first page, and saw the entry was dated 1910, although no month was given. She lowered the book for a few moments, calculating backwards—father, grandfather, great-grandfather...

Connell McCafferty could be her great-great-grandfather.

She'd always meant to learn more about the family, to trace her roots; when she'd had Jeannie, she'd vowed to research the family tree and present Jeannie with the information when she was old enough to appreciate it. But somehow, in the rush of raising a child and working and living, she'd never gotten around to it.

She did know that her great-grandfather, Ewan, had come to America from Scotland in 1925. Could Connell be Ewan's father?

She glanced down at the book again, and her eyes began to move over Connell's fluid script:

"'Tis time to talk of Hallowmas—Samhain to some—and thus 'tis also time, I think, to talk about the great unspoken secret, the McCaffertys' tragedy and curse. I didn't believe it myself until this year, but even in late summer you could feel a change in the air that had naught to do with autumn, a change that told us all something was coming, something very bad."

Merran looked up from the book, startled, at the sound of footsteps on her walk. It was a small boy, no more than four, dressed as a tiny cowboy, and apparently as shocked by her response as she was by his arrival. He hesitated, until she forced a smile.

"Trick or treat," he said, so quietly Merran barely heard.

She held out candy. He snatched it and then ran while his father, out on the sidewalk, chided him.

But Merran wasn't listening. She was pondering the book.

Where could this thing have come from?

She could only imagine that Jeannie had found it somewhere, stashed in some old trunk or box, maybe in the attic, and that she'd thought it would make a fine Halloween prop.

She couldn't have known how right she'd been.

Merran glanced up and down the street again, saw no groups of kids headed her way, and so she settled down onto the porch to read the journal of an ancestor she'd never known, describing a family history she'd never learned...

THE JOURNAL OF CONNELL McCAFFERTY— THE BEGINNING

'Tis time to talk of Hallowmas—Samhain to some—and thus 'tis also time, I think, to talk about the great unspoken secret, the McCaffertys' tragedy and curse. I didn't believe it myself until this year, but even in late summer you could feel a change in the air that had naught to do with autumn, a change that told us all something was coming, something very bad.

I'll set the story down here just as my father told me, just as his father told him, back through two hundred years of McCaffertys. Back to 1710, when it was Michael McCafferty who oversaw the family, and Jamie, his fine young son of eighteen years. The family lived out by Glen Creachan, and they'd prospered under Mike's fine hand.

So it was on Hallowmas Eve of that year that the McCaffertys held a party, inviting all the young folk from the parish. They had nigh on fifty guests, 'twas reckoned, and they held all the games that the season called for: Snap-apple, bobbing for apples, pulling the kale, burning nuts, sowing hemp seed, casting yarn into the kiln. Just as now, most of the games were about revealing the face or name or nature of the one you'd be marrying someday. I played a few of those games myself, I did, when I were younger, and I can tell you that most of them were but an excuse to sneak up on the lass you fancied and whisper your own name in her ear.

It was late in the even, but before midnight, when Red Rab showed. His name was really Robert Fraser, but he'd been called Red Rab from birth due to his crimson hair...and fiery temper. Rab was no ordinary fellow on any account: He'd been born twenty years earlier on a Hallowmas Eve like this one, near to midnight, and his mother—God rest her soul—had died just minutes after the birth. Rab had been raised by his father alone, and Widower Fraser had a heart of coal—he took to beating the boy on a regular basis. Of course there were those who said the beatings were not without reason: That Rab was a queer one because of his birth, that he had second sight and could commune with things that surpassed a normal man's vision. But then the Scots have e'er been a superstitious folk...

As Rab had grown, he'd become a great hulking figure of a man, tall and with a laborer's broad shoulders. There were, it's said, a few of the lasses who found him quite striking, with his red hair and strong arms, but Red Rab had eyes for only one: Mary Bruce. Sadly for Rab, Mary wanted naught to do with the likes of him, and anyway she already had Jamie McCafferty, who was happy to be had by her.

So, you can probably imagine that the entrance of Red Rab Fraser into the McCafferty All Hallows party filled no one with joy. Rab had quite clearly started drinking earlier in the evening, and he kept at it, putting away cup after cup of the McCaffertys' strong punch.

Finally Mary brought out a barm brack she'd made herself, and one into which she'd baked a ring; the custom (as it still is) was that whomever should receive the slice with the ring would be first to wed. Rab had stood back most of the night, but now he angled forward with all the rest, hoping to get that piece of the cake that would tell him Mary would soon be his.

But the ring was not to be uncovered by him. Instead Jamie finished his cake, and pulled forth the ring, holding it up with a grin directed at Mary, who blushed five shades of crimson but didn't look away.

Rab got it into his head that he'd been cheated somehow, and he began to have words with Jamie. The two came to blows, and although Rab was big, Jamie was faster and smarter. He knocked Red Rab down in two hits, and told him in no uncertain terms to leave. Rab, who was bleeding from a broken nose now, spit to the side, told Jamie Hallowmas wasn't over, and made his exit.

What comes next in the story couldn't actually have been witnessed by anyone, because none of the main folk involved survived that night, but the story's come down to us as stories will, with moments that somebody had to make up, and that's just how I'll report it here:

So just before midnight, Mary and Jamie went out to a haystack, intending to practice the old enchantment where you draw a straw to see who you'll marry. Jamie, of course, probably had something worked out in advance, because he told Mary to close her eyes and he guided her hand. Just as she felt the hay under her fingers, she heard a strange kind of "whoosh" noise, then felt something warm on her face. She opened her eyes—

—and saw Red Rab standing there with a scythe in his hands, and Jamie's headless corpse falling to its knees, and Mary realized the warm stuff on her face was Jamie's blood. She began to scream, of course, and Rab, he dropped the scythe, gathered up Mary, and hustled her into a wagon he'd got waiting. Jamie's people, hearing Mary, came a-rushing out of the house just in time to see Rab's wagon disappear down the road.

They found Jamie's body (and, some yards away, his head), and old Michael McCafferty set his jaw, grabbed his gun, and jumped onto his horse. His next eldest son, Cameron, and a few of the other men did likewise.

There was about eight of them who arrived at the Fraser farm twenty minutes later. There was no sign of Rab's wagon, but just to be sure they went into the barn—where they found Rab's father hanging, tied up by his wrists and completely skinned, just as Rab had left him before he'd set out for the McCaffertys'. His flesh had been tossed into a bloody corner, more blood had pooled around the old man's feet…but the Devil must have loved those Frasers, because the old man was still alive.

He told them of a bog about two miles distant where Rab liked to go, then he begged one of them to shoot him. Michael nearly had half a mind to let him dangle there until he died in agony, but—being as decent a Scotsman as ever lived—instead he stepped up and put a bullet through Fraser's head, ending his suffering.

The McCafferty riders arrived at the bog, and sure enough spotted Rab's wagon, although at first there was no sign of Rab. They found Mary in the back of the wagon, where she'd been tied and assaulted by Rab, who'd had his way with her and left her bruised and bloodied. Just then Rab called to them from out in the bog:

"Ah, so it's the whole McCafferty clan, is it? Good! Because I've got a final gift for you this Samhain!"

The McCafferty patriarch pulled his gun, but couldn't get a proper line on Rab from where he stood. "If you give yourself up now, Rab Fraser, I'll promise you a quick death."

"Like what I gave your brat, Jamie?"

That was too much for the father, who fired anyway, with a howl. The bullet flew wide, and Rab laughed.

The younger McCafferty, Cameron, stepped forward. "Might as well give yourself up, Rab. There's only more bog behind you, and you'll never make it."

Rab laughed again, a sound so demented that it must have raised the hairs on the back of every sane man's neck. "You're fools, all of you. I've no intention of running away, nor of giving myself up to the likes of you, either! Have you all forgotten that I was born on this day?"

Mr. McCafferty started trying to trudge through the fetid bog. "Then we'll come and get you—" But he only made it a few feet before quicksand tugged at his legs, and three of the other men had to leap forward and pull him out.

Cameron whispered to his father, "He knows these bogs, Father—I've heard tell before that he spends time here. We'll have to wait for him to come to us."

But the elder McCafferty would have none of waiting or reasoning. "I don't care what day you were born, you syphilitic dog, I'll see you dead for what you've done to my son tonight—"

"Ahhh," Rab called back, "but that was nothing compared to what's coming. You see, my being born on this day gifted me with certain abilities the rest of you couldn't begin to comprehend. Including talking to demons."

"Rubbish," answered Cameron.

"In fact," Rab said, ignoring the young man's insult, "there happens to be a very powerful demon that resides in this very bog. Surely you've heard of...the Samhanach?"

A hush fell over the eight men, until Michael spoke up: "A tale to frighten children, nothing more."

"Then you're about to be revealed as eight small bairns, my lads. Witness my servant—the Samhanach." With that, Rab gestured behind him, grandly.

As Michael and Cameron and the other men watched, the brackish water behind Rab began to glow with a hellish orange light, bubbling up with a sound like molten lava. A shape thrust its way up out of the muck, a dark figure that towered over Rab by at least two feet, and had the twisted face of a carved turnip lit by candle from within.

"What trickery is this?" cried out the senior McCafferty.

"No Halloween trick, this," answered Rab, "but a demon shapeshifter come to do my bidding. At each Hallowmas, the Samhanach will find the McCaffertys. It may only jest, or it may kill. It might show its true form, or it might arrive disguised. It might take your first-born back to the otherworld, or it might not. It won't matter where in the wide world you try to hide, it'll find you, at All Hallows, and you'll never know what it'll do until 'tis done."

With that, the demon raised a long clawed hand, and slit Rab's throat.

The look of surprise on Rab's face was near well worth the terror of seeing a murder; he'd obviously never expected that which he'd summoned to turn on him. But it did, and as Rab fell, clutching his gushing throat, so did the monster fall on him, ravaging his flesh, feeding itself from him before the bog claimed the remains.

Finished with Rab, the thing rose and started forward, each step taking it three yards, nearing the frozen watchers—but suddenly it paused, and its hideous features contorted, with something like frustration, or disappointment. It turned back the way it had come, and, as swiftly as it had risen, vanished down into the bog again until it was completely gone.

Young Cameron forced himself from his paralysis and pulled a pocket watch from his waistcoat. "Midnight exactly."

With Hallow's Eve over, the McCafferty group gathered up

poor Mary, and returned home.

But Rab's mayhem hadn't ended. Two months later, Mary realized she was with child. Knowing the bairn could only be Rab Fraser's—and conceived in a bog on Hallow's Eve, to boot—she ended her own life with a noose strung from a barn rafter.

Come next October, the McCaffertys grew full of dread. Nearly a year had passed since that night, but none who had been present for the scene in the bog had forgotten Red Rab's words. There would be no Hallowmas celebration this year, no lively party or joyous games. This would be a year of prayers and loaded guns, shuttered windows and shaking fingers.

Dusk came on the 31st, and the family hunkered down, starting at each creak of wood or bird call. Time seemed to slow to a snail's pace as they waited, girding themselves.

Seven o'clock…eight o'clock…ten…

The last hour was the worst, especially the final few minutes. Would the Samhanach appear with a single minute left to Hallow's Eve, wreak great havoc, and then vanish?

No.

The clock struck twelve, and they knew they were safe.

They still spent the remainder of the night edgy, doubtful, but morning revealed that they'd passed the evening without incident. The animals in the barn were unharmed, the house and outbuildings sound, the entire family safe.

Over the next week, they discussed it endlessly. Had Rab's death ended his own curse? Was he too weak after all to direct a demon to do his bidding? Or had Mary's sacrifice resulted in a greater good that she couldn't have foreseen?

They were still cautious at Hallowmas the following year, but again the night was uneventful. As it was the year after that, and after that.

By 1715, the McCaffertys knew they were safe.

They were wrong.

MERRAN

Merran paused as a knot of trick or treaters approached, and she was oddly grateful to see a bumblebee, a Snow White, a SpongeBob and a policeman; no monsters or jack-o'-lanterns.

I thought I was supposed to be doing the scaring here.

After she'd passed out candy, she set the journal down. There was more—much more—and she was curious now, but also frightened on a level that went beyond demonic creatures:

There was madness in her family.

At least that was the only way to read this journal. Right now she couldn't tell if the madman was a figure from the 1710 story, or her great-great-grandfather, Connell McCafferty, calmly relaying a story that even the most gullible of believers wouldn't swallow. Demons and curses and haunted bogs?

The only other possibility was that this was an elaborate Halloween joke, but Merran couldn't think of anyone who would invest the amount of time and effort involved in something this detailed. Will certainly didn't have the talent for it, even if he'd wanted to (and she doubted that he did, because that would have involved thinking of her in some way). And besides, the journal seemed too authentically old, the pages brittle, the binding antiquated and worn.

No, she thought it was real. Which brought her back to a McCafferty insanity gene.

She'd never heard anyone mention Connell, and she wondered if that meant he'd been stricken from family histories, like a black sheep who revealed an ugly truth...

Merran thought about other members of her family, and realized she'd never been told any other stories of mental illness. Oh sure, there'd been old great-aunt Lizzie, who'd never married and had died at the age of 94 surrounded by over a hundred cats...but that was hardly the level of dementia that involved murder and a belief in demons.

Perhaps the entire family had been duped.

That explanation settled best with Merran, and she opted for it. Given how she'd fallen hard and fast for Will (who she'd since realized had lied to her from the beginning of their relationship), she could believe a strain of gullibility in the McCaffertys.

She also felt a brief, sinister moment of déjà vu as she realized that the events she'd just read about had occurred exactly three hundred years ago on this same night.

Merran saw a small mob of kids approaching, and was grateful for the distraction. She'd continue reading later, but right now she was happy to lose herself in the pleasant modern day rituals of American Halloween.

THE THREE BOYS

Luke Ehrens, Jay Saunders, and Manny Posada stood in the Saunders' expansive backyard, passing a joint. Reflections from the swimming pool lights rippled across their faces as they glanced from time to time at the house.

The spliff reached Luke, who hesitated as he reached for it. "Hey, man, your parents…"

Jay, irritated, reached and grabbed the joint back. "…Are busy with all the little kiddies, dude, I told you that." Jay sucked down smoke, held it in, smiled.

Luke, though, still wasn't satisfied. He hadn't liked the way this whole evening was going. Halloween had once been his favorite day of the year, but ever since he'd outgrown trick or treating, he'd felt lost on October 31st. Jay and Manny had promised him a party, but sucking down so-so weed in Jay's park-sized backyard wasn't Luke's idea of fun. He would have been happier at home with a pizza, a six-pack of Coke, and a stack of horror movies.

"So what else, man?" asked Manny, almost mirroring Luke's thoughts.

Jay exhaled. "What do you mean?"

"What else we gonna do tonight? I mean, it's fuckin' Halloween, man. We can stand back here and smoke any night. C'mon, let's fuckin' do something. Go fuck something up. I'll drive. Maybe we can find one of those pussy haunted houses and really scare the shit out of somebody…"

Luke thought that sounded way better; at least it involved a simulation of action. "Sounds good to me."

"Nah," Jay said, blowing on the end of the joint, "I got somethin' else in mind."

"Like fuckin' what?"

"Like…" Jay let a dramatic pause go by, then went on: "…like wait and see how drunk Mrs. Kazanian gets."

Luke stifled a groan. Mrs. Kazanian and her 82-year-old husband, a dry cleaning mogul, had moved in next door two years ago. When the old man had died six months ago, leaving behind a 30-year-old widow with a trophy wife's figure, Jay had become obsessed with Mrs. Robinson scenarios; but Luke couldn't imagine anything she'd find attractive in a posing, inexperienced, spoiled rich brat.

Manny apparently agreed, as he stamped his feet in anger. "That's lame, motherfucker."

Luke didn't try to hide the contempt in his tone. "Motherfucker's what he wants to be. I think it's more like right-hand-fucker."

Jay shot a hand out toward Luke and pushed him hard enough to make him stagger. "Hey, asswipe, you were supposed to bring the tequila, and you showed up empty-handed. At least I got the J like I said I would."

"Fuck," Luke exclaimed, regaining his balance, feeling his face burn, "I told you—my father locked the liquor cabinet. Not much I could do about that, now, was there?"

"Fine. Then go steal one from the corner liquor store."

Luke held up his hands dismissively; he was done. "You know what? This whole night sucks. I think I'll go watch the little kids—at least they're having fun."

He hiked up his jeans and turned to go. Manny had driven them here tonight, but at this point Luke was more than happy to walk the three miles back to his middle-class neighborhood. He hated to admit that his parents could be right about anything, but Jay and Manny really were losers.

His mind made up, Luke headed for the side gate—and stopped after two steps.

A girl was just coming through.

She was drop-dead gorgeous, and caused all three boys to freeze in astonishment. She looked to be a remarkably well-developed, was dressed like a prostitute, and carried something in a white plastic grocery bag. She took three steps into the yard, then looked around in surprise.

"Oh shit. I thought this was the party. Sorry."

Before she could turn to go, Jay leapt forward, nearly tripping over his own feet. "Yeah, no, this is it. I mean, this is a party. Now that you're here."

The girl tossed Jay a knowing grin, and wavered indecisively. "Cute, but...I'm looking for my friends, and..."

Now it was Manny's turn. "We'll be your friends."

Luke was closest to her, and he knew the other two boys were probably expecting him to chime in, but his voice caught in his throat.

Something was wrong here. And it wasn't just the possible danger the girl was walking into.

It was the girl herself.

She was too perfect, too sexy, too knowing. The way she lowered her eyelashes as she looked at each of them in turn, the one hip that was cocked, the tiny twist to the lips…she simultaneously turned Luke on and made him feel like he'd just stepped in something long-dead.

"I don't know," she purred, and Luke already knew she'd be staying.

And as much as his internal warning signals were screaming at him to GO, GET AWAY, RUN…he knew he'd be staying, too.

"We're not so bad," he said to her, trying to summon up a smile.

"Well, maybe for a little while. Who's got the joint?"

Grinning from ear to ear (*Why doesn't he notice this is wrong?*, Luke wondered), Jay handed her the spliff. She took it and sauntered over to set her bag down on a patio table, then she leaned against it, provocatively, holding out the stick.

"Light?"

Manny and Jay both jumped forward, lighters at the ready. Jay reached her first, and Manny grudgingly accepted defeat, then watched, envious, as the girl clamped her red-nailed fingers around Jay's wrist while he lit the joint. The end flared to red, and she sucked on it, drawing the weed's strength into her lungs, finally releasing it with a luxurious sigh.

"Not bad," she murmured, and Luke knew she was lying. She kept the joint, took a second hit, then passed it back to Jay.

"What's your name?" he asked her.

"After two hits of that, I don't remember," she said, with an overdone giggle.

Manny bounced on his feet. "Well, all fuckin' right."

"So what are you guys doing tonight?"

Jay gave her a leer. "Waiting for you."

She rolled her eyes, but stepped closer to him, brushing her hip against his. "That's a pretty dumb line."

"Not if it worked."

She eyed him for another moment, then reached back for the

bag. "Weed always makes me hungry. I made this for the party, but…fuck it, let's eat it now." She reached into the bag and withdrew something dark, on a plate, covered in plastic wrap. Luke squinted at it in the dim light, and saw it was a cake.

"This is a traditional Halloween thing called a barm brack. I found a recipe for it on the internet and thought it sounded weird."

Luke asked, "What's in it?"

"I don't even remember…y'know, flour, pieces of fruit, all that kind of shit. You're supposed to bake a ring in it, and whoever gets the ring will…like…have good luck or something. But I baked something better than that into it."

"Like what?" Jay asked.

"A condom."

Manny and Jay almost split their faces with their grins. Luke still didn't like something about the girl, but he had to admit—he was experiencing a constrained erection under the denim of his pants. "Oh, c'mon," he said, trying to retain some composure, "you baked a condom? It probably melted."

She shrugged, a gesture that conveyed more than doubt, since her shoulders were left bare by the thin tube top she wore. "Maybe. It's still in the foil. I guess whoever gets that slice will just have to tell us for sure."

Luke saw Manny and Jay both shift their stances, and he knew they were as hard as he was. "So you gonna cut it for us?" Jay asked.

The girl unwrapped the cake, then produced a knife from the bag, and Luke experienced another jolt of alarm. The knife was huge, a butcher knife, too big for just slicing a cake, and the way she waved it around…he didn't know if she was stoned or just careless, but only fast reflexes saved Jay from getting nicked on one cheek.

"Hey, watch it with that thing!"

She put on a fake pout that she knew was even more erotic, with lower lip thrust out and eyes strategically averted. "Sorry."

With three quick strokes she efficiently sliced the cake into six large pieces, then selected one for herself. "Dig in."

All three reached for their own wedges, biting into them with the gusto of multiple hungers. "This shit is weird," muttered Manny, around mouthfuls.

"I like it," Jay fired back, throwing a look at the girl.

Luke hesitated, holding the cake halfway to his mouth, but when he saw the girl swallow her first taste, he followed suit. It took him a few seconds to place the flavors: Spices, sugar, strong tea. Unusual, but not unpleasant.

The boys finished in seconds, nothing left but crumbs. "Fuck," muttered Jay. Then he glanced at the girl, saw she was still eating. "Hey, what happens if you get it?"

She arched her eyebrows, finished chewing, and said, "Then it's my choice I guess, huh?"

A hooded look—the oldest expression of male aggression—passed among Jay, Manny, and Luke. Luke was shocked to realize that for an instant he'd wanted to beat Manny and Jay to a pulp, all for a girl, and again he wanted to leave, but something else had him in its grip; whether that was lust or some sort of magic, he couldn't say, and figured they might even be the same thing.

Then she'd finished her piece, and had also come up empty-handed. They followed her look as she gazed at the two chunks left on the plate. "Huh...only two pieces left...now how do we work this?"

Jay laughed, then stepped forward. "Simple." He grabbed one slice in each hand and simply crushed them, working his fingers through the cake, remains littering the lawn beneath.

Both Luke and Manny cried out: "Hey—!"

But before they could do anything else, Jay was shaking crumbs from his left hand, and holding a foil packet in his right. "Looks like I win."

"Fuck you, dog," Manny said, his meaty hand forming a fist.

"Probably melted in there anyway," Luke added, then let himself fall into a lawn chair, defeated.

"Yeah," Jay said, fixing the girl with a hard stare, "but what if it's not?"

"Then," she said, drawing out the pause, letting her tongue linger on her lower lip, "the trick'll be a treat for you."

"Well, then," Jay said, trying to match her sexually-charged speech and failing, "let's find out."

He held the packet up, and slowly tore it open. When nothing was revealed, he raised the packet up to his eyes, peering inside.

"What the—?!"

Manny gasped and Luke leapt out of his chair, knocking it

over, as they both saw something black swirl up out of the packet and into Jay's open mouth. He clamped his jaws shut, but too late—something had entered him, something that was already making him sweat and stagger back.

The girl smiled and stepped forward, staying with him as he stumbled, stricken. "Okay, I confess: This has all been a little Halloween trick, because that was certainly no condom…and my costume is way better than you could ever guess."

Jay was drenched already, shaking and panting. "What the fuck was that?"

The girl's face was subtly altering even as the boys watched, becoming more feral, her eyes taking on a malignant glow. Luke desperately tried to will his feet to move, but somehow he also knew he had to stay to witness the finale of this drama, to see a real Halloween haunting.

"That," the girl-thing answered, "was a little something of my own creation, a sort of concentrated form of the bubonic plague. You know what they call it in the history books, don't you? The Black Death."

Jay's hand shot to his neck as something bulged there, and Luke realized his friend's skin was now covered with large protrusions, oozing blood and pus.

The tormentor continued, lightly, as if describing an amusing scene. "I thought it was appropriate for tonight, because we owe some of Halloween to the Black Death. You probably didn't know that, did you? All the stuff with skeletons and skulls? That comes from the art that was inspired by the plague, the 'Danse Macabre' drawings—"

Jay leaned over and vomited, splattering barely-digested cake across his collectible Nike shoes and the manicured lawn.

The girl frowned. "You interrupted me. And just when I'm in the middle of teaching you something important—"

Manny's paralysis broke, and he soundlessly turned to flee. He made it almost to the gate before she caught up to him; Luke hadn't even seen her move. She snagged Manny's collar and hauled him back as he screamed, high-pitched shrieks that didn't sound as if they could issue from a masculine throat. The girl-thing didn't even struggle as it thrust him towards Jay, who had now fallen and lay writhing in agony. Manny's screams turned to "No, no, NO" as she pushed him inexorably closer to Jay.

"They say the Black Death was passed by rats, but I figure your idiot friend will do just as well."

She ground Manny's face down into Jay's bloody neck, then released him. Manny reared back, his cries now sobs of terror and pain. He clawed at his black t-shirt, and literally tore the sleeve frantically trying to reach the pustules that had sprouted under his arm.

Luke stood in frozen horror, watching his two friends die, waiting dumbly for his turn. He knew he wouldn't make it if he tried to run or fight. This was the end of his life. No one would come to help—if anyone had heard the screams, they'd dismissed it as a Halloween stunt. He'd die here, tonight, at sixteen, and he regretted how little he'd done, for himself or anyone else. His siblings hated him, he'd disappointed his parents, and had accomplished nothing. Now there'd be no chance to fix any of those things.

He didn't know he was crying until the girl-thing turned to him and laughed. "Tears for your friends. How sweet."

He couldn't even speak, couldn't tell her the tears weren't for them. He just wiped his eyes and looked at her.

"You know Merran McCafferty."

The words—not even phrased as a question—took him so completely by surprise that his crying stopped instantly. At first he didn't recognize the name, then he remembered: The attractive, newly-single mom who lived at the end of his block, the one Jay had called "milf" earlier tonight. When he'd still been alive.

He thought her name was Merran, although the last name sounded wrong. Wasn't it something like Allman? No—Alstead. But that first name...how many Merrans could there be?

"I think so. I mean, yes."

Her voice changed, becoming deeper, stranger, acquiring an accent—British. *No*, Luke thought—*Scottish*.

"You're being allowed to leave here alive to deliver a message to her: Tell her the Samhanach has come tonight."

"The...Samhanach...?"

Then the creature before him transformed visually as well, growing, darkening, until it was an eight-foot-tall nightmare with the face of a demonic jack-o'-lantern.

Luke didn't have to wait to be urged to leave. He turned now, freed from his stasis, and ran, arms flailing wildly, breath coming in great gulps. He ran three blocks until his legs stopped working and he dropped in the middle of the street. When he could breathe normally again, he realized a car was honking at him and anxious trick or treaters were staring, and he picked himself up, then started walking quickly. He was three miles from home, so it would take him an hour...

...but he would find Merran McCafferty and deliver the monster's message.

The Samhanach had come.

MERRAN

Merran shivered—the night was cooling rapidly—and went into the house to retrieve a sweater and her phone.

Once she'd returned to the porch, she sat down and ran an internet search on the term "Samhanach." She found a website called *The Halloween Encyclopedia* where the Samhanach was described as a Scottish "bogie," or demon, that appeared only on Halloween, performed malicious mischief, and stole children.

It was almost eight, and she was surprised that Keesha wasn't back with Jeannie yet. She had a flash, a presentiment of danger—*something is wrong*—then quickly dismissed it. They were trick or treating. Taking their time. Enjoying the evening.

As she should have been doing.

Looking for something to occupy her thoughts (not think about her daughter in peril), Merran picked up the journal, and opened it to where she'd left off.

THE JOURNAL OF CONNELL McCAFFERTY—1810

It was a century before the trouble started again.

By the end of the 1700s, the McCaffertys had truly prospered; they'd left behind the farming life and were succeeding as merchants in the growing city of Inverness. They had a lovely house on a street not far from River Ness, and they were liked and respected in the community. Brian McCafferty was 43 years old, in good health, and still in love with his wife, Maeve, who'd recently given birth to their fourth child; tiny Ceana joined her six-year-old sister, Fiona, ten-year-old brother, Murdock, and fifteen-year-old Niall.

Halloween held only happy memories for Brian and Maeve, who had wed after a Halloween when they'd thrown two nuts onto a fire, and the nuts had burned together until both were ash. This year they'd decided to keep their annual gathering intimate, just the immediate family and the serving people and their kin. As the sun set on October 31st, 1810, there were a dozen present in the warm central room of the McCaffertys' home. A fire was burning merrily in the hearth, nuts were readied nearby, a tub of apples for ducking waited, a barm brack cooled in the kitchen, and the adults drank the traditional lamb's wool.

Little Murdock was the first to call for ghost stories, and although his sister Fiona blanched, the servants' children all echoed the cry. Brian laughed, settled into a chair before the fire, and leaned forward.

"Do you know of the Samhanach?" he asked.

Maeve frowned. "Brian, that story isn't for wee ears—"

He cut her off, nodding at the circle of young listeners gathered around his feet. "Nonsense, Maeve. They're all old enough to hear it. Besides, it's part of their family history—they should know it."

Maeve leaned back, unsettled, but silent.

"What's the Samhanach, Papa?" asked Murdock.

"Well," Brian began, rubbing his hands together, "a hundred years ago the McCaffertys weren't so well off as we are now. Your great-great-grandparents lived out in the country, where they were farmers. But they loved Halloween, and every year they held great parties that were famous for three counties.

"This one year—1710 it was—there was a bad man in the neighborhood, a villain named Red Rab. Rab, he had a long-standing feud with the McCaffertys, and this Halloween it came to a head. Rab got into a fight with one of the younger McCaffertys, who whipped him and made him run. But Rab, he wasn't one to give up so easily; he hid outside, and waited for that unfortunate young man to come out, and when he did…"

Brian paused dramatically until little Fiona exclaimed, "What? What happened?"

Swinging his arms dramatically, Brian said, "Red Rab cut off his head with a reaping scythe!"

The children all gasped, and Maeve started forward. "Brian, that's enough—"

"Oh Mother, can't we please hear the rest?" said Murdock.

Maeve hesitated, then returned to her seat, offering an angry look to Brian. "Their nightmares tonight will be on your head!"

Brian grinned. "It's Halloween—we should *all* have nightmares."

"What happened next?" said the usually-quiet Niall.

"Well, the McCaffertys of course went after Rab when he fled. They went to his home first, and found out he'd killed his own father.

"Then they followed the black-hearted rascal to a bog, a *haunted* bog. Rab, you see, had been born on this very night—on Halloween—and as we all know, those who come into *this* world on that day can sometimes see into the *next*. Rab had second sight, and other powers, too…he could call up wicked wichts."

Another collective shiver rippled through Brian's audience. He let it pass, then went on:

"And that's what he did, there in that bog on Hallow's Eve. He summoned forth the worst of all the bogies: the Samhanach. In the old tongue, 'samhanach' meant 'giant,' and that's what it was—taller than the tallest man by at least another yard. It had skin like a rotting turnip, and features that glowed with hellfire.

"Eight of the McCaffertys were there to behold the monster, and they all swore to exactly the same thing: that the Samhanach turned on Rab himself, ripping him apart before the clock hand moved to twelve; midnight struck, and the demon returned to the otherworld—"

A scream cut the story short. It'd come from the kitchen, and was followed by the sudden appearance of Bridget, the cook, hands in the air, face white as milk.

"Bridget—!" Brian jumped from his chair and went to her.

"Sir," she gasped out, between pants, "I just spied something out the kitchen window, something horrible, moving outside the house…"

Brian led her to a chair and bade her sit. "There, there, I'm sure 'tis gone, whatever it was—"

His daughter shrieked, pointing to a window beside the front door. "A bogie!"

Brian's eyes shot from his daughter, who now clutched, trembling, at her mother. "Brian…" Maeve said, a growl of disapproval in her voice.

"I swear I don't know what's—"

There was a knock at the front door. It was so strong it shook the whole house, and every one of those present could feel that knock vibrate in their chests.

The knock came again, then continued, slow, steady, deafening. Maeve's expression had now changed to fear. "What *is* that?!"

Brian moved towards the door. "I don't know."

"You're not going to open it—!"

He waved her to silence and tried to peek carefully through the small window by the door. After a beat, he tentatively reached for the knob, rested his hand there, swallowed once—and then yanked the door open.

An ancient, decrepit beggar stood there. He was nearly black from grime, his hair long and matted, toothless mouth sunken, clothes tattered, body bent. He leaned heavily on a gnarled old walking staff, and there was a filth-crusted bag slung over one shoulder.

He peered up at the astonished Brian, squinting his red-rimmed eyes. "Pardon me, sir, I did nae mean to frighten ye…"

"Yes? What is it?"

The beggar thrust out a shaking hand. "Could ye spare a soul-cake to a poor man for All Souls Day?"

Brian stared at the man's hand—the nails were so long they extended at least an inch past the ends of his fingers—and he felt a mix of repulsion, pity, and curiosity, the latter engendered by the man's reference to All Souls, still two days off.

"Good sir…?"

"Oh." Brian shook himself from his reverie, and gestured back to Bridget. "Bridget, prepare a plate of food for this man."

Bridget shook her head and stared in disbelief. "Sir, I don't—"

Brian turned to look back at her. "Bridget, don't be silly. Just—"

The beggar began to laugh. Brian spun back to him, and as the laughter grew, the beggar changed—his limbs and torso lengthened, his eyes went from red-rimmed to emitting their own fiery internal glow. The laughter took on gale proportions, and Brian braced himself in the entryway; behind him, the fire went out in the hearth, all the candles and lamps throughout the house were extinguished, and he was dimly aware of a chorus of screams behind him.

Gathering his strength, Brian began to push against the door, struggling to block the unnatural wind that roared in. It took him several seconds, but finally the door was shut and he threw the lock, then leaned back against it in the sudden darkness, panting, trying to get his bearings.

He realized that the laughter and wind had ceased, as had the screams from his family. He heard confused voices: Maeve crying out for someone to light a candle, a muttered curse as someone banged a shin, something crashed to the floor. He made his way carefully into the room, found a flint, and soon had a candle going.

"Is anyone harmed?"

He received denials and questions. He lit lamps and candles, passing them around, until the room was nearly as bright as midday. He saw pale faces, wide eyes, shaking fingers. Maeve was just setting Fiona down, and the child suddenly ran to him, wrapping her arms around his knees. "Was that the Samhanach?"

Brian put a hand on his daughter's head, but had no answer for her. He was trying to make sense of what they'd just experienced, when his wife uttered a sound far worse than any scream, a groan that sounded as if part of her soul had been ripped out, and then she fell, senseless, to the floor. He ran to her, his heart in his throat, and he realized with dread what she'd been looking at:

The new baby's crib.

He peered down into the little wooden bed, trying to prepare himself, but seeing it was both better and worse than what he'd feared.

The crib was empty. The blanket had been tossed carelessly into one corner, but there was no sign of his infant daughter, Ceana.

Niall spoke from behind him. "It took her, didn't it?"

Brian couldn't answer. He could only stare down, stunned, helpless. He heard Fiona move up to join her brother. "What took her?"

"The Samhanach."

Brian said nothing, because he knew it was the truth. The Samhanach had come, and it had taken his baby.

And someday it would return.

THE PARTY

Rick Joosten paused by the kitchen to chat up Emmy Kazanian. The woman was already drunk, and Rick guessed that by the end of the evening she'd have a convenient wardrobe malfunction and fall out of the top of the leather corset she wore, trying to pass herself off as a dominatrix. Of course Rick was dressed in a white medical jacket and red rubber gloves; his gynecologist costume included a long-handled mirror he used to stir drinks.

He exchanged idle flirtation with the young widow for a few moments, and gave his red gloves a snap that caused her to shriek and slosh vodka onto his carpet. She didn't seem to notice.

He briefly considered sending her a carpet cleaning bill, then excused himself and pushed through the party guests to see Shirl at the front door, doling out candy to another group of kids. A small boy accepted the chocolate, then stared up at her in confusion.

"Who are you s'posed to be?" he asked.

Shirl thrust out a hip and threw her be-wigged head back. "Recognize me now?"

The kid still looked confused, then turned and left.

Rick desperately wished he could go with the boy. He'd spent the early part of the evening watching in horror as his wife, determined to be a popular African-American singer, had applied dark skin makeup to her exposed arms, neck and face, and he'd tried not to suggest that perhaps he should have dressed as Al Jolson. He wondered how many of their guests tonight would find the get-up to be in extraordinarily bad taste. At least his choice came with a sense of humor.

It certainly made him laugh, if not openly: That he would be dressed as an OB-GYN practitioner, mixing drinks and teasing the ladies...and all the while trying not to think solely of Joey Simonetti.

Joey was the newest salesman Rick had hired to work at North Valley Toyota. At 25, Joey had the features and build of a Roman god. He was a decent salesman (he could almost always close a deal with any female customer), had an easy, gleaming smile, and there was no wife or girlfriend in his life. Once or twice Joey had thrown Rick a look that'd made the middle-aged manager's head spin, and fantasies Rick thought he'd outgrown in college had manifested again, leaving him avoiding Shirl and taking long showers masturbating to thoughts of Joey's hands on his body.

He'd invited Joey tonight, of course, and Joey had promised to come; every knock at the door snapped Rick's head up, but it was invariably just another group of trick or treaters, or more neighbors coming for the party, neighbors who thought of Rick as their local flirt and jokester, the guy who always had a wink for their wives. They thought he was Rick Joosten, successful general manager of a car dealership, devoted husband and father (of two grown kids, now off at college), good Republican and Protestant, a stand-up guy.

Which was why he knew it'd been slightly dangerous to invite Joey tonight. He'd have to remind himself to exercise caution. He knew Shirl would basically have to catch him sucking dick before she'd believe it...

...but at this point in his life, with more of it unhappily behind him than ahead, he wasn't sure he'd mind being found with his lips wrapped around Joey's rod.

He just wasn't sure how Joey would feel about that.

There was another knock on the door, and Rick waited, breathless, as Shirl opened the door—to reveal someone dressed in a very realistic Grim Reaper outfit, complete with a cowl that completely obscured their face and an authentic-looking scythe, with skeletal fingers wrapped around it.

Skeletal?

Rick smiled to himself at the success of the illusion; they'd obviously glued a real skeleton hand to the handle of the scythe, and were holding the other end of the arm bones, hidden by the folds of the draped sleeve.

Shirl gaped for a second, then stepped back. "Oh, hello...let's see, is that Pete Lavesh in there?"

The Reaper didn't respond, except to step past Shirl soundlessly. She caught Rick's eye, shrugged, and closed the door.

Christ, that isn't...?

Rick almost went up to ask the new arrival's identity, to make sure it wasn't Joey hidden under there...but somehow he couldn't see the beautiful young man covering himself with all that black cloth.

Can't be him.

Just then Shirl edged past, whispering a reminder that he

should be bartending. He nodded, pushed through the crowded living room to the wet bar, and lost track of the Grim Reaper as he began mixing cocktails.

Several martinis and cosmopolitans later, he heard a shrill cry from the kitchen, loud enough to pierce the hum of party conversation. He couldn't place the voice's owner, and considered trying to sidle through the mob to investigate, but just then he heard a rich baritone ask, "How ya doin', boss?"

He looked up—and dropped the cocktail shaker. It hit the floor with a loud clatter and the two halves separated, spilling ice and booze. But Rick didn't notice.

Joey was there—dressed as a gladiator. He wore a tight leather tunic that left his arms and legs bare, boots with shin guards, and a sheathed sword strapped to a belt. He'd moussed his hair to give it the proper sweaty Roman curl, and the leather bands strapped around his biceps flexed and shifted with his muscles.

"Hey, whoops—let me help you with that…"

Before Rick could protest, Joey had joined him behind the bar and was retrieving the parts of the shaker, bending over, exposing his defined upper thighs, and Rick actually had to grasp the edge of the metal sink to stay upright.

He forced out, "Thanks," as Joey handed him the shaker, then the young man backed away, eyeing the party.

"Looks like you're the hit of the neighborhood."

Rick cleared his throat, feeling suddenly clumsy and exposed, and asked, "Did you come alone?"

Joey lifted his shoulders, and even that simple gesture sent a wave of desire roaring through Rick. "Yeah. I'll probably meet up with some friends later."

Rick wanted to ask about those friends, if they were female or male, gay or straight, platonic or…instead, what he said was, "What can I get you to drink?"

"A beer's fine. Whatever you've got."

Rick found a bottle, opened it, and handed it to Joey, trying to keep his eyes from settling on the outlines of Joey's chest beneath the leather.

"Hey, Shirl looked great," Joey said, leaning over to be heard above some insipid dance tune that was now drowning out the sounds of conversation.

Rick just nodded. He felt neither like fighting with the music nor lying. Instead, he leaned over to Joey and said, "I can't hear a thing in here. Can we go outside to talk?"

He felt shock well up as the words left his mouth; he felt as if someone else, surely not Rick Joosten, had spoken through him, even though they'd said exactly what he most wanted to say. Even more to his surprise, Joey nodded, smiled, and started to push through the crowd.

Rick followed, energized by an adrenaline rush of equal part exhilaration and terror. What was he going to say? What else might come rushing past his lips once they were outside, away from the throng, out in the romance of a cool autumn night?

He moved past Joey to the sliding glass doors at the rear of the living room. They were already open and the party had spilled out onto the patio, but the backyard was still empty on the far side of the pool. His heart hammering, mouth dry, Rick led the way to two lounge chairs. "Take a seat," he said, gesturing.

Joey dropped into the low chair, drank from his beer, then turned that smile on Rick, and it made Rick weak as he sat.

"So what's up, Mister Rick? Or should I say…Doctor Rick?"

Rick feigned a laugh. "God, this was a bad choice. It was kind of a last minute thing…"

Joey tilted his bottle to Rick in a toast. "No way. You look very dashing."

Sweat exploded on Rick's face.

He blinked as some trickled into one eye, then he wiped a coat sleeve over his brow. Joey noticed, and leaned forward in concern. "You okay?"

"I don't know. That's actually part of what I wanted to ask you…"

"Anything, boss. You know that."

I want you, thought Rick, staring unhappily at this feet, *I want you so goddamn bad I can't even stand up when I'm around you, I want you so bad I'm willing to risk everything, a marriage, a career, forty-six years of a life that's been a lie, I want you so bad I'd die for just a single touch…*

"I may be coming down with something. Can you work for me tomorrow if I can't make it?"

In that moment Rick hated himself, especially when Joey leaned over and rested a hand on his shoulder in concern, and Rick had to bite the inside of his cheek to keep from taking that hand in his own.

"You know it. Don't worry about it, okay?"

Rick nodded, feeling sick over his own cowardice.

"Was there anything else?"

"Uh...yes..."

Joey waited, and finally Rick inhaled and turned to him. "Joey, are you gay?"

The young man blinked in surprise, and a wry, slightly bitter smile formed on his rugged face. Rick rushed out more words: "It's not—you know, a job thing, but—well, it's just something Shirl was wondering, and I..."

"Yeah, I am."

"Ah...because...well, frankly, Shirl and I haven't been happy for quite a while..."

Joey hesitated, then said, "Are you...coming out to me?"

"Yeah, I guess I am."

Then Rick was grinning. He felt delirious, feather-light, and he realized that he'd only needed to say that much, that the rest—how Joey made him feel—didn't matter anymore, not after admitting a truth he'd hidden for 46 years.

Joey grinned as well—

Screams erupted from the living room.

Rick's head swam for an instant as he was yanked from euphoria to alarm, then he was on his feet and running around the pool toward the house. Before he reached the door, Emmy Kazanian staggered towards him—and then crimson gushed from her neck, which he realized was slit ear to ear. They shared an absurdly surprised look, then she collapsed and fell at his feet, spraying blood on his white lab coat.

"Holy shit," Joey said, beside him. The last thing Rick ever thought was that he could face anything now that he was free of his dreadful burden and had Joey beside him.

Then the scythe whistled through the Halloween night and buried itself in Rick's chest. There was a flash of incandescent pain, followed by intense cold and a shift in his vision as his body sank, unfeeling.

The last thing he saw was Joey's blood-splattered face hitting the ground next to him.

DANSE MACABRE

Luke Ehrens had slowed to a walk, winded from a three-mile jog, as he reached the street where Merran Alstead lived. He turned the corner, started forward—and stopped.

Something was wrong.

He was briefly puzzled by his own behavior. Nothing was obvious. The lights were on in the houses; jack-o'-lanterns flickered on porches; bad dance music echoed from Rick and Shirl's.

But there was no one on the street. No groups of trick or treaters. No adults heading for the party. No parents waiting in doorways. There wasn't even the sound of laughter coming from the party; in fact, there were no human voices at all.

Luke almost turned and headed for his own house, a few blocks away. He could lock himself up in his bedroom, hide in a corner with his baseball bat. But he'd been charged with a task, something that he knew no mere cheap toy would keep at bay. After tonight, he believed in demons, absolutely, and he believed that one would come after him if he failed to deliver the message he'd been given. If he hid, it would find him. If he ran, it would catch him.

So he took a deep breath and started down the street, senses stretched taut, eyes darting from side to side.

He passed one silent house…two…Rick and Shirl's was next…

The music coming from their house changed. Without any segue, it transformed from 21st century pop to something far older, but with an even faster rhythm. The music reverberated in him somehow, as if he'd secretly known it all his life but forgotten it, because it was only supposed to be recalled at life's end.

Luke froze as the door to the house burst open, and a line of people stepped—no, *danced*—out. Leading them was a tall figure in black, clutching a blood-stained blade that somehow Luke identified as a scythe. The figure moved in an awkward, jerky way, and Luke thought he made out the clatter of bones along with the music.

Then he saw the line following the black-cloaked leader—and he began to shake.

He knew some of the people in the line—there was the widow Kazanian, there were the Nichols from his own street, there was Rick, clutching the hand of a man dressed as a Roman gladiator—but they were all covered in blood, and some dangled their own intestines as they danced to the maniacal tarantella.

Luke saw their ghastly wounds and pale skin and unseeing eyes, and he knew they were all dead.

Then the thing in the lead stopped fifty feet away, and he saw its hooded head. Bony fingers pushed the cowl back, revealing a perfect white skull, eyeless sockets fixed on Luke. It pointed a bony finger down the street—towards Merran's house—and then returned to leading the horrific dance.

For an instant, Luke thought he'd seen an image of the girl from Jay's backyard superimposed over the skull, and then he realized they were one and the same.

He stood, waiting, as the abominable line of nearly thirty dead danced behind the Samhanach, until they curved around past a fence and were finally lost from view.

When his senses returned, Luke felt something warm and wet on his legs, only now aware that his bladder had released itself. But none of that mattered now.

All that did was getting to Merran McCafferty.

MERRAN

Merran looked up from the book, distracted by a sound.

She thought she'd heard screaming. Not the childish shriek of Halloween glee, but adult voices—many of them—raised in terror, coming from down the street.

For some reason she thought of Rick and Shirl's party, and was glad she hadn't gone. After a few seconds, the sounds stopped, and she shrugged off her unease.

Seeing that there were still no approaching trick or treaters (*Strange*, she thought), she returned to the journal.

THE JOURNAL OF
CONNELL McCAFFERTY—1910

And now we come to my part of this history.

After his wee Ceana was stolen, Brian McCafferty was a changed man. He no longer saw to his businesses. The McCafferty clan, that had been well on its way to becoming one of Scotland's wealthiest families, fell into ruin and misfortune. The famines at mid-century didn't help; nor did the McCaffertys' insistence on staying in Inverness when so many others were fleeing to America.

By 1900, the McCaffertys were reduced to peat collecting. Which is where I found myself, in 1910.

It hasn't been a terrible life. My family has a small house out on the moors, near a peat bog. We spend our days digging great blocks of the stuff out of the earth, loading them onto the backs of carts, and taking them to market. A lifetime of hard labor took both my parents from me at a young age, but I have my beloved wife, Gillian, and we have...had...our two wee ones—Ewan, 12, and Aileen, 6. We had happy times with the bad; we had holidays and gatherings.

And then there was Hallowe'en.

I knew Brian and Michael's history, just as I've set it down here, and I *believed*. I saw how the curse had struck once in 1710, and again in 1810, and I knew that if the pattern continued, it would surely return in 1910. By October of this year I was the oldest surviving member of the McCafferty clan, so I knew the demon would come for me. Or rather...

For my darling little Aileen.

Now Ewan and Aileen held Hallowe'en in great esteem. Last year, for the first time, Aileen had been allowed to join the house-to-house festivities. Ewan had taught her what she'd need to know, and on the 31st the two of them had taken a cork from a bottle of wine, blackened it, then smeared the soot about their faces, until they looked barely human. They'd dressed in tattered castoffs kept just for this day, and joined with four of their friends, going to neighboring houses and presenting their own version of "The Old Horse," a play guisers had put on in this area as long as anyone had memory. At the conclusion of the play the house's residents had applauded and filled their bags with nuts and fruit, and they'd returned home at the end of the evening, happy and excited, with stories about the evening.

But that had been 1909. Now it was 1910. October 31st, to be precise. And there would be no Hallowe'en celebration this year.

I'd told Gillian, of course, the stories of the curse and the demon, and even though she had her doubts, she stood by me when I told the children we couldn't hold All Hallows' this year, that

I'd already made plans to send Ewan to his aunt and uncle's two parishes over.

Aileen would be staying, though. Because I knew it would be her who the Samhanach came after, and I wouldn't imperil another. Besides, I wanted to do what I could to protect her.

I'd spent the first nine months of that year talking to all the oldest locals, asking for any tales about the *sidh*, the mischievous fairy people, and their realm. I heard the tale of Tam Lin, who was rescued from the fairy queen by his lady love, Janet; I heard of the young man in the fairy knoll, who'd watched a foolish friend be seduced by fairy enchantment until he danced himself to death. I heard of the host of the dead, who came forth with the fairies only on November Eve, and I heard of mighty heroes of auld who'd fought the "good neighbors."

What I didn't hear was any way to kill a fairy demon.

Still, come the day of the 31st, we prepared as best we could.

We laid branches of rowan across the entry. We tied kale stems over the doorway. We made sure to throw out any water well before sundown.

I cleaned and loaded my shotgun.

Then we bolted the doors, shuttered the windows, tried to make merry with a feast of *fuarag* and barm brack, and waited by the hearth with Aileen clasped tightly in Gillian's arms.

All light left the sky, and the evening wore on. Gillian and I jumped at every creak of board, or scratching of mice. Aileen, thankfully, dozed off, disappointed at missing the main Hallowe'en activities, but blissfully unaware of the state her parents were in.

The clock had just passed eleven when it began.

First there was a light outside, too strong to be a lantern carried by man or carriage. Its rays penetrated through the shutters, striping us with a vivid amber glow that made Gillian and I blink. My wife clutched our little one tighter, and I rose, cradling the ready shotgun.

After hearing from my granddad of Brian's account, I moved to the front door, bracing myself a short distance from it...but then one of the front windows exploded, glass and splinters of wood shutters blowing inward, causing Gillian to scream and instinctively shield Aileen, who blinked in sleepy incomprehension.

I ran to the window, but before I could so much as lift the gun something hit me in the chest, hard enough to send me reeling back into the nearest wall. I rebounded, and saw something huge and dark bent over Gillian, who screamed and struggled. I raised the shotgun, but feared hitting my wife or child, so instead I ran forward, ready to swing the gun as a club—

Suddenly the thing turned to me, and the face was as terrible as Michael McCafferty's recollection: A vicious smile, lit from within by a fearsome light, with skin like a rotted vegetable rind.

And it had Aileen in its arms.

It turned and headed for the sundered wall; behind me Gillian screamed at me, "Shoot it! SHOOT IT!"

I did. I unloaded both barrels of the gun into its broad back. It didn't so much as stagger from the blows.

Instead it stepped outside, and began to run.

Its speed was immense, and I knew I could never hope to keep up. But I thought I knew where it was headed: On the other side of the peat bog was a small hill that some folk said was a fairy barrow, an entryway to the Otherworld.

I ran as fast as I could for that mound, and reached it a few minutes later. There was no sign of the thing that had wrested my daughter—

—but the mound was glowing, and there was an opening that had never been there before, like the entrance to a vast cavern.

I didn't stop to consider (as a wiser man would have), but ran for that doorway, my thoughts only on Aileen.

Inside was a cave, with glittering walls that seemed to be their own source of illumination. I made my way through the tunnel, around twists and turns, ducking stalactites and dodging iridescent pools, until finally the cave opened on the other side…

In the Otherworld.

And that's where I am now.

I'm not sure at this point how long I've been here, searching for Aileen and the Samhanach. The things I've seen…God himself has surely abandoned this place. Were it not for the fact that my mind is focused on finding my daughter, I'm sure I would have been driven mad long ago.

At some point I realized I still had this journal in a pocket, and so I've recorded everything into it that I can think of. I don't know if there's a way to protect future generations with this, but I—

MERRAN AND LUKE

"Ms. McCafferty—?"

Merran, startled, sucked in her breath and looked up from the journal to see a boy standing at the edge of her lawn. It took her a few seconds to place him: Luke Ahrens, one of the three delinquents who'd trudged by earlier in the evening. But something had happened to him since. He was completely white-faced now, his breath coming in shallow pants, and the front of his pants were wet.

"Yes…?"

The boy was shaking, too, and when he spoke there was a tremor in his voice. "I'm supposed to give you a message: I'm supposed to tell you that the—" he struggled a second before getting out the next word, "—the Samhanach has come tonight."

He'd turned the word into a strange guttural sound, with something like a "v" in the middle and a hoarse syllable, almost a cough, on the end, and so it took her a few seconds to connect it to the name she'd been reading in the journal:

The Samhanach.

How could he know that name?

Before Merran could form a question, the boy was heading off down the sidewalk at a rapid pace. Merran ran to the front of her yard, calling out after him: "Please, wait!"

The boy didn't turn, but gestured back at her. "I've got to get home."

"How did you know that name? Did something—?"

He cut her off this time. "I'm really sorry that I can't help you."

Then he started to run.

Merran considered going after him, but saw how fast he was moving (*he's got twenty years on me, I'll never catch him*), and gave up on that plan of action. Instead she pondered the message:

The Samhanach has come tonight.

The kid—Luke—must have been in on some elaborate practical joke, even though the terrified look on his face told Merran that he'd been a victim, rather than a perpetrator. Someone—surely it had to be Will, for whatever fucked-up reason—was trying to scare her, with stories of ancestral curses, and a mythical creature that stole children—

Oh God. Jeannie.

Alarm shot through Merran's system at the thought that her daughter might be part of some malicious prank. Before her heart could take another beat she was running for the house and the cell phone that was charging on the front table. It held Keesha's number in memory, and Merran's fingers were clumsy with panic as she flipped the phone open, punched a button and waited.

After a few seconds Keesha's cheery voice answered. "Trick or treat!"

Merran's heart slowed, slightly, in relief. "Jeannie is with you, right?"

Even over the cell phone connection, she could hear the perplexity in Keesha's tone. "Of course. She's forty feet away from me right now, extorting candy from another homeowner. Is everything all right?"

"Where are you?"

There was a beat, as Keesha apparently looked around. "We're on Houston, in front of 4452."

Merran calculated: That was about three blocks away. "Keesha, can you start heading for home now? I'm coming to you—meet you at the corner of Houston and 43rd."

"Okay, but…is something wrong?"

"I'll tell you when I see you. Just start home—don't go to any more houses or talk to anyone."

Merran snapped the phone shut, shoved it in a pocket, and ran.

THE WITCH AND THE OLD MAN

Keesha's two kids were already at the door of the last house, shouting out, "Trick or treat!" but Jeannie was still halfway up the front walk. Her nose was falling off again, and she paused to adjust it.

"Hurry up, Jeannie," she heard Keesha call from the sidewalk, "your mom wants you home."

"She does?"

"She just called. Something's going on. Let's make this the last house of the evening, okay?"

Jeannie shrugged, then finally got her long, wart-encrusted nose properly aligned, and dodged Darren and Marissa as they ran by her. If this was going to be the end of trick or treat for another year, she was going to make sure she looked perfect and was well compensated in return.

The porch, lit only by a very large, flickering jack-o'-lantern, was a little spookier than Jeannie liked, but she felt powerful in her witch costume, confident that she could banish either human or monster. She rang the doorbell, called out the classic solicitation—"Trick or treat!"—and extended her plastic pumpkin, waiting.

After a few seconds the door creaked open, revealing the dim outline of a very old man. Although most of him was in shadow (they didn't seem to have any lights on inside the house), she could tell he was long and bent, with a nearly bald head.

"Well, well, well," he said, and Jeannie was relieved to hear that his voice sounded nice, not mean or creepy at all. "What have we here? A little witch?"

"Yes, sir—I'm the Halloween Witch!"

The old man chuckled softly. "My goodness, I had no idea I was in the presence of such an important personage. And let me get a look at that costume…"

He stepped out onto the porch, and Jeannie felt a moment of irritation—why didn't he just hand her the candy? She'd said the right thing, and her mom was waiting.

But the old man was whistling as he eyed her costume, and she *did* enjoy being admired. "That is very good. Very, very good."

He bent closer, and now Jeannie could see the lines in his face and tufts of white on the sides of his head. He wore little round glasses that made his milky eyes look huge as he squinted at her. "Why, I think this is the best outfit I've seen all night. Say, I don't suppose you'd like to do me a favor?"

"Uh…I'm kind of in a hurry…"

"Oh, it wouldn't take long." He gestured at the dark open doorway behind him, and for a second it reminded Jeannie of a big, hungry mouth. "My wife can't walk, but she loves trick or treaters, and I know she'd love to see your costume. Do you think you could come in and show her?"

He stepped back, throwing an inviting arm toward the lightless living room.

"Why is she in the dark?" Jeannie asked, trying to peer past him.

"Oh, if you come in, I'll turn on the lights so she can get a good look at you."

Jeannie considered for a moment, and looked back, hoping Keesha would make the decision for her—but she couldn't see Keesha on the street, or Darren or Marissa.

"Uh," she started, then faced him, bucking up the courage to turn down an adult, "sorry, but my mom doesn't let me go into strange houses."

"You wouldn't have to come any farther than just the living room."

Jeannie was starting to feel something more than just irritation; a tiny snowflake of dread was forming inside her. "I can't. Sorry, but I have to go—"

She started to turn, but the man called after her, "Wait!"

She reluctantly looked at him again. He backed up a step, reached inside the doorway, and retrieved a camera. "May I at least take your picture to show my wife?"

"I guess." Seeing the old man poised at the entrance, Jeannie remembered why she'd come up to the house in the first place. "Do you have any candy?"

He barked a short laugh. "Oh my—we have something much better!"

He thrust an arm back into the house, and produced a perfect red apple, which he dropped into her bucket. Jeannie stared at it, perplexed. "An apple?"

The man nodded. "The oldest of Halloween symbols."

"I don't think my mom will let me have anything that's not wrapped."

"Oh, that's just not right. Apples have been a part of Halloween for thousands of years. Even the Celts included apples in their celebrations."

Jeannie frowned. "The who?"

The man smiled wryly. "Right you are—they've been gone for a very long time now."

He held up the camera, preparing to snap the shot, and Jeannie eyed it curiously. It was a strange, boxy thing, like no camera she'd ever seen. It had a glass lens, yes, and a viewfinder that the old man peered through, but it seemed to have *two* flashes that popped up like eyes on either side of the black body. Something about it made Jeannie uncomfortable, and she thought about just going, running back to find Keesha, and then her mom…but she had been given an apple. And she felt bad for the man's sick wife.

"Say 'Samhanach,'" the man murmured, finger poised over the shutter release button.

"Huh?"

There was a small click as the button was depressed—

—and then there was the sound of a small detonation, and a thousand suns exploded in Jeannie's eyes. She cried out and instinctively dropped her bucket as her hands moved to her face, knocking her fake nose off, but she was blinded, completely. She felt herself lifted, tucked up under an arm that was like an iron band around her waist, and now she couldn't see or move, but she could SCREAM, as she was carried off by something that ran, something that couldn't have been the bent old man who'd moved so slowly and cautiously. She clawed at the arm holding her, and the flesh felt strange under her fingers, like the tough rind of a pumpkin.

All that was left to her was to scream.

MERRAN

Merran heard her daughter screaming. But the sound came from behind her.

She was at the corner of her street and Houston, ready to head west and find Keesha and Jeannie—but then she heard that terrible sound. She whirled, and saw something huge and awkward rush out of a side street behind her, heading back towards her house.

She reversed course and ran after it, every nerve set on fire by the sound of Jeannie's shrieks.

"Jeannie!"

The screams paused for a moment. "MOM!"

Merran tried to increase her speed, her lungs already ragged and burning, but that didn't matter. What did was catching the thing that held her daughter underarm. It was a good eight feet tall, with misshapen head and too-narrow shoulders, and it ran with loping strides that were easily increasing the distance between it and Merran.

No…faster…

But she was nearly middle-aged, and human, and she saw that this thing would soon lose her...

...until it turned into a yard that, even from half-a-block down, she knew was hers.

It went into MY house?!

But she didn't let that question slow her down. She kept her speed until she reached her front yard. She effortlessly cleared the bordering hedge, dodged lit jack-o'-lanterns, and paused as she reached the porch, panting.

The front door was still closed, just as she'd left it.

But she'd been panicked enough that she hadn't locked it. She threw the door back, racing quickly through the house, but knew in seconds that the monster and her daughter weren't there.

She ran back outside, her eyes darting about the yard. There was nothing there, just innocent jack-o'-lanterns lighting a quiet lawn. Nowhere that something that big could have hidden, and the sound of Jeannie's screaming had vanished. She felt desperation and horror boiling up, threatening to overwhelm her, to set her screaming louder than Jeannie—

—and then her eyes fell on the ring of toadstools in the dark corner of her lawn.

The ring was glowing.

She stepped up to it, and felt something change subtly; hairs on the back of her arms and neck stood up, the air charged with ozone.

There was power here.

Something surged into her consciousness, something from her college days, when she'd studied the folklore of olden times: Fairy rings, formed from toadstools, were dangerous places, especially on Mayday or Halloween. Mischievous elves could lure unwary humans into the rings and trap them there. The rings would mysteriously disappear a day later, along with the ethereal pranksters.

Merran knew: The circle formed a gateway to the fairies' realm. The Otherworld.

The Samhanach (for such it could only be) had taken Jeannie, and escaped back to its own world here. Her only chance at regaining her daughter was to step through, attempt to follow it. Part of her urged her forward without hesitation, and she suddenly stood at the edge of the circle, a foot poised in mid-step to enter...

She drew it back. She had to think this through. To enter another world, unprepared, un*armed*, could do Jeannie more harm than good. No, she had to do this carefully. But quickly, because she remembered Connell's journal, how the demon had disappeared at exactly midnight on Halloween. She glanced at her watch.

It was 9:24. How had it gotten to be that late?

Merran turned away, trying to remember those folklore classes, nearly two decades back. Demons…fairies…pranksters… what had protected against them?

Something about…iron. Or was it silver?

Did a modern, urban American even have access to either?

She thought about iron, and could only come up with the term "tire iron"; she had a crowbar in the car, but had no idea if it was actually made from iron or not.

Silver…she had silver jewelry, certainly…

Sterling silver. She had the McCafferty family's sterling silver flatware set, stashed in a drawer in the kitchen. It was supposedly nearly 150 years old…and it included a long, sharp, carving knife.

She ran to the kitchen, tearing drawers open until she found the velvet roll that held the silverware. She shook it open, disregarding the clatter as spoons, forks, and dull butter knives spilled out onto the floor. There—the serving fork, and—

The knife.

She snatched it up, examining its surface. She'd been meaning to polish the set for years, to research the manufacturer's marks and the value, but—as with so many other things—she'd never gotten to it. The knife still gleamed though, with a long blade and tapered, sharp point. She ran a thumb along the edge, and although it didn't cut through the flesh, she thought the point, driven into something with the weight of her body behind it, could prove quite lethal.

Merran wasn't sure if the entire implement was silver—she thought the blade might be stainless steel. Which meant it was an alloy of iron…so the knife had a silver handle, and an iron blade.

It would do for a weapon.

Grabbing a canvas bag from a cupboard, Merran threw the knife in, and—after quick consideration—added a lighter, a small container of butane, her cell phone, and Connell's journal. She pocketed only her house keys—she wanted to keep the pockets of her jeans as free as possible, so nothing could impede her ability to run.

She glanced at her watch again—9:30 exactly—and left the house behind. As she locked the front door, she tried not to wonder if she'd ever be back.

Frankly, she didn't *want* to come back if she didn't have her daughter.

Slinging the bag over one shoulder, Merran strode to the ring of toadstools—still glowing softly in the too-quiet evening—and hesitated. Then, taking a deep breath, she raised a foot, and stepped through.

THE FAERIE REALM

Nothing happened.

Stifling an urge to scream out of sheer frustration, Merran looked around carefully. This was her lawn, there was her porch, the front door of her house, the jack-o'-lanterns…

Wait—something *had* changed:

It was the pumpkins. They had subtly altered, becoming larger and more malevolent looking. It wasn't, perhaps, immediately obvious, but Merran had carved every one of them, and she was sure she hadn't carved *that* one with an expression that looked like a pedophile's leer, and surely *that* pumpkin weighed close to 40 pounds, while she knew she hadn't bought any that were even half that big. And the glow coming from each one seemed brighter, with more orange and red—

Then the closest one widened its grin and rolled its eyes at her.

Merran felt a thrill, made up of equal parts fear and wonder. She really *had* stepped through a fairy ring on Halloween night and traveled to some other place, where demons lived with stolen children and pumpkins wore living faces. She was in a world of magic, where anything was possible…

One of the jack-o'-lanterns snapped at her ankle.

Merran felt something brush her leg and heard a *thunk* as rind-covered teeth clamped together, and she stumbled back, looking down at the pumpkin that now opened its mouth wide again, ready. Another sound came from behind her, and she spun to see two pumpkins leaning forward, trying to reach her.

She scanned the yard, looking for a path to clear the pumpkins; all around, she could hear the sound of their thick, fleshy mouths closing, and a strange groaning, as if their shells were trying to expand, stretching beyond what they were designed for. She thought she saw a way to reach the relative safety of the porch, but it would involve jumping over some of the jack-o'-lanterns...and she certainly didn't want to go near the cobwebs she'd strung earlier in the night, once fake but now alive with skittering shadows...

She ran for it.

Some of the pumpkins were large enough that leaping over them was difficult, and Merran tried not to think of them beneath her airborne feet, turning for a mid-air bite, their carven eyes shifting to follow her, candle-heated air erupting from triangular noses.

With a long, final leap, she reached the porch. She paused to catch her breath and turned to look back, half expecting to see the damned things now growing legs or sprouting wings—but instead they were again inanimate, almost serene.

She resettled the bag straps on her shoulder, then considered her situation. She had no idea which way to go, no way of knowing where the monster had taken Jeannie. As long as she'd reached the porch, she turned and looked at the front of her house...

And saw that the door was ajar.

That was impossible—she'd clearly remembered locking it, just minutes before, wondering if it was the last time she'd see her house. But now it was open, and even creaked slightly in the evening breeze.

Merran reached into the bag and withdrew the knife. She clenched it tightly in her right hand, then reached out with her left to push the door slowly open. Even before she'd moved the door more than an inch or two she saw something was wrong—the light coming from within the house was different somehow, softer and with a hint of green.

She kicked the door all the way back on its hinges, and froze in astonishment at what she saw. Any expectations of a sudden attacker like some costumed ghoul from a cheap Halloween haunted house were dashed instantly.

The doorway opened onto not her comfortable living room,

but the stony interior of a cavern. Stalactites and milky water dripped from overhead, and the light was provided by the walls themselves; Merran couldn't tell if some mineral in the stone was phosphorescent, or if some sort of fungus or moss covering the walls provided the greenish glimmer.

The cavern narrowed ahead to a single tunnel, just big enough for a man (or woman) to pass through. Merran wondered briefly if the Samhanach could really have come this way—it would have had to bend nearly double to pass through the tunnel—but then she remembered that she was dealing with an immortal shapeshifter.

Yes, the demon had almost certainly come this way.

Holding the knife out before her, Merran walked through the open cavern, then ducked several long stalactites and stepped into the tunnel. After just a few feet it twisted sharply left; then, another yard or two on, a hard right. The path turned out to be serpentine, bending and curving constantly, keeping Merran on edge. She led into every turn with the knife blade held before her, expecting an attack to come from around every new bend, but the only footsteps she heard echoing in the tunnel were hers, the only other sound the susurration of water dripping. The glow from the walls occasionally changed hue, moving through the cool end of the spectrum: green, blue, violet.

After a few minutes of making her way through this underground labyrinth, Merran had the sensation of being lulled into a kind of hypnagogic state; it was almost as if she were journeying into the center of a vast dream. Or—given how this cave felt strangely familiar—a collective subconscious.

Just when she was wondering if this cave had any real destination (if she turned back, would the way out still be there, behind her?), it startled her by abruptly ending. She turned a final corner and stepped out of the cave...

She stopped, surveying her new surroundings. She was outside, in a small clearing at the edge of a great forest. Overhead, a full quarter of the night sky was filled with a cyclopean harvest moon, its pumpkin-orange surface bathing the landscape in an amber light. It would have been lovely, romantic even, had it not been for the forest.

The trees, which grew up to the edge of the clearing, barely ten yards away, were dark even under the strong golden glow, and Merran thought the wood would be black even by daylight. They stretched out long twigs and branches like skinless fingers, and the bark on the trunks waved in strange directions, forming shapes and, almost, faces. The trees grew close together, and Merran shivered at the thought of venturing into that forest, trying to find her way in the dense growth, where little light penetrated…

And there were the sounds. The forest was alive with them: howls, cries, barks, snarls. Merran could barely guess what sort of animal any of the noises belonged to—bird, mammal, reptile, human, or inhuman. She instinctively recoiled, not relishing coming up against anything that could make that ululating wail, or that guttural growl.

She had no idea which way to go. Behind her was a rocky cliff so tall she couldn't see the top; the cave had spilled out from the base of the cliff, and she could just make out a few other openings in the granite wall. To her right was a small path that bordered the cliff; she thought she saw several trails leading off into the forest.

She turned back to the cave, wondering if it was possible she'd missed a turn somewhere. She glanced at her watch—it was now after ten—and knew she couldn't afford to make a wrong decision.

"Oh my God—Merran?"

She jumped, startled by the voice, and whirled to spot a figure emerging from the trees. The voice…she knew the voice…but it couldn't be…and yet, as he stepped into the moonlight, she saw it was—

"Will…?"

"Yeah. It *is* you."

He stepped forward, stopping a few feet from her. He looked pale, anxious, and was dressed simply, in a white shirt and black slacks. Merran lowered the knife, and tried to find words.

"How can you be here?"

Will looked around, perplexed and afraid. "I don't know how I got here. What is this place?"

Merran shook her head. "I don't know." She *did* know, in a way, but she couldn't answer him because of his mere presence. Why was he here? To help? Had some force for good brought Jeannie's other parent here to take her back, keep Merran from having to face this nightmare alone? She hated to admit that she was glad to see Will again, but under the circumstances...

He suddenly fixed her with his eyes. "Is Jeannie with you?"

"No. God, Will, something took her—she was out trick or treating, and—"

"What do you mean, 'something took her'?!"

There was a hint of anger in his voice, and Merran felt her own body tense for a coming fight, a reaction she'd come to know all too well in the last year of their marriage. "Some kind of—I don't know exactly what it was, but I followed it here—"

"Wait, hold on." Will took a step closer to her, and she saw now that his eyes were hard, his jaw set. "Are you telling me that you let something take our daughter?"

Merran tried to answer—she wanted to shout at him to help, to not start an argument now, not when their daughter was in the arms of a monster—but her jaw only hung open in disbelief...and guilt. She felt anger burning, and frustration; she was ashamed by tears welling. "Goddamnit, Will, *no*—I didn't 'let something take our daughter.' She was *kidnapped*—"

"Were you with her when it happened?"

"No, I..." As the first drop slid down her cheek, she hurriedly brushed it away. "She was with Keesha—"

He cut her off, no longer trying to contain his own rage. "I don't fucking believe this—you're telling me you left a six-year-old with someone else on fucking Halloween?!"

The tears came freely now, and Merran sagged back against the rock behind her, unable to look at him any longer. "Will, we have to go get her..."

"And I suppose you know exactly where she is in this—well, whatever the fuck this place is..."

"No, I don't. I don't have a clue..."

"Great. That's just fucking great, Merran." And then he was standing only inches away, shouting down at her. "HOW FUCKING STUPID COULD YOU BE TO LET THIS HAPPEN?!"

She'd failed. She'd failed as a wife, as a mother, as her daughter's protector, and now she'd fail as her daughter's rescuer. Will had managed to target her greatest fear with a single perfectly-aimed bullet, and now she collapsed, sinking to her knees, rendered helpless by her own overwhelming sense of inadequacy.

Will bent over her, looming, and opened his mouth for

another salvo. "YOU'RE A FUCKING DISASTER OF A MOTHER—"

THUD. A rock flew out of nowhere and hit Will on the side of the head.

He staggered, his eyes glassing over briefly, then he spun, searching for his attacker. In that instant, another missile connected with his face. Merran blinked, then hurriedly wiped away tears as she saw Will start to change. He stumbled back, thrown off balance, and even as he did he was shrinking, his limbs shortening, head and chest collapsing inward like deflating balloons. His clothing melted away, and his skin changed color, from cream to pale blue. His mouth grew outsized fangs, curling over his purple lips, and a snakelike tail sprouted from his back.

When he was no more than two feet tall, he hissed at something off to Merran's right, then scuttled into the sanctuary of the great forest. He was lost from sight within seconds.

Still gaping in astonishment, Merran struggled to stand, then turned toward the sound of a male voice that was asking, "Are ye unharmed, lassie?"

A man stood at the head of the path to her right. He had long brown hair, waving down to his shoulders, and an equally long beard; he still clutched another stone in his right hand, and his eyes darted from Merran to the edge of the forest.

"I…yes…"

The voice was gruff, as if seldom used, and thick with Scottish brogue. "Ye'd best follow me. 'Tis nae safe out here, wi' the bogies 'round."

"Is that…that was a…"

He nodded. "Aye. I could see its real form, even if ye could nae. But ye'd been magicked."

This was too much to take in. Merran walked towards him, dumbly.

His eyes moved from her face down to her right hand, and suddenly went wide. Merran looked down, and realized she still held the knife, forgotten during her confrontation with the thing that had mimicked her husband.

"Oh…I…sorry…" She started to return the knife to her bag.

"Ye've got a knife." The statement was made with astonishment, and a hint of sheer joy.

"Yes…"

"May I see it?"

Merran started to extend it toward him, then caught herself: *What if he's another monster in disguise? Do I just hand over my only weapon?* "Why do you want it?"

He glanced from the blade to Merran. "Good. That's the attitude ye'll need in this place. And t' answer yer question: My interest in yer knife is that it's the first decent weapon I've seen in a year." He narrowed his eyes and bent closer. "And it looks like ane I once owned..."

She raised the knife so he could see the hilt. "This has been in my family for a long time."

He leaned forward, trying to examine the knife by moonglow. "Aye...very like, it is...wha' might yer name be?"

"Merran. Merran Alstead."

He looked briefly disappointed, until she added, "My maiden name was McCafferty."

He froze in astonishment, then grinned and jabbed a finger in her direction. "Aye. I thought I could ken tha' chin. We're kin, lassie—I'd be Connell McCafferty."

Now it was Merran's turn to stare, incredulous. "Connell... you're Connell?!"

"At yer service." He thrust a hand at her, and Merran took it, feeling a strong, calloused grip. Just then something large cried out from dangerously nearby, and Connell changed the friendly grip to a firm tug. "We'd best nae talk here. I've a safe place nae far. Come."

He released her to move quickly down the narrow path between cliff and forest, and Merran followed, caught between wonder and apprehension. Could this really be the great-great-grandfather she'd first met via his journal? He had ended by saying he'd crossed over to this world, but that had been a hundred years ago, and this man was still young and vital...

A few minutes later, Connell was lifting a camouflage of branches and leaves away from the cliff, revealing another cave mouth, artfully hidden. He motioned her in, and she complied; she saw a cave that widened and went back perhaps 40 feet, with a small fire flickering at the far end. Various homemade weapons and tools lined the floor, and herbs and dried meat hung from the soot-blackened ceiling.

She stepped aside as Connell followed her in, then moved the camouflage back in place, followed by a heavy wooden barrier. He strode down the tunnel to the fire, gesturing about him.

"Nae quite a' the comforts o' home, but it's been my home for ane year now." He gestured at the ground near the fire. "Now, s'pose ye rest and tell me about how ye came here, Merran McCafferty."

Merran didn't take the floor, but instead held up her wrist and watch. "I need you to answer me a question first: Will the gate or door or whatever back to my world close at midnight?"

"Aye..." then Connell squinted at her digital watch. "I've nae seen a timepiece quite like tha' one..." His gaze moved suspiciously up to her face. "What year have ye come from?"

"2010."

Connell looked as if he'd just been sucker-punched in the gut. He let out a long breath, then sank to a sitting position by the fire. "2010...a hundred year...dear Lord, a century passed, as I feared..."

She crouched beside him, laying a reassuring hand on his shoulder. "Connell, you know about the Samhanach, right?"

When he looked at her, his eyes were hooded with a deep-seated loathing. "Aye. Tha' demon is why I'm here..."

"And me, too. It's got my daughter. Do you know where it is?"

Connell ground his jaws together for a few seconds, then looked at her. "Aye. It lives nae far from here. I've watched it every day for a year..."

"But you've been here...."

He gestured at a rock wall nearby, and Merran saw hundreds of tiny slash marks etched into the stone. "A year by my reckoning. But, as I'd feared—time flows weirdly between the twa worlds. A century at home is only a year here."

Something clicked in Merran's head. "Then that's why the Samhanach only shows up once every hundred years..."

He nodded. "Aye. Because but a year has passed here. An' it can only cross over on Hallow's Eve. Once a year."

Merran couldn't help but glance at her watch again. "So if I don't get out of here in just over an hour..."

Connell's gaze darkened again. "Ye'll be trapped here, as I've been."

Remembering, Merran reached into her bag and produced the small book. "But you managed to get your journal to me..."

He peered at the book and blinked in dismay. "My what…?"

"Your journal."

Shaking his head, Connell said, "Nae mine. I've never larned t' read or write. I'm naught but a poor workin' man without schoolin'. I fear ye've been tricked."

Merran stared at the journal, stunned. "But…why?"

"Our adversary is a great trickster, he is. An' a nasty one. Just takin' yer child was nae enow; this way the bogie's trapped ye here as well. I ken he's got more fun planned for ye."

Merran dropped the book back in her bag, and hefted the knife. "No. I'm getting my daughter back and leaving here, before twelve."

Connell squinted at the knife. "Well, tha' does have a steel blade, as I recall…and steel's mainly iron, which a' the stories say the faerie kind dinnae like. Ye came better prepared than I did, lassie, and we might ha'e a chance…" He moved with sudden resolution, picking up a long homemade spear in one hand and a torch in the other. "We'd best move quickly."

Merran grinned, and followed him out of the cave.

THE McCAFFERTYS AND THE SAMHANACH

They talked, in soft tones, as Connell led her on a well-defined path through the forest. He asked about her life, what America and her world were like. She asked how he'd survived here for a year, and he told her that it was different in the daytime—almost idyllic, with plentiful game and good water.

But mostly they talked of their children. Merran had to sadly admit that she knew little of Ewan, who had passed on by the time she was born; Connell told her he was sure little Aileen was still alive, because he'd heard her cries at times, although he'd been unable to reach her.

It turned out that most of the journal had been reasonably accurate; Connell confirmed the stories of Michael and Brian McCafferty, and how the family's fortune had fallen. Merran realized she liked Connell a great deal, and was proud to call this man her great-great-grandfather.

At one point something reached out for them from the darkness, and Merran caught only a glance of a misshapen paw before

Connell swung the torch. There was a squeal of pain, and after a second to make sure their would-be attacker had retreated, they continued on, undisturbed.

Finally, the path emptied out of the trees onto the edge of a large, flat clearing—which Merran realized was a swamp only when she stepped out and felt something sucking her foot down. Connell was there to pull her back; once he'd steadied her on solid ground, he spoke in a desperate whisper.

"This is the demon's bog."

Merran saw only black liquid and low-lying vapors. "How do we get through this?"

"We don't. It'll find us." After a few seconds, Connell nodded at the knife. "Merran, d'ye not think I should have tha'? I've had more experience here, I can handle a knife—"

"So can I." He looked at her with some measure of surprise, and she added, "Women are equal in 2010, Connell."

He shook his head in disbelief. "Mus' be a strange world indeed."

They waited in silence a few seconds, then Merran cried out in frustration. "Where the hell is it?! You're sure this is the right place?"

"I told ye, I've been here every day for a year. 'Tis the right place."

Her watch read 11:31.

She performed a quick mental calculation in her mind: It'd taken them ten minutes to get here from Connell's cave, and she thought it'd taken her about ten minutes to get through the cave. She was looking at 20 minutes minimum, then, to get back to the toadstool ring.

Unless whatever was going to happen, happened soon…

"I'm not going to make it—"

She broke off as the surface of the swamp eight feet away began to churn. Something breached the water and continued to rise up, up, and she saw the oversized head with blazing features, the apelike limbs—and, clutched against the hollow chest, a child-sized bundle wrapped in some sort of translucent skin. Like a birth caul.

"No, Merran," came a voice like a fierce wind grinding down a rock wall, "you're not going to make it. Not you, nor your child."

"Jeannie!" She tried to make out features through the strange, oily sac, and she thought she saw her daughters face, the mouth opening and closing slightly.

"Your child now belongs to me, to do with as I will."

Connell stepped forward, his own voice a harsh growl. "Demon! Wha' of my child, who you stole from me a year ago?!"

The Samhanach's mouth twisted in glee. "Ahh. That one now dwells with the faerie queen and her court. I doubt if she even remembers you."

Connell cried out in distress and swung the torch, but the Samhanach was still three feet past Connell's reach.

The bogie moved its scarlet gaze down towards Jeannie, who either slept or was held captive in the caul. "As for this one, I'm still undecided. Perhaps a gift to the great carrion birds of Cruachan, who are always hungry—"

Merran stepped forward and gestured with the knife. "Let go of my daughter!"

The demon eyed her with vicious amusement. "Are you sure?"

Her body tensing, Merran answered: "You've tormented my family for three centuries, you bastard. It ends tonight."

The Samhanach uttered a deafening sound that caused Merran to flinch, and that she could only assume was its laughter.

Then it dropped Jeannie.

For a split second, Merran stared in disbelief as the bog began to pull her daughter's immobile body beneath its black surface. Then she leapt, all rational thought fled, banished before the image of her daughter lost forever in the depths of a lightless bog in a world of monsters. She reached with her left hand for Jeannie, even as she felt the swamp tugging at her. Her hand clamped onto the sac around the child, and it felt hideously organic, like a skinned animal. She tried to haul Jeannie out, but she was fighting both the sac and the swamp. So she raised the knife, and drew it along the surface of the caul. The membrane split beneath the blade, and suddenly Jeannie was crying and reaching out.

"Ha'e her ta'e this!"

Merran looked back and saw Connell extending his spear. She pulled Jeannie free from the sac, and let the swamp take the horrible thing. Then she saw Jeannie's hands grasp the wooden haft, and Connell was pulling her to shore; she was free—

The Samhanach reached after her.

Merran saw the hand move past her, and she swung out

blindly with the knife. It connected with the thing's sinuous arm, and the bogie shrieked, wounded, as hot ichor splattered the swamp around Merran.

She wasn't going to let it retreat. The swamp surface was almost up to her chest now, and this would be her only chance. She rallied the last of her strength and swung the knife in a great overhead arc. A wild exhilaration surged through her as she buried the knife up to the hilt in the Samhanach's midsection, and its scream of rage and terror and agony told her that she'd wounded it badly, even mortally. She withdrew the knife and stabbed again, and again, and then the thing was sinking into the bog, still shrieking, and she was being dragged down with it. The swamp closed over her mouth, nose, eyes...

And it was acceptable, because Jeannie was safe, and even though Connell couldn't take her home, he'd make sure they both survived here, and the Samhanach would never answer another call for vengeance—

She felt something slap her left hand, the only part of her still left above the swamp's surface.

It was Connell's spear.

She wrapped her hand around it. She didn't think she'd be able to hang on, but she found new reserves of strength as she was pulled up, out of the bog. Her head broke the surface and she gasped for air.

"Both hands now!"

That was Connell. She squinted through the muck in her eyes, and saw him crouched on shore...

With Jeannie standing beside him, looking bedraggled and desperate.

She thrust her right hand up out of the swamp, and saw it still held the knife. She tossed the knife up onto the bank, then grasped Connell's spear with the other hand. He groaned as he put his weight into pulling, and slowly, so slowly, she came free of the bog, her shoulders on the shore, then her chest, waist, and finally she pulled her legs free.

Connell collapsed beside her, panting in exertion and relief. Jeannie's hands were around her neck, both of them covered in the bog's thick, dark slime. Merran allowed herself a moment of relief, then she remembered—

Her watch said 11:43.

"Oh God." She lurched to her feet, much to Jeannie's surprise. "Mommy—"

"Baby, we've got to go. NOW."

Connell was already on his feet. He paused just long enough to retrieve the knife and the torch, then he took the lead on the path. "This way."

Merran knelt before Jeannie. "Can you move?"

Jeannie nodded, her eyes wide.

And so they ran.

COMING HOME

They ran through the forest, and nothing tried to stop them. When Jeannie stumbled, Merran picked her up and ran with her, even after every muscle threatened to snap and every breath scorched her lungs.

At 11:51, they reached the cave mouth.

"You won't need the torch," Merran told him. He nodded silently, tossed it aside, and they entered the cave, Connell in the lead.

They made their way through the same glowing maze, around corners and beneath low-hanging stalactites.

At 11:57, they left the last twist of the cave and saw Merran's front door.

She threw it open, and there was the faerie version of her yard, complete with grimacing jack-o'-lanterns.

The toadstool ring was glowing so brightly it was incandescent, causing Merran to squint. She started down the porch steps, saying to Connell: "Be careful of the pumpkins—they're alive."

"Merran..."

Something in his tone caused her to stop and turn back. Connell stood on the porch, her knife still clenched in his hand, his features creased in anxiety.

"I cannae gae."

She stopped, staring at him silently for a moment; in Merran's arms, Jeannie also looked on, still wiping silt from her eyes.

"Connell, of course you have to come. You can't stay here..."

"I've no choice, lassie. D'ye nae remember the old tales?"

Merran hesitated, thinking back to the Scottish folklore, stories of those who returned from trips to the Otherworld, stepped back onto home ground—

And died instantly from old age. Of course—Connell would be over 130 years old in the human world.

"Oh God. Oh, Connell, I'm so sorry…"

He stepped down and gave her a gentle push. "Ye've no time lef'. Go now."

She nodded, feeling the tears again, but knowing she couldn't afford that luxury right now. Clutching her daughter tightly, she leapt quickly over the pumpkins until she'd reached the edge of the blinding white ring. Then she turned to look back one last time.

Connell smiled and gestured with the knife. "Oh, if ye dinnae mind—I'll keep the knife. It might help when I find Aileen."

"It's yours, anyway."

She and Connell shared a last look, of grief and victory and mutual blood.

Then she stepped into the ring.

BY DAWN'S LIGHT

Merran blinked, the afterglow of the faerie circle still burned onto her retinas…

So it took her a moment to realize the sky overhead was light, pale blue, brighter to the east.

Sunrise.

When her vision cleared, she looked down at the ground. Although it was still dim, she could see that the toadstools had withered, become nothing but tiny dried caps buried in the grass. The unlit jack-o'-lanterns lay scattered about the lawn, now just outdated decorations.

Merran toed one just to be sure.

Convinced that she was home and safe, she staggered to the front porch and sat there, cradling Jeannie in her lap. "You okay?"

The little girl nodded. "Are we home?"

"We're home, baby."

Merran glanced at her watch, saw that it read 12:02. She'd have to remember to re-set it.

The dawn was chilly, and she hugged Jeannie tightly, for

warmth and love. Her thoughts kept returning to Connell, left behind in an inhuman world, searching for his own daughter armed with nothing more than a knife.

In time, she hoped she'd be able to think of him without feeling regret, loss, even guilt.

At this moment, though, she knew she had to focus on herself, on Jeannie. Things would be different. Will was a minor boogeyman now, nothing but a scuttling lesser imp. She had more important things to deal with, like her own life, and her daughter's.

But most of all, she tried not to remember the other old stories, of changelings, those stolen by mischievous sprites and switched with unearthly children. Merran's mind kept returning to the image of Jeannie in what looked like a birth sac, held in the arms of the Samhanach as it taunted Connell with the notion of his child now an alien thing, lacking memories of her former humanity. Merran promised herself that she wouldn't watch obsessively for signs of odd behavior on the part of her daughter, that she'd always love her, no matter what the future might bring.

Then she sat on the steps of her own home, with her daughter, and watched the sun rise over the quiet neighborhood, the beginning of a new day.

FINDING ULALUME

When the message came, it was simple enough:

SCSSAR Team needed. Please proceed ASAP to end of County Route 24. There were GPS coordinates after that.

It was the fourth Search and Rescue I'd been called for since I'd volunteered two months back. A lot of folks got lost up in the mountains—hikers took a wrong turn, maybe a bad tumble into a ravine, and it was our job to save them.

But this time I wasn't going to the mountains. I knew damned well what was at the end of Route 24:

Weir Forest.

As a child, it has been forbidden territory. My grandmother, who we all called Grams, lived at the edge of the place, and sometimes my parents would drop the two of us—my sister Anna and I—off for the weekend with her, loaded down with warnings about children who'd disappeared in the black, pathless interior of the woods. At night, as the silhouettes of the trees grew below the starlight, Grams told us stories about how things got worse the farther in you went: First, there were ghosts; then ghouls, half-demons who craved the taste of human flesh.

But there was something in the very heart of the woods,

something too terrible to even speak of. When Grams mentioned that last, awful thing, she dropped her voice to a whisper, which was sure to produce a shiver in us. It was near the lake, Auber. No one knew what it was exactly, because to know it would be to die.

Anna was a year older than me, and an elegant tomboy; she wore boys' jeans and flannel shirts, but kept her hair long and pulled back, and moved with an uncanny grace. She was as brave as any of my male friends, and so of course she and I challenged each other to enter the woods. We'd tell Grams we were taking our bikes into town to get ice cream or batteries, but we'd ride a half-mile down the county road, turn left onto the dirt trail that led through the cypresses and crab-apples, pedal to the end of the path, and then look into the dense brush that picked up where the road ended. Through the mass of brambles and vines and rotting logs, shadows formed a patchwork with squares of dusty sunlight. Things flickered, skittered. We didn't know *what* things.

We never went beyond the end of the road, into the brush. There didn't seem to be anywhere to go—no obvious trail, not even openings to pass through.

"Go in," I'd dare Anna.

"I'd get scratched up in there."

"Chicken."

Anna would turn and sneer at me. "If you go in first and keep the thorns away, I'll go in."

I didn't, of course. After a few minutes, we'd get back on our bikes and ride into town, feeling proud of how close we'd come to mystery, to certain danger.

Once, we'd been there later in the day, as the sun crouched down behind the trees. We were standing, smelling the mulch, watching the pollen swirl in the last rays of light, when something *big* crashed through some of the branches. We both stepped back involuntarily, gripped our bikes' handlebars tightly, preparing to flee should something (*a ghost*) come roaring out of the woods, but after a few seconds we heard a few smaller sounds, as if the creature that had come near the border of Weir Forest were retreating again.

"Whatever that was, it was big," Anna said, her eyes wide when she looked at me.

"What do you think it was?"

Anna shrugged. "A bear, maybe…"

I don't think either of us really believed it was a bear.

ooooo

Anna went missing two years later.

She'd just turned thirteen, and the way the jeans and flannel shirts looked on her made boys consider her with something other than preadolescent disdain. When Anna hadn't reappeared after a few days, some of those boys even fell under suspicion. Police interviewed them; they stammered and squirmed, but none of them knew anything about Anna.

They asked me, too. I told them I didn't know.

I didn't tell them what I really thought: that Weir Forest had taken her. She'd finally gone in there, alone, and it had kept her like a possessive lover.

They found some threads on a blackberry bush on the rim of the forest. The threads might have been from Anna's shirt. It was the only clue they ever had.

After Anna's disappearance, my parents kept me from visiting Grams again. I only saw her when she visited us. When she died, in her house, I hadn't seen her for nearly a year. She'd been dead for a week before her mailman asked the sheriff to check.

I grew up after that, went to college, got a degree I would never turn into a career, took a job in a chain drugstore I would never manage. I was one more millennial burdened with student loans and no real future, a smart phone in my pocket that interested me more than my friends-in-the-flesh. I lived in my parents' house (the same room I'd grown up in, next to Anna's old bedroom on the second floor), and on Saturday nights I drank alone. I drank alone and thought of those who'd vanished from my life. Or those who'd never appeared in it at all, who'd left me alone and unfulfilled, whose names I didn't know but who I missed with terrible longing.

One of my few joys was simply being outside. The most useful skills I'd learned at college were from friends who taught me how to hike and camp. Just before graduation, one of my friends had told me about how much he'd enjoyed being a volunteer with his hometown search and rescue team, so I signed up when I came back from college. By the end of my fifth week, I'd been involved with finding a runaway kid who was hiding out in a cave on Mount Yaanek, I'd rescued a family dog from a bear trap, and I'd tracked down a grandfather with Alzheimer's who'd wandered away from home one night. It was mid-day when I located Grandpa Henry, so the poor old guy had spent the long October night in Weir Forest, turning this way and that, with no idea where he was or why he was there. When I spotted him, he was standing beneath the shade of a sycamore, facing the trunk, chattering. I made out part of it before he knew I was there. "… They're all here, I seen 'em but goddamnit I can't remember the names, but I knowed *every goddamn one of 'em*, and—"

I said, softly, trying not to frighten him, "Henry?"

He stopped muttering and turned to me. Squinting, he asked, "Who are you? Are you alive?"

I would normally have laughed at the absurdity of the question, but here, on the perimeter of the forest, it didn't seem so funny. "Yes, I am. I'm with a search and rescue team that's been looking for you, Henry. Your family is very worried about you."

"My family? Hell, they're all dead."

"No, sir, they're not. They're fine, and they're waiting for you…" Henry, at least, was docile and let me lead him back to his home, but he muttered the whole way and occasionally glanced back over his shoulder, as if expecting to see something following him out of the woods. One of the last intelligible things he said before I left him was, "Tell them to stop laughing…they laughed all goddamn night…"

That'd been last week, before Halloween.

Today.

I'd been scheduled to work, selling plastic bags full of bubble-gum eyeballs and flame-retardant masks, but when the SCSSAR text came through, I called into the store sick. There were other team members who could take this one, but I knew where Route 24 led.

Weir Forest.

It took me thirty minutes to reach the destination. After I turned onto County Road 24, civilization thinned out—houses gave way to isolated farms to abandoned shacks to nothing human. It was the end of October, and even though the tree branches were barren, their leaves already fallen and crisp, the brush around the sides of the road was so thick that it was impossible to see more than a few yards in. I passed no other cars in either direction, saw no one walking or biking. Soon the trees met over the road, creating a shadowed, organic tunnel, blocking out the gray skies.

I rounded a final curve, and saw two other cars already parked before a metal barrier with a sign reading ROAD ENDS. I parked and walked up to two of the county sheriffs, Sam and the tall Asian one who was still new—Cheng. They turned and smiled at me, and Sam gave me a mock salute. "Morning. You're the first to arrive."

"What've we got?"

Sheriff Sam gestured at the car parked beyond his sheriff's cruiser, near the barricade at the end of the road. It was a big black SUV that looked like it had just rolled off the lot. One of the doors was open; there was no one inside.

"That SUV belongs to a company called Durand Enterprises—sound familiar?"

"As in…Mark Durand?"

Sam nodded, a cynical half-smile curling his mouth up on one side. "The same."

Mark Durand…everyone around here knew that name. He was a tech billionaire who'd decided to move his company headquarters to our little county, and the influx of hundreds of jobs had cheered some but left others anxious. Then, last month, Durand had made a deal with the state to lease a huge chunk of unincorporated land—which was most of Weir Forest. There'd been a few attempts to turn it into a national park in the past, but they'd all failed. The area had no landmarks, no renowned monuments or natural beauty; there was a lake, Auber, at the region's heart, but it was surrounded by marshland and largely inaccessible. The state was only too glad to let Durand take Weir Forest off its hands.

Sam nodded at the black SUV. "Durand wants to start developments out here, so he sent a surveying crew—three guys and their equipment—out here yesterday. Then, when they didn't come home last night, we sent one of our guys out to check, and sure enough—there's the van, but no sign of the three. Their equipment's gone, too, so we figured they made their way out into the forest and, being city folk, just got turned around."

I shrugged. "If they're surveyors with equipment, you'd expect them to be able to find their way out again, wouldn't you?"

Sam took a swig from his travel mug (emblazoned with the logo of a local golf course) and peered into the trees. "Maybe. It's Weir Forest," he said, as if that explained everything.

The new sheriff, Cheng, said, "It's supposed to be full of ghosts or something, right?"

Nobody answered. Sam and I looked away. Cheng hadn't grown up around here, but we had. We'd heard tales of Weir's ghoul-haunted woodland for as long as we could remember.

I turned to look back, gesturing at the empty road behind us. "The others are coming, right?"

Sam glanced at his phone. "Got affirmatives from eight of you, and Bill Morse should get here soon."

Bill Morse was the only one of us civilians who'd undergone actual SAR training, so he usually took lead on these operations. But this time I didn't want to wait. This time it was Weir Forest.

I tried to sound casual as I said, "I'm just going to go scope out the immediate area a little."

"Fine. Just don't go too far. It's darker than a dog's ass in there."

I heard Cheng offer up some comeback about wondering how Sam knew so much about dogs' asses, but I was already pulling on my pack's shoulder straps and heading for the woods.

I stepped off the asphalt (badly cracked where it ran up against the forest), around the metal barricade with the ROAD ENDS sign, and let my eyes adjust—it was as if I'd entered an unlit structure. There was only one clearing in the brush, the closest thing to a trail leading away from the road, and I walked to it. Pausing, I peered along its length; it entered the forest, but seemed to be an actual animal track of some kind, the easiest way in. If three surveyors had decided to inspect Weir Forest, they would've had to come this way.

I walked maybe a hundred yards along the path, which veered between winter-drained trees and deadfalls, as thorns and twigs clawed at me. At one area where the trail broadened slightly and moved over a rotting log, I pulled out a Maglite and knelt to inspect.

There was a shoe imprint in the mushy top of the log, its treads almost clear enough to name the brand.

So they *had* come this way.

I pulled out my cell phone, intending to send a text back to Sam to let him know what I'd found, but I had no reception. That seemed odd; my reception had still been fine when I'd parked, and I hadn't come that far.

I knew I should go back now. I should let everyone know I'd found some sign of the missing persons.

I should have. But I didn't.

Weir Forest was before me, and it was time to accept its challenge. Its mysteries pulled on me; they always had, just as they'd pulled on Anna. But I wasn't Anna. I wasn't a teenager, alone and unprepared.

So I stepped over the marked log and set off into the murkier depths of Weir.

I walked on, although at some point I began using my Mag just to find the path before me. What time was it? It was October, the last day of the month, and the withered branches entwined above me should have allowed in more light, but it remained dank, dismal, and I moved slowly. I stopped at one point, saw my breath exit in a thick puff. When had the temperature dropped? I zipped my down jacket all the way to the neck, shrugged out of my pack, and removed a water bottle. As I took a long swallow, my gulping sounded amplified, and it took me a few seconds to realize why: I hadn't heard another sound for a while. Normally a forest like this was full of bird sounds, leaves crunching as animals dashed through them, wind soughing in high branches.

But Weir was completely silent.

I recapped the bottle, stowed it, shouldered my pack, and decided I was anxious enough now to go back. Entering Weir had been a mistake.

Turning around, I pushed back down the path, away from the decaying heart of the forest. I walked, my breath in vapors. The woods grew no warmer, no brighter. It all looked the same, but none of it looked familiar. I walked. Sweat turned to a layer of damp chill. I walked.

And went nowhere.

I tried my cell phone again. I tried scaling a tree for a better view, but the bark repelled me. I searched the thick organic carpet of the forest floor for traces of my own footprints, but there were none. I hadn't come this way.

I was lost.

As that realization sank in, I stopped, dropped my pack, squatted down to think. What time was it? I was reaching for my phone when I saw something in the trees nearby, a whiteness that shone against the dark gray tree-shapes.

I rose slowly and moved to the side, where I could see it better. It was a person, another human being. I nearly choked in relief, started to run forward, to call it—but my voice froze in my throat when my Maglite swung up and settled on the face.

It was Anna. My sister, Anna. She was still thirteen, still dressed in the sweatshirt and denim skirt she'd worn the day she vanished.

"Anna?" I staggered forward. She didn't move or speak, just looked at me.

"Anna?"

I smelled something dead then. The force of the stench hit me like a blow, and I turned aside for a second, coughing. When I turned back, Anna was gone.

First there were ghosts...

"Anna," I said, and gave in to the frigid tears that spread down my cheeks.

∞∞∞

After some time—as even the vague light of the forest faded and full night came on—I found matches in my pack, gathered material, and lit a fire. I hoped Bill Morse had the SAR team looking for me now. Maybe they'd already found the surveyors, and would find me soon. Maybe a fire would help.

Its warmth did little to dispel the chill, but the orange glow was welcome after the silver daylight. I was leaning forward to warm my hands, contemplating eating a protein bar, when I heard it:

Laughter. High-pitched, distant, tittering, but clearly laughter.

I almost put the fire out, but whatever had made that sound could probably find me in the dark. Besides, I wanted to see it, and my Maglite was dying.

I waited, feeding more stripped branches into the flames.

The laughter came again, closer, and from multiple throats.

The ghoul-haunted woodland.

They appeared, edging forward out of the darkness into the circle of pumpkin-colored light. Three of them, ashen-colored, bare-skinned, with crimson eyes and jagged teeth. Adrenaline coursed through me, my hand instinctively sought a burning branch to use as a fiery weapon, but they kept their distance, leering. After a few seconds, one of them beckoned me, gesturing behind, into the woods. They wanted me to follow them.

I debated. If I didn't, they could well turn on me, tear me to shreds in seconds. Or they might abandon me here, to die alone, to join my sister in a frozen afterlife. But what would they show me if I followed them?

The truth was, I wanted to know. I thought it might be a secret revealed, a question answered.

I picked up the longest, thickest branch from my fire, one with a flickering end that would make an effective torch. I hefted it, stood, and moved toward them. They tittered and leapt off into the night-black woods.

The ghouls kept up a quick pace and I stumbled more than once, but tried to be careful of the flame, tried to hold it up and keep it going.

At last I saw the fire glint off something before me. I pushed past a final stand of brush that tore through my jeans and gloves, leaving sharp, throbbing scratches, and then I saw where we'd come: Water. A lake. Auber. The heart of Weir.

I gazed across its expanse, the flat ebon surface reflecting only my faint light, and then I heard my monstrous guides utter their grotesque amusement again. I turned, moved toward them, holding out the torch, feeling the ground beneath me change from sodden mash of leafy detritus to sucking, damp shore—

And then I saw the three surveyors…or what was left of them, because the ghouls had already feasted. Limbs were reduced to bones with a few bloody shreds; clothing, which was apparently not to the ghouls' taste, hung in tatters or littered the ground. The remains had been stacked in a pile, a pyramid shape with three severed heads on top. The eye sockets were all hollow, the orbs sucked out.

I retched. Leaning over the tarn, I convulsed, producing only a thin string that sizzled as it hit Auber's surface. I panted, wiped the back of my hand (which had lost its glove some unknown time ago), and tried to straighten up. My eyes were drawn back to that hideous collage before me, to the ridiculous thought that Weir would never be charted, never be neatly divided into squares on a map, to be flattened and paved and populated.

One of the ghouls touched me. I leapt back, crying out, nearly lost my balance on the soggy ground, but then saw that the creature merely wanted to direct my attention away from the gore-covered pile. I followed its pointing finger, and saw something near the shore of Auber, something that glinted without need of starlight or moon's glow.

It was a stone edifice, a marble square with columns and a metal gate.

A tomb.

As I neared it, I saw a word carved into the front, a name. I stepped closer until I could read the name by the ethereal light: *Ulalume.*

And then it was as if I fell headlong into a tunnel, a passage through lives and centuries, a backward, descending spiral. I rushed past other versions of me—a 1960s soldier, a 1920s dance girl, an 1890s Edwardian matron—back, back, down, until I came to the bottom and the beginning. To Ulalume, who I'd once loved and lost and buried here, on another night such as this so long ago. Ulalume, who appeared now before the tomb, who had seized the surveyors and given them to the ghouls as a sacrifice on this night, to bring me here. Ulalume, whose loss I now understood I'd felt throughout my life, even though I couldn't put a name to that loss. Ulalume, whose hand was cold fog in mine, but strong enough to pull me toward the black waters of the Auber. Ulalume, who I would join now, at last, united forever here in the ghoul-haunted woodland of Weir.

My beloved. My Ulalume. My destiny.

Ulalume, found at last.

ALIVE-OH

HAUNTED HOUSE

The sign was crudely hand-lettered on a flattened-out cardboard box and nailed to an old signpost, but Mason smiled when he saw it.

Just like he said it was, he thought, as he followed the arrow at the bottom of the sign onto a dirt road, *out in the middle of fucking nowhere. This is going to be IT.*

The discussion board posting at Mason's AmericasGotHaunts. com website had been from a new user, HalloweenJoyRide, and had claimed to have found the most terrifying haunted attraction in the country—"My girlfriend and me couldn't sleep for a week." Normally Mason was skeptical about postings that sounded like sales pitches, but he'd never heard of the haunt, and from the directions HalloweenJoyRide had provided, it was clearly located in the countryside, at least an hour from anything. It had to be pretty outrageous to turn a buck in the boonies. And it had no website, which somehow intrigued Mason even more.

He'd driven for four hours to get there. It'd been a long drive without Kat.

The dirt road led to a parking lot that had obviously once been the spacious front yard of a home. The house itself stood at the far side; once a prim and proud farmhouse, it was now a dilapidated blight, with splintered porches, empty windows, and a crumbled chimney.

They're not taking us through THAT, surely...

Then Mason saw more crudely drawn signs, with big arrows pointing around the house. He drove further and saw a huge, old barn, still standing and lit up.

Aaaahhh. A barn. She would have loved this. Her loss.

He parked the SUV, then debated about bringing the camera bag. When he encountered a new haunted house, he usually went through it once first with Kat—

No, that wasn't right. Kat was gone now. Mason felt regret pricking at his thoughts.

"You don't really care about anything but this Halloween shit, Mason. Yes, I think it's fun, too—but it's more than that for you. I think you want it to be real. Sorry, but I don't."

For the last two years, Kat had come with him to every haunted house. He realized how much he'd counted on her, even just for help with carrying a bag or pointing a light.

Fuck it. AmericasGotHaunts.com doesn't need her.

He decided to go through the maze alone first, to get a feel for it, then he'd go through a second time with the camera.

If they gave him permission, that is. Or didn't catch him doing it without permission.

He knew they might have a no-cameras policy. Even the smallest neighborhood haunted houses had photos and videos online—"Here's our Freddy Krueger scaring those stupid kids from next door!"—but this haunt didn't even have a name.

Mason locked the doors and looked around. He'd timed it right; it was early in the evening, and there were only a few other cars parked around him. The barn stood maybe a hundred yards away. A faint echo of ghostly music and wails drifted over towards him, and there were tables set up near the front of the barn.

He forced himself not to rush toward the entrance. He wanted to take his time, to watch other customers leaving the maze. They were usually the first indication of how high the fear factor was—so frightening that they were still laughing nervously, girls clinging to their boys, the boys grinning like pale wolves? Were jocks slapping each others' backs too hard and making bad jokes about lunatic chicks in nightgowns and gay killer clowns?

Mason spotted a couple coming towards him, moving away from the barn—twenty-somethings, maybe even married. The man had his arm around the woman, who was sobbing quietly. He looked ashen and said nothing; they didn't glance up as they passed Mason.

What the fuck…?

He wanted to stop them, ask them what they'd seen, but he knew he'd find out soon enough.

A small group of college boys walked out of the barn and started towards him. Mason deliberately veered slightly towards them, listening intently.

"…Telling you, that shit was real," said a broad-shouldered boy with a flannel shirt.

His friend, sporting a hoodie with a band logo on the back, barked a single sharp laugh. "'Course it's not real, doofus. It's make-up. I read about how these haunted houses get all these make-up guys from Hollywood now who've been put out of work by computers."

"I dunno…"

The third boy, with a wrestler's body, had his head down and hands thrust in the pockets of his jeans. "Just shut up," he muttered to his friends before speeding up to reach their car first.

"What the fuck's eating him?"

Then the boys passed out of earshot. And Mason felt his interest growing.

These people are all seriously effed up. This is going to be good. Maybe great.

But as he neared the front of the barn, he was hit with a series of small disappointments. The music was a tinny, cheap Halloween CD that he recognized as one cluttering seasonal bargain bins all over the country; it was being played over an old-fashioned boombox set up on a folding tray. Parked nearby was a well-used RV, paint chipping from its sides, but with new tires that told Mason it was still being driven. The barn doors were closed, with a few paper Halloween decorations glued to them. An older man sat behind another table with a metal cashbox before him. The only impressive part of the scene was the giant who stood before the doors; he had to be at least eight feet tall, and his massive feet, poking out from the bottoms of stained overalls, were bare. He gazed at Mason impassively, and Mason realized he was a kid—he couldn't have been more than fifteen or sixteen.

"Happy Halloween," said the older man behind the table.

Mason looked down at him, and saw that his lined, weathered face and gray hair betrayed a man who'd worked hard in life and received little in return.

"This your place?" Mason asked.

"The haunted house, yes. The farm...nobody owns it. Been abandoned for a few years now. You here for Halloween?"

"Oh, yes, sorry." Mason almost asked for two tickets, then caught himself. "One, please."

"Ten dollars."

At least the ticket price was reasonable. Mason handed the man a twenty, and received two fives in exchange along with a warning. "No pictures inside. We're pretty strict about that."

Mason shrugged, but was already planning his approach when he was ready for the second go-around: "I run the largest haunted house site on the web. We get half-a-million hits a week in October. Just let me post a few photos, and I guarantee your business will go nuclear." Damn it—if he'd still had Kat, he knew she could've worked magic on the old duffer. He'd seen her do it before.

If there was really anything worth covering here.

The old man nodded at the giant, who reached for the barn doors. Mason's excitement started to spike. The familiar anticipation, that sense of both tension and glee, began to pulse in Mason like a black star. He even forgot for a few seconds that Kat wasn't beside him, her hand in his, sharing his joy.

Mason stepped through the door, which closed behind him. The music from outside was shut off by the heavy wood, and he was surprised by the lack of sound. Most haunted attractions reverberated with pounding music, shrieks, chainsaws...but this place was almost silent.

Ahead was a long, straight aisle; on the right side were the stalls that had once held livestock, and down the left was a hastily-installed wall, simple wooden flats placed there to form a narrow walkway. The flats were decorated with crudely-done Halloween paintings—lopsided jack-o'-lanterns, skeletons missing a lot of bones, devils who were probably supposed to be leering. It didn't look like the usual maze; Mason couldn't make out any

twists or turns, just a single one-way path. There were a few other customers visible at the far end—two couples. They gazed at
whatever lay within one of the stalls and whispered to each other.
Whispers? What kind of fucking place is this?!

For a second, Mason had the horrible feeling that it was a "hell
house," and he was about to be presented with a series of scenes
badly acted by youthful members of a church in which he'd be
told about the horrors of abortion and raves and gay marriage. If
this was a hell house, he'd turn around at the first stupid fucking
stall, march back out the way he'd come in, and demand his ten
bucks back. *Assholes.*

But no, whatever the quartet at the far end was watching was
quiet, so this couldn't be a hell house.

Mason took a deep breath, starting to feel a less happy apprehension now, and stepped forward, already turning to look into
the first stall.

For a few seconds, he couldn't quite parse what he was seeing:
The wall between two of the stalls had been removed to make
a larger space, and a platform constructed from sawhorses and
sheets of plywood had been set up in the center. On the platform
was a large glass aquarium—Mason guessed 20 gallons—but it
was only partly full of water. Most of the tank's space was taken up
with a gray, scaled mass, something like the hide of an unremarkable snake. The mass was large, though, and had arms, legs—and
a human head peering at Mason. Mason stared dumbly, trying to
figure it out. Was this a setup for a scare? Something would pop
out, surely, or perhaps swoop down from overhead on a zipline.
But then Mason felt his gut clench when the thing in the tank
blinked its large, liquid eyes, and he knew it was alive. It repositioned itself in the tank slightly, and issued something like a sigh.
Okay. Well, at least it definitely isn't a hell house...whatever it is.

Mason moved on to the next stall. In this one, a teenaged
girl was sprawled stomach-down on an ancient, tattered couch,
reading a magazine by flashlight. She wore low-rider jeans and a
t-shirt that had been positioned to allow her sinuous, four-foot-
long tail to wave lazily above her. As Mason stopped, gaping,
she glanced back at him once, then returned her attention to the
magazine. It was a mindless celebrity rag sheet, its pages stuffed
with photos of television and film stars.

Mason had been to exactly 212 other haunted houses. He'd

covered everything from theme parks that hosted hundreds of thousands of visitors to home haunts that delighted trick or treaters one night a year; he'd been to trade shows and workshops, and he knew everything about hydraulics, wires, ghost glass, infrared sensors, latex appliances, blood squibs, and projections.

And so he knew the girl's tail was real. He watched it twitch in the air, its tawny, soft pelt undulating, and there was no question that it was a part of her.

"Hey," he blurted out, softly.

The girl turned and looked at him, but didn't say anything.

"What's the deal here?" Mason asked.

"We're not supposed to talk," she said, and her voice was a normal teenaged girl's, high and lyrical, with a light regional accent he couldn't place. She went back to her magazine.

The next three stalls held a young man with feet the size of steamer trunks, a little girl completely covered in thick fur who was more interested in her Barbie dolls than Mason, and a boy with four seemingly normal arms.

In the last cubicle was a girl of maybe seventeen, wearing a large, loose t-shirt featuring innocuous smiling kitten graphics. At first she looked like any other girl, and Mason wondered why she was here. Then he felt a stab of shock as her shirt rippled. She glanced at Mason, pulled the shirt up—and revealed a fist-sized head and tiny chest and arms extending from her torso, just below the rib cage. The twin—for Mason knew it to be that—looked at him, wiggled its tiny fingers, and giggled. The girl bent her head for a moment as if listening, then she also glanced up at Mason and snickered as well.

Mason turned and stalked out.

He heard Kat's voice in his mind—Kat, who worked with special needs children, and who'd left him because he was more interested in searching out horrors than working for progress. Well, maybe he could make progress happen here, and then he could tell Kat what he'd done, and she'd—

"Hey!" He'd reached the front table again, where the tired man and the teenaged giant stood. They both looked up at his shout.

"Maybe a lot of these other suckers you're selling tickets to don't know what this is, but I do, and it sure as hell is not a haunted house. It's a goddamn freak show. All you're missing is a barker standing on a platform shouting out, 'All living, all alive, alive-alive-oh!'"

The ticket seller's shoulders repositioned, as if some weight had just been laid across his back. He reached into his cash box and withdrew a ten, which he extended to Mason. "I'm sorry, sir. Here's your money back—"

Mason ignored the bill. "I don't care about the money, asswipe. See, I know a little something about the history of these things, and I know freak shows are illegal in most states, probably like this one. And some of these people—Christ, they're just kids! These aren't even adults you're putting on display in there. Where the fuck are their parents?"

The tall boy took a half-step forward and a jab of fear shot through Mason's gut, but then the older man rose and put a hand up to the massive chest. "It's okay, Jack—I'll handle this." The kid glared at Mason, but didn't advance.

The older man stepped from behind the folding table and extended a hand. "My name's Andrew. And you are…?"

Mason didn't accept the hand. "Just give me one good reason why I shouldn't call the cops right now."

"Because I'm the legal guardian of all these children."

"You're kidding."

"No. I've adopted all of them. This is my family."

Mason flung a gesture at the barn. "So in other words…these are your own children you're displaying like animals."

Andrew winced slightly. "Please understand: It's not cheap to raise so many special little ones. This is our one big chance every year to make money."

"They should be in…special homes or something."

"Institutions, you mean."

The word sounded mean coming from Andrew, and Mason shrugged, suddenly feeling guilty. "Some place where they can be taken care of."

"I take care of them. We take care of each other. We do all right."

"What did the girl—the one with the tail—mean when she said, 'We're not supposed to talk'? What is it you don't want people to know? Are you abusing them?"

"Abusing…?" For a second, Andrew flushed, and Mason

wondered if he could outrace the giant, make it back to his car before those hubcap-sized hands were on him, lifting him like a doll. Then Andrew inhaled, and turned toward the RV parked a short distance away. "There's something I'd like to show you."

Without another word, the older man started towards the side entrance door to the RV. Mason hesitated, then saw Jack eyeing him, and decided to follow. Andrew opened the door, stepped up into a dark interior and motioned for Mason to wait. "Hang on," he said before turning to the shadows and saying softly, "Kevin, are you awake?" He listened for a moment, then turned on a light somewhere inside the RV. He disappeared from view for a few seconds, and then returned, motioning Mason to step in.

Inside, Mason saw a small kitchenette, closets and cabinets, a table, and a large, padded dog bed on the table. Andrew had turned on a single light over the table, and he whispered to Mason. "He's asleep, so we'll have to speak quietly."

Andrew waved Mason forward until they both stood over the dog bed. "I'd like you to meet Kevin."

Mason looked down into the bed—and felt his dinner from two hours ago climb halfway up his throat.

Inside the soft, downy interior of the bed was something that looked like a raw puddle of semi-translucent flesh about the size of a terrier, but without fur. There were longer, gelatinous-looking extensions that might have been arms and legs, and a rounded knob on one end that was some sort of head, but it was almost not even recognizable as anything human.

"Kevin," the old man whispered, looking down at the thing with eyes that gleamed wetly in the dim overhead light, "was essentially born without bones. He's almost six years old, and it's a miracle that he's still alive. A friend found him when he was three months old; his parents left him out in a snowy field on a January morning to die."

"God," Mason muttered, and he was shocked to realize that he could understand: The young parents, faced with a lifetime, not knowing whether it was short or long, of caring for this child that would never run, never play, never even go for a walk or sit up. "Why didn't they...take him somewhere?"

"Where? Please don't tell me some government-run home or hospital, because there aren't any, not since all the budget cuts. We've got wars to finance—we can't afford to give away precious money to children like Kevin. And his parents…they had nothing, not even health insurance. There was no way they could take care of a child like him."

Mason wanted to look away, but he found his eyes drawn again and again to that alien form, impossible and yet alive. It was jarring when he realized Andrew was speaking again.

"Kevin, you see, is not comfortable around large groups of people, so it's his choice not to participate in our performance. His brothers and sisters all enjoy it."

The boy in the bed shifted slightly. Something in the head rolled, and Mason's fascination curdled as he realized he was looking at an open, pale blue eye that had fixed on him…an eye that was intelligent and measuring.

Andrew reached down a comforting hand and rested it lightly on the child's back. "Oh, we woke him. It's all right, Kevin, go back to sleep. I just wanted our friend here to meet you, but it can wait for another time." Andrew looked back at Mason, and added, "There are going to be more like Kevin, and Lizzie, and Jack, and Dolly and Missy, and Terence, and Michael, and Abby, you know. They're a product of a world that's been poisoned, and that world's not interested in offering them the antidote. They're the future."

One of the rubbery arms slid across the soft covering of the dog bed, and Mason realized that Kevin was trying to reach for him.

Mason staggered back, horrified at the thought of being touched by this little monster. He collided with a closet behind him, rattling it loudly, and from the dog bed came a high-pitched whine of anxiety. Andrew leaned in closer, shushing the child, while Mason stumbled to his left, trying to find the exit, the goddamned exit that he knew was here somewhere, and—

"Shhh, Kevin, it's all right, he's just…well…"

Mason didn't wait to hear the rest. The door was behind him suddenly, and he pushed against it so hard that he fell through it backwards, landing in the barnyard dirt. Jack loomed over him, and Mason gasped and found his feet, then turned to run, and Andrew was behind him, standing in the doorway, shouting, "Please, mister, just let us live…"

Mason ran, not looking back to see if a giant pursued him like some ogre in a dark fairy tale. He reached his car and restrained an urge to vomit, then dug his keys out and climbed in. By the time he'd made the main road, leaving a trail of dust, he knew he would never make any phone call—whether to the police or Kat it didn't much matter, because Andrew and his family would be gone by the time the police arrived anyway, gone until next season, when they'd set up in some other town and make just enough money to see them through for one more year. And someone who'd read about them online, in some forum, would show up and try to take a photo, and Jack the Giant would grab the camera so Andrew's family would remain mysterious and safe.

And Mason wouldn't call Kat, because she already understood: That the world was broken and the future twisted.

Mason drove on through the dark countryside, towards the comfort of artificial monsters.

SUMMER'S END

OCTOBER 31, 2012, ALMOST MIDNIGHT

My name is Lisa Morton. I'm one of the world's leading authorities on Halloween.

And this year I discovered that everything I thought I knew was wrong.

OCTOBER 31 / OCTOBER 20

It's been less than two weeks since the world started to fall apart.

During the third week of October, I received an e-mail with the subject line "Samhain query." I get a lot of e-mailed questions this time of year: requests for interviews, reporters searching for illustrations for Halloween articles, someone trying to identify and appraise an odd Halloween collectible. This year I had a new Halloween history book out, so I was trying to set up book signings. I'd even been invited to sign at a store in Salem, home of America's own home-grown witch-hunting tragedy, although they couldn't find me a place to stay—hotels there book up a year in advance for the October festivities.

But two things stood out about this e-mail: The first was that it asked not about Halloween, but about the holiday's ancient Celtic forebear. The second was that the sender's address ended in "ucla.edu."

I clicked on the message and read:

Dear Ms. Morton,
I'm a linguistics professor at UCLA specializing in Latin, and I'm currently working with a team from Ireland to translate a manuscript discovered in a recent archaeological dig. The manuscript was written mostly in Latin, but was believed to belong to an Irish Druid circa 350 C.E. It includes numerous references to Samhain, many of which I'm frankly having difficulty making sense of. I found your book, *The Halloween Encyclopedia*, in the campus library, and you seem to have extensive knowledge of Samhain. Your bio says you're in the Southern California area, so would you be open to a meeting? Thank you. My contact information is below.
Sincerely,
Dr. Wilson Armitage[1]

I checked the e-mail headers to make sure this really had come from UCLA, because otherwise I would have smiled and dismissed it as an early Halloween prank. The Celts' Druids—essentially their priest caste—were notorious for passing all of their lore verbally; they didn't believe in writing anything down. To have a Druid "manuscript," then, was virtually impossible. And in Latin?

---

[1] Dr. Wilson Armitage is the author of *Latin: A Comprehensive Study of the Language*, now in its ninth edition.

There had been cases of Celts who had integrated into Roman society and become quite adept in Latin, but they were from the Gaul tribes of continental Europe, not Ireland.

But, if this was real…

Scholars frankly know little about the Irish Celts, and less about Samhain. What we have are the tantalizing bits passed down in legends transcribed by early Catholic missionaries. Stories about heroes who fought malicious *sidh*, or fairies, on Samhain Eve[2]. Horror tales involving hanged corpses that returned to vengeful life on that night and asked for drinks, which they spit into the faces of those who were foolish enough to supply them, causing immediate death to their benefactors[3]. Romances about princesses who turned into swans on October 31st and who flew off with their true love[4]. There were suggestions that the Celts had celebrated "summer's end" (the literal translation of "Samhain") with a three-day long party of drinking, feasting, and horse-racing. One debate raging among those who study Halloween questions how much our modern holiday owes to the Celts; some believe that the festival has a completely Christian history, and that its grimmer aspects derive from the November 2nd Catholic celebration of All Souls. Myself, I fall largely on the side of "summer's end"—I think Halloween unquestionably inherited some of its lore from Samhain, like belief in supernatural forces being prevalent on the evening of the 31st, or the notion (held mainly by the old Scots) that fortune-telling was likelier to be successful if performed on All Hallows' Eve.

There's another camp, however, which holds that Halloween is little more than a pagan festival renamed; fundamentalist Christians go so far as to condemn the holiday as a celebration of "Samhain, Lord of the Dead."[5] What the fire-and-brimstone preachers don't know is that their "facts" stem from the fanciful work of one Charles Vallancey, an eighteenth-century British engineer who was dispatched by the government to survey Ireland. He fell in love with the Irish/Celtic language and culture, and spent most of the rest of his life collecting information, which he transcribed into a massive opus (pretentiously) called *Collectanea de rebus Hibernicis*. Except…Vallancey was frankly an arrogant fool. He was obsessed with the notion that the Celtic tongue could be traced back to Indo-European roots, and in his quest to find connections

---

[2] "The Coming of Finn"
[3] "The Story of Nera"
[4] "The Story of Oengus"
[5] http://www.churchesofchrist.net/authors/Walter_Porter/Halloween.htm

he frequently disposed of the facts. He somehow decided that all of the other scholars (and there had already been many, even by 1786, when his Collectanea was published) were wrong, and that Samhain had not been a new year's celebration and in-bringing of the harvest, but was rather a day of judgment when the Celts offered sacrifices to their dark god "Balsab." Vallancey's books found their way onto library shelves around the world, next to volumes that both reiterated and decried them, and so Vallancey inadvertently created a strange alternate history of Halloween. By the 1990s, some American church groups were calling October 31st "The Devil's Birthday" and had banned trick or treat. I wondered if they were simply miserable people who didn't want their kids to have any fun, either.

So now I had been presented with what could potentially, possibly, change our understanding of Samhain and perhaps finally lay the ghost of Vallancey to rest. My schedule was pretty booked, but tomorrow would be a rare free night, and my significant other, Ricky, was working on a movie that was shooting down in South Carolina (he's an actor, and is most well-known for his performance as "Henry the Red" in *Army of Darkness*). I answered Dr. Armitage and told him I'd be happy to meet to discuss his project. He responded within minutes, suggesting a time and providing his UCLA office address.

At least Armitage was legit, and he wasn't likely to be the kind of man who could be fooled by a scam. What would I find out? Was Samhain mainly an administrative function when the Celts extinguished all their home hearths and relit them with an ember from a fire kindled by Druid priests (for which services they were duly taxed)? Was it really a three-day kegger? Was it possible that human sacrifice had been performed?

I was twenty-four hours away from finding out.

OCTOBER 21, EVENING

Wilson Armitage turned out to be one of those college professors who you knew had girls fighting to sign up for his classes—he was maybe 35, with a charmingly ragged haircut, a quick smile, and clothes straight from Urban Outfitters. His office was more old-fashioned than he was, full of language reference books and stacks of papers and jars of pencils, only one small laptop on the desk offering evidence of the 21st century.

If I liked Wilson immediately, I was less sure about the man with him: Thin, fifty-something, with narrow features and a perpetual scowl. Wilson introduced him as Dr. Conor ó Cuinn, the archaeologist who had overseen the excavation at which the manuscript had been found. He'd flown over from Ireland with the actual artifact, which UCLA was still in the process of scanning. Wilson did most of the talking, but Conor never stopped staring at me. It occurred to me to wonder if he simply mistrusted women. Or perhaps American women.

Wilson started by offering me a chair, then turned his laptop around to let me look at pages of the manuscript while he talked. The photos on the screen showed a continuous scroll, broken into frames for scanning, with edges chewed and uneven; the parchment or vellum was covered in neat handwriting that I just barely recognized as Latin. The scroll had been wrapped in oiled cloth and laid within a metal box with sealed edges—a box still clutched by the bony fingers of a long-dead female corpse. A poor farmer in Northern Ireland had discovered the remains while digging peat blocks out of a bog; fortunately he'd had enough sense to call the authorities, who'd brought in ó Cuinn. The excavation had been brief—there'd been nothing else at all in the bog—but the scroll was remarkable. The author had been named Mongfind[6], and claimed to have been the last of the Irish Druids.

"Well, right off the bat, something's odd," I said. "That's a female name, and most of the Druids were men, although there are isolated historical recordings of female Druids."

The two professors exchanged a quick glance, and then Wilson smiled. "You're going to be in for a few surprises, I think. According to this…exactly half the Druid caste were women, and they were essential to the Druid rituals."

I couldn't even answer, not right away. *Half the Druids were women?!* "How do you know this isn't a fraud?"

Wilson shot a glance at his Irish companion, who nodded back to him. "We've got everything from carbon dating to Mongfind's body to confirm this."

---

[6] Mongfind is a legendary sorceress and warrior queen who supposedly died one Samhain when she ingested poison meant for her brother.

"So you think the body you found this with was Mongfind herself?"

"We believe so—Mongfind mentions several...uh, *peculiarities* of her body that matched up to the corpse found in the bog. We've even got autopsy results on the body confirming how she died, how old she was, and what she ate for her last meal. And, of course, Dr. ó Cuinn is a highly-regarded specialist in his field. No, the evidence is incontrovertible."

ó Cuinn spoke up, and his brogue was thick and obvious, even with only three words spoken. "The tongue..."

Armitage made a quick grimace, then added, "Of course. One of those 'peculiarities' mentioned in the manuscript is that Mongfind's tongue was cut out. The body we found had been mutilated in that manner."

"Why was her tongue cut out?"

Armitage took a deep breath and then said, "What do you know about the conversion of the Celts to Christianity?"

I shrugged. "As much as anyone, I guess. Gregory the Great taught his missionaries the doctrine of syncretism[7], of incorporating existing pagan practices rather than stamping them out. All Saints' Day was probably moved from May 13th to November 1st to help Catholic missionaries in Ireland convert the Celts[8]."

ó Cuinn asked, "Have you not wondered why the Celts would have so easily converted?"

In fact, I had. I figured that more often than not, conversion had been along the lines of the conquest of the Aztecs, when Cortez had ridden into their lands with a banner that read, "We shall conquer under the sign of the cross," and a large force of men with superior armor, weapons, and diseases that the Aztecs couldn't fight. "Sure, I've wondered that, but I figured they probably kind of bought them off with a combination of gifts and threats."

"According to this—" Armitage gestured at the laptop screen, "—the Catholic missionaries had studied the tactics employed by Roman troops against the British Celts, and they learned. When they were ready, they moved into Ireland with a hired army and started by slaughtering all of the Celt warriors, then moved onto the Druids. Only a few escaped; the remaining Celts converted easily."

---

[7] In a famous letter from 601 A.D., Pope Gregory (later known as Gregory the Great) instructed the Abbot Mellitus, who was then bound for Britain, to leave pagan temples standing, because "if those temples are well built, it is requisite that they be converted from the worship of devils to the service of the true God."

[8] May 13th had probably been chosen as the original date for All Saints' Day because it had marked the climax of Lemuria, a Roman festival honoring the dead.

"So you're telling me this document reveals that early Catholic missionaries were basically mass murderers?"

"Well, more in the nature of...conquerors," Wilson said, squirming, then riffling through a stack of printouts on his desk. "Listen to this: 'Yesterday the Catholics offered a gift of a great man built of wicker. This figure could hold fifty men, and the Catholics suggested we should tour it from the inside. When fifty of us were within, they sealed the entrance and set the wicker man afire. The rest of us tried to save our fellows, but our enemies had sunk traps in the earth, and many of our tribe died impaled on great spikes. Those of us who suffered neither stakes nor flames were forced to listen to the dying screams of our brothers and sisters.'"

I couldn't suppress a laugh. "This is all going to go over well with modern Catholics."

But bitter jokes aside, my head was spinning. Hadn't it been Caesar who had ascribed wicker men to the Celts[9]? But now we had something saying the infamous giant figures were not Celtic, but had been used as a trick by Catholic missionaries...who were also ruthless invaders. "So...are you suggesting that all of the other histories..."

ó Cuinn leaned forward, his pinched features eager. "...Are false, re-written by later Christian scribes who were instructed to hide the truth."

"Why?" Even as I asked it, I knew the answer.

Wilson confirmed. "Don't the victors in every war write the history they want? The Catholics probably weren't comfortable with a society in which women held half the religious offices and..."

"And what?"

Wilson abruptly dropped his eyes and fidgeted; he was uneasy talking about whatever came next. I looked to ó Cuinn, who slid a USB stick across the table to me. "It might be easier if you just read what Dr. Armitage has translated thus far."

I picked the stick up. "I can take this?"

They both nodded, so I put it in a pocket. "Okay. But...you called me in with questions about Samhain, and you haven't even mentioned that."

Nodding toward the stick, Wilson said, "Read that and you'll

---

[9] *The Conquest of Gaul*

see. According to our Druid priestess Mongfind, Samhain was a little more than a new year's party. It was…" He trailed off, unsure, or simply unwilling to tell me.

"What?"

ó Cuinn filled in. "According to this…the Druids could perform real magic, and on Samhain they communed directly to their gods."

I'm sure my mouth was open as I stared at ó Cuinn; I expected him to wink, or laugh.

He didn't.

OCTOBER 21 / OCTOBER 22

I am Mongfind, daughter of Fidach of Munster, and a devoted sister of the Morrigan. I was once the Arch-Druid of Ireland, but now I am simply the last Druid. Last night was Samhain, and I attempted to speak to the gods. I failed. When I have finished writing this, the Druids will be no more.

That was how the manuscript began.

I stayed up all night reading it. Wilson had translated around 30,000 words so far—he was still working through the rest—but I understood now why they'd made me sign a nondisclosure agreement before I'd left the office.

This would change everything. Not just our knowledge of the Celts, but of the Romans, the Christians, and much of what came after.

Mongfind began by talking about her childhood, focusing on how she'd begun training in the Druid priesthood from the age of six. She memorized thousands of pieces of history, religious ritual, law, and herbal knowledge. By the age of sixteen, she could recite thousands of lengthy chants, or prepare potions that would cure any disease. She described a world of golden palaces and well-fed, happy citizens, of bards who performed magnificent poems, and noble warriors who fought off enemies with ease. According to her, the Celts had skilled astronomers who had already charted the solar system, seamen who regularly visited America, and farmers who could produce grains and vegetables that remained fresh through the dead of winter.

She also claimed that the Celts owed their good fortune to their gods, who were quite real and visited each Samhain.

The original manuscript had been a mishmash of Mongfind's own life, the history of the Irish Celts, and Druidic rituals; as the manuscript progressed, the sections on her own life had become less detailed, more rushed, and I soon found out why.

The missionaries had timed their armies to arrive shortly before Samhain, when they knew the warriors would be settling into their winter quarters and the rest of the country preparing for the festivities; the Samhain rituals in essence renewed the Celts' contracts with their gods, and the gods' communion with their mortal worshippers was at a low point just before. The invaders' strategies had been thought out for decades, and were carried out with ruthless efficiency; they laid waste to the Celts' nobility and warriors, silenced and imprisoned the Druids, and enslaved the rest. The Catholics had inadvertently killed many of the Druids when they'd cut their tongues out to ensure that they would be unable to call for their gods. Mongfind had been mutilated with all the rest, but had found one piece of luck the others hadn't: A sympathetic Catholic missionary. From her journal:

> One day I arrived at the place where I thought I would spend the remainder of my life: one of our great halls, now a home for our conquerors. My cell here was better—I was provided with straw to sleep on, and there was a high window large enough to permit nearly an hour of sunlight to penetrate each afternoon.
>
> The man in charge of this place visited me as soon as I arrived. We were of course unable to communicate—even if we knew each others' languages, I had no tongue to convey words with—but he gave me to understand that he intended me no harm. The others treated him with reverence, and I realized he was in charge of this place. He pointed at himself and said the word, "Jerome,"[10] which I took to be his name.
>
> He made sure I received generous amounts of food and blankets, and I soon began to recover some of the health I

---

[10] Abbot Jerome is apparently lost to history. Strangely enough, the timing—mid-4th-century—coincides with the life of St. Jerome, an early church father who was involved with translations of the Old Testament from Hebrew; however, it seems extremely unlikely that St. Jerome ever journeyed as far north as Great Britain and Ireland, so this is evidently another Jerome. It's also worth noting that Mongfind's journal contains no mention of Ireland's patron saint, Patrick…but then it would be unlikely to find Patrick in her journal, since he historically appears in Ireland almost a century later. Perhaps Patrick was always intended to be sent in as a sort of compassionate, unifying figure after the horrors of the earlier missionaries.

had lost after my initial capture. As he visited me each day, he brought long rolls of paper, ink, and quill, and taught me words from his language, which he called Latin. I was at first unwilling to use the quill, but reconciled myself soon enough—how could it be against the gods to learn of his world and language?

I quickly became quite adept at writing in Latin, and Jerome—whose title was "Abbot," while his house was called "monastery"—was very pleased. He began to urge me to write of my people and our history. At first I refused, and he accepted my explanation that we didn't believe in committing to mere paper that which we held sacred.

But one day Jerome arrived at my cell very early in the morning; it was not yet sunrise, and he woke me. He said he'd just received word that the Church had issued orders for the remaining Druids to be put to death.

Then he took me from the cell, led me out of the monastery, and brought me to where he had a horse waiting. He told me that this was the only time he'd disobeyed his Church, and that he would spend the rest of his days begging his God to forgive him. He'd provided my mount with supplies, including food, clothing, tools…and ink and paper. I thanked him profusely, told him he would have made a fine Druid, and left him forever.

I knew not this part of Eire, but a day's ride brought me to uninhabited woodland, with plentiful game and water. I was well trained in Celtic survival arts, and knew I could make a home here. Whether I could avoid the Romans forever… well, only the Dagda and the Morrigan[11] knew that for certain.

It was a hard life, and lonely, and I did not fare well as the year grew colder. I was able to call upon the *sidh* for some assistance, and when I needed to hunt I allowed the Morrigan to fill me…but without a Druid of the opposite sex, I was unable to call down the Dagda or even bring the Morrigan's full powers into play. Samhain came and went, and I could offer only a small sacrifice—a fox I'd captured and held for

[11] In Celtic religion, the Dagda and the Morrigan are basically the father and mother gods (respectively). They were thought to couple at Samhain to ensure fertility for the next year's crops and livestock, and they figure prominently in a number of existing Samhain legends (the Morrigan, for example, was also a warrior who, together with her son Oengus, drove the monstrous Fomorians from Ireland one Samhain).

that night. It was not enough.

Within a month I knew I was dying.

Although Jerome's consideration had led me to believe I was healed, the mutilation of my mouth by his fellows began to plague me, and with the onset of winter cold I fell ill. I knew I could hold on for a short time, but doubted I would live to see Beltane[12].

Beyond my own death, however, loomed a greater horror: If I was the last remaining Druid, all of our knowledge would die with me.

Unless I committed the greatest of sins and recorded it all.

I could, with the language and utensils Jerome had provided. I knew I wouldn't have time to write all I knew, but if I began now, I might have just enough left for the most important things, the rituals and stories and formulae that every Druid learned in their first year.

And so I begged the gods' forgiveness and I wrote.

It was more difficult than I'd expected, especially as winter set in. I built small fires for no other reason than to thaw my ink and my cramped fingers. I resented time taken away from the task of writing—time to hunt, to prepare food, to attend to other bodily needs. I realized my thoughts were not organized, that recollections of my own life (which I selfishly thought important enough to commit here) were bound with the true knowledge.

Yet it kept me alive. Even as I grew weaker and thinner, even as the spittle I coughed up began to contain more blood than other fluid, I kept writing. I burned with the need to record, and my own heat carried me through to Beltane and beyond.

But as another Samhain approached, my fingers finally refused to work, and my eyes grew dim. It was enough; I'd written only a fraction of our learning, but it would do. What was here could provide a new beginning, should it be found by one of understanding.

As my body failed me, I settled on one last plan:

I would journey to a nearby bog, and on Samhain I would offer myself as sacrifice there, asking the thick waters

---

[12] In the Celtic calendar, Beltane—which takes place on May Eve, exactly six months apart from Samhain, or Halloween—was the great spring/summer counterpart to the fall/winter holiday.

to preserve me and hide me until one would come who was worthy of receiving this, the last of our real soul. I will wrap these pages carefully in animal hides and a box Jerome provided, and take them beneath the water with me, trusting in the gods to keep us both.

Forgive me, holy ones. I know I've failed you twice now and damned the world to a new darkness, but perhaps one day our light will shine again, if my sacrifice is accepted.

I dream of a new world.

There were still pages after that—apparently Mongfind had remembered a last few items to commit to history. But her story really ended there, in the bog where she and her pages were found, more than fifteen hundred years later.

And she'd been right about at least one thing: The world had descended into "a new darkness." The Dark Ages settled over Europe and continued for a thousand years, ten bleak centuries of ignorance and confusion that climaxed as the Black Death raced across the continent while the Church burned tens of thousands of so-called witches and tortured heretics.

Despite the Enlightenment and the Renaissance and the Industrial Revolution and the Digital Age, I couldn't help but wonder if the world had ever really recovered. Especially recently, as I passed each year more convinced that mankind was entering its own final chapter, that centuries of greed and ecological devastation were finally leading to a planet that would no longer be able to sustain so many of us.

I was less certain what to make of Mongfind's accounts of encounters with *sidh*, of using magic to ward off foes (before the missionaries had slain the Druids), and especially of blood sacrifices on Samhain to propitiate the gods. The knowledge Mongfind had recorded was a mix of what seemed to be practical information—which healing herbs could be gathered in a forest, when to plant certain crops, how to create "needfire," or sparks engendered by friction—but other parts of the recorded lore read like a fantasy novel. There was an account of a Samhain when the *sidh* had appeared in the king's throne room, demanding tribute of food and slaves, but Mongfind and a male arch-Druid name Mog Roith had sacrificed a black sheep and a young warrior who'd offered himself to invoke a fearsome and powerful death-spirit named Balsab, who had driven the *sidh* back to the barrow they'd come out of. Mog Roith and Mongfind had spent the next two weeks not sleeping or eating, but working first to banish Balsab, and then to create a spell that would seal the barrow forever.

Balsab…Charles Vallancey's "lord of death." There was more about Balsab and Samhain: Apparently each Samhain, sacrifices were offered to Balsab to ensure his cooperation throughout the coming year. If they bought him off with a few small deaths at the end of every summer, he apparently spared the Celts from plagues and wars and pestilence the rest of the year.

Dear God. Vallancey's ludicrous ramblings suddenly didn't seem so ludicrous anymore. Instead, he'd been right all along. We were the fools, not Vallancey. The alternate history of Halloween was the *real* history.

All of this was presented in Wilson's straightforward, matter-of-fact translation, which made it all sound perfectly plausible. I really didn't know what to think of it.

I was going over it again when my phone rang. Checking the caller ID, I saw "Ó CUINN, CONOR." I'd given Wilson my number, but somehow I wasn't entirely comfortable knowing that ó Cuinn had it.

The conversation that followed didn't do much to dissuade me in finding Dr. ó Cuinn unnerving. He wanted to meet. His Irish accent was anything but lilting; he sounded excited and anxious. I asked what he wanted to meet about.

"Have you read the journal?"

"Yes. Or at least most it."

"What do you make of it?"

"I'm not sure."

"Well, maybe I can help. I've got some ideas on it, but…well, we should discuss it in person."

I debated for a few seconds. I could tell him I was busy (which was true; in fact, I had two book signings and four interviews scheduled over the next week). I could ask that he just e-mail me whatever he had to say. But then I reminded myself that this man was a respected archaeologist, an expert in a field I'd once seriously considered pursuing. He undoubtedly did have some insight into the find, and I was curious to know why he wanted to share his thoughts with me.

"All right," I told him. "Did you have somewhere in mind?"

He had his own temporary office at the UCLA campus. He wanted to meet tonight.

I almost said no. I'd attended UCLA as an undergraduate, and the place hadn't changed much since then. This was a Monday night in fall, so the campus would be quiet, no sporting events or film screenings at Melnitz Hall, no crowds of students to feel safe within. It was spread out and dark, with parking structures nowhere near any of the buildings. When I'd attended the school, I'd lived in one of the dorms to the west of the grounds; they'd routinely issued warnings to female students about the dangers of walking alone after dark. I'd even written a recent short story in which a male student had been attacked here by a transgendered rapist.[13]

But I was intrigued—did he know something about Samhain? I'd googled Conor ó Cuinn, and his credentials were solid; not overwhelming, but he'd overseen enough excavations around Ireland that he was considered something of an expert in Celtic history.

That brought up a new question in my mind: Why had they called me in? There was surely nothing I could offer above what was in my books. There had to be some other reason they hadn't revealed yet. Maybe they were just doing a documentary for The History Channel and needed another talking head.

So I said yes, and by 8 p.m. I was parked and making my way across the campus grounds. It was a mid-October night in L.A., which meant it was still warm enough to need only a light jacket. The campus was mostly empty; in fact, it seemed *too* empty. Surely classes were in session in October, and a state university must have certainly offered some evening classes...? I saw only a handful of students, all hunched over and hurrying somewhere as if anxious to escape a chill that didn't even exist.

I was just passing a thick growth of shrubbery ringing the edge of one of the great brick-built halls when I first heard it: A slight rustling of the leaves. The night was still, there was no breeze to blame, and I swallowed down a small jolt of unease. I scanned the low bushes, trying not to appear too obvious, but saw no movement, nor heard anything else. A squirrel, then, or maybe a cat strayed over from the surrounding residential area...

Something struck the brickwork ahead and to the right of me.

---

[13] "Dr. Jekyll and Mr. Hyde" from Monsters of L.A.

The tiny, metallic clang was followed by what sounded for all the world like a stifled laugh.

This time I did stop, peering into the dark corner from which the sounds had emanated. I wished then that I carried a flashlight, one of those little Mags that dangles on a keychain, or even a lighter. As it was, I could make out nothing in the black shadow surrounding the looming three-story building.

I waited for a few seconds, ears straining, but heard nothing else. The echo of a distant cell phone conversation, yes; or something coming from within the building, possibly traveling through a ventilation duct. That was it.

I continued on; the hall where ó Cuinn had said his temporary office was housed couldn't be more than a hundred yards off. I was sure it was the next building ahead, and I'd be safe once I was inside—

Something scuttled through the bushes just a few feet to my left now, and all speculation was done. I reached into the jacket pocket where I'd put my car keys, and wrapped a fist around them; if I had to fight off an attacker, they might think twice after getting a key wrapped between two knuckles in the face. But I still starting walking *fast*, toward the building, trying not to look over my shoulder, trying to ignore the obvious sound of something now following me, something getting closer with each step. Suddenly I was shivering, and my breath puffed out in front of me—*how was that possible?*—and I almost ran the last of the way to the double doors leading into the hall, to the warmth and safety of the well-lit interior beyond—

What if the doors are locked? That thought flickered through my growing unease as I leapt up the five steps to the landing, reached out for the door, tried not to imagine being caught there, in front of the doors, alone, by whatever tracked me—

I flung the door open and stepped through.

As the door closed behind me, I turned and looked out.

There was nothing there.

I walked right up to the glass, scanning the night. I'm not someone who frightens easily; maybe it's because I explore fear so often in fiction. I have no phobias, and being a lifelong city dweller (and occasionally working as a screenwriter in the film industry, where the writer was everyone's doormat), I'd developed a tough hide. I'd been followed before...but I'd never been followed like *this*.

"Ms. Morton?"

I spun so fast I nearly tripped on my own feet. Conor ó Cuinn stood behind me; I'd been so intent on looking outside that I hadn't heard him approach. I have to say that as much as he put me on edge, he was still preferable to whatever had just followed me.

"Are you all right?"

"Yes, I...sorry, I think someone just followed me here."

ó Cuinn's reaction to that was unexpected, to say the least—he glanced quickly past me, and then *smiled*. "Yes, well...perhaps we can talk in my office."

It was such an inappropriate response that I wanted to shout at him; I would've turned around and left, except that *something* was still out there. Something that didn't seem to shock Dr. Conor ó Cuinn.

It crossed my mind then to wonder if what had followed me had been ó Cuinn himself. Could he have somehow beat me to the entrance, or used some other way into the building? Or even put someone else up to it? But why?

"Dr. ó Cuinn..."

"Call me Conor." He gestured down the hallway. "Please."

I followed him. At least that way he was ahead of me, always in sight.

ó Cuinn's "office" turned out to be little more than a storage closet, with boxes lining two walls, a window with the blinds drawn over it on a third wall, and a beat-up metal desk and threadbare chair against the fourth. On the desk were a tablet computer and plug-in keyboard, a pen, a pad of paper, and a few books. He gestured at a metal folding chair pushed up against the cardboard crates, and he took the ancient rolling chair behind the desk.

"I'm sorry, I don't have anything to offer you." He waved a hand around the space, indicating the lack of coffee maker or even water cooler.

"That's okay, but I..." I decided to be honest with him and see how he reacted. "Something was definitely after me just now, outside."

He peered at me for an instant, and I found myself disliking his narrow features and dark eyes (black Irish) all over again. After a few seconds, he looked away and asked, "So, you said you've read most of the manuscript?"

"Most of it, yes. I haven't looked at some of the longer sections in detail yet, the…"

"Spells?"

"Well…yes." There were lengthy sections of the manuscript that seemed to be little more than very precise descriptions of rituals and ceremonies, or how to gather and dry certain herbs, or how to enact what could only be called "spells." I'd glanced at a few of them, but had tuned out when I'd seen words like "wand" and "sacrifice."

I should probably mention here that I'm a confirmed, die-hard skeptic, and always have been. I've never believed in ghosts, UFOs, Bigfoot, Nessie, reincarnation, conspiracy theories (most of them, anyway), demonic possession (although I'd like to—it would explain a lot), Echinacea's ability to prevent a cold, Mount Olympus, trickle-down economics, chupacabras, magic (other than illusion), vampires, werewolves, or any religion you'd care to offer up. I'm a longtime subscriber to *Skeptical Inquirer* magazine, and for entertainment I enjoy watching YouTube videos of James Randi debunking various so-called "paranormal" happenings.

I mention all this to explain why I'd done little more than scan Mongfind's descriptions of various occult practices and ceremonies. And to offer some insight into my reaction when ó Cuinn said, "You should read the spells more carefully."

"Why?"

"Because then you'd know about the one I've cast tonight."

I smirked. Perhaps it wasn't polite, maybe it was rude and condescending, but I couldn't avoid it. "You cast one of the spells in Mongfind's manuscript?"

"Yes."

"I hope it was something on how to brew beer."

He answered only by nodding at the covered window. "Pull up the blinds."

What the fuck?

I almost refused. I almost got up and left, whatever was outside be damned. ó Cuinn was playing with me, and I've never been much for games.

"Why should I?"

"Because it'll make the rest of what I have to tell you easier to believe."

Or it'll give me the power to tell you, Conor, that I'm out of here and don't want to hear from you again. I reached out and grabbed the cord that controlled the blinds and pulled.

The blinds drew up—and beyond the glass, outside in the night, something was peering in at me. The face was so white the skin was slightly blue, the ears were long and with pointed tips poking up through lank, pale hair, and the corners of the thing's grin reached all the way to the bottom of those ears. The teeth were jagged and sharp, the eyes red.

It vanished almost instantly, but it'd been enough to send me up out of the chair and stumbling back. ó Cuinn leapt to his feet and moved behind me, whether to steady me or keep me from running I wasn't sure.

"It's all right, it won't hurt you," he said.

I turned to look at him. He was confident, even smug. "You're going to tell me that was the spell...?"

"Yes. I summoned the *sidh.*"

"The *sidh*..." I'm sure my mouth must have fallen open for a second in disbelief. An esteemed archaeologist was standing here, in a cramped but well-lit office in the 21st century, trying to tell me that he'd performed an ancient magic ritual and had called down the *sidh*—the Little People, the Good Neighbors...fairies. "That's ridiculous."

"Then what did you hear outside? What did you see just now?"

As I stared at him, his gaunt, stubbled cheeks and sunken eyes and shock of coal-colored hair, I wondered: What was he trying to do? Why had he tried to scare me? Was this about to become a pitch to finance some project of his? It wasn't uncommon for people who only knew me through my work to assume that I was pagan, that I believed in the things I wrote fiction about. Was ó Cuinn pagan and thinking I was a fellow believer? Or had he thought maybe he could scam me?

"What is it you want?"

He looked genuinely perplexed (*He's a good actor*, crossed my mind), then he said, "I want you to understand. It's very important that you do."

"Understand what?"

"What Mongfind has left us. What your role in this is."

Is he coming on to me? That notion forced me to stifle a shudder. "What if I say I don't want a role in...whatever this is?"

"You will, when you see what we have a chance to do. And you and I are the only ones who can do it, because we're the last Druids."

Now this had taken on such epic proportions of lunacy that I openly laughed. "We're Druids...you and I..."

"Yes. Think of what a Druid was: Someone who studied Celtic ways for years, who stood apart because of the specialized knowledge they possessed, who could create something from nothing."

"If I could create something from nothing, I'd have a lot more zeroes on the amount in my checking account."

"What do you do whenever you write? What else is fiction but a form of magic?"

That stopped me, because it was something that even I—the hard-bitten skeptic—believed. Even if I accepted that writing was just neurons in my brain firing, an immensely sophisticated organic computer transforming tiny electrical sparks into thoughts, thoughts that my fingers then translated into letters, it *felt* like magic, and I was the magician, creating (from nothing) whole worlds that would eventually be shared by others. Yes, writing was a form of magic, and a powerful one at that...but I wasn't about to believe that my ability to tell stories somehow made me a priestess for a long-dead people.

But Conor believed that. Absolutely and without question, he believed that he and I were Druids and that he (we) could perform spells that would create more than just words on paper. I had a moment then of pity for him; I could only imagine he must have been a lonely and lost man.

I looked down at his left hand, and saw that he wore a simple gold band. "Are you married?"

He blinked in surprise. "I was. My wife died three years ago. A rare form of cancer. We had six weeks after she was diagnosed." He turned the laptop towards me so I could see the desktop photo, which showed a fair-haired young woman, a baby, and Conor, who was not just younger, but almost a completely different man, with a fuller face and bright, almost kind eyes. Ó Cuinn had been hollowed out by grief.

"You have a child?"

He nodded, and the smile that touched his lips made me want to like him, despite my misgivings. "Alec. He's five now; I brought him with me, to America. He's in our temporary apartment just a mile from here, with a student I hired to help me look after him."

I started walking toward the door, letting him know I was done here. "Go spend time with your little boy. I don't know why you're trying to scare me—" he started to protest, but I cut him off, raising my voice as I went on, "—but we're done. I don't think you really need me for this project anyway."

I left and he didn't stop me; but when I reached the hall, he stepped out behind me and called, "Try one of the spells yourself. That's all I ask."

I stopped and turned, ready to respond with some quick sarcastic remark, but all I could manage was, "That's crazy. Really. The Druids have been gone for fifteen-hundred years, and they were really just tree-huggers, not magicians."

I walked out then. I'd convinced myself that Conor had some confederate who'd followed me before and who'd popped up outside the window; I hadn't really seen the face for more than an instant, and it *could* have been a mask, or even a complete fake head. I knew whoever was working with him was probably still outside, but I'd be less polite if they tried to follow me again.

Curious, though, I did walk to the point where Conor's office window faced out, and tried to examine the area beneath it. There were bushes masking the ground and the brick wall, and the growth was certainly thick enough to conceal someone crouching down. "Oh, and by the way—fuck you, too," I said, before turning to walk away.

I made it back to my car without incident and drove home still percolating with anger. By the time I crawled into bed, I'd decided that in the morning I would call Wilson Armitage and talk to him about Conor ó Cuinn.

What I didn't know then was that Wilson Armitage was dead.

OCTOBER 23 / OCTOBER 24

When I called Dr. Armitage's office in the morning, a male voice I didn't recognize answered. "Yes?"

"Hi, this is Lisa Morton calling for Dr. Armitage."

"What did you need to speak to him about?"

Something about the voice was wrong—it was too gruff, too harsh to belong to anyone who worked at a university. "I was consulting with him on a project."

"Well, Ms. Morton, I'm afraid I have some bad news: Dr. Armitage is dead. My name's Lieutenant John Bertocelli, and I'm investigating his death."

Oh God. "How did he die?"

"He was found here on campus last night. It looks like he was attacked by some sort of wild animal, but we're not ruling out murder yet."

*Wild animal…*maybe something with a too-wide mouthful of jagged fangs, something that moved unseen through the night…

And I'd been there. If they found that out, would I be a suspect? Would it look better for me if I told them now? "I was at the campus last night."

"What time would that have been?"

"I came to talk to Dr. Armitage's associate, Conor ó Cuinn. I was there from about eight-thirty to not quite nine."

"We think that's about the time Dr. Armitage was killed."

"Something followed me last night."

There was a pause, and I imagined the detective waving his partner over, or grabbing a notepad. "You mean something followed you last night while you were on the school grounds?"

"Yes."

"But you didn't see it?"

"No. I'm sorry."

"Don't be. If you'd gotten a look at it, you'd probably be dead today instead of Dr. Armitage." He asked a few more brief questions, then took my contact information and hung up.

After several seconds of just sitting, staring (*Did Conor kill him?*), I googled UCLA news and found a brief mention on a local news website of Armitage's death. It didn't add much to what I'd already heard from Lt. Bertocelli—that he'd been found dead outside Haines Hall late last night, his body mauled and covered with what looked like bite marks.

That could have been me.

Maybe I'd been wrong about the face I'd seen outside the window. Maybe it had been an animal—a mountain lion? A maddened, injured dog?

But Conor had known it was there.

Had Conor meant to kill Wilson Armitage? Why?

I was interviewed by Lt. Bertocelli a day later, in an ugly little office with scratched furniture and sickly-green walls in a Westside police station. They told me they were still leaning toward a wild animal attack, but they had some questions...mainly about Dr. Conor ó Cuinn. Apparently he and Armitage had argued earlier in the day, about something to do with what was now being called "the Celtic manuscript." Students who'd overheard the confrontation mentioned a loud, "Yes, I *do* intend to try it," in Conor's accent, to which Armitage responded, "You can't be serious."

The fact that I'd been with ó Cuinn at the time of Wilson's death—it'd been put precisely at 8:40—ruled him out as a suspect. And they told me repeatedly I was not a suspect.

But they said they might have more questions.

That night, a mountain lion was spotted in wealthy Bel Air, just to the north of the UCLA campus. It happens sometimes—predators are driven down out of the few remaining patches of Southern California wilderness by hunger, thirst, wildfires...maybe loneliness. In another few hours, the story would probably end the way these stories always did: Some cop would claim his dart gun had jammed, and he'd just kill the poor cat instead. Meanwhile, we'd all know: That the cop, when faced with a 140-pound, yellow-eyed carnivore, had reacted on the most primeval level possible, that his every instinct had said "Kill or die," and he'd opted for the gun that he knew would put the beast down permanently. An armed caveman.

The news was already speculating that the big cat had savaged Wilson Armitage. Bel Air was within (human) walking distance of UCLA, separated only by Sunset Boulevard. It might provide a convenient close to the case.

But I knew a mountain lion was not what I'd heard following me. And it certainly wasn't the grinning, red-eyed specter I'd seen outside ó Cuinn's window.

OCTOBER 27

I was too busy to think much more about Wilson Armitage and Conor ó Cuinn. I had signings to attend, interviews to give, and blog posts to write. There were Halloween haunts to visit, decorations to photograph, and stores to shop in. I have a soft spot for cheap, completely useless Halloween kitsch that makes me laugh.

I imagine the laborers at the manufacturing plant in China slaving over miniature Halloween skateboards and goblin finger puppets, and thinking that all Americans must surely be mad.

Then an e-mail arrived, with a generic name from a gmail account. I almost dismissed it instantly as spam, but the subject heading read: "Samhain query."

Don't open it. That was my first thought.

But, of course, I did.

It was from Conor ó Cuinn. The gmail account suggested he was probably still under suspicion, and had sent this from some public computer. It was a simple message:

"Scroll to page 147 in Armitage's translation. Read the next ten pages. And remember what I said about us being the last Druids."

Delete it and forget about it. I considered telling ó Cuinn not to contact me again. Maybe I should send it to my new detective friend, Bertocelli.

Instead, I opened the Mongfind translation file.

Page 147 started by recounting the moment when the Celts realized their new Catholic friends were actually an invasion force, bent on conquest. The initial attacks took out many in the warrior caste; the survivors were trying to rally their forces. And so they called on Mongfind:

I saw our dead, our dying, our wounded. These men had now revealed that they came with no purpose other than to slay us and subjugate us. My people turned to their Arch-Druids—Mog Roith and I—in this hour of need.

I sought out Mog Roith, and yet he was nowhere to be found. Our path was clear: We had to invoke the Dagda and the Morrigan and take them within ourselves. Only they would be powerful enough to lead the opposition.

We searched quickly, but came to believe that Mog Roith must already be dead, although he had not been found among the corpses yet. Finally, we could tarry no longer—we had to hope the Morrigan alone would be enough.

And so, protected by a ring of our strongest remaining warriors, I performed the ritual to call forth the Morrigan. Fortunately, the year was close to Samhain, and the Morrigan was near at this time.

She answered my summons, and filled me. Her power! Her strength, her resolution gave me fresh hope. Sharing your body with a god is one of the most ecstatic experiences for any Druid; it is neither possession nor loss, but is instead a bonding that exceeds anything experienced by ordinary men and women. It is one of the ultimate rewards for the years of training and learning the Druid must undergo. It is among the holiest of our rites, and may be practiced only then by the male and female Arch-Druids.

The invocation was accomplished quickly and successfully. The Morrigan, instantly awake and aware within me, began issuing orders to our soldiers. Then she took a spear and shield, and led them to the battlefield.

I felt everything with her as we cut a bloody swath through the opposing troops. Our speed and skill were unmatched. The first row of enemies went down beneath spear thrusts and a shield wielded as a second weapon. Gore soaked us; we shook it from our eyes and kept going, bloodlust increasing our power. We raged through their ranks, and behind us the Celtic warriors were renewed, screaming their battle cries. The invaders began to panic; many tried to run, only to collide with their comrades behind them. Our shield sprouted arrows like deadly quills, but nothing could harm us. We were invincible. We would win.

Eire would remain ours forever.

But then the enemy forces began to scatter for another reason—something was coming up from behind them, something they *wanted* to let through. The Morrigan and I sensed an intelligence approaching, familiar and usually welcomed...

The last of their rows parted, and Mog Roith stepped through; Mog is blind, but because he moved among the soldiers easily, I knew that the Dagda had joined him and given him sight.

"Mongfind," he said—except "Morrigan" impossibly came from his mouth at the same time—"we must cease this fighting."

I felt the Morrigan's disbelief surge through me, and I shared it. The Dagda and the Morrigan were the great

defenders of Eire; they'd fought against Fomorians and
sidh, they were the most valorous warriors of the *Tuatha
de Danaan.* The Dagda would never call for an end to de-
fending our land.

"No," the Morrigan and I answered, "we must drive them
out."

Mog Roith smiled, sadly…and then raised the great club
he held and brought it down on our head.

When I awakened, a day later, the Morrigan was gone, I
was bound and gagged in a dank cell, and I knew the invaders had won.

Eire was theirs.

Mog Roith had betrayed us. He had summoned the
Dagda and then used the god's power against us. I never
found out why, I never knew what the Catholics and their
god could possibly have offered. I did find out that shortly
after he bludgeoned me, he staggered from the battlefield to
an oak grove, took a sacred knife and slit his own throat. Or,
likely, the furious Dagda took over and repaid Mog Roith's
betrayal. One may partner with the gods, but one cannot be-
tray them and expect the forged bond not to shatter.

I'd read this account earlier, but hadn't really looked at what followed it: Instructions for performing the ritual to invoke the spirit
of the Morrigan. It was a comparatively simple procedure, requiring none of the paraphernalia (a rod made of ash, a wand fashioned
from an oak twig) of most of the other spells I'd glanced at. Fasting
was suggested, but I knew Mongfind had performed it successfully
without that; the rest consisted of assuming a posture known as
the heron stance, and meditating while inciting an invocation. It
reiterated that only a female Arch-Druid could successfully invoke
the Morrigan.

I had no idea why ó Cuinn wanted me to read this passage. Yes,
the account of Mongfind laying into her Catholic enemies while
possessed by a goddess was stirring fiction, but what did any of this
have to do with me? Did ó Cuinn actually believe that he and I
were Arch-Druids?

I tried to focus on writing an article I had promised an online
news site, but my thoughts kept circling back to ó Cuinn's suggestion. It was ludicrous, the thought of me standing in the middle of

my living room floor, one foot braced against the opposite knee, trying to keep my balance while reciting words that sounded like a Lewis Carroll poem…I couldn't foresee that ending with anything but me collapsing onto the carpet, cursing my own innate clumsiness.

Still…what could it hurt? It wasn't as if this ritual required the sacrifice of a child, or even a blood oath. Fifteen minutes of my time, and it might be an interesting experiment; perhaps it would help me to understand, at least in some small part, how ecstatic states could be reached in shamanistic practices. Maybe I'd feel a little of what Mongfind had felt, nearly two millennia ago. Maybe I'd understand how she could have possibly believed that she'd been in communion with a goddess.

The chant was simple[14]; it only took me a few seconds to memorize it. I stood, walked to a clear space in my living room, raised one leg, and tried to concentrate.

The first few seconds were disastrous. I wobbled; I lost the pose; I laughed; I almost returned to my desk, thankful that no one had been around to witness my attempt.

But instead I opted to remain as serious as possible; I was, as I mentioned, curious about the state it would theoretically produce in the practitioner.

I held the pose, one leg bent, the foot resting against the other knee, thinking about engravings I'd seen of Celtic warriors in this pose, and Australian aborigines…and after a time of struggling to stay upright, my difficulties seemed to fall away and were replaced with calm steadiness. My eyes closed, the chant continued to flow past my lips, becoming more effortless with each recitation. With every passing second, it became easier to concentrate solely on the words…the invitation…

Awareness seemed to simultaneously fall away and expand. I was calm, focused…open.

Something was in the room with me. I felt it like a blanket, or like a luxurious wrap made of the most exquisite fabric. It was warmth, and strength, and comfort. I didn't open my eyes, because there was no need; there was nothing in this sensation to alarm me, to cause anxiety or dread.

The chant continued, and so did the presence. It enveloped me;

---

[14] I'm not including the actual chant here because…well, even though it can supposedly be performed only by a Druid priest or priestess of the highest level, let's just say I nonetheless have some safety concerns. Don't try this at home, in other words.

it spoke without words, telling me it—or, rather, *she*, because there was something quintessentially feminine about this presence—had come at my bidding. The no-words conveyed admiration and love, and surprise, because it had been millennia since she had been thus called.

The Morrigan.

At this point, my skepticism was laid to rest by desire—I wanted nothing more than to join with this power, to feel it within me, infusing me. I wanted nothing so badly as to feel what Mongfind had felt, as she'd strode onto a battlefield without fear, striking down her foes with grace and divine skill.

The warmth was inside me, then, and

OCTOBER 27, TIME UNKNOWN

first are the smells, my head is flooded not just with the scent of cooking meat from the apartment below but the half-wrapped chocolate bar I left on my desk and the jasmine soap from the bathroom and the odd chemical tang of dishwashing liquid and detergent from the kitchen (and how is it possible I've never noticed before how intense that is and how it grates) and I can feel every fiber of the carpet beneath my bare feet and the air on the skin of my arms and face and the sounds—so many, so loud—the sounds of music thumping from somewhere nearby and a helicopter *whup-whup-whupping* overhead and a bass rumble which it takes me several seconds to identify as my own heartbeat and I still taste the wine I drank an hour ago and the brightness of my computer screen nearly forces me to turn my head away but it's *glorious*, a fire that glows unlike any we've seen before and it is "we" now, because I share these wonders with another who has fit into me like a sleek hand into a glove and I can feel the energy she brings with her throbbing and pushing fire through my limbs and she tests them, moves my arms and then my legs and we're outside, running through the October night, no shoes but it doesn't matter because nothing can hurt us, not the speeding cars that we leap away from, clearing the hood of a parked truck as easily as stepping over a bump in the ground, we run, reveling in the rush of our own blood as it flows through muscles that *she* has made flexible and fit, and it's not just the particle-thickened Los Angeles air we can feel on our flesh and within our lungs, but we can feel the veil, too, the membrane that separates our worlds, and we can almost glimpse what lies beyond it, the grimacing *sidh* and the shadowy dead ones, the things with shifting form like smoke and with black hearts that seek to suck and devour, and we see how thin that veil is, because it's almost the end of the month (of summer, and of the year), it's only a few nights from Samhain, when that skin will be thinnest, and one with craft—one like a Druid—could reach past, but that world doesn't interest us right now because we've heard something coming from one of the intersecting streets ahead of us, a voice raised in anger, and that tone reacts within *her* like a flammable chemical set on fire and we follow, moving so quickly that the houses and apartment complexes and parked cars are a blur, we run three blocks to where the buildings are a little older, a little more in need of repair, and coming from a bottom-floor apartment is the voice of a man shouting obscenities at a woman, who offers nothing but weak, sobbing responses, and we draw closer, standing outside the door of the apartment, listening, and something within crashes and shatters, and the woman cries out, and then the door is flying open (it was so easy to break its flimsy lock), and there's a man, young, heavy-set, wearing a stained t-shirt, drawing back a fist, but the woman is already bleeding from the nose, her eyes wide as she sees us, and he turns and swings at us instead, but we catch the blow and laugh at the expression on his face as we squeeze his hand, grinding the fingers against each other until he screams, and we force him down while the woman stands back, silent now, staring in disbelief, and then with our other hand we strike him again, in the temple, and he wobbles but doesn't fall, and I know one more blow will kill him and we're pulling back our arm a second time and I know I can stop this now, I can take control and we can leave, return home before we take this man's life, leave him to prey upon her until she dies at 28 or 32 or (unlikely) 40, beaten down and used up, but I don't stop it, I want to feel this happening, to rid the world of this abuser and to know what death feels like, and so I let her draw back our fist and bring it down again and this time his eyes roll up and he falls like a butchered steer, and we can no longer hear his breath or his heart so we know he's dead, and we turn to the woman, and I understand that by tomorrow she will describe us as a male, six feet tall and tattooed, and we turn to leave, half-drunk on violence, and her influence is ebbing as she takes us home again on middle-aged legs that pump now with a failing rhythm, and as we reach home I notice the blood on my fingers and the panic I feel is mine alone and she leaves then, and in that instant, when all that she brought with her is suddenly taken from me, my legs give way and my eyes lose focus and

OCTOBER 28, DAY

The first thing I noticed when I woke up in the morning was how much my hands hurt.

Then I realized I'd fallen asleep fully dressed on the couch in the living room. I sat up, aching from the cushions, bleary-eyed, blinking against morning sun. I raised a hand to rub away the sleep—and saw the blood crusted across my fingers.

I…we…killed a man last night.

The memories washed through me, a toxic rain poisoning whatever it touched. I remembered all of it.

Or did I?

I ran to my computer and googled "North Hollywood Crime News." The search took me to a local news station's updates… and there it was, under the headline "NORTH HOLLYWOOD MAN FOUND DEAD BY ABUSED WIFE, SUSPECT SOUGHT." They were looking for a male, approximately six feet tall, medium build, brown hair.

It had happened. Exactly as I remembered it, down to the Morrigan using her influence to guarantee the wife's unwitting complicity.

There was something else there: Last night, I'd apparently typed the account of the possession, while it was still fresh.[15] I had only a vague memory of doing it, in some sort of dreamlike state.

I ran to the bathroom, turned on the shower, and stepped in, still clothed. There wasn't much blood on me—mainly on my hand, and some of that was mine—but I still planned on washing these clothes after, then driving to some distant dumpster and disposing of them.

As the hot water flooded over me, turning pink when it swirled around the drain, I began to remember more. The Morrigan had left me with thoughts tucked away, thoughts I pulled forth as I

---

[15] The previous chapter was exactly what I found on my computer.

relaxed beneath the steady warmth:

I saw, clearly, an archaic, idyllic settlement, perched on a green hill. Spacious houses built of wood and stone clustered about a palace ornamented in gold; I recognized the geometric spiral ornamentation as Celtic in origin. Smoke curled from a hundred chimneys, the people wore heavy torques over fine robes, and they glowed with health and happiness. I understood that an old man, still hardy, his white beard and a few wrinkles the only clues to his longevity, was more than 150 years old. I saw a school where young men and women studied history and lore, and I felt a strange kinship with them.

This was Mongfind's world, before the invaders came.

Another memory appeared in my mind's eye, and I saw a Samhain ritual. A great cake was prepared, cut into small portions, and one portion was rubbed with charcoal on the bottom. Warriors and young nobles lined up to choose pieces, and when a handsome young man turned his over to find the blackened underside, he smiled and received the congratulations of those around him. At night, the Druids led him to a pond; there, as he stood quietly, dressed in the finest jewels and raiments, they began the Samhain ritual. Mongfind and Mog Roith used chalk dust to draw a protective circle around those present, while they invoked sanctuary. First, the two Arch-Druids offered a black sheep; they moved in perfect, long-practiced unity, and the animal died almost instantly. Then, with great dignity, Mongfind knotted a rope about the neck of the handsome young man as she chanted a prayer to Balsab, the Lord of Death. At a signal from her, the sacrifice knelt by the side of the bog, his expression serene. Mog Roith stepped up, and while she tightened the noose, her male counterpart thrust a ceremonial dagger into the young man's chest; then, together, they pushed his head down beneath the waters of the bog. He was, in effect, simultaneously hanged, stabbed, and drowned, satisfying the classic Druidical obsession with the number three.

With the sacrifices completed, a weight filled the air. The fires ringing the bog darkened; even Mongfind was plainly unnerved.

Balsab had come.

I felt Mongfind's anxiety as she waited with the others. The air literally thickened, pressurized; one young man's knees buckled and he sank to the soggy ground, gasping. A noxious odor arose, the scent of spilled blood and decayed corpses. Mongfind fought back an urge to gag, then withdrew her own knife, ready to offer herself should the protective circle prove insufficient.

Seconds passed like small eternities. The future hung on this void; if it found the offerings unworthy, it could release horrors beyond death on the people. Mongfind offered up silent prayers to the other gods, but this was Balsab's moment.

The dark god's overpowering presence vanished abruptly, and the gathered Druids all exhaled in relief. Balsab had accepted the sacrifices, and ensured another year of prosperity for his worshippers. A feast would commence now, and even if the *sidh* should cross over, Mongfind and Mog Roith would be ready. The Celts would enjoy another year of prosperity, until next Samhain.

Samhain…Halloween…four days away.

I finished showering, dressed, walked to the living room on legs gone numb, didn't even correct myself when I missed the couch, and sagged to the floor.

True. All of it, true.

The Morrigan had possessed me last night, and together we'd committed murder. I'd just washed our victim's blood from my hands, and yet that wasn't what had taken the feeling from me and dropped me:

I couldn't deny what had happened last night—*any* of it. There was a world beyond ours—a world of violent gods and ancient magic and hunger for human life. History is a lie and reality a thin sheet, beyond which we sometimes glimpse shadows that strut and grasp at us. Nothing in Mongfind's journal was fantasy or deception—it was the truth, not what I'd spent my life experiencing and believing.

And ó Cuinn…he'd known exactly which spell to send me to, the one that would provide an encounter so intimate that even the most confirmed of skeptics wouldn't deny it. This couldn't be explained away as a cheap Halloween mask, or even the finest special effects trick created by a master wizard.

Or could it?

I still couldn't accept it completely. A drug, perhaps; certain psychotropics were widely used to induce ecstatic states. Could ó Cuinn have somehow slipped me something? I thought back to everything I'd eaten and drunk yesterday—tea from my own supply, Thai food from the same restaurant I ate at twice a week, wine from a bottle I'd just opened. It didn't seem likely, but…

What if he hadn't tampered with my food? That meant he was right—that we were both Druids, that he had called up the *sidh*…

That they'd murdered Wilson Armitage.

Had ó Cuinn meant for that to happen? Or had he been unable to control his guests once they'd arrived?

After some time I found the strength to rise, and resolved to continue with my schedule as planned. I'd taken this week off from my day job as a bookseller to focus on my Halloween commitments, and I wouldn't abandon those now. I had a phone interview set up with the BBC in thirty minutes—I'd be damned if I'd give that up because I'd had a psychedelic trip into fairyland.

Even as I thought that, I hoped I wouldn't be damned for other reasons.

OCTOBER 28, EVENING

Somehow, I managed to get through the day. In between interviews and answering e-mails, I packed last night's clothes into a trash bag, drove to an alley thirty minutes away, found an open dumpster, tossed the bag in, and came home again.

Night fell, and I drove to Dark Delicacies, a nearby genre specialty bookstore, for a signing. I didn't like the idea of being out at night, but this wouldn't be like walking across a large, empty campus; even if I had to park a short distance from the store, I'd be walking past other stores on a heavily-trafficked street.

The signing was pleasant, if under-attended (aren't they all), and afterward I ended up walking with friends to a coffee shop two blocks away, where we gabbed over tea and dessert. For an hour or so, I was able to forget about goddesses and murder and pagan rituals as we lost ourselves in the simple, mundane pleasures of gossip and jokes.

At 11 p.m. (how had it gotten to be that late?), the shop closed up and kicked us out. We said our goodbyes on the sidewalk, and I turned to head for my car, now parked several blocks away. It was late enough that the other stores had closed, and few cars drove by. In the distance I could hear the ever-present sound of sirens (in an area as big as L.A., there's *always* a catastrophe happening somewhere) and the thrum of freeway congestion.

I came to an intersection, and even though I couldn't see any approaching cars, I waited for the crosswalk light to turn green—the last thing in the world I needed right now was for a hidden cop to nab me for jaywalking.

"I'm really sorry, officer, and—what? No, that's not blood under my fingernails, of course not..." My rational mind assured me that there was no visible blood beneath the nails of the hands I'd scrubbed until they were raw and red, but I still wasn't taking any chances. I waited.

The shop on the corner was one of those little cluttered gift shops, the kind that you glance in and you can't imagine buying any of this kitschy nonsense and you wonder how they stay in business. Because it was Halloween, their front display windows were full of little papier-mâché pumpkins (some were sprayed with glitter or even wore little aprons, which offended my highly-honed sense of Halloween decorum), cute witch and cat figurines, and gingerbread-scented candles. There were Halloween salt shakers and mugs and hand-towels.

Near the bottom was a jack-o'-lantern that made me stop and stare. It was white, almost the size of a real pumpkin, and lit with some sort of reddish glow from within. It also bore one of the most grotesquely carved faces I'd ever seen—eyes with knitted brows, a huge snaggle-toothed grin, two slits for a nose. It didn't begin to match the other items in the window, all of which would have been more at home in an Anne Geddes photo book than a Stephen King novel, and it was the only piece that seemed to be lit.

I was bending down to look more closely at it when it turned and looked directly up at me.

Now I knew why it looked familiar. I'd seen it before, outside the window of ó Cuinn's office.

But this time it didn't vanish abruptly—I think it *wanted* me to see it. Its rictus grin widened, spilling even more crimson light out around it, although I couldn't make out the rest of its body. I took one, two steps back—

HOONNNK! I'd backed right into the street, and hadn't even noticed the car barreling through the intersection. Heart hammering, I leapt up onto the curb and the car sped off into the night.

When I looked back at the window, the face was gone.

It was coming for me.

Fuck it—I ran then; ran against the red light and regardless of who might see me and wonder what I was running from. I didn't look into any of the other windows I passed, or listen for the sound of tiny footsteps coming up behind me, closer and closer…I ran, digging into my purse as I neared my car, trying to find my keys which always fell to the bottom of the voluminous bag, requiring precious extra seconds to dig them out—

I had them. I flipped up the car key, jammed it into the lock, threw the door open, and fell into the front seat. I slammed the door behind me, pressed the lock button—and flinched as something hit the door outside *hard*, making the whole car shake. I heard a high-pitched squeal.

Somehow, I managed to get the right key into the ignition, start the car, and take off, burning rubber. I'd driven two blocks before I realized the parking brake was still on. I ran one stoplight (got lucky), then risked a glance in the rearview mirror.

Nothing but a quiet street of closed shops. A few headlights in the distance. Nothing chasing me, no sign of anything unusual.

Five minutes later I was home. I waited a few moments before I opened the car door—what if it had somehow attached itself to the car, or followed where I couldn't see it? Did it even need normal laws of physics? Could it simply wish itself here, to continue its mischief…or worse?

When it proved quiet, I opened the door and stepped out. Still safe. Closing the door, I glanced down—and saw a dent in the door panel.

So much for the drugged theory.

I walked, fast, to my front door, got in, closed it behind me, and checked all the locks, then collapsed onto the couch. I'm not used to adrenaline rushes, and I was surprised to realize I was shaking. My little tortoiseshell cat, Roxie, helped by sitting at my ankles and mewing at me in gentle concern. The simple of act of stroking her warm back and feeling her purr beneath my touch calmed me. We sometimes forget the power of the most common acts, don't we? This ancient communion with another species, something that has been part of human life for thousands of years, was its own kind of magic, with a peculiar power to restore and heal.

The phone rang, jarring me from my brief peace. I got up, stepped around Roxie, and checked the caller ID—it was Ricky, calling from North Carolina.

Hearing his voice was another gift, but—after exchanging the usual greetings—his message was disturbing. "I had the strangest thing happen tonight, and I knew you'd appreciate this."

The film had put their cast and crew up in a nice hotel in downtown Wilmington. Ricky had a room on the fifth floor, and we'd already joked about how they called the view from his window "Cape Fear Riverfront." It was too bad he wasn't making a horror movie.

"I had this nice dinner tonight with a couple of guys from the crew—we found this little seafood place you'd love—and then I came up to my room. I was just getting ready for bed when I thought I heard something on the other side of the window, so I looked—and there was some kind of strange face out there. I only got a glimpse of it before it disappeared. It must have been one of the guys punking me, because they know about you and Halloween—at least that's all I can figure."

Cold rushed through me, freezing me to the spot. "What did this face look like?"

"Well, that was kind of the giveaway: It looked like a jack-o'-lantern. I figure they probably picked up one of those battery-operated things that are in all the stores right now and lowered it down on a line. In fact, it was probably Dave from Effects—he's been teasing me all week."

A jack-o'-lantern. Of course. It was so obvious, and yes, I'd missed it—*they* looked too much like malevolent, glowing jack-o'-lanterns for it to be sheer coincidence.

"Hon...you there?"

"Sorry. Long day. You're not going out again tonight, right?"

"No. Why?"

What could I say? That what he'd seen hadn't been a cheap Halloween prop, that he was being threatened by otherworldly forces because of me? Because of something that an Irish archaeologist in Los Angeles had unleashed? Something that pulverized the well-ordered, rational world we both believed in...or, at least, *used* to believe in?

And then there was his job—this film was important to both of us. It was a good supporting role in a serious movie, with a young writer/director who we liked and admired. And, frankly, the money would make our lives much easier. If I told him now I was in trouble, he'd leave the movie and come home. We couldn't afford that...but I also wasn't ready to involve him in this. There was only one person who could help, and I would need to deal with him alone.

"Just be careful."

"Are you okay?" He knew me too well, and his warmth thawed the chill that had paralyzed me.

"Yeah, I'm fine. Just another long day."

We spent the rest of the call talking about my signing, the interview I'd given today to a Montréal radio station, a nice customer review that had gone up at Amazon for my book. We said the things that parted lovers have said to each other in letters, on phones, in text messages, for centuries. Then we hung up.

I checked the locks again, risked a glance outside, and decided to try to sleep, even though I knew it was unlikely. And if I did… would my dreams leave me more exhausted and unsettled in the morning?

OCTOBER 29

A strange whining sound from Roxie woke me in the morning.

It was earlier than my usual waking time, but the sun was already up, and I was surprised to realize I had slept.

But that sound—I'd never heard her make anything like it. She was in the living room, so I couldn't see (or imagine) what would have caused her to act that way. "Roxie?"

She didn't stop—she sounded almost like a small child uttering a string of nonsense syllables. The sound brought last night's unease hurtling back, but the fact that it was already light outside was reassuring.

I got out of bed, ventured into the living room—and saw instantly what had provoked the sound from my cat:

Outside, on my enclosed, second-floor balcony, a large carved pumpkin rested. The jack-o'-lantern's face was a small masterwork of carving skill, exuding vicious glee.

I picked up Roxie, trying to calm her, and together we stared at the sinister objet d'art beyond the glass. After a few seconds, I saw that the shadow around the base of the pumpkin wasn't just dark—it was dark red, and thick. The thing was oozing blood. And as I knelt so I could see through its empty grin, I saw there was something inside, something with fur.

Whatever was in there wasn't moving, but it was still bleeding.

The thin shape just visible through one eye socket might have been a tail, a pointed extension was possibly an ear.

A cat. Maybe still alive. Probably not, but…

If it was still alive, I couldn't stand there and watch it bleed out. Yes, Ripley went back for the cat in *Alien*, and I'd risk a dangerous encounter now to check on an animal that wasn't even mine. That's one of the things about compassion—it trumps both fear and common sense.

Because I knew, at that moment, exactly what I was confronting. There was no question that the jack-o'-lantern and the bloodied animal were not the work of ordinary pranksters. For one thing, my balcony is difficult to reach, accessible only by going through my living room or coming down from the apartment building's roof. The pumpkin was a large one, and would have been hard for even a strong man to carry down a ladder. And I didn't want to accept that any humans were capable of inflicting gruesome harm on a small animal and then stuffing its corpse into a hollowed-out squash.

No, I trusted then that if I stepped outside, I might be facing vicious, inhuman things.

I locked Roxie in the bedroom, then went to the hallway closet and found the baseball bat stored there. It was a good, solid wooden Louisville slugger, and had been given to me years ago as a gift after I'd called the police on a psycho who'd threatened a friend with it. It had heft to it, and gave me enough confidence to slide the glass door open and step out onto the balcony.

It was still early, but the day was already warm and clear, and it was hard to believe anything more threatening than a hungry squirrel would be nearby. I was guessing the *sidh* moved at night and had left this before vanishing at dawn, but I didn't know that for sure.

And…there might be something hurt and alive inside the pumpkin.

I used the bat to reach down and knock the pumpkin's top aside. A smell assaulted me, a thick, musky odor that I knew from an emergency visit to a veterinarian to fix an injured cat: The smell of fear and feline blood.

I bent over the pumpkin and looked in. I could see there was a small animal within, black, unmoving. A black cat. I poked at it tentatively with the bat, but there was no response. I went back in for a heavy towel and then returned. I laid the towel by the pumpkin, picked it up gingerly, and tilted the cat out onto the towel.

Now it was clear: It was dead. Its throat had been slit. Gore matted its soft black fur.

I understood then how the *sidh* had earned their reputation as savage pranksters: A black cat was not just a classic Halloween icon, it was also the source of one of the most common urban legends—that Satanic cults kidnapped black cats every Halloween and sacrificed them in diabolical rituals. There was no basis to that story whatsoever.

Until now, that is.

The *sidh* had slain an innocent cat to taunt me. The message was clear, and my response would be as well.

I took little comfort from the fact that I didn't know this cat—it didn't belong to a neighbor, it wasn't a local stray I'd glimpsed from time to time. I wrapped up the small corpse in the towel and placed it in a plastic bag; later on, I'd find a nice patch of yard and bury it. I'd deal with the pumpkin and the blood later. I had something more important to do now.

I found ó Cuinn's phone number and called him.

He answered on the first ring, and sounded wary when he heard my voice. "The little friends you called up are stalking me," I told him.

"Can we meet somewhere?"

I knew he was worried about the police still possibly tracking him, but right then I didn't give two fucks about him or the cops. "No. Just reverse this shit, Conor. I don't care what it takes, get rid of them. *Now.*"

There was a pause before he answered, "I can't."

"What do you mean—you can't, or you won't?"

"I mean, I *can't*. Look at the manuscript yourself—the banishing spell is only partial. That section of the manuscript is illegible."

"You're kidding." I paced my living room, wishing I could reach through the phone and strangle ó Cuinn. "You called these things up *before* making sure you could get rid of them?"

"I...I really didn't think they'd be a problem. What exactly are they...what—"

I cut him off. "They left a dead, mutilated cat on my balcony this morning, just for starters."

"Are you sure it wasn't the work of pranksters?"

I had to laugh at how our roles had suddenly reversed themselves: two nights ago I'd walked out on this man when he'd told me we were both Druids, and now he was arguing in favor of human mischief while I advocated for the supernatural. "I've *seen* them, Conor."

"Oh. Dear God. I never thought—"

I hung up on him. He was an irritating idiot. He was the fool in every bad horror movie who read the ancient spell out loud, who taunted the killer, who had sex while a madman lurked in the shadows. I'd solve this without him.

I brought up the manuscript on the computer, and found the banishing spell. He was right about that, at least: The beginning of it was there—it involved a rod made of ash and a spoken command—but the rest was lost.

I'd find another way, then. Could I still use logic against something that was essentially illogical? At this point, didn't it make the most sense to accept the irrational, to just acknowledge that the supernatural did exist? But could that doorway be only partly opened? If the *sidh* were real (they were), what else was behind that portal? I'd met one goddess already—how many more were there? Was there one single God, watching impassively?

Unless He was going to intervene now, I'd have to wrestle with that question later on. Right now I needed to come up with some way to fight the deadly tricksters Conor had called up. I needed to think about practical magic, not impractical theology.

I tried to remember everything I could about Samhain encounters with the *sidh*, and later Scottish stories of fairies on Halloween. A few tales talked about silver or iron; one odd legend mentioned wearing your clothes inside out. Mostly the old folklore suggested avoiding them.

I pulled down some of my reference books and flipped through them, but everything that I found described ways to protect yourself from the *sidh*, not get rid of them. Or even hurt them.

But I knew there was a way—Mongfind had recorded one, but I only had part of it. A rod of ash…a command…what else?

I glanced out my balcony at the bloody jack-o'-lantern, and the sight of it triggered a realization: The *sidh* had carved the pumpkin in a recreation of their own faces. Their heads, in fact, with the oversized, round shape and glowing features, looked like living jack-o'-lanterns.

Was it possible that the classic Halloween jack-o'-lantern—that most beloved of the holiday's symbols—had been based on the faces of the *sidh*? Or was there even more to it than simply remembering the *sidh* in folk art?

Before bringing Halloween to America[16], the Irish had carved turnips into jack-o'-lanterns. Common wisdom held that the vegetables—with a candle placed inside—had been used to startle passersby on Halloween night, but now I believed they might have served another purpose:

What if the jack-o'-lanterns had originally represented the ultimate defense against the *sidh* on Halloween night? Were they perhaps used in Mongfind's ritual? Were stories of Irish lads smashing their sculpted turnips on Halloween night indicating more than just sheer playfulness?

The baseball bat was made of ash…it would certainly be very effective in smashing a pumpkin…

Somehow I knew this was right. Maybe it was some part of the Morrigan, still residing in me; or my own intuition, telling me that the connections I'd just drawn were simply too strong.

Maybe it was Druid knowledge, buried deep within me. Magic encoded in DNA, like musical ability or language skills.

I would wait until evening, when the *sidh* were present again. I knew I'd be putting myself in peril, but I also thought it might be the only way to banish them—would they react to a command and a banishment ritual during the day, when they didn't seem to be present?

No, I had to risk it. At sundown, I'd use the bat—my rod of ash—to shatter the pumpkin they'd left me as a cruel taunt, and I'd command them to return to their own world.

And if I was wrong and it didn't work…then come Halloween, the *sidh* would make any human terrorists look like preschoolers.

OCTOBER 29, EVENING

I spent the rest of the daylight hours going over Mongfind's manuscript, paying attention to the charms, spells and rituals that I'd only glanced at before.

---

[16] Mainly in the mid-nineteenth century, after the Great Potato Famine devastated the food supply in Ireland.

Most of them were little more than recipes or instructions: How to prepare a tea that would cure nausea, how to make a poultice for a leg wound, how to keep berries picked in October from spoiling by November.

But then there were the more serious magicks as well. These included:

- Shapeshifting
- Communicating with the dead
- Enchanting a spear so it would never miss its target
- Creating a cup that would never empty of mead
- Traveling via an astral body
- Invisibility
- Invulnerability in battle
- Passing into the Otherworld, or the realm of the *sidh*

A few of the incantations were missing key words; despite Mongfind's precautions, parts of the manuscript had blurred with the passage of time. A few sections were spattered with something dark that covered the writing—probably Mongfind's own blood, coughed out as her lungs had failed her over that long final winter.

There were some instructions on creating protective wards, in case I failed in my attempt at performing the banishing ceremony.

I should perhaps make clear that none of these practices were presented as symbolic acts; this wasn't some new age book in which transforming into a wolf meant you'd been granted a license to be- have a little wildly in the sack. No, in Mongfind's book transform- ing into a wolf meant you grew hair, got down on four paws, and grew teeth as sharp as knife tips. This wasn't bogus spiritualism; this was the real deal.

As the sun dropped in the sky, I made sure the (now empty) jack-o'-lantern, its base stained red, was placed squarely in the cen- ter of my balcony. I moved everything—chairs, potted plants— well away, so I'd have room to swing the bat. I took down wind chimes and the cute orange lights Ricky had strung around the eaves. Then I stepped in, closed the glass door, and waited.

Five p.m....five-thirty...six, and the sun was gone. The sky overhead glowed like burnished steel, leaving the ficus and mag- nolia trees to stand in mute silhouette. I made sure my lights were all on, my front door locked, my bat in hand.

I hoped I wouldn't need to worry about my own cat; she'd been fed an hour earlier, and was now probably curled up on a corner of my bed, sleeping off dinner.

Or so I thought, until I heard her *screaming*.

The shriek was piercing, and sent me rushing into the bedroom; it sounded as if she was still on the bed, and now the cry was punctuated with hissing. I reached the bedroom—

The lights went off in the apartment.

The terrible sound of the cat's shriek redoubled.

By the light coming in through the bedroom blinds, I saw a flash of something moving around the edge of the bed.

Of course: they *could* come into a building. I'd been stupid to think that somehow doors and walls could keep out things that came from another dimension.

I felt my way to the apartment's breaker panel in the hall, threw back the hinged cover, and started flipping switches. The power returned, the lights came back on—

Something rushed past me, leaving the skin of my leg chilled through my jeans. I heard a high-pitched tiny cackle from the living room, echoing as if it came from the far end of a cave.

Clutching and lifting the bat, I stepped cautiously into the living room. Behind me, the cat quieted and I heard her paws hit the floor as she leapt from the bed and scurried beneath it in alarm.

Good girl.

That left me needing to get through the living room to the sliding door, and the balcony beyond. Meaning, of course, I just had to get past what waited for me somewhere in the living room.

One step...two...

I heard something skitter behind a bookcase to my right. I edged to the left, trying to move away from it—

And heard a snicker below the couch to my left. Followed by a tiny cry from behind the desk in front of me.

There was more than one of them. In fact, they were hidden throughout the entire apartment.

One brushed against my ankles. I jumped and swung the bat, which crushed a corner of the coffee table but nothing else.

I turned, seeking them, determined to take a swing at the next little fucker who touched me.

But—

Their voices came from all around me now. They whispered

together, but because there must have been dozens of them circling me the whispers became a single loud pulsing hiss.

I felt a sharp sting in my right calf, and knew I'd been bitten. I kicked backwards, but only managed to nearly throw myself off balance and go down.

How long before they'd all be on me, with their claws and jack-o'-lantern grins—

Of course: The jack-o'-lantern. They'd almost made me forget my original purpose.

I ran to the glass door and slid it open. Behind me, talons raked both ankles while they cackled in feral glee.

But they were too late—I'd reached my goal. I raised the bat and turned to face them. The lights were out again in the apartment, and through the glass I saw their eyes, glimmering, savoring what they thought was their victory.

The command was simple: I ordered them to return to their own world, and then I brought the bat down. The pumpkin caved in, spraying orange pulp in a wide circle.

The *sidh*'s chortles turned to shrieks. The glow of their eyes faded. And behind them—

I saw their world, for an instant that has proven to be unforgettable: A black, starless sky looked down on a lifeless landscape. Gray, leafless trees sprouted from depthless bogs, stones sculpted into shapes like headstones with leering faces rose from mounds of soggy earth—and then the stone faces turned to leer at me. The *sidh* scuttled among it all like maggots on a rotting corpse, and before the gap between us closed, I saw from the way they glared at me that mere prank-playing wouldn't be involved should we meet again.

It was over. The lights in the apartment flickered back on, the bat dropped from my fingers into the mess of the shattered pumpkin, and the pain ignited in my legs.

I moved into the light to examine the damage they'd inflicted on me. There were three striped claw marks on my left leg, and four pinprick puncture marks on my right. They were trickling blood, although none seemed deep enough to require stitches. But…

Were the *sidh* venomous? Did they carry disease, had they succeeded in killing me in a way that would just take longer…and be even more painful?

I swabbed the wounds out in the bathroom, but stopped before bandaging them, wondering if Mongfind's writings could offer any aid. Upon checking, I found a recipe for a poultice that would cure "the bites of dangerous creatures of all kinds." It required a few herbs I didn't have, but that I thought I could find at a nearby health food market.

I put Band-Aids on and stepped out the door. A moment of apprehension caused me to wait halfway down the stairs, ears straining...but I was reassured by the normal night sounds: Cars, dogs barking, a neighbor's inane television sitcom.

I'd successfully performed a banishment ritual.

As I headed to the market, I felt fresh confidence, and I knew I would survive the *sidh's* wounds.

I could create and control magic, even better than Conor ó Cuinn.

I was a Druid.

I was living inside one of my own Halloween stories.

I've written two Halloween-themed novellas[17]; both are about ordinary, middle-aged adults who find themselves surrounded by ancient, malevolent supernatural forces on Halloween. In both, the protagonists fight to hang onto something (a child, a business). In both, the fight climaxes in another world.

What was I fighting for? I wasn't fighting to protect my (dis) beliefs; they'd already been taken from me.

There was something bigger at stake. *Much* bigger.

But now I felt fever setting in, and I had to concentrate on making it to the market, buying what I needed, getting home and putting together Mongfind's poultices. By the time I crawled into bed, the heavy packs of herbs taped against the burning wounds, I was shaking and sweating. If Mongfind's cure didn't work, whatever else was at stake wouldn't matter, at least not to me.

OCTOBER 30, BEFORE DAWN

Fever dreams:

I soar into the night sky, but instead of more stars appearing the higher I go, they disappear, one by one, then whole galaxies, and I realize something huge has reared up between me and space. Something completely black and lightless, huge and freezing.

---

[17] *The Samhanach* (2010) and *Hell Manor* (2012)

Balsab. Lord of Death.

I look down, and the Earth is below me, but it's no longer my Earth—I'm in the past now, looking down on the ruins of the great Celtic palaces. It's Samhain, and there are no Druids left to sate Balsab's hunger, so he takes his sacrifice in other ways. He waves a vast limb, and the portals to the Otherworld open, releasing the *sidh*. They ravage through Europe, bringing the Black Death with them; when wise women attempt to banish them, they fester in the minds of neighbors, judges, priests and inquisitors, who torture and burn the women. The witches.

Centuries pass, and Balsab's voracious appetite continues unabated. He finally tires of letting the *sidh* do his dirty work, and he takes to whispering in the minds of great men, infesting their brilliance with visions of mass destruction. Those he seduces produce ever more powerful weapons—catapults, cannons, nerve gas, nuclear bombs.

Where are the other gods? Why do they allow this?

"Because we must," answers the Morrigan, and I feel her presence beside/inside me.

"Why? Why can't you stop him?"

"He is Death. Death, more than any of us, must continue. Without Death, there would be no balance."

"But…" I struggle to find the words. "The world wasn't always like this."

The Morrigan's sadness courses through me like tears in a creased cheek. "No. And it need not be this way now."

"How?"

But I know. Even as I ask it, I know.

"Even Death can be forgiving," she says, before disappearing.

I awoke, then. It was early in the morning, still dark outside, but my fever had broken and the pain from the cuts was gone. I got up to drink some water, then returned to bed, still weak. Before I drifted off again, I made my plan:

I'd call ó Cuinn in the new day.

OCTOBER 30, DAY

Conor was surprised to hear from me.

"We need to meet today," I told him.

155

We made arrangements to have lunch at a coffee shop near me. We'd meet there at two—it would be fairly empty by then. We'd need to talk where we wouldn't be heard, because we'd be discussing murder.

ó Cuinn was right on time. I knew the waitress—Ricky and I ate here frequently—and asked her for a back booth. The place was quiet, just us and a few other groups closer to the front. Conor ordered black coffee, I asked for an iced tea.

"You look tired," he said, once the waitress left with our drink orders.

"More than tired—I fought the *sidh* last night. They got in a few good jabs, but I won."

The way his jaw dropped would have been comical under other circumstances. "You—you banished them?"

I nodded. He forced his jaws closed. "How…?"

"I improvised. It worked. They clawed me in a few places, but Mongfind left a cure for that, and it worked, too."

"So…?" He left his question unasked, but I knew what it was.

"Yes," I told him, before adding, "so let's talk about the Samhain ritual."

The grin that crossed his face made him look uncomfortably like the *sidh*, and for a moment I regretted this meeting.

"Well, that's brilliant. You know it won't work without you."

"Do you have…everything?"

He was about to respond when the waitress brought our drinks. Conor stopped abruptly, averting his gaze, nervous and guilty, and I wondered how he'd possibly stayed out of jail if he'd acted this way with Bertocelli. Once she'd gone, he leaned close and whispered, "Yes, everything's been arranged."

"Everything," of course, included a human sacrificial victim. One I would be required to help kill.

I almost asked him how he'd manage that part—maybe he'd lure a junkie or transient with money; he was slightly built, and I couldn't picture him physically subduing anyone—but I really didn't want to hear details.

I know now, of course, that I was an idiot. I *should* have asked him. If I'd known what he had planned…

But I didn't, whether from cowardice or simply revulsion. I didn't ask him who we'd be killing.

"There is one thing only you can bring," he said.

"What?"

"Recall that the ritual indicates the use of a wand—it's crucial in creating the circle that will protect us. I can't supply you with that—you must find your wand on your own."

"Is that Mongfind or J.K. Rowling?"

He grimaced briefly, then added, "Children's fiction aside, magicians often speak of wands finding them, rather than vice versa. The wand is most likely found near a special tree, or forested area."

"Why do you know that? How long have you been studying this stuff?"

He actually reddened at that, revealing a secret passion. "I…it was just a purely academic study. Until…"

"Of course."

He reached into his jacket and removed a long bundle wrapped in a white handkerchief. "This is mine. I acquired it several years ago, from the area of Tara[18] in Ireland." He pulled the white linen away to reveal a surprisingly plain, sturdy foot-long twig. The only unusual feature was a sort of groove that wound around the narrower half. "This is ash. The spiraling around it is the result of vines growing in the trees; finding something like this is quite rare."

"Have you used it, Conor?"

He looked away, abashed. "Only once…"

"When you summoned the *sidh*."

"Yes."

"Well, at least we know it works." I enjoyed mustering that sarcasm; I still didn't like Conor ó Cuinn, despite the fact that we would soon be partners. "So…have you thought about where… *this*…will happen tomorrow?"

He nodded. "Mongfind specifies that it must occur in a sacred oak grove. There isn't much sacred here in Southern California, but at least there are plenty of oaks."

Touché. I had to admire the way he'd just repaid my sarcasm. "Thousand Oaks[19], perhaps?"

"Actually…yes. I'll e-mail you directions."

We sat silently for a moment; when we weren't discussing the supernatural, we really had nothing in common. After a while, Conor said, "You understand that there is an element of danger to us in this."

I wasn't sure if he meant the ritual or kidnapping someone to be

---

[18] According to Celtic mythology, Tara was the ancient seat of kings.
[19] Thousand Oaks is a suburb to the west of the San Fernando Valley, about forty minutes from Los Angeles.

offered as a blood sacrifice. "Do you mean...?"

"Summoning Balsab. That's why the first part of the ritual calls for the creation of a protected space."

Of course I'd read Mongfind's description of encountering Balsab, but I realized only now that I'd still thought of it as fiction. A real encounter with a physical representation of Death...do any of us know ourselves well enough to perfectly anticipate how we'll react when confronted with something genuinely terrifying?

"Then we'll just have to be sure we create that space well, won't we?"

That shut him up.

The rest of the meeting was devoted to lunch. We ate quickly and quietly. A last meal? Or the last meal of an old world?

As we finished, Conor asked, "Do you know where you'll look for your wand? Maybe you've got a special park you like, a garden...?"

"I do know, but it's...neither of those things."

He realized I had no interest in sharing a private plan with him, and he accepted that without further argument. "Well...tomorrow afternoon, then."

He left. I followed him out of the restaurant, climbed in my car, and headed toward the 5 freeway. Even though it was just past three p.m., traffic was heavy, and I headed south at barely ten miles an hour.

What will this all be like, if we succeed? Will there still be traffic jams, road rage, smog, hundred-degree fall temperatures thanks to global warming, gas at five dollars a gallon, increasing ranks of homeless, greedy corporate heads, ambitious politicians, junkies, cancer, and all the other things that grind us down every day even as we take them for granted?

It was hard to imagine a renaissance in the middle of the SoCal metro sprawl.

OCTOBER 30 / OCTOBER 31

I left the freeway at Cesar Chavez Avenue and headed east. My destination was only a mile away.

When Conor had mentioned a "special tree," my thoughts had immediately gone to a photo I'd taken sometime in the early 1980s.

Back then, I'd briefly considered going into professional photography for my day job, and I'd worked to assemble a portfolio. One day, completely by accident, I'd stumbled across an amazing cemetery just east of downtown L.A. At the time I didn't know that Evergreen Cemetery was the oldest extant cemetery in Los Angeles, but its melancholy beauty, age, and hodgepodge of monuments and headstones had yielded some of my best photos.

My real prize, however, was a picture of a gigantic spreading oak that overlooked a significant chunk of the graveyard. In the final black-and-white print, the tree looked impossibly huge, and somehow wise.

I knew exactly where to find my wand.

At this time of the afternoon, on a weekday, the cemetery was mostly deserted. I was also saddened to see that it had fallen into some disrepair in the years since I'd last visited, but I spotted the oak easily enough, and parked as near to it as I could.

Evergreen dated back to 1877 and supposedly held some 300,000 interments. There were no superstars resting here, no shining beacons of Hollywood history, but Evergreen was home to many of L.A.'s more interesting historical figures. A tall, white monument marked the plot of the Lankershim family; Isaac Lankershim had once had a town named after him, until that town was renamed North Hollywood in 1927.

I strode across the lawn, and was saddened to see patches of dying grass and headstones that had literally fallen in disrepair. A few graves were clean and well kept, testament to longstanding families that still honored their dead.

I passed the quaint, cobblestone cottage that would be opened for funerals, and elaborate granite memorials that were taller than I was. In some places, the headstones were so crowded together that it was hard to see ground beneath them. I passed a stone angel I'd shot thirty years ago, and saw it was now missing most of one upraised arm.

The oak had been significantly trimmed back, but it was still there, providing a surprisingly lush green canopy for those resting beneath. The sun was slanting in from the west now, but there were still areas beneath the oak hidden from light, perhaps permanently. The ground was spongy here, and I sidestepped around a large gray mushroom cropping up from the cracks in a plaque that marked an 1892 burial.

I didn't know what I was looking for, really, so I searched for a place to sit. There were no benches in this area, and I finally opted for a small patch of dry grass without a marker. Was it nonetheless a grave, one for which the marker had crumbled or been removed? I offered a silent apology to the resident beneath me, if that was the case.

I'd picked a spot in the sun, but the day's autumn warmth faded quickly, even as the sun's light did not. I shivered once, wondering why the temperature was dropping when sunset was still hours away.

The first tiny nudge—it wasn't truly a physical sensational, but I can only compare it to that—came then. I turned, expecting a visitor or a guard, but there was no one to be seen nearby, just a few distant joggers on the path that encircled the cemetery. A leaf, perhaps, that had fallen from the tree...

It happened again, this time feeling more like a small puff near my ear, like a sentient breeze trying to whisper its secrets. Then I remembered something from Mongfind's book about contacting the dead:

"The new Druid will experience the initial attempts by the dead to reach us as the smallest of touches or sounds, or perhaps a movement half-glimpsed when nothing's there...those with experience, though, will understand that the dead are anxious to communicate, and that we need only open ourselves to them."

*Open ourselves to them...*I wasn't sure what that meant, and I wasn't sure I wanted to find out. Weren't close encounters with death at the heart of most great horror fiction? I'd certainly written about it myself dozens of times, everything from a story about a haunted bookstore[20] to flesh-eating zombies[21]. Again, I had to ask myself how much deeper I wanted to explore the real version of my fiction.

Yet I felt no fear about this potential meeting. Perhaps it was the gentleness of the approaches; there was something timid about it. Maybe the ghosts were more afraid of *me*.

And I hadn't come here to parlay with spirits; I was in search of a tool. But I had no idea how to go about finding what I needed; perhaps one already dead would know how to help me deal with a Lord of Death.

It was—paradoxically—too bright to see them, so I closed my eyes.

Whether what took place was dream or reality or trance or

---

[20] "Blind-stamped," from *Shelf Life: Fantastic Stories Celebrating Bookstores*
[21] I confess I've written more zombie fiction than I care to list here.

some other state, I can't say.

It was:

Gray, as if all light and color had been leeched from the world. And in this gray realm were gray people—hundreds, *thousands*, of them. They were dim—not translucent, not see-through shades with faint blue glows, not cheap movie effects, but rather like someone you'd glimpse from a distance standing in an unlit corner of an attic. I could see just enough of them to make out a few details—an out-of-fashion cut of hair, a nineteenth-century uniform, a woman's dress from the 1940s. Some of them moved slightly, wavering as if they were underwater. It was hard to tell how much awareness they possessed, but a few seemed to be murmuring. I could hear their voices, but too faintly to make out any words.

I watched them for a while before I rose to move among them. They didn't react...nor did I. There was nothing frightening about them; if anything, they seemed...sad. Stuck. How many of us feel like this in our lives—drained, trapped, unaware? Death should be different, but perhaps it was just an extension of life.

As I walked through them, I saw a change happening, slowly: As the sky darkened, they brightened. Colors faded in on their clothing and skin; some took tentative steps.

And they began to notice me.

I wasn't sure when the first pair of faint eyes locked with mine, but I knew that they followed me as I walked by. More began to track me. A small, wizened woman in a shawl stretched out a veined arm as I passed.

I realized it was night now, and that was why *they* had changed, become slightly more substantial. I still felt no menace from them, but I did wonder how it was possible that night had settled in at the cemetery and I hadn't been asked to leave. Didn't they lock up graveyards at night? Wouldn't they have at least noticed my car, even if they'd somehow missed me?

I considered trying to find my car, seeing if I could leave, but I still didn't have what I'd come for. I'd walked out now from beneath the oak tree, and thought perhaps I should return to it.

Somehow I'd lost my bearings, and everything looked different in the gloom of night. Was that my tree ahead...or was it that silhouette against the sky behind me? The figures around me now were almost all Asian, some dressed in obsolete robes, and some in the loose-fitting clothing of nineteenth-century railroad workers. I

161

also saw westerners here and there, but they didn't look like those I'd passed in other areas of Evergreen—these people were noticeably poor, with gaunt frames and threadbare garments of another age.

Potter's Field.

I remembered something I'd read about Evergreen: That it had once housed L.A. county's Potter's Field, where those too impoverished or too forgotten to be buried elsewhere had been interred. But it wasn't just the transients and addicts and outlaws who rested there—back in the nineteenth century, L.A.'s ruling whites had refused to integrate Chinese into their graveyards, and had charged the immigrants to be buried with the indigents. Now their spirits stood side by side, taking no notice of each other, proving that intolerance died with living skin.

A colder breeze caused me to tremble, but it wasn't just the temperature—that wind was tinged with something else, the mental equivalent of the smell of rotting meat. Then I saw the spirits being pushed aside by some greater mass. Something was flowing up out of the ground of the Potter's Field, something that was far blacker than the night sky. Even the dead were distressed now—I saw mouths open in soundless horror, hands upraised to ward off whatever it was that came.

What the fuck was I seeing? I ran down possibilities—an unidentified murderer or rapist who'd been interred in the Potter's Field, an accumulation of the misery the poor had suffered while alive—before the answer came: Surely this could only be Balsab. The black cloud was exactly what Mongfind had described, and a sense of immense hunger radiated from the heart of the thing. I turned to run, with no clear direction except away from it. My legs moved as if in a dream—they pumped furiously, my heart hammered, but my forward momentum was slow. Perhaps running through ghosts dragged on me, or Balsab had the power to pull me towards him.

I knew he would be on me in seconds; reason was replaced by the flight impulse. There was something mixed with Balsab's palpable hunger: he emanated glee at my panic, and I knew that if he caught me, he would toy with me, torture me, linger over every shriek and shiver, and it wouldn't end with my physical death. My suffering would make the pathetic souls of the Potter's Field seem blessed by comparison.

This was why the Druids had protected themselves before calling on him.

I could feel him closer behind me. My feet caught on headstones and tiny hills in the grass; I stumbled, but didn't go down. If I fell, it would be my final act.

Then, among the shades before me, I saw a woman who possessed more color than the rest. She faced me, fearless; she wore a sort of frock dress, and held something in one hand. I instinctively ran towards her, and she didn't falter as she turned her attention to my pursuer. She raised her hand, which I saw held a narrow rod, and she pointed it at the Death that came for me.

There was no sound or explosion of light, but the sensation of nightmarish pursuit vanished immediately. I knew without question that she'd somehow driven Balsab back, with only a gesture. I envied that confidence and power, regardless of the fact that she'd been dead for at least a century.

I walked towards her, full of questions, but when I opened my mouth I couldn't seem to speak. *Who are you? How did you do that? Can you teach me? Are you a Druid?*

She smiled as I approached, and held out her hand—no, not her hand, but the length of wood in it.

The wand.

At first I thought she meant to cast some sort of enchantment on me—a protection, perhaps—but then I realized her true intent: She wanted me to take the wand. I held up my own hand, looked at her tentatively, and she nodded. I reached out, wrapped my fingers around the slender length of wood—

And woke up.

OCTOBER 31, MORNING

The sun was in my eyes, I was stiff and cold, and damp from morning dew.

I was still in the cemetery, where I'd apparently spent the night. That shouldn't have been possible…yet, as I sat up and looked around me at the headstones, the morning joggers, my great tree… it had happened.

The fingers of my right hand were tight. I flexed them—and something dropped from my grasp. I retrieved it.

It was the wand—a foot-long section of oak, twisted in a perfect spiral shape, with a neat nob at one end and a tapering point at the other. It was possible that it had fallen from the tree above me naturally—the wood felt a little rough, there was a slight center bend to it—but I recognized it without question:

It was the tool that my savior used during the night to drive Balsab back.

I didn't even ask myself if it had really happened or if I'd merely dreamed it. At this point, the answer didn't really matter.

I was relieved to find my car where I'd left it, and the gates to the cemetery were open. I drove out without seeing a caretaker or guard.

It was 7:33 as I left Evergreen, the morning of Halloween. The day was clear and already warm, with just a trace of L.A.'s perpetual smog blanket. I was surprised to find that I wasn't tired or aching from my night on the ground. In fact, I felt…well, I can only call it hyper-aware. I saw every detail as I drove towards the 5 freeway: Every yard of cracked asphalt, every scrap of trash, every used hypodermic needle or empty bottle, every man who staggered along the sidewalk too young to have dead eyes, every woman who carried a jar of Vaseline in a cheap purse and looked for her next trick, every kid whose heart hardened a little as he saw the bullies coming, and wanted to join them.

At first I was glad to leave the city streets behind and ascend to the freeway that ran above the urban hell, but the morning rush-hour traffic was in full force and presented its own grim scenes: A woman on the shoulder, staring with grim desperation at her broken-down car; a man in a Lexus with a perfect haircut shrieking into a Bluetooth so loudly that I could hear him across two lanes of idling cars; honking horns, blaring ranchera music fighting discordant rock, a helicopter beating the air overhead.

This world was mad.

Two-thousand years had led to this. It seemed ridiculous to think any of it could be reversed. The everyday difficulties of life, small and large, are too interconnected; severing one link can't destroy the chain. But if part of the chain can be weakened, then maybe we can begin the act of freeing ourselves. Isn't that why we vote, why we volunteer, why we donate?

What part of the chain would break if an ancient death god were appeased?

An hour later, I finally reached home. Roxie meowed unhappily at me, understandably upset over missing dinner last night, but even her irritated, shrill little cries lightened my mood. The world couldn't be so bad when different species could share their lives together, with joys and upsets, experiences and those rare times when simply nothing happened except each other.

I fed Roxie, then she settled in at my feet, purring and grooming herself, as I checked e-mail. There was the message from Conor, with directions; he'd provided a map of the location where we were to meet. It was forty minutes or so to the west, but I'd be joining the going-home traffic and so doubled the time. I'd need to leave here at around 3:30, then.

I had six hours to prepare.

And no idea what "preparation" should be.

OCTOBER 31

I spent part of the day apologizing. I'd missed two interviews, one last night and one this morning. I'd disappointed a New Jersey radio station and a Boston newspaper. And my publisher.

I called Ricky, but he only had a few minutes between takes. I lied, and told him everything was fine.

I studied the Samhain ritual in the journal. We'd begin with a prayer to the gods, we'd sanctify our space, we'd offer an animal in sacrifice, and then…I had no idea how Conor expected us to create the triple-death that the Celts had employed, the simultaneous strangling/stabbing/drowning, unless we were breaking into the backyard of someone who had both an oak grove and a swimming pool. Southern California isn't exactly known for its bogs and bodies of water. Here I was considering participating in a murder, and I was more concerned with the method than the act.

I left early. I couldn't stay in the apartment anymore, thinking about what was to come. I took the wand and the netbook that had Mongfind's manuscript. Conor said he'd have everything else.

An hour later, I'd driven into the hills, down a road marked for construction, but which was still surrounded by undeveloped land. I parked, and hiked a short trail to the spot Conor had indicated. I had to admit that he'd chosen perfectly: The area was hidden in a slight depression, was surrounded on all sides by gorgeous old oak trees, and would be a lovely area to kill someone in.

You have to stop thinking that way.

Sacrifice has been practiced by cultures throughout history and around the world. Among the Celts, it had been considered a great honor to be chosen; those who were accepted death willingly to ensure the prosperity of their clan.

This is the right thing to do.

But no matter how many times I repeated that to myself, it still felt like a lie.

I spent an hour there, trying to enjoy the sun, wondering if it would rise again tomorrow, watching a small brown lizard scuttle up the trunk of a tree, before ó Cuinn arrived. I heard an engine, and was surprised to see a rented four-wheel-drive SUV come bouncing up to the edge of the grove. Conor parked and got out.

"Ah, good—you're already here." He moved around to the rear of the SUV, opened it up, and revealed a cage holding a small goat. There was also a metal tub, a five-gallon bottle of water, and a duffel bag. Aside from the goat—a little gray-and-white kid who kept squalling piteously—he was alone, although I couldn't tell if there was someone else in the SUV.

"Aren't you…missing something?"

He nodded towards the front of the car. "I told our special guest to wait until I called for him. I thought that might be easier on you."

I started to walk toward the SUV to look in, but realized Conor was actually right about that. "Yes, it probably will be." The kid pressed its little face against the wire mesh of the cage and bleated at me. "A goat? Doesn't Mongfind mention sheep?"

Conor shrugged. "There aren't a lot of sheep in the L.A. area. The goat was hard enough to find. I don't think it much matters exactly what species the animal is."

"I hope you're right."

He set the tub in the middle of the grove, opened the five-gallon container, and poured the water into the tub. "Ahh," I said, watching him, "so that's how you plan to satisfy the drowning requirement."

"Yes. Again, when in L.A., like a good actor you learn to improvise. What about you—did you have any luck with the wand?"

I showed him my find, and his eyes narrowed as he examined it. "Where did you get it?"

"A cemetery, just east of downtown."

"You just found it there?"

"Well…not exactly…it was given to me in a dream, by a woman. I still had it when I woke up."

"A woman in a dream?"

I nodded. "Yes, but not Mongfind, or the Morrigan, if that's what you're thinking. From her dress, I'd guess this woman had lived about a hundred years ago, and I'm assuming she lived in L.A., since her grave is here."

Conor touched one finger lightly to the wand, held it there for a second, as if somehow gauging it, and then pulled his hand away. "She must have been a powerful wise woman. A witch, I guess you'd say."

I remembered how easily she'd repelled Balsab. "Yes, she was quite powerful."

"And now," he said, moving his eyes from the wand to my face, "so are you."

If he'd meant to flatter me with that, it didn't work. All he succeeded in doing was making me uncomfortable again; although I certainly had no objections to accruing power in some areas, magic I hadn't even believed in a week ago wasn't one of them. "Any power I have is…an accident."

"No. Not an accident. Call it what you like—destiny, fate, luck—but I believe that you were born for this night, just as I was. Most people go through life wondering if they have a real purpose; well, yours and mine is to set history back on its proper track. Tonight."

No, I wanted to say to him, *I'm a writer. That's my purpose. Not this.* But I wasn't interested in arguing with Conor ó Cuinn, so I kept quiet.

Overhead, the sky had started to dim, the blue taking on the deeper, almost metallic shade of approaching dusk in autumn. The sun was dipping below the hill that defined the west side of the grove, and Conor turned his attention to the duffel bag. "We need to move quickly. It's almost time to begin."

He handed me what at first looked like a white sheet. "Put that on." I shook it out, and realized it was a simple robe, fashioned from bed linen, probably by Conor himself. I pulled it over my head, and he handed me a large sash I used to belt it. He'd even picked up three cheap lanterns that he now lit and set on the ground.

He put his own robe on, handed me a printed out version of the ritual, picked up his own copy...

We began.

SAMHAIN

I won't give you the details here of the first part of what we did. It was hard not to giggle through some of it, although I thought of Balsab as we created the protective circle and any derisive laughter died in my throat. I'm not proud of my part in killing the goat. The poor little animal kicked and cried and shook, and even though its life ended quickly, it seemed like hours for me. Somehow assisting Conor with the sacrifice of the goat affected me far more than sharing a murder with the Morrigan had. I grew up with a hunter and tried to imagine this as no more than cleaning fish with dad, or watching him dress a deer; but I thought even my father would have a difficult time with a small, howling goat.

Conor, however, seemed to have no such compunctions. He performed his part of the ritual with clenched-jaw efficiency. I wondered if he'd done it before.

The goat's body, head submerged in the tub of water, had just ceased trembling when the air in the grove changed. The sky, still a faint shade of purple, abruptly darkened, the temperature dropped, my skin goose-pimpled.

Conor's steel melted. He looked up, eyes widening. "My God..." he breathed.

Yours, maybe. Not mine.

Balsab had arrived.

I went over the protection spell in my mind, hoping we'd done it right. The Lord of Death's unrelenting appetite would easily take us if we hadn't. We waited a few seconds, breathless—but the circle held. Balsab would be taking only what we offered.

"Let's finish this," I said to ó Cuinn.

His attention snapped back to me, and for a minute I saw

him sag. After the way he'd dispatched the goat, I expected the next sacrifice to be easy for him. He didn't move, but only gazed towards the SUV.

"Conor…?"

Without a word, then, he trudged off to the parked SUV, opened the middle door, and reached in.

When I saw our intended victim, I understood his hesitation. My own resolution, which I'd spent the day—days—trying to build up vanished instantly.

Because it was a five-year-old boy he'd brought out of the SUV. The little boy—Alec, I remembered—looked like Conor, but like the Conor I'd seen in the photograph on his desk, younger, fuller, happier. The boy still clutched some sort of little talking stuffed animal in one hand. He seemed small even for five.

Five.

"No," I said.

Conor clutched his son's hand in fingers still stained with goat's blood. At least his voice broke when he said, "We have to."

"No. This isn't what we talked about."

"It has to be an…extraordinary offering. We're trying to correct two thousand years of mistakes with one night."

I felt Balsab roil with anticipation above me. I felt the Morrigan's lingering presence within me, telling me Conor was right. This would work.

"Daddy?" said Alec, his accent thick even in two simple syllables. He looked up at his father with love and confusion.

I tore off the robe.

"What are you doing?" Conor released his son and started towards me.

"I'm leaving."

"You can't. I can't finish it alone. The ritual requires both of us."

I'd nearly reached the edge of the circle then. "I know. That's why I'm leaving."

"You won't be safe once you step out of that circle."

I knew that, too. And I'm ashamed to admit that I'm enough of a coward that I stopped. For a second. Long enough to say, "None of us are."

Then I stepped past the lines we'd drawn and walked out into the night.

I expected Balsab to engulf me. The last thing I'd feel would be agony, or intense cold, or the breath of eternal suffering.

Instead there was nothing. As soon as I was out from beneath the oaks, the sky returned to normal, I heard the distant sounds of freeways, saw the glow of the valley to the east...

And knew that I'd just damned the world.

HALLOWEEN

It's nearly midnight now on Halloween night. Two thousand years ago, the Samhain sacrifices would have been completed, and the feast celebrating summer's end begun. The Celts would have rested well knowing that they'd earned another year of prosperity and peace. The Lord of Death would visit them only for those whose long lives were at a natural end.

It won't be that way for us, though. Did I fail tonight? Could I really have granted the world a return to that kind of serenity?

At the beginning of this journal, I said this: "It's only been two weeks since the world started to fall apart." I realize now that sentence, while dramatic, is not entirely correct. The world fell apart long ago. And yet we continue to live in it, as messy and dangerous and ugly as it is, we somehow continue along, occasionally finding moments of joy, love, or just quiet reflection. We share love that joins two of us together, and we share stories that one of us has created from nothing. We bond with non-human species, and we feel horror when we cause them harm.

I don't accept that I've condemned the world, because any world that requires giving the lives of children (or adults, or animals) to gods is frankly not worth living in. Gods are too arbitrary for me. Even the Morrigan's righteousness came with a vicious price.

I know Conor might try again, that he might find another woman who possesses skills greater than mine and the constitution to commit bloody sacrifice. If he succeeds, and the world improves overnight next year, or the year after that, then I will think of a young boy whose soul is owned forever by a black abomination, and I won't regret my decision.

I won't erase Mongfind's manuscript or break the wand I was gifted with, but I have no interest in casting spells or pursuing any other magical goals.

The world is already magical enough.

TAM LANE

The old newspaper building was haunted.

At least that was what Janet had always heard about May O'Greene's extraordinary 1910 masterpiece. Tucked in a forgotten corner of downtown L.A., wedged in somewhere between the Garment District and the endless cheap appliance stores, it had stood for over a century, long after the *Daily Examiner* had folded and the structure's original purpose had vanished. Three stories tall and occupying most of a block, its once glittering turrets and graceful, swirling archways were grimed over with decades of accumulated urban grit and neglect.

Still, it stood out enough that, as a youngster driving past it with her father, Janet had asked him about it. "I'll buy it for you one of these days," he'd told her.

With her father, that was no joke. Edward Carterhaugh III probably owned more of Los Angeles than any other mogul; he bought and sold properties, redeveloped and repurposed and renovated and demolished and rebuilt. The Carterhaughs' own home was a classic Greene and Greene Craftsmen house; as a child growing up in it, Janet had gotten used to seeing strangers peering in through the fence, taking photos.

It was almost remarkable that eight years passed between the time eleven-year-old Janet had asked about May O'Greene's monument to journalism and her father's acquisition of the same. During that time, Janet had developed an obsession for architecture that had transformed into a career choice. Now in the second year of her major, she had favorites (Gehry, Paul Williams), but none she admired so much as May O'Greene.

When her father mentioned at dinner one hot August night that his offer on the old *Daily Examiner* building had been accepted, Janet's eyes had widened and Carterhaugh laughed. "I thought that might pique your interest."

"I've always wanted to get into that building."

Edward wiped his mouth with a napkin, took another sip of his dirty martini, and said (with a slight smirk), "They say it's haunted, you know."

Janet returned his smile. "All the better."

Their housekeeper, Maria, placed plates before them. She squinted at Janet. "You don't eat enough. Too thin." It was an old joke between them. Maria had been with the family for a dozen years—she lived in a bedroom just off the kitchen—and Janet loved her like an aunt.

"It'll be your fault when I weigh three-hundred pounds," Janet said. Maria smiled and returned to the kitchen.

Edward picked up a knife and fork, resuming the conversation as he cut into his rare steak. "There's a film crew shooting on the ground floor right now—it's been used mainly for movies over the last thirty years, I guess, but only the first floor. The two upper floors are pretty useless."

"I want to see it."

Edward nodded. "I'll have Amy call in a pass for you tomorrow." He paused, a forkful of Maria's good beef halfway to his mouth, then lowered it and added, "I'm thinking of converting it to office lofts. Might be a great first job for a young architect..."

"Are you serious?"

He nodded. "You're welcome. Just don't embarrass me."

Janet knew this was probably where she should have risen and hugged him; that was how the scene would have gone in a movie, or even a lot of real households. But there'd been tension between them since Mother had died four years ago. It had been a miserable death—a month-long coma following too many years of too many prescription drugs, until finally the coma had ended in seizures and a lonely passing in a hospital bed. Janet secretly blamed her father for her mother's dependence on self-medication, and she'd wondered if he didn't feel the same about her.

At least he's trying. Of course he probably just knows I'll be the cheapest architect he can get.

Whatever the circumstances—whatever unearned privilege, whatever paternal guilt—Janet was still happy, the next day, to walk into the grand *Daily Examiner* building. She'd spent the rest of last night reading up again on May O'Greene's history. The *Examiner* had been her last major work; it had taken her nearly ten years, as she'd overseen every detail, every tiny bit of tile and ornament and fixture. Many critics felt the *Examiner* lacked the sheer spectacle of some of May's earlier work, especially her Santa Monica amusement park, Sealight, which had been completed in 1898 and torn down in 1942, its wood and metal used in the creation of war machinery instead. Sealight had been called "a fairy palace"; the *Examiner* had been dismissed as "a wealthy Indian's brothel." It combined Art Nouveau and Orientalism in ways that hadn't always pleased architecture buffs; Janet, however, found it sensuous (as she thought O'Greene had likely intended). O'Greene's reputation should have been as great as Williams's, or certainly Julia Morgan's, but Janet doubted if most of the film crews that shot in its ground floor recognized the brilliance they stood within.

The guard at the building's entrance found her name on a list and admitted her. It was an uninteresting side entrance. Once inside, Janet found herself jostled by frantic assistant directors and grips hauling apple crates and coils of cable. She passed a row of glassed-in offices where she glimpsed cameras and actors (dressed in white lab coats). A few of the crewmembers eyed her curiously, but something about her—some indefinable aura of confidence, status—kept them from approaching her.

She moved past the crew, and the hallway she was in emptied out into the *Examiner*'s front lobby. She stopped and gazed around, stunned; here, she could finally commune with O'Greene's glorious designs. The spacious interior went up three stories to skylights; curving flights of stairs flanked either side. Rich, original tile, in burnished earth tones, graced the floor; dual Moroccan-style turrets framed the carved oak front doors, locked for decades against the Los Angeles streets. The handrails on the stairs were rich mahogany, rubbed to a deep, nearly decadent finish from a century of use.

Janet stood unmoving, breathing it in. The sunlight that penetrated through the skylights and turrets was filtered by heavy dust (the building had never been designed for air conditioning); behind her, the sounds of the film crew had sunk to a constant low thrum.

It was easy to believe this palace was haunted.

Janet remembered, then, why she was here. Her father wanted her to lay waste to this space, to turn its offices and storage areas into the large single-room apartments he liked to refer to as "artists' lofts."

For a second the idea sickened her. She hated the job. She hated her father. It was a sacrilege.

But then she reconsidered. She could, after all, keep the lobby; it was functional as well as beautiful. It would provide pleasure to those tenants ("artists," she reminded herself) with enough soul to appreciate its art.

She was sweating as she climbed the stairs to the second floor; it was August in Southern California, and she was in a building that kept only part of its ground floor acceptably cooled. Here, on the second floor, the temperature rose sharply. Janet picked her way through ancient offices, most empty, a few strewn with trash. In one back room she found the remains of a party—a bag full of empty bottles of cheap red wine and a used condom. It was hard to tell how long they'd been there. She began to feel better about rededicating the *Examiner* to a purposeful existence.

A twisting back staircase led her up to a third floor that had plainly seen even fewer visitors in recent years. From her online study of the *Examiner*, she knew that the third floor had once housed the executive offices; May O'Greene herself had even had a suite up here. Motes glittered in the air, turned opalescent by afternoon sunlight. Later, Janet would come back with a camera and tablet computer and begin planning; today was purely exploratory.

The heat on the third floor was stifling. Janet was wiping sweat from her brow when she poked her head into a room... and gasped:

She looked into a sitting room that could have stepped out of a silent film. Low tables, chairs, writing desk, vintage sofa, and cabinets all squatted, as clean as the items in a showroom. On the desk were a shaded lamp, a blotter, pens, an elaborate Art Deco paperweight. On one gorgeous teak end table was something that looked for all the world like an original Tiffany lamp. Even Janet, who'd grown up with wealth, wondered what the lamp alone was worth.

She stepped into the space, running her fingers lightly along the fixtures, astonished by the lack of apparent age. Surely they were all reproductions, but…why? Who would install all of this in an unused office on the third floor of a nearly-abandoned building? Some eccentric film exec, maybe? She nearly pulled out her cell phone and called her father's office to ask if they'd forgotten to tell her that part of the third floor was rented out, but somehow she knew the answer would be "no," followed by questions she didn't want to deal with.

Was it possible that this room was just miraculously forgotten and preserved, a happy accident of time and environmental circumstance?

Janet reached the desk and picked up one of the items she found there. It was an antique fountain pen with a silver scaled finish like a metallic lizard. Curious, she pulled the cap off and ran the nib across a sheet of cream-colored paper; it produced a clean, perfect dark line. Janet often made preliminary sketches in pen before rendering them in software; she somehow felt more connection to her work when she used ink instead of pixels. The idea of sketching out her designs for the *Examiner*'s new artists' lofts in a pen she'd taken from it appealed to her, and so she replaced the cap and was lowering the pen into her purse when a voice sounded behind her:

"That's not yours."

Janet jumped and turned, trying to find the source of the words. It was a young man, seated in what looked like a genuine Louis XVI settee. White light streamed in through Venetian blinds behind the man, rendering him into a striped silhouette.

Janet struggled to make him out as her heart pounded. How could she not have seen him there before? Startled, nervous, she held the pen up, jiggling it. "Oh, I'm so sorry—is this yours?"

"Yes." The man rose now and stepped forward, and when his face caught the light Janet nearly gasped.

He was the most beautiful man she'd ever seen. Light brown skin, glossy black hair that fell onto his forehead in charmingly unruly locks, golden eyes whose shape hinted at an Asian parent, dazzling white teeth that Janet didn't even think were capped. He was dressed in an Oxford shirt that defined his sculpted, hard surfaces, and simple khaki pants.

There was also something familiar about him, something that tugged at the back of her mind, tickling. She caught herself before she used the hackneyed, "Have we met before?" Instead, she said, "I…didn't expect to find anyone up here."

"Well, I don't get many visitors. But the ones that I do are…" he reached out to take the pen from her, and when his fingertips brushed over her skin, Janet shivered—they were impossibly cold, icy, "…always *special.*"

He stood there staring at her, a look that caused Janet's pulse to race.

Trying to cover her nervousness, she asked, "Just what *are* you doing here?"

"This place is mine."

Janet laughed, then said, "I'm sorry to disillusion you, but it's not. My father just bought it. It's in escrow already. We'll be turning it into artists' lofts."

"'We'?"

"Yes. I'm an architect." She felt like a fraud saying that, in this place, but it was too late to take it back.

"Like May O'Greene?"

"Yes," Janet said, before blurting out, "I mean, no! May O'Greene was a genius. I take it you're a fan…?"

The look that crossed his perfect face then was unexpected, full of fear and regret. "I can't really say I am."

"Oh…then, what…?"

Abruptly, he grinned again, apparently anxious to move past the mention of the architect. "My name's Tam—Tam Lane. And you are…?"

"Janet Carterhaugh," she said.

She placed her hand in his…and lost herself. His skin was chilled, but the sensation of it on hers ignited fire. He squeezed her hand, lightly, and it was enough to leave her weak-kneed and desperate. Janet was hardly virginal—her own aristocratic beauty had made many boys seek a place in her bed (when her father wasn't home), and she'd given it to a few of them—but she'd never experienced a need so all-devouring that it made her forget where, who, what she was.

"Tam," she breathed out.

"You know," he said, stepping closer to her (and that action alone flooded her with fresh arousal), "I did catch you trying to steal from me. I think I'm owed something."

"I already apologized."

He placed two fingers beneath her chin and tilted it up. "That's not what I had in mind."

He took his payment as a kiss. Janet returned it; even as she did so, feverishly, some small part of her whispered, *Something's wrong here…walk away. No—RUN.*

But she didn't listen to that part. All she heard were the soft, moist sounds of their lips and tongues, her own breath, his.

When, several moments later, he lowered her to the velvet couch as his fingers sought her buttons, she let him.

ooooo

After, as they lay together, unclothed, her bathed in sweat, his skin only slightly warmed, she turned to him and asked, "Why do I feel like I know you?"

He answered, "I confess: In a former life I was an actor. I starred in a television series called *Thorn in the Roses*—"

Janet cut him off. "Oh my God—I used to watch that show every week! It ran for—what, four years?"

"Five."

Pictures came together in Janet's mind, like two etched images lining up to form a moiré pattern. A beautiful boy, with dark skin and eyes the color of certain clouds at sunset. Every girl she'd known had had a crush on the star…Tommy Lane, she remembered.

Tam Lane.

"You were so young on that show…"

He nodded. "I was only sixteen when it ended."

"And what did you do then? I don't remember any movies, or…"

His expression darkened, and Janet instantly rued the question; she would, in fact, have rued anything that caused distress to crease that face. "I...well, I'll tell you some other time."

The last ray of light faded; the room plunged into shadow. For a second, Janet had the unsettling thought that all the other furniture had vanished, that the couch beneath her felt old and sprung...but then her eyes adjusted, she made out the shapes of the desk and tables and chairs, and velvet caressed her where Tam didn't. "I should be getting home," she said.

Tam said nothing.

Janet untangled herself from him, feeling suddenly modest as she sat up, gathering her discarded clothes. She dressed in silence and then turned to look down upon him. In the room's semi-darkness he looked unreal, like an out-of-focus photograph, or fog.

"Come with me," she said, even though she knew Daddy would throw a fit if she walked in with a man.

"I can't," he said.

"Oh." The thought struck her: She'd just had unprotected sex with a man she didn't know. She nearly turned and ran, so strong was her urge to be home, safe, away from...*whatever was so wrong here.*

She had nearly reached the doorway when he called after her, "Wait."

She turned, saw him rise and walk to the desk, where he picked something up. Even in the room's darkness, growing stronger with each passing minute, his beauty—freed from cloth-ing now—shone, paralyzing her.

"Here." He held something out to her, and, numb, she reached a hand up. He placed the object in her palm. "Your pen."

"Will I see you again?"

"I truthfully don't know."

The last of the day vanished. Janet stumbled out, feeling her way blindly along the walls, shivering as her fingers scraped away chips of paint; something sticky clung to her like a poisonous spider's web. The floorboards groaned beneath her; she felt their rot and wondered if they'd hold her. The silence was otherwise complete.

Janet forced herself to remain calm, to find her exit. She had a good memory for layout and located the staircase; she stumbled twice negotiating its creaking turns in the dark, but soon she was on the ground floor, filing out with the last of the film crew. Some of them cast side glances at her, and Janet wondered what they saw: A disheveled woman with a shell-shocked look, perhaps?

When she reached the sanctuary of her car, she cried.

After ten minutes she stopped. She wondered, with a turn so complete she couldn't begin to understand, why she'd been sobbing.

She started the car and drove home.

ooooo

On the way, she stopped at a pharmacy and bought two items: A bottle of juice, and a pill that would prevent pregnancy.

She swallowed the pill with the juice and disposed of the box in the drug store parking lot.

When she got home, she took a forty-minute shower, let Maria feed her, then fell into bed. Her sleep was black, dreamless.

ooooo

The next day she asked her father's secretary, Amy, to find out if anyone was renting part of the *Examiner*'s third floor. Amy checked. The answer, of course, was no.

She googled Tommy Lane. It turned out that his show, *Thorn in the Roses*, had been canceled because he'd disappeared, not the other way around. His parents claimed they knew where he was and that he was in good hands. Speculation was that he'd run afoul of drugs, been shipped off to a very quiet rehab somewhere. After a time, mentions of him stopped altogether.

Amy arranged a permanent pass into the building; after all, she was now lead architect. The next day she returned to the *Examiner*, her heart in her throat as she climbed the spiral staircase to the third floor. She was shaking by the time she reached Tam's corner; she half-expected to look in and see nothing at all, no furnishings, not even a trace.

The furnishings were still there. But Tam was not.

She called his name. She sat on the couch, quivering as she remembered the feel of his icy fingertips on her shoulders, her breasts, between her legs. She jumped to her feet, trying to ward off arousal, calling again, again. "Tam! Are you here? Tam?"

He didn't appear.

179

As night fell, she left.

Over the next month she visited the room as often as she could, working her trips in around classes. When a good-looking PoliSci major named Matt asked her out, she politely declined. The next day she sat on the velvet cushions in Tam's room and talked to thin air. She told him about Matt. She told him she'd turned down the invitation.

She told him she wanted him.

He didn't appear.

A month passed, and the memory of their lovemaking became more precious to her, not less. August spilled into September, and one morning Janet woke up sick. As she knelt over the toilet, one hand instinctively clutched at her belly. It was too soon, of course, to show anything there but she knew.

October arrived, and the sickness continued. Janet tried to be quiet, but she'd never been able to hide anything from Maria. "You sick a lot lately," the housekeeper said, looking away.

Janet had no answer.

Maria came out of the bathroom with a load of towels for the laundry. She stopped before Janet. "You know you're like family to me, Miss Janet..."

"Of course. You, too."

"So you'd tell Maria if anything was wrong? If you needed help?"

Janet's throat was dry, her tongue useless.

Maria kissed her gently on a cheek and left the room.

ooooo

A day later, Janet sat on the couch in Tam's room and cried. "Tam, goddamnit, I really need to see you. I...I think I'm..."

She couldn't say the words, not to empty air. And emptiness was all there was.

ooooo

A home pregnancy test confirmed what she already knew. It shouldn't have been possible, but it had happened.

She finally gave up going back to Tam's room. She grew distracted and missed classes. She wondered what Maria's offer for help meant. She was afraid of the answer.

The boy at school, Matt, asked her out again, this time to a Halloween party. Was it really October already? She politely declined. As she walked away from him, she laughed.

Halloween party? Sure…I could go as Stupid Pregnant Girl. I won't even need a costume.

One morning she awoke to a knock on her bedroom door. She was sprawled on her bed, looking at old pictures of a handsome young television star named Tommy Lane on her tablet. "Yes?"

The door opened and her father entered. Janet thumbed a tab on the screen to switch to another website, then set the computer aside. "Oh, hi, Daddy."

"Hi, sweetie. Listen, I've got some bad news: the *Examiner* failed inspection, and I mean as in epic fail."

Dread crashed down on Janet, nearly suffocating her. "So what does that mean?"

"I'm sorry, I know you've put a lot of work into this, and I really liked your ideas, but…the lofts aren't gonna happen. The building's just too far gone—it would cost more to bring it up to code than it's worth."

"So…?"

"It's going to have to come down."

"When?"

"Demolition starts tomorrow—"

"You can't!" Janet leapt from the bed, face flushed, fingers clawed.

"There's really no choice."

Of course there's a choice, she wanted to say. *Spend the money to bring it up to code. Honor the building.*

Love your daughter more than business.

Instead, Janet pleaded, "Can't you at least postpone it?"

"Why? What difference will that make? There's nothing left to get out of that building, Janet."

Janet strode past him, pausing only long enough to grab a jacket. "Yes, there is."

He reached out as she ran by. "Don't go down there—"

But she was gone.

The side door Janet always used was secured with a heavy chain that had been added since the last time she'd been here, three days ago. She wouldn't be getting in that way.

But she knew the *Examiner* now; it had become an old and dear friend. She knew its secrets, the hidden ways in and out. She knew about the rickety door next to a loading dock in the back that gave easily when she applied pressure.

The ground floor was dark, but she'd brought a mag lite. She turned it on, heading for a back stairwell.

She shivered.

It wasn't cold; October in L.A. never was. But something in the *Examiner* had changed. It was no longer the friend she'd come to know intimately. It felt charged with fear, electrified with dread.

It felt haunted.

Janet remembered what day it was and forced herself to smile. *Right…it's Halloween and I'm in a haunted house. All I'm missing is a jack-o'-lantern full of candy.* But the thought didn't cheer her; it didn't dispel the *Examiner*'s newly-acquired aura.

She was relieved when she reached the third floor and sunlight spilled in through a few windows, wan but enough to reassure her that there was a world outside where kids were putting on costumes, laughing, looking forward to their night of mock terrors.

Tam's room looked the same. She knew crews had toured every room in the *Examiner*, and she wondered what they'd seen here. A Tiffany lamp? Antique fountain pens? She guessed not.

"Tam…goddamnit, Tam, you need to hear me! The building's coming down tomorrow!"

Nothing.

She paced the carpeted floor of his room, desperate. She'd called him once before, hadn't she? She tried to recall exactly what she'd done on that sweltering August afternoon. Of course she'd tried this before, dozens of times, but she had to try again. She'd come in…she'd gaped…she'd admired the lamp…she'd picked up a pen…

The pen.

It had to be the pen. But she'd tried this before, on so many other days. She'd picked up one of the other pens (there were still half-a-dozen on the desk), even waved it around…but nothing. No Tam.

There had to be something else—

Wait—I tried to steal it.

Janet grabbed one of the pens and shoved it into a pocket of her jacket.

"I've been waiting for you to figure that out."

She turned as Tam rushed forward to embrace her. "God, Tam, I've got so much to tell you…" she began, her voice husky, but she broke off as his mouth found hers. They were ravenous for each other, and the need to speak gave way to other, more urgent desires. She fell back over the desk, he moved between her legs, and two months of separation vanished.

It was over quickly, and then Janet's rush of words came out. "Tam, you have to leave here, tonight, my father's tearing the *Examiner* down tomorrow and I can't stop him—"

He put two fingers to her lips, gently. "Just slow down…"

She looked into his eyes, and she saw compassion, a hint of mischief, love…and a trapped animal. She lifted herself from the rough wood of the desk, pulled clothing back into place. "I'm sorry, it's just that I have so many questions, and with the baby and all—"

"Baby?"

The ability to make coherent words left her. She looked at him, uncertainly. Would he mock her? Question if it was his? Dismiss her?

Instead, he pulled her to him. "Janet…my Janet…"

She let him hold her for a few seconds before pulling away. "Tam…what exactly *are* you? Why are you here?"

Tam sighed, a slight expression but enough that she felt his breath on her skin. "I'm something both more and less than human. Remember that show, *Thorn in the Roses*? We shot the last episode here. I was a stupid kid, sixteen. I got bored once while I waited for the cameras to set up, and I wandered off to the third floor. This was where I met *her*."

"Who?"

"Who else? May O'Greene."

Janet's mind raced back to the biography she'd read months ago. "But…May O'Greene died in something like 1912, not long after she finished the *Examiner*."

Tam shook his lovely head. "No. She can't die, because she's not human."

"What…what is she?"

"She's had many names. Titania...Oona...Mab...Maeve... May...Queen of the Fairies."

Janet couldn't suppress a sharp laugh. "Fairies? Now I'm supposed to believe in fairies?"

Tam took her hands, kissed her fingers (sending another ripple through her), said, "Nowadays people would call us ghosts. We're the ones who live on the outside...or, maybe more accurately, tucked into the edges of your reality. We never die, but we don't really live, either."

"But you..."

"Ahh, yes...the boy who wandered away from the film crew. Well, it was a Halloween—like today—and May came through the veil between the worlds and took me back with her. She laid magicks on me first and then on my parents, so they lied about knowing where I was. And she kept me prisoner, or rather—*collected*, a pretty trinket she can look at when she's bored."

"But if the hotel is torn down..."

Tam's look contained almost inexpressible weariness. "I'll go with it."

"How do we get you out of here, then?"

"There's one way, but..."

He turned away from her, and Janet walked to his front, forcing him to look at her. "I don't care. What do we do?"

"Do you know about Halloween, I mean, its real meaning beyond silly costumes and pumpkins? It's the night when fall becomes winter, when sun's life turns to night's death, when the veil between worlds is thinnest. You sense it, don't you?"

Janet thought about the walk from the first floor, how she could almost feel a vibration in the air itself. "Yes."

"At midnight, that veil will be the thinnest and you might be able to pull me through, but May will try to stop you."

"Stop me? How?"

"By tricking you. She'll tell you you can have me...if you can hold me. Then she'll try to frighten you into letting go. She'll change me three times, and each transformation will be worse than the last."

Janet's hands moved to his face, his cold skin. "I don't care. If I get you out..."

He encircled her wrists with his hands. "You can. But don't make the mistake of underestimating her, Janet. It will be the hardest thing you've ever done. Just remember: *don't let go.* When I return to my true form, wrap me in your jacket and it'll be over."

She nodded, too overwhelmed to speak. He smiled warmly at her. "You can do this."

She wished she shared his confidence.

ooooo

They spent the rest of that day talking, holding each other. Tam asked her questions about what had happened in the ten years that he'd been May's prisoner. Janet talked about her life, her plans, how she both loved and hated her father.

As the sun set, the Tiffany lamp glowed softly, casting the room in the soft shades of its colored glass squares. The light would have been pleasant under any other circumstance, but as the time drew closer to midnight, the oppressive atmosphere intensified. Janet felt it like a low frequency hum in her midsection, setting her on edge, making her want to flee.

But she didn't. She stayed with Tam as he spoke to her, soothing her, telling her that May had treated him well (for a prisoner), and that he believed she loved him.

"Who wouldn't?" Janet asked.

Janet glanced at her phone, and saw the time was just after 8 p.m. "Four hours to go," she said, setting the phone up where she could see it.

She glanced out the window—and her heart skipped a beat as she saw eyes looking in at her. Yellow eyes that didn't blink, that weren't shaped like any animal she could name.

"Tam!"

He followed her wide gaze before pulling her close. "It's starting. The veil is lifting."

"But it's too early, it's only—" She looked at the phone.

It read 11:58.

"That's not possible. It was just eight o'clock—"

The building began to rumble, as if a small earthquake were happening. The Tiffany lamp blinked out, so that the only light in the room came from the glowing eyes of whatever watched them from outside. Janet clutched at Tam, her breath quickening; the temperature plummeted, and steam puffed from her with each exhalation.

The other side of the room began to glow, softly, a bluish light that might once have been seen above a dank graveyard, or in the heart of a darting will-o'-the-wisp.

"Tam...?"

"It's her."

Something moved in front of the glow—a feminine shape. Tall, dressed in some sort of full-length dress or gown, hair flowing... "Well, now, Tam, what's this?" asked a husky feminine voice, with a hint of old world accent.

The glow moved to reveal her face, and Janet gaped—the photo of May O'Greene she'd found hadn't begun to capture her extraordinary face. Her features were too sharp—almost feral—to be truly beautiful, but her eyes glinted with both youthful passion and the madness of great age.

Janet saw that even Tam was unnerved by May. "This is Janet, and we're leaving."

May laughed, a sound that was every Halloween witch's shriek mixed together. "Oh, dear Tam, are we actually going to do this?"

Tam ignored her and turned to Janet. "Are you ready?"

She nodded and put her arms around him. He whispered into her ear, "Remember—*don't let go.*"

Whatever Janet expected—a snake, a giant spider, a flame that might scald her—she didn't anticipate Tam trying to pull away from her.

Except it wasn't Tam's voice that said, "What the...Janet? Where am I?"

She pulled back as far as she could without releasing him, and saw the college boy who'd asked her out. "Matt...?"

Even in the dim light, she made out the terror on his face. Her first instinct was to release him, tell him to run, this wasn't his fight... "*No.*" She held him tighter.

May said, "That's one..."

Janet closed her eyes. Maybe if she kept them shut, if she didn't look at whatever came next...

"Janet, look at me," said her father.

Her eyes snapped open involuntarily, and Janet gasped and shrank back at what she saw: It was her father, but his features had altered, become savage, almost demonic. He leered at her and pulled her to him; she felt the bulge in his crotch and cried out wordlessly. "There's been nobody but you since your mother died," he said, and he ran his tongue down her cheek.

Janet willed her knees to hold her up, her arms to keep their circle around him. *It's a phantom...it's not my father...*

"You've disappointed me in so many ways," he said, and she hated the tear that she felt trace down her cheek, "but you could still make it right, if you're good to me..."

He ground against her. She swallowed back a scream, turned her head, but finally forced out, "I won't let go!"

"Oh, really, child?" May asked. "How about now?"

Her father's face melted away, the figure in her arms grew smaller, more compact, until Janet saw that she held—

Herself.

She stared in confusion. It was like looking into a mirror, except she felt the body solidly in her arms—*her* body. How was this supposed to scare her? It was strange, yes, but hardly fearful enough to make her relinquish her hold—

The face began to shift. To *age*.

Twenty...twenty-one, an adult now, and doubt etched itself in her features...twenty-three, twenty-six, and she saw anxiety, premature lines...twenty-eight, thirty, thirty-three, and failure was deeply graven, the eyes half-lidded and sunken, the mouth turning down forever...

Janet sobbed as she realized this could be her life with Tam. Joyless and careworn, burdened with a child at too early an age—

Thirty-eight, forty, forty-five...

She looked like her mother. Her unfocused eyes and sallow cheeks were testament to prescription drug abuse, and she knew she'd be dead soon, dead like her mother, worn away by life...

But she could have life back if she let go. The next thirty years didn't have to go like this.

Let go...

"No!" It was a shout of desperation, but it worked. It roused her to realization: *A trick.*

She tightened her grip.

And she felt bare, warm skin beneath. She held Tam again. He looked drained, barely conscious. Janet reached one arm to the desk, found the jacket she'd placed there, and draped it around him. He fell against her. She lowered him to the floor, kneeling with him, keeping the jacket in place.

May O'Greene didn't shriek, or storm. Instead she sobbed.

"You've won him, girl," she managed, between cries. "Be good to him."

She blinked out. The world changed. The eyes at the windows were gone, the lovely furnishings vanished, the smothering sense of wrongness replaced by the ordinary air of a world that held a future for her again.

"Is it over?" Tam muttered, trying to re-gather energy he hadn't possessed in ten years.

"It's over," Janet said as she bent to kiss his head.

Or, she thought, as she felt a lifetime's worth of happiness wash over her, *it's just beginning.*

THE HALLOWEEN COLLECTOR

"It's not vintage," said the Halloween Collector as he peered closely at the papier-mâché jack-o'-lantern. "It's a reproduction."

The man was right—Danny had made the piece himself—but he had no intention of backing down easily, especially not from this clown. "What makes you say that?"

The slender man with the strange neck tattoo—a vine with partly-ripe pumpkins attached—glared at Danny. "I know." He held up a large shopping bag. "Fortunately, there are plenty of other dealers here who have good authentic material, so I'll just continue dealing with them."

The Halloween Collector started to saunter away, and Danny caught the eye of his wife, Ellie, seated behind the table. She arched her eyebrows and nodded at the Halloween Collector. Danny leaned over to speak to her softly. "You're sure that's him?"

"It's him. After he left the last show, I was missing the three German noisemakers—and they *weren't* reproductions."

"Okay," Danny said, as he edged out from behind the booth, already fingering his car keys.

Ellie saw his anxiety and said, "Just remind yourself that those three missing pieces were worth close to a thousand dollars. Plus

189

who knows how much this creep's stolen from everybody else."

"Right. I'll be back."

As Danny walked away from his booth, he tried to push down the knot in his stomach. They'd spoken to half-a-dozen dealers who'd all agreed that the man he was following was a thief; his *modus operandi* was to buy something small, pay cash, put the purchased item in his own bag along with one *not* purchased, and stroll off quickly. No one had actually seen him do it, so they didn't have enough to call the cops; and no one knew his name, so they could only exchange descriptions and warnings. They called him simply "the Halloween Collector."

Enough was enough, Danny had decided. If no one else would do anything about this douchebag, he would.

Staying well behind his quarry, Danny followed the Halloween Collector past tables selling old candles, ceramics, figures, and postcards. He nodded to the dealers he knew; two pointed at the Halloween Collector and gave Danny a thumbs-up when he indicated he was trailing the man. He'd be a hero if he pulled this off.

The Halloween Collector left the small civic auditorium and threaded his way through cars parked in the lot. Danny put on sunglasses as he headed for his own car. He reached it, unlocked the door, dove in, started it up, and backed up so fast his tires squealed. He saw the Halloween Collector in his car—an old Mercedes-Benz—turning left out of the lot. Danny gunned his engine and sped through a yellow light to follow.

They drove for miles, heading into the hills, past fewer and fewer houses. At one point Danny lost sight of the Benz on a winding road, but when he rounded the curve he saw the car pulling into a driveway. Danny kept driving past. When he was out of sight, he parked, picked up the heavy crowbar he kept for emergencies, and got out.

The sun was setting as he approached the drive, and he was thankful for the cover the evening shadows provided. Crouching down behind a surrounding hedge, he saw the Halloween Collector enter the house.

When the front door closed, Danny pushed through the hedge, silently cursing the scraping twigs, and jogged across the front yard to a living room window. He knew he could just write down the address and leave, but he wanted some sort of confirmation. He knelt beneath the window and slowly raised himself up until he could look in.

The interior of the house was brightly lit. Danny saw a wall lined with display cabinets…cabinets full of vintage Halloween collectibles. There were hundreds of them—composition-material jack-o'-lanterns, die-cut snarling black cats, table decorations of paper witches cackling over cardboard cauldrons. It was the most astonishing collection Danny had ever seen.

And there, on a shelf to the right, were the three German wooden noisemakers topped with grinning pumpkins that had been stolen from him last year.

Danny dug into a pocket, found his phone, raised it, and snapped a photo of the shelf.

The flash went off.

Cursing his mistake, Danny turned to run, but he'd gone no more than three yards when something tripped him. *What—? Wasn't that ground flat?*

The front door opened and the Halloween Collector stood framed there. "I wondered when you'd arrive. Come in."

Danny reached for the crowbar, but the sun had set and the yard was thrust into darkness too complete to be mere twilight. Forgetting the crowbar, Danny gained his feet and confronted the other man. "You've been stealing from us!"

"Yes, I have. I'll show you why."

Invisible hands clamped around Danny's wrists. He cried out in alarm, especially when he was pulled toward the house. "Let go—!"

The Halloween Collector stepped back as Danny was brought in. He closed the door and walked up to stand before Danny. Danny stared at the tattoo on his neck—was it moving, sliding slowly across his skin? And hadn't the inked pumpkins *grown*?

"Now," said the Halloween Collector, "I'll show you why I need to possess these things and the rest of you don't. Because, you see, the real Halloween, the *authentic* Halloween, isn't safe. If you could tell vintage from modern, you'd know that."

Danny struggled against the invisible bonds holding him. "I don't know how you're doing this or what you're talking about, but—"

The man cut him off. "Trick or treat?"

"What?"

The Halloween Collector stepped closer, his voice a whisper. "*Choose.*"

Something pricked Danny's arms, and he yelped in pain, then cried out, "All right, all right: Treat!"

The Halloween Collector moved back.

Behind him, all the vintage collectibles opened their mouths in hungry anticipation.

THE DEVIL'S BIRTHDAY

INTERLUDE WITH THE DEVIL #1
Scotland, Halloween Night, 1785

The girl left the party just before midnight. No one had much noticed her during the earlier festivities, as they'd burned nuts at the hearth and tried to bite apples hung from strings; she had a scarf pulled up around her head and the lower part of her face, leaving only her oddly gold-colored eyes visible. They paid her no mind when she slipped out the door, away from the warm candlelight of the farmhouse, and into the cold October night.

It was Halloween, and parties were easy to find in the Highlands. Young people all over the country were drinking and dancing and telling fortunes. Those who were yet unmarried had dozens of methods that could reveal the names of their future true loves; grandmothers, meanwhile, sat in rockers in the corner and entertained the smallest children with ghost stories.

Most of those attending old MacAvoy's All Hallows' Eve gathering had just spent the season laboring on his farm; many would soon be traveling on, looking for other work with harvest done. The girl in the scarf might have come from her own harvest, looking for work as domestic help; or she might have come with one of the others, who'd drunk enough ale to forget their companion. Being forgotten, however, was not why she left the party.

On Halloween night, there was nothing unusual about unmarried men and women stealing out of the farmhouse. Some went to the lime kiln with a ball of blue yarn, hoping their future spouse would yank the other end once they tossed it in; some went to the kale patch, waiting to see what the root of the plant they pulled would reveal about the character of their intended.

The girl, however, went to the barn. She meant to try a divination that left weaker souls crossing themselves and muttering.

Pulling her scarf tighter around her head and over her face (for the night was already cold, and it grew colder with each passing quarter-hour), she opened the door of the barn, hefting the lantern she carried to examine the interior. It was a small structure—really more of a storage shed—and would serve her purposes ideally.

She crossed to the far door and unlatched it, then threw it back. With both doors now open, she set the lantern down on a barrel and walked to a wall where various farming implements hung from nails. She chose a two-foot wide, round, short wooden tray—the wecht, used in the harvest to separate the grains of oat from the chaff.

Returning to the center of the barn, the girl took a deep breath, tucked her scarf firmly into place, raised the empty wecht in one hand, and called out, "I winnow this corn three times in the name of the Devil, that I might know the name of my husband-to-be." She took the wecht in both hands and mimed throwing grain into the air with it. Then she waited.

It didn't take long.

A wind sprang up, rushing through the barn, lifting her heavy skirts and shawl. She set the wecht down and turned to face the door she'd come in through. The wind gained in strength until she was forced to squint against it.

A figure appeared in the doorway, apparently impervious to the gusts. It walked forward, silhouetted by the light from the farmhouse, and the shape was *wrong*. It was too tall for a man, something bulged from the head, and the knees seemingly bent backward.

The girl backed away, toward the lantern. The figure entered the barn, and suddenly the door slammed shut behind it, stopping the wind.

The Devil stepped into the circle of light cast by the girl's lantern. She gasped as she saw his horns—thick, long and curving, like a ram's—his pale skin and glowing eyes, his bare chest and heavily furred legs, with an animal's joints and tall, black hooves. Something hissed behind him, and the tail that swung into view was topped with an open-mouthed, fanged serpent's head.

"Well, lass," he said, grinning, revealing pointed yellow teeth, "so you've called me on Hallowe'en in order to know the name of your husband, eh?"

The girl stared in mute terror, one hand holding her scarf in place.

The Devil walked closer to her, running his eyes over her body. "Are you sure you're wanting to know this? You'd not prefer to find out…the *natural* way?"

The girl shook her head, trying to remain resolute.

The Devil tilted his head back and laughed, a sound that held the crackle of flames and grating brimstone. "Very well, then, girl. The name of your future husband is…THE DEVIL!"

The girl gasped and ran for the barn's back door, but it slammed shut before she reached it. She tried to open it, but it wouldn't budge; she rattled it, putting all of her weight against it, but it remained fixed.

She felt heat on her shoulders, and whirled to see the Devil standing right behind her, leering at her. "You're a fool—you forgot the most important part of this spell: You have to remove the doors from their hinges. Otherwise, I can still close them…and you have no way out."

He began to advance on her. She backed away, her eyes wide. He reached out, and she ducked as one claw scraped the air where her cheek had just been. "You're mine now, lass. Mine until sunrise, although I doubt you'll last that long…"

The girl staggered as her back hit the wall of the barn. Her hand groped frantically around behind her, seeking escape.

The Devil pressed closer, and his musky scent nearly gagged her; the snake-head peered around his side, eyeing her hungrily. "Now, let's see what my All Hallows' bride looks like under all those clothes—"

He broke off as three raps sounded on one of the barn doors. He frowned and listened, seeking the source of the sound. "What...?"

The girl spoke for the first time. "Ah, good—that'll be Father Hume."

The Devil squinted at her. "Father...? What are you playing at, girl?"

The girl reached up and tore her scarf away, revealing a lustrous auburn mane and caramel-hued skin. "Hello, Auld Nick—it's been a while."

The Devil cried out in anger and backed away, his eyes blazing. "Sathariel!"

She cast aside the concealing shawl, revealing both her broad, muscled shoulders and the long sheathed dagger in the belt around her waist. She plucked the dagger free and the blade gleamed in the lantern's light. "Good—I was beginning to think you'd forgotten me. After all, that scarf wasn't really much of a disguise, but apparently you're too arrogant or stupid to see past it."

He tried to remain indignant, but his eyes kept returning to the dagger. "Actually, I hoped you'd given up this nonsense. Our paths haven't crossed in fifty years..."

"I try to find you every Halloween, you old demon, but you've eluded me. A bystander might think you were afraid."

"I'm not afraid, Angel, but I'm also not interested. There are others calling my name who really are deliciously foolish humans, so I'll just bid you farewell and I hope you enjoy all the saints on the morrow."

Satan gestured at the nearest door, which opened. He ran for it, moving so fast he was a blur – but he pulled up short at the threshold. He frowned, tried to walk forward, but something barred his way. "What is this?"

"It's what my friend Father Hume was busy with outside while you pranced and gloated. As soon as he knew you'd arrived, he made a circle all the way around the barn with holy water."

Outside, a man in a priest's cassock stepped into view. He smiled and saluted the Devil with a nearly-empty bottle of holy water. Satan spun to see Sathariel behind him, toying idly with the dagger. "I'm afraid it's now *you* who are trapped in here... with me."

The Devil uttered one harsh bark of dismay before turning on Sathariel. "Now, this is just cruel! I'm allowed this one night a year to come to earth—that was the deal I set up with your former Superior, so who are you to get in the way?"

"Yes, you get to come to earth…but that doesn't mean I can't try to stop you from committing mischief, especially the kind that scares young girls half to death."

"Oh, come, now—you know *half* to death is all I can do. I can't even touch them while they're alive. Angels, on the other hand…"

Sathariel groaned, found her abandoned scarf, and picked it up, holding it out. "I've a mind to gag you so I don't have to listen to this all night."

The Devil flicked a wrist in the direction of one of the barn's walls, and a long scythe mounted there flew into his waiting hands. "And I've a mind to cut off your hands if you try it."

Grinning, Sathariel said, "Then try it I will." She leapt forward.

Satan swung the scythe; it should have cut Sathariel in half, but she'd already twisted to the side, and the long blade whistled through empty air. He tried again, and this time she ducked under the arc, coming up with her dagger. He blocked the blow by bringing the scythe handle down, but Sathariel countered with a kick aimed at one knee. The Devil sprang back, and the kick connected only with air. He suddenly spun, his back to her, and just as Sathariel was about to rush forward the snake's head shot up, its jaw clamping down on the cloth of her blouse. She pulled back and stopped, considering her options. The Devil turned to face her.

"We can go on like this all night, you know," the Devil said.

"Sounds like a fine way to spend an All Hallows' Eve." Sathariel crouched. The Devil ran at her, swinging the scythe.

She stepped aside, and as he ran past she grabbed a pitchfork that was propped against the wall; in one fluid motion, she whirled, raised the tool, and hurled it at her opponent. It struck him in the back and drove him against the far wall, pinning him there. Sathariel ran forward before he could squirm free; she put her weight against the pitchfork and drove it further through the Devil and the barn's wooden wall. He shrieked and writhed, but couldn't escape. The snake went silent and buried its head between his woolly thighs. Sathariel reached back for the scarf, which she wrapped around his face three times, silencing him.

"There," she said at last, "I can endure you until sunrise now, and then Hell is welcome to have you back."

She spotted a length of hemp rope, and wound that around his legs and hands for good measure, then she found a comfy hay bale and sat back to wait. From outside, Father Hume called out, "Are you all right in there, miss?"

"Aye, Father, and I thank you for your services, but I've got it under control now."

The priest answered, "Then I'll be on my way now. Might I see you at the mass on the morrow?"

"I doubt it, Father."

She thought she heard him offer a small sound of regret, and then the night was silent again.

Sathariel reached into a pouch at her belt, produced tobacco and a small pipe, filled the bowl and lit it with a straw from the lantern's flame, and settled back to while away the night. After a few puffs, she raised her eyes up and asked, "One sign from You, you know…that's all I ask. Just one nod to let me know You approve, that I'm on the right path…"

There was no response. After a few seconds, the Devil began to laugh through his gag, low and guttural.

"Shut up or I'll cut your throat," Sathariel murmured.

Chapter 1
Los Angeles, October 29, 2014

The young man with the spiky blonde hair glanced up and down Temple Street again. Satisfied, he whipped a can of orange spray paint out of his satchel and began to apply it in even strokes over the intricate stencil he'd already taped up to the side of the boards around the construction site. When he was done with the orange, he snapped the cap back on and exchanged it for black. The stencil showed a blocky graphic portrait of a popular politician who'd just been indicted on corruption charges, and at the bottom it read, in jagged letters, "TRICK OR TRICK." The artist finished, put the can away, stepped back to admire his handiwork, and was pleased. He heard a distant siren, reminding him that his mission here was still at risk. He ripped down the large stencil, and replaced it with a smaller one that had a stylized logo reading

"K-Os."

He was midway through painting the logo in red when a voice startled him. "You not touch my place!"

He spun and saw an Asian man behind him wielding a double-barreled shotgun. The painter dropped the can, which hit the concrete sidewalk with a clatter as he raised his hands. "Hey... hey now..."

The Asian man nodded back at a storefront behind him, the one to the immediate right of the construction site. It was a small, cheap appliance store, with half the lettering in a language the boy couldn't read. "You not paint my store!"

The young man tried to back away, shaking. "No, I wasn't—look, I was doing the construction site! Believe me, dude, I wouldn't touch your store—"

The man cut him off, anger ramping up. "You not care about anybody else place, all you. I work hard—" He raised the shotgun and sighted along the barrels.

The artist dropped to his knees, quivering from head to toe, certain he was about to be splattered all over the filthy sidewalk in a dingy part of downtown Los Angeles. "Please..." It was all he could manage.

The store owner stepped closer, the gun barrel came nearer the young man's face, he closed his eyes—

A woman's voice interrupted. "Now, now, there's no need for that, is there?"

The store owner spun.

The shotgun went off.

The blast hit a woman behind him and blew a large hole in her chest.

The young man gaped in disbelief.

The scene froze for a few seconds before the store owner lowered the barrel. "I not...I—"

The woman, impossibly, was still upright. She was auburn-haired, brown-skinned, young, dressed in a tattered military green jacket and khaki pants, a backpack strung behind her. Her head was lowered, and the boy expected her to fall any second... but as he watched, the scene lit by the garish yellow light of the street lamps, the wounds in her chest simply closed as tattered skin grew together. When she looked up, she was calm, unfazed.

The store owner fired the other barrel. It took off part of her shoulder and destroyed a strap of the backpack, which hit the ground with a dull thud. "Damn it," said the woman, looking down at her ruin of a shoulder. "This was a good jacket."

She shrugged out of what was left of it and tossed the shredded remnants aside. Again, the injured flesh simply reknit.

The store owner began to mutter curses in his own language. When she took a step toward him, he dropped the shotgun and ran for his store, disappearing around the side of the building. The woman kicked the shotgun into a nearby storm drain, waiting until she heard it hit the sewer ten feet underground. "He won't be trying *that* again," she said, before turning away. She paused only long enough to pick up her ruined backpack, which she clutched to her chest.

When the young man realized she intended to walk away, he leapt up from his kneeling position and called out, "Wait!"

She stopped, and when she turned around again, the artist realized she was without question the most beautiful woman he'd ever seen, with bone structure that might have belonged to a Renaissance temptress. Her face was classical, and reminded him of something…

"Raphael's Madonna, only darker," he suddenly blurted out, without really meaning to.

The woman peered at him curiously. "What?"

For a few seconds he was dumbstruck by her; then he forced himself into action again. "Please, don't leave." He dug into a pocket of his paint-spattered jeans, removed his phone. "I'll call 911, you—"

She interrupted, "There's no need. It wasn't buckshot, or even rock salt. It didn't hurt."

The young man hesitated with his fingers poised above the screen; he knew she was lying, that she'd plainly taken two close shotgun blasts, that her clothing had been shredded but not the skin. He didn't know why she would lie, but neither did he much care. "Are you sure? I mean, your jacket, and—"

"Really, I'm fine."

She started to turn away again, and he realized he didn't want to lose her; beyond her extraordinary face, he had a sense that she was somehow important to him, to his future. "You saved my life. At least let me offer you coffee or something. I live two blocks from here."

She hesitated.

He added, "Please."

The woman eyed him carefully, and her gaze was so frank it nearly made him blush. Her eyes ran down past his face and over his entire body. "All right," she said.

Relief flooded him, as if he'd just been told by a doctor that his disease was not terminal. He thrust a hand out. "I'm Eddie Jones, but my street tag is K-Os."

She took the hand, and the touch of her flesh on his nearly made Eddie swoon. "Sathariel."

"That's an interesting name."

"I'm fairly interesting."

Eddie giggled nervously when he realized, several seconds later, that he still held her hand. He released it, stuttering, "I…I… uh, yeah, I noticed."

CHAPTER 2

Eddie lived in an artist's loft on Alameda. The building, he explained to Sathariel, had once held a toy factory.

His loft was a classic artist's studio, with wooden trestle tables, easels holding half-finished pieces, and color-daubed walls. A double bed with rumpled sheets took up a far corner near a floor-to-ceiling window that looked out on the downtown streets, four stories below. The factory's original ducts had been left in place, overhead, and only a bathroom was separated from the rest of the main space.

Eddie led the way in, gesturing to a battered couch. Sathariel ignored the couch to examine the art, which were mostly portraits that exaggerated the worst features. "They're all politicians, aren't they?"

Nodding, Eddie said, "Yeah. I want my art to comment and wake people up. After I get the portraits right, I transfer them to the stencils."

"I like them."

Eddie watched her silently for a few seconds before asking, "Are you sure you're all right?" He looked at her shoulder, plainly visible now through the remnants of her unadorned white t-shirt.

"I'm fine, although…"

"What?"

"Is there any chance you'd have a spare shirt?"

Eddie ran to the room's only closet, rummaged through it briefly, returned with a t-shirt emblazoned with a graphic of a surfing zombie. He sniffed it before handing it to her. "This one's clean."

"Thanks."

"Don't you have another shirt?"

"I like to travel light."

Eddie was prepared to avert his eyes while she changed, but she didn't move, just finished with the art and lowered herself to the couch, casually draping the shirt over the back cushion.

After a short, uncomfortable silence, Eddie asked, "How'd you do that thing with the shotgun? Really? Am I being punked or something? I mean, I *saw* the way it hit you—"

He broke off as Sathariel rose and stood before him, only a few inches away. "Look for yourself, Eddie. My shoulder's fine."

Being this close to her nearly overwhelmed Eddie. He tried to keep his eyes on her bare, flawless shoulder, but somehow they roamed without his consent—along the curve of her neck, the coppery sweep of her hair, down to the round trace of breasts…

She startled him when she asked, "How old are you?"

"Twenty," he answered. He wondered if she expected older, younger, different…just what *did* she expect?

"Do you have anyone in your life? Girlfriend? Boyfriend?"

Eddie shook his head too rapidly, forced his gaze up to her eyes. "No."

"Good."

Sathariel put her arms around his neck, drawing him down to her…but not all the way, and Eddie understood that she'd made the offer, but the decision to accept was his.

There was no decision to make. He kissed her, slowly at first, savoring the wonder of her in his arms, her warmth, her willingness. After a few seconds, she *did* pull him down, with increased heat. Her hands moved lower, and Eddie had to pull away, breathless, incredulous, when she started undoing his black jeans. "Really?" he asked, watching her nimble fingers work his zipper.

She laughed, a low, throaty sound, before kissing him again and then saying, "Really."

"Oh boy," Eddie said, before she silenced him with another kiss.

CHAPTER 3
Los Angeles, October 30, 2014

The sky outside was just turning light as Sathariel climbed from Eddie's bed. The loft was cold, but even though she was naked she didn't notice the chill.

She sat on the edge of the bed for a moment, looking down at Eddie with affection. He was snoring softly, buried beneath the covers. Only his head was visible; he smiled slightly.

They'd made love twice. Eddie had been frantic and nervous the first time, but the second time had been long and slow and left him exhausted. He'd fallen asleep almost immediately.

She hadn't, of course—she didn't need sleep—but she'd learned over millennia how to be still and quiet. She enjoyed being near Eddie, hearing the changes in his breathing as he moved through the different stages of sleep, smelling him, seeing the slight blue glow of his aura. The aura, in fact, was what had first attracted her: It was pure, focused, guileless, lacking the muddied patches of greed, envy, neuroses that plagued most people. Eddie's had the red glint of anger, but it was contained and channeled, a useful essence instead of a psychic drain.

Sathariel rose and padded silently across the loft to the small kitchen area. She found her backpack, opened it, and removed a large plastic bag filled with curled, dried leaves. In a cupboard she found a mug that bore the logo of a famous coffee company; she filled it with water and put it in a small microwave oven for a few minutes.

When the oven's bell sounded, she removed the hot cup, threw a pinch of leaves from the bag into the water, and waited.

Five minutes later, she poured the tea out, being careful not to spill out any of the unfurled leaves that now lined the cup's interior. Normally she would have enjoyed the tea first—it was an expensive oolong, purchased from a tea shop hidden away in a corner of the San Gabriel Valley—but this morning she was too anxious for whatever the leaves might reveal.

She moved to the couch and seated herself. She tried to erase her mind, to empty it of other thoughts. When she felt ready, she looked down into the cup, examining the shape of the leaves.

The images came so fast and so violent that Sathariel gasped. As they unfolded within her, she had to restrain the urge to set the mug aside—no, to *hurl* it away. Instead, she held it and let the secret revealed by the leaves fill her.

CHAPTER 4
Los Angeles, October 1, 2014

"Martin? Get your ass in here, boy!"

Martin Boyer rose from his armchair as if he bore a great weight on his shoulders. Even though he was only 34, he was already stoop-shouldered and shuffling as he walked. "Coming, Daddy."

He trudged into his father's bedroom. The old man lay sprawled in his stained sheets and yellowed tank top, wrestling with the oxygen tube that was supposed to feed into his nose. "This fucking thing—it came out again…"

Moving mechanically, Martin crossed to the bed, leaned down, reinserted the tubes. "You gotta stop picking at 'em. And they're not that hard to get back in…"

"Are you fucking with me, you little shit?"

"No, sir." Martin turned away to check the oxygen machine.

Martin's father raised his voice to a mocking falsetto. "'They're not that hard to get back in.' You try it when you're the one stuck in this goddamn bed with emphysema and nobody but a useless halfwit kid to help you out."

Martin endured the insult in silence—just like he always did—before asking, "Is there anything else you need?"

Daddy flapped a hand around. "No, there's nothing else I need from you. Go back to your internet porn or whatever the fuck it is you do out there so you can ignore me rotting away in here." Daddy grabbed his remote and turned up the sound on the inane sitcom cluttering up the television screen.

Dismissed by laugh tracks and bad jokes, Martin wandered back to the living room, where he had his own programs playing: He liked cop shows, especially the real-life ones about homicide detectives and forensics experts. He picked up his half-empty bottle of Bud and settled back to watch.

The current show was about a husband who thought he'd pulled off the perfect murder of his wife; unfortunately, he'd left blood stains in his car, and apparently hadn't thought anyone would find out he'd recently purchased both a gun and a life insurance policy.

As Martin watched, the usual thoughts crowded into his head: *I could have been a forensics guy—a pathologist, maybe, or a blood spatter specialist like Dexter. I could have been a detective, figuring out the cold cases that nobody thought would ever be solved. I could've done any of that, if only Mama hadn't died ten years back and then Daddy got emphysema and I had to give up my job to take care of him. And so what if I was just a clerk in a hardware store. If Daddy hadn't gotten sick, I could've gone to college and then into the police.*

But tonight, a different voice intruded on Martin's thoughts. It sounded like his voice, but it was saying things he'd never really thought before: *You could still do all those things, Martin. You're a smart guy, and you're still young, although you won't be for much longer, especially not given how Daddy's wearing you down. In fact, it all comes back to Daddy, doesn't it? Everything that's missing in your life? Isn't the answer obvious?*

Kill Daddy.

Martin squirmed and set his empty beer bottle down. *Kill Daddy?*

That other voice answered, *Sure. You'd probably be doing the miserable old bastard a favor, and you'd certainly be doing the right thing for yourself.*

Martin glanced at the television screen, where a technician was running a special light slowly along a length of car upholstery, stopping when he found a tiny blood splotch.

They'd find out. I don't want to go to prison.

Martin, you're assuming anyone would miss your father. Does anyone ever come to see him, call about him, even ask about him? Nobody but you and his doctor, and the doctor doesn't have the time to check up on him.

Martin thought about this for a second. *That's true. So...I'd...*

Simple: You go in there and put a pillow over his face until he stops moving. Then you roll him up in plastic trash bags, seal the door and window with tape, and don't go into that room again. His pension and social security checks will keep feeding into his bank account, and no one has to find out.

The voice stopped after that. Martin tried to go back to watching his show, but Daddy started in again, wanting, demanding, taunting, threatening. Martin was exhausted by the time he fell into bed. In his dreams that night, he was a powerful predator running free and wild on endless plains, taking down all the lesser creatures he encountered, sinking his strong teeth into hide and fur.

In the morning, Martin awoke, rolled out of bed, walked into his father's room, yanked the old man's pillow out from beneath his balding head, put it over his face, and held it down until Daddy stopped struggling. He held the pillow down another full minute, putting all of his weight down on it, just to be sure.

It was only a little after 8 a.m., but Martin went into the kitchen, got a can from the fridge, and started his day with it. Later on, he could roll up the body and seal the doors and windows. For now, however, he just wanted to enjoy the first hour of his new life with the King of Beers.

CHAPTER 5
Los Angeles, October 30, 2014

Sathariel started at the feel of a hand on her shoulder. She pulled herself up out of the vision of Martin Boyer and turned to see Eddie behind her, jerking his hand away. "Whoa, sorry, didn't mean to scare you."

She tried to smile at him reassuringly. "You didn't. I was just... somewhere else."

Eddie bent over her and peered down into the mug. "Tea?"

"Um-hmm. I'll make you some, if you like."

"That's okay—I'm more of a Coke man." He padded to the kitchen, wearing only a pair of boxer shorts imprinted with designs of rolling dice. He reached into the refrigerator, pulled out a can, and was in the process of opening it when he stopped and stared at her.

"What?" she asked.

"Wow, I just...you're not dressed," he said, then added, "It's a nice view." He took a seat at a trestle worktable, sipped the soda, and asked, "How did you sleep?"

"Oh, I don't really sleep."

He hesitated halfway through a swallow, then gulped and shrugged. "Okay. Is there...uh...a reason for that? You don't, like, have a drug problem or something, right?"

"No." As she rose, she said, "Eddie, it's time I tell you the truth about what you saw last night…"

Eddie took a gulp, set the can on the table, turned his full attention to her. "Okay, I'm ready. Lay it on me."

"I'm not human."

Eddie stared for a moment before saying, "So, uh…what do you think you are?"

She walked past him silently, pulled open two kitchen drawers until she found a steak knife, put her hand on the kitchen counter, and drove the knife through it.

Eddie leapt from his chair, crying out. He was heading toward her when, gritting her teeth, she yanked the knife out and held up her hand to show him.

There was no blood. There was no wound, not even a red cut. Nothing.

Eddie froze, his face pale. "How'd you do that?"

"I didn't *do* anything. It's *me*. Watch…"

She suddenly flipped the knife blade around and drove it into her own midsection. As Eddie watched, stunned, she pulled it up and sidewise, gasping in pain. He saw the knife plainly embedded in her, moving through her flesh, but there was no gush of crimson, no glimpse of glistening organs, no pain or shock on her face. After a few seconds, she withdrew the knife and tossed it to the table in front of him, then collapsed onto the couch, gasping.

Eddie picked it up, holding it gingerly before glancing at her. "Well, the sun's up, so I guess you're not a vampire…"

"I'm an Angel."

He set the knife down. "You mean, like…of the heavenly variety?"

"Not exactly—I was cast out of Heaven."

Eddie abruptly looked sick. "Are you here for my soul? Because what I do is *art*, you know? It's street art, it's not vandalism, or—"

She looked at him with amusement. "No, nothing like that. Eddie, even though I'm fallen, I'm not evil. Two hundred of us were cast out because we fell in love with humanity and wanted to give you knowledge, but we acted against God's wishes. Some of us *were* evil—Semjaza, probably Azazel although I've never been sure—and God sent his loyal Angels to bind them. The rest of us were simply cast aside. To this day, four thousand years later,

I don't really understand why what we did was so bad, but I've learned that not even Angels can know what's in His mind."

Eddie gestured at the two of them. "I'm guessing he probably doesn't look favorably on what you and I did last night, either."

Sathariel shrugged. "I really don't know. I just know that I can't see any evil in it. And sometimes I find that physical closeness makes this truth-telling part of it easier."

"I thought Angels were all guys—you know, Michael, Gabriel…"

"In Heaven, we had no gender. When we came to earth, we all chose our sex and appearance. I wanted to interact with as many of you as possible, so I created an appearance that I thought melded many of the varieties of humankind. And I thought it was quite obvious that women were the stronger sex."

Eddie peered at her with something like wonder. "So are you…are you immortal?"

"Yes, I am. When we were cast out, we were stripped of many of our abilities, but left with others. I'll never get sick or be wounded or die. Because I once spoke the tongue of Heaven, I can understand every language on Earth. And I can tell by looking at anyone how much goodness they possess."

"Do you eat? Or sleep?"

Sathariel shook her head. "No, although I experience physical sensations like heat or cold, taste or smell, pain…or pleasure."

"Oh, good, glad to know you weren't faking all that." Eddie ran his fingers through his straw-colored hair and asked, "So you've spent four thousand years doing…uh, what? I'm guessing it was more than seducing a string of hot guys."

She laughed. "A little more. I want to redeem myself. I've spent four thousand years traveling the world, doing whatever good I could. Sometimes I get clues about things I'm supposed to do by reading tea leaves, or listening at a crossroads at midnight, or laying out cards. Like you, for example: I was sent to save you last night, but I was almost too late because the messages are sometimes incomplete or fuzzy."

"You came to Los Angeles to save me?"

"No, I was already here. This time of year is always active. Satan—the original Fallen Angel, who was banished from Heaven long before I was—is usually confined to reaching humans via their dreams, or their thoughts. There's only one night a year when he is allowed to come to earth and interact with humans face-to-face..."

Eddie stood up, moving to his kitchen, opening cabinets in a useless search for food. "Halloween? You mean the fundies who don't let their kids trick or treat are right and it really is 'The Devil's Birthday'?"

Sathariel enjoyed watching him, and was surprised by a sudden rush of affection for him. She liked his playfulness, his kindness, his honesty, his attentiveness to her. "No, but it is the night when seasons change, days grow shorter and darkness takes hold, the barrier between our world and the one that comes after can be breached and Satan crosses over, until sunrise. This year, though, something's different; I think he's got something big planned, but I'm not sure what. It'll happen here, in Los Angeles...that's all I know. And *that's* why I came here."

"Great." Eddie slammed a cupboard door and turned to her abruptly. "There's not a fucking thing in here to eat. Let's go out—I'm starving."

Sathariel rose and moved to him. "So am I," she said, reaching under the band of his boxers.

Eddie groaned as he instantly grew hard again. "Food can wait."

CHAPTER 6

The Pantry was an L.A. institution. The venerable restaurant had been around since 1924, and it still retained much of its original design, with a counter near the front and tables with vintage wooden chairs. It was relatively quiet on a weekday between the breakfast rush and the lunch hour, so they had most of the back area to themselves. Eddie had ordered fried chicken, while Sathariel nibbled from a peach cobbler.

Between and around mouthfuls of food, Eddie answered questions about his own life. He told Sathariel about his rich father, who paid for the loft because he still thought Eddie would come to his senses and go back to college soon. He told her about his art, about artists who inspired him, about how "K-Os" already had a small cult following, and what he hoped to achieve beyond that. He told her that he wanted to spend the rest of his life creating art that would provoke and enlighten; when he reached the point where he could support himself, he planned on telling his father to kiss his ass and stop paying his rent.

Sathariel listened, and at last commented, "We're very much alike, aren't we? Both rebelling against our fathers and trying to do good."

Eddie smiled, reached out, squeezed her hand.

In that moment, she looked down at the casual arrangement of bones on his plate—

They began to form into shapes: A man's profile. A room. A gun...

She let herself drift away from reality, following the vision.

CHAPTER 7
Los Angeles, October 19, 2014

Martin Boyer grew restless watching the television, as he did every night.

The murder shows no longer fascinated him; now they irritated, like poison ivy. It'd been over two weeks since he'd snuffed out his father's life with a pillow, and overall the plan had worked—no one had asked about Daddy, the checks had been deposited this month. Martin hadn't opened the door to Daddy's bedroom, although he'd been somewhat curious about the body—had it decayed like a television zombie, or bloated like a drowning victim? Would it still look like Daddy, or had it morphed into some unrecognizable, putrescent thing?

But that wasn't the thought that really obsessed him, that stayed with him nearly all the time, that kept him from enjoying his shows.

What he kept thinking about was how good it had felt. He'd liked knowing that Daddy's life was his for the taking, that he really *did* possess some power. He liked knowing it was a secret power, like a superhero's. He knew it was morally wrong, but he didn't care.

Still, he hadn't really considered acting on it until today. He'd been at the supermarket, doing his weekly shopping for beer and microwaveable meals, when he'd spotted a boy in the frozen foods aisle, chatting away on a smart phone. The boy was maybe sixteen, wearing board shorts and a Minecraft t-shirt; he was so tanned and blonde that he could've stepped out of a Beach Boys song. Martin stopped and openly stared until the boy glanced up, frowned, and walked away.

He thinks he's something special, but I could take him, he thought. *I could put a bullet into his stomach, not enough to kill him but it'd knock him off his feet, and then I could straddle him and feel his fear as I put the gun up against his head and pull the trigger.*

The thought had left Martin so happy that he'd complimented his cashier, who giggled as she rang up his items.

At home, he was still thinking about the boy as the evening's cop shows began. The murders seemed too cold and distant, too calculated, and he was uninvolved. He was more than willing to listen when the voice started up in his head.

You could do it, Martin. You could buy the gun and do it a lot. And you deserve it, after the way Daddy made you give up your own life, the rotten fucking old bastard.

I don't know anything about guns, though.

The voice in his head laughed. *Martin, you're a smart man, and even dummies can use guns. It'd take you about three minutes to learn how.*

Who are you, Martin mentally asked, *and how are you in my head?*

I'm just you, Martin. The part of you that's genuine, and true, and knows what you really want.

Martin considered for a few moments.

You know you want it. It's yours for the taking. Halloween's coming, and that means trick or treat. Who gets the trick and who gets the treat this year, Martin?

Finally, Martin turned off the television, rose, and walked to his home computer. He googled California's gun laws, and found out that there was a ten-day waiting time for a buyer to take possession of a handgun.

He didn't really want to wait that long, but he supposed he could if he had to. After all, today was October 19th, so if he bought the gun tomorrow...

He could still have it in time for Halloween.

Martin didn't really understand the last thing the voice said, but in time he thought he would:

Just don't forget to distract the Angel before the main event.

CHAPTER 8
Los Angeles, October 30, 2014

"...Hello? Anybody home?"

Sathariel heard Eddie's voice, the sounds of the restaurant rushed back in, and she shook the vision out of her head. "I...I saw something..."

And it hit her: She'd just been told that someone nearby was a serial killer-in-the-making who was obsessed with young blonde men. Satan was stoking that man's madness, poking himself into Martin Boyer's subconscious like a blacksmith's tool into the slow-burning embers of a fire.

"*...Distract the Angel...*"

Eddie was the distraction. Martin Boyer was going to be gunning for him.

Or already *was* gunning for him. "That was the 19th...ten days ago..."

She felt nausea she hadn't experienced in decades, not since she'd been on a European battlefield during the last world war. There was no way Satan could have known, ten days ago, about her and Eddie; even the Great Adversary didn't possess clairvoyance. That could only mean that Satan had set up the Korean store owner, and had sent Sathariel the vision that had drawn her to save Eddie last night. Satan had surely known she'd be attracted by Eddie's essential sweetness, his boyish handsomeness...

She'd been set up by her enemy.

"Oh no. Oh, Eddie, I think I've done something terrible, that I may have just fallen for a terrible trick and exposed you to the worst kind of danger."

Eddie set down his fork, swallowed a last mouthful of food, and said, "What...danger?"

"I'm not sure, but..." She searched the visions for clues, came up only with, "Satan."

"Satan?"

She nodded. "He's up to something. Whatever it is, he's been setting up a madman to come after you. Today, that man, whose name is Martin Boyer, acquired a gun."

Eddie looked scared, but also confused. "But you can stop some dude with a gun, right? I mean, you stopped the guy last night..."

Sathariel thought for a moment before answering. Finally she reached across the table and clutched his hand tightly. "Do you trust me?"

He shrugged, as if he barely understood the question. "Of course."

"Then I need you to come with me. There's someone who can help us."

They flagged down the waitress for their check and left.

Eddie had always loved The Pantry; now he wondered if he'd ever see it again.

INTERLUDE WITH THE DEVIL #2
Lubbock, Texas, Halloween Night, 1992

Sathariel stood in the long line of (mostly) teens waiting to get into the "Hell House." It was in an abandoned factory just outside of the city limits, but distance hadn't kept the thrill-seekers away.

Two giggling girls who couldn't have been over fifteen were in line in front of her. "I heard they have an abortion scene with real human fetuses!"

Her friend looked concerned. "I don't know about this, Mary Lou. You sure it isn't gonna be *too* scary?"

"You're such a wuss," the first girl said, pushing on her friend's shoulder hard enough to make her stagger.

Sathariel tuned out the rest of their conversation, thinking instead about the clues that had led her here. She didn't normally have much luck with scrying glasses, but this year it'd yielded up the tantalizing suggestion that she'd find Satan here, tonight.

Forty minutes later, she was inside the haunt. A man in a bad greasepaint job was pretending to be "the demon Billzebub" and leading them into a sort of stage setting, where a group of thirty onlookers lined up behind a rough wooden barrier and watched a badly acted scene in which a girl, attended by blood-drenched nurses and doctors, feigned undergoing an abortion. Sathariel heard the girls spout disappointment at the obviously fake fetus, plainly a child's doll covered in stage blood.

Billzebub proceeded to take them through eight more tableaux. A girl, taunted by voices from her computer, killed herself. A young man in a hospital bed, dying of AIDS, regretted his "lifestyle choice." A pair of girls went to a rave and took drugs, only to be murdered on the dance floor. Although she applauded the goal of bringing viewers to God, she didn't enjoy the use of tawdry scares to do so. It was tacky and depressing, and judging by the responses of other attendees Sathariel wasn't alone in feeling that way.

Things livened up when the final scene was revealed to be Hell, complete with papier-mâché brimstone, lurid lighting, piped-in screams, and the Devil holding court in the center as the line of attendees wound around him. Sathariel thought at first that the Devil might be real, but his aura was unremarkable. Plus, he employed melodrama and exaggeration that the actual Satan would have found laughable.

On the far side of Hell, they filed through a door and into a brightly-lit room set up as a chapel, with benches. They were directed to sit; Sathariel was near the front. When the benches were filled, the door behind them was shut and three men stepped to the front of the room.

The man in the center began preaching. He introduced himself as Pastor Bob Fagleson, and he explained to them that they now had a choice: They could accept God into their lives and ascend to Heaven, or they could live like the sinners they'd just seen and burn in Hell.

Pastor Fagleson had one of the darkest auras Sathariel had ever seen. It pulsed with sickly greenish channels, throbbing, churning. She'd seen similar emanations on businessmen, laborers, criminals...it was a particular strain of evil.

"Excuse me, Pastor?" A voice shouted from the back of the room, interrupting the sales pitch.

The pastor broke off. "I'm sorry, son, but this isn't the time for questions." He gestured to the two blandly smiling men on either side of him. "In the next room, Deacon Kirk and Deacon James will be happy to discuss any questions you might have..."

"I'm not sure if they'll discuss this one, though..."

Sathariel turned to see the questioner—and froze.

It was the Devil. He'd taken on the guise of a teenaged boy, one with pierced cheeks and leather jacket, but there was no mistaking the ring of orange, fiery glow that surrounded him. He saw Sathariel staring at him and winked at her; she gritted her teeth in ire, but kept her seat. To attack him here, in plain view of forty others, was not an option.

He continued, "I was really wondering about all those boys you had kneel before you and blow you at summer camp last year. I think Bobby Joe Seacrest, for example, was only twelve, wasn't he?"

The Pastor blanched. For a second his jaw worked uselessly, then speech returned. "I'm afraid I'm going to have to ask you to step out…"

The two deacons started moving toward the boy/Devil. He stood, made sure his voice was loud and clear when he said, "It's okay, I'll leave on my own—as soon as you tell us exactly why Zeke Dodd's family left town after he got back from that camp…"

The deacons were on him then, each firmly taking one of his arms to escort him out, but the damage was already done—a twenty-something woman in the front row muttered, "Yeah, I'd like to know, too—I was dating Zeke's brother, and they just lit out."

"Is that true about Bobby Joe?" shouted someone from the side.

The whole place began to erupt in questions, confusion, accusations. Pastor Fagleson's aura pulsed in anger as he attempted to wave the crowd down.

Sathariel rose and went after the Devil.

She caught up to him as he was picking himself up from the dirt he'd been flung into outside the Hell House exit. He saw her and grinned. "How'd you like *that*, Angel? Huh?"

She snarled, was about to hurl herself at him when she stopped, realizing…

He was right.

Of course his goal had been to disrupt the church's attempt at recruiting members, but in the process he'd exposed a monster who didn't deserve to speak for God.

"Tricky, eh? Why don't you just think about it for a while, and maybe I'll see you again in a year." With that, he'd tipped an imaginary hat to her and sauntered off.

And she'd let him.

CHAPTER 9
Los Angeles, October 30, 2014

Eddie drove them into the Hollywood hills, Sathariel directing him around winding canyon roads he hadn't even known existed before this.

She finally told him to pull up before a large wrought-iron gate tucked into a hillside. There was a strange symbol worked into the bars that Eddie couldn't identify.

Sathariel got out of the car and walked up to an intercom. Eddie didn't hear the exchange, but after a few seconds the gate began to open and Sathariel returned to the car.

They drove past the gate (which closed behind them) and down a short road that curved around before a massive, multi-level house sprawled along the hill. As they got out of the car and approached the house, Eddie had to work to keep his jaw from dropping. "So who does this belong to, exactly?"

"Her name is Magdalena San Pietro. She's highly placed in a secret organization called the Order of the Light. And she's got Nephilim blood."

Eddie was about to ask what that meant, but he broke off as the front door opened and a woman stepped out to greet them.

Magdalena was seven feet tall, with ebony hair and eyes even blacker. Her age was impossible to guess, but she exuded the authority that only came with experience. "Sathariel," she said, waiting for the Angel to reach the landing at the short flight of steps leading up to the door before embracing her. "Such a pleasure to see you."

"Magdalena." Sathariel gestured at Eddie. "This is my friend Eddie Jones."

The woman eyed Eddie with cool regard, almost contempt. "Hmm. Are you sure about this one, dear? He doesn't look like much."

"All I know is Satan deliberately put him in my way. He's important."

Magdalena offered Eddie a final dismissive glance, then led the way into the house. "Well, come in. We've got much to discuss."

The interior of the house was as sumptuous and elegant as the outside, if slightly too baroque for Eddie's taste. He guessed the floor was real marble, the paintings in the ornate gilt frames were genuine old masters, the furnishings true antiques. It made him nervous to move among these things, as if he might brush against something and destroy it.

They entered a sitting room, where Sathariel and Eddie shared a brocade couch while Magdalena lowered her massive frame into a comfortable armchair.

"Why don't we see more of you, Sathariel? You know we want to help you."

The Angel shrugged, and Eddie knew instantly that she wasn't comfortable, although he couldn't guess the reason. "I walk my own path, Maggie. You know that."

"True. So what brings you here today?"

"Something big is happening. Our Great Enemy is mobilizing. He's got something planned for this Halloween, it's going to go down here in L.A., and whatever it is, he needs to distract me from it. I need to know what that thing is."

Magdalena listened for a moment, considered, finally said, "You know more than I do, but if I had to guess...I'd say it involves Azazel."

Sathariel blinked in surprise. "Azazel?"

"Yes. You know he escaped, don't you? We're still not sure how, but it happened a few months ago. He might have been found and freed by Kasdaya."

Sathariel had to look away, but Eddie saw the pain in her tensed shoulders. "Kasdaya..."

"Poor, mad Kasdaya. A number of your fellow Fallen have suffered that fate."

Sathariel didn't speak.

Magdalena continued. "Azazael, however, is likely to be as cunning and resourceful as ever. He knows enchantments that no one else does, even Satan. It's possible he's working with Satan now..."

Sathariel drew herself straight and said, "Azazel and Satan...?"

"Well, as I said, it's just a possibility. We won't know for sure until we can find Azazel. We've been looking for weeks, using everything from hacking into security networks to sending messages via Ouija boards—"

Cutting her off, Sathariel said, "I need to see a friend who might know something." With that she rose and Eddie joined her.

Magdalena stayed seated, impassively watching as Sathariel led Eddie from the house. "You should use us, Sathariel. We can help you..."

Sathariel didn't answer. She didn't turn back, but she heard Magdalena's heels on the marble as she came after them. "Will you at least share your information with us?"

Sathariel called back over one shoulder, "Let me make sure first that it's worth sharing."

Once they were out of the house and halfway to their car, Eddie nearly running to keep up with the Angel, he asked, "I'm sorry, but—is she seriously one of the good guys?"

"She's Nephilim, meaning she's descended from some of the Fallen who took human wives. Because she's not fully human, I can't see her aura, so I don't know just how good or bad she is. But I do know that she's smart and ambitious and likes being rich and I wouldn't trust her any further than one of the Devil's minions."

"So who's this...Azazel?"

They reached the car, climbing in as Sathariel answered. "He was one of our leaders. In fact, it was really his idea to give our knowledge to man. At the time, I thought he was selfless and noble; now I realize I was a fool, and he really just wanted to be God. That's why he got the serious punishment and the rest of us were just left to our own devices."

Eddie started up the car. As he pulled away from the house, he looked in the rearview mirror and saw Magdalena standing just outside, watching them. He shivered, trying not to imagine her running after them, or even sprouting black wings and soaring in pursuit. He was relieved when they reached the gate, it opened, and they drove through. "So how will you find this Azazel?"

"I don't have to find him—I already know where he is."

"Where?"

"Here, in L.A. He came to see me after Kasdaya found him and turned him loose."

"And you didn't tell your friend Mags?"

"Would you tell her anything?"

"Good point."

Sathariel looked out the window, studying the urban canyons. It was late fall in Los Angeles, a time of year when sunsets were long and golden, days still warm, nights just starting to cool...but today, here, somehow the light seemed lesser, tinged with incipient dark. "I once put a great deal of faith in Azazel—too much. Maybe I should have let Magdalena's Order take him again, but…instead I helped him, after he led me to exile."

Eddie stopped the car at an intersection, looked over at her. "You loved him. That's not a bad thing."

The intersection cleared, and Sathariel said, "Do you know how to get to Union Station from here?"

"Why? Are we taking a train somewhere?"

"We're going to see Azazel."

Eddie glanced at her in alarm. "You mean…now?"

Sathariel nodded.

They drove in silence for a few blocks before Eddie asked, "What could Azazel give Satan? Something that would make it so he could really hurt people on Halloween?"

"I doubt it. That's not his modus operandi; Satan would rather concoct serious mischief. Besides, I don't think Azazel has that much power. But Satan's Halloween pranks can be deadly even without him being able to touch anyone."

"How?"

"Well…let's just say I may still harbor some affection for Azazel, but if I have to choke an answer out of him, I will."

Eddie made a mental note to never piss her off.

INTERLUDE WITH THE DEVIL #3
Minneapolis, Minnesota, Halloween Night, 1933

Jake Svensson, Klaus Horvig, and Billy Clanton had just finished throwing eggs at old man Jorgensen's house; they'd run, laughing, into the night until they were two blocks away, then they'd stopped by the vacant lot next to Billy's house to catch their breath.

Still laughing and panting, Klaus asked, "Did you see the look on his face when he came out onto the porch?"

Billy, at ten the smallest of the trio, still looked anxious. "You sure he didn't see us?"

Jake, the unofficial leader, swiped a finger through the soot darkening Billy's face. "Even if he did, he wouldn't recognize us in this, remember?"

Billy shrugged. "I hope so...'course I'm still in trouble if my Mama finds those eggs gone. She told me they were all we got to eat right now."

Klaus began to cluck like a chicken, bucking his arms and stepping about in a comical, bird-like fashion.

"Aww, cut it out," Billy said, not really expecting Klaus to stop.

But he did when a new voice interrupted. "I think you're all chicken."

They looked up to see a boy standing ten feet away, eyeing them with amusement. He was a few inches taller than Jake and maybe two years older, and none of them recognized his undisguised face. He wore knickers with suspenders, a plain long sleeved shirt, and a tilted newsboy cap.

Jake took a few steps toward the newcomer, trying to make himself as big and threatening as possible. "What do you know about it?"

"I know that throwin' eggs on Halloween is kid's stuff."

Klaus moved up by Jake's side. "Oh yeah? So what do *you* like to do—read poetry and drink tea?"

Jake snorted. But the newcomer didn't back down. "I'm just sayin' that if you wanna play pranks, then make 'em *good* pranks, not egg-throwing." He nodded at a wooden spool on a string that Billy held in one hand. "And sure not ticktacks—those things are just plain dumb."

Billy held the ticktack up defensively. "But the noise 'bout scares folks to death..."

"You really wanna scare folks? C'mon, I'll show ya somethin'..."

The boy turned around and strode off confidently. Billy and Klaus turned to Jake, who shrugged and followed the older boy. Billy and Klaus fell into line.

They all marched to the end of the block. The newcomer paused at the intersection and looked around. On the cross street, there were a few older people out walking: Workers returning after a long day, shoppers coming home with packages, teens heading to Halloween parties.

The boy found a stretch of sidewalk where there was a picket fence and hedge on one side, and a parked car on the other. He gestured to Billy's ticktack. "Here's what you do: Take that piece of string and tie it between the car and the fence."

Billy examined the string, then the sidewalk. "But somebody might trip…"

"That's the idea, genius."

Nobody moved. After a few seconds, the newcomer waved at them in disgust. "Aww, you boys are all sissies. I'm done with you."

He started to walk off, but Jake suddenly leapt forward, snatching the string from Billy. "We ain't sissies." Jake tied the string about two inches above the ground. He finished and stood back, surveying his work; the string was hard to see by the glow of the street lamps. "So now what?"

The boy nodded at the hedge. "Now we hide and wait for somebody to come along."

Klaus and Billy looked to Jake, who nodded and leapt over the picket fence, crouching down behind the hedge. The older boy joined them.

They didn't have long to wait. Just a few seconds later, a man came along the sidewalk toward them. Peering through the leaves and twigs, they saw it was Mr. Dearborn, the lawyer who never gave his staff holidays or vacations. Dearborn was dressed as he always was: In a proper three-piece suit with newly shined shoes and a hat, a leather case clutched in one hand.

They held their breath as he drew nearer…nearer…and then he was crying out as he went sprawling. He landed on all fours; when his case hit the ground, it flew open, sending papers careening across the sidewalk.

The new boy whooped and leapt up from behind the shrubbery, and the other three swiftly followed. As they all laughed and hollered, Dearborn shouted at them while attempting to gather his papers. "You hooligans! If I find out who you are, I'll sue every one of you for physical distress!"

The boys didn't hear the rest; they had already run far enough that Dearborn's threats were lost. They took shelter in the darkness of an alley, where they laughed, clutching at their sides, exchanging descriptions of the look on Dearborn's face. "Did you see how he snarled…?" "His hat flew right off!" "I reckon he's still back there picking up all those papers…!"

After a few seconds, the new boy peeked around the corner and came back. "Hey, guess where we are?"

Jake slapped the brick wall behind him. "This is Dr. Butcher's office, right?"

Dr. Bletcher was the town dentist, and the terror of most of the younger population. He was a bachelor with an intense dislike of children, and there were those who thought he enjoyed sending little ones out of his office wailing in terror and pain. Because of this, he'd been nicknamed "Dr. Butcher" by most of the boys, and more than a few of the parents.

The new boy grinned and nodded. "Yeah." He bent over, scrabbled in the darkness, and they heard a scraping sound. He stood up, holding a chunk of paving he'd pried up from the cracked alley surface. "Here," he said, handing it to Jake. He bent over again, finding two more fist-sized pieces he passed to Klaus and Billy.

"What do we do with these?" Klaus asked.

"Oh, c'mon, don't tell me you're *that* lacking in imagination."

Jake looked skeptical, but little Billy walked resolutely to the end of the alley, and they followed. Billy stopped on the sidewalk in the front of the large plate glass window that was stenciled, in curving script, with the name "DR. GEORGE BLETCHER— DENTIST."

"He made my whole mouth hurt," Billy said, drawing back his chunk of stone, "and then called Mama bad names when she said he'd overcharged us. He deserves this." Billy hurled the missile.

It impacted with the glass, but Billy'd always had a weak throw, and it only cracked the window. Klaus stepped back, cocking his arm. "Here, let me try."

Jake joined him. "Me, too."

They threw their rocks almost simultaneously, and a deafening *CRASH* followed as the large window shattered. They ran again, this time hearing a police whistle blowing a block behind them. They ducked in and out of fences and yards and garages, and finally came to rest in an empty building that had been a popular diner until the Depression had come along and folks had stopped eating out.

"Boy, that was *great!*" Billy said. The younger boy's eyes were unblinking, wide, uncreased despite his smile.

"Ready to try something *really* big, then?" The older boy reached into a pocket, pulled out a small box, tossed it to Billy.

Billy eyed the box, held it up for Klaus and Jake to see:

Matches.

"Let's make a fire," Billy said.

The newcomer grinned, the expression so wide it threatened to wrap around the sides of his head. "That's the spirit."

Billy had just removed a match when a voice interrupted: "You call these pranks?"

The boys all turned to see a woman framed in the open doorway of the old building. She wore a plain dress and shabby coat, had a satchel like a hobo's draped over one shoulder, but she showed no fear or hesitation confronting the boys. "Looks more like vandalism to me."

The older boy saw her and bolted, leaping through a window the boards had fallen away from.

She ran after him.

He ran no more than a hundred feet away from the building, then stopped and turned to face her. "Well, Sathariel, you arrived just in time."

"In time for what?"

"To witness the end of my best Halloween prank ever."

The *whoosh* sound of flames came from behind Sathariel. She turned and saw the rattletrap diner going up in flames. Inside, boys screamed.

She rushed to the structure just as the roof collapsed. Disregarding the sensation of her own burning flesh, she tried to push aside timbers and fiery debris, but she was too late—all she could see of the boys were splayed limbs beneath flames, the skin already charring.

She staggered out of the conflagration, smelling of smoke and covered in ash. The Devil, wearing the form of a thirteen-year-old boy, waited for her, looking satisfied. "Oh, golly, that's too bad—they'll never have the chance to repent now, will they?"

"You bastard," was all Sathariel could say.

"I win," said the Devil.

CHAPTER 10
Los Angeles, October 30, 2014

Sathariel directed Eddie to Union Station, L.A.'s famed downtown train hub.

"Are we taking a train to see Azazel?" he asked, only half-joking.

"Not exactly."

They parked in a nearby lot, walked past Olvera Street, with its kiosks and shops selling Mexican kitsch and food, crossed Alameda, and entered the huge structure, still impressive despite more than 70 years of constant use. As they strode through the waiting area, with its lofty ceiling and retro-style, heavy square chairs, Eddie finally voiced something that had been irritating him. "I gotta ask something: Why is it up to you to stop the Devil on Halloween? I mean where's...well, you know...*God*, in all this?"

The pain that flickered across Sathariel's face almost made Eddie regret the question. "I don't know," she said. "After four thousand years of being here, among all of His creations, I feel as if I understand Him less, not more. None of it makes sense to me. I try to do good, but more and more, I find myself wondering why. There's a reason other Angels like Kasdaya have opted for just going insane. That frequently sounds fairly appealing to me."

Eddie danced in front of her, put a hand out to stop her. "Hey, none of that. You're probably the sanest person—or, well, whatever—I've ever met. If we can't do good, help each other, love each other, there's really not much point in going on."

"That's not exactly very comforting, Eddie."

"Maybe not, but..." he paused to take her hands in his, "all I know is that as long as you're here, I want to help you, and *that* is worth living for."

He kissed her, and she returned it. Travelers walked around them, some envious, some pleased, most not caring. But it was enough.

Sathariel finally broke away, stepping around him to lead the way. "Let's get this over with."

They walked past signs pointing to the subways and went down to the lowest level. A few dozen passengers waited, spread out along the length of the platform. Tunnels stretched off into darkness at either end; the distant sounds of trains rumbling along the tracks echoed around them.

Sathariel went to a far end of the platform, away from those waiting. She stopped and faced an innocuous framed poster displaying route information. "This is it," she murmured, glancing to the sides.

"This is what?"

She spoke to Eddie over one shoulder. "Only I can pass here, but it should work if I carry you." She knelt down. "It's probably easiest if you climb onto my back."

"What?" Eddie laughed and looked around nervously. "What are you talking about?"

"I'd also urge you to close your eyes when we reach the other side. Azazel's got some surprises set up that might be…disconcerting."

"Seriously?"

Without rising, she motioned at her back. "Eddie, just do it."

Looking embarrassed, he leaned over, put his arms around her neck, and she grabbed his legs. She was strong, but still struggled slightly with his weight as she rose. "Get ready," she said, adjusting her grip slightly.

"For what—"

He was interrupted as they stepped through the wall.

He made an unintelligible sound as she set him down. They were in an ancient tunnel, the walls lined with crumbling old brick, a rickety wooden staircase going down below them; the only light came from there, a yellowish glow barely limning the stairs.

Eddie looked around, wondering how anything this obviously *old* could exist in L.A. "What is this place?"

"It used to be part of a series of tunnels beneath the old Chinese district, before they moved it a little northwest. Azazel has been kept chained underground for the last four thousand years, and he hasn't adapted to open spaces or sunlight yet, so he picked this for his temporary home. No one else even knows it's still here."

A sound came from overhead, then, something skittering and hissing. Eddie tried to peer up into the gloom, but couldn't make anything out. "What's that…?"

"Eddie, I told you to close your eyes—"

He didn't, and so he screamed when the horse-sized spider dropped down in front of him.

It was black, furred, with softball-sized, glowing eyes and fangs as long as butcher knives. It swung from a thread as thick as a finger, blocking the staircase. Sathariel leapt between the nightmarish thing and Eddie. "Don't look at it."

"This is your idea of 'disconcerting'?!"

"It's not real, Eddie. It's an illusion, created by Azazel to warn off any who might somehow wind up here."

"It's not real?"

"Trust me."

He closed his eyes, but every hair on his body stood to attention as he continued to hear the thing hiss, its eight long legs rasping against the brickwork.

Sathariel took his hand. "We're going down the stairs now. I'll tell you when to open your eyes again."

The old wood sagged beneath their weight, menacing creaks joining the sounds of what hung just inches above. Eddie's heart threatened to hammer through his chest with each step. Once, he thought he felt something brush through his hair and he cried out in alarm, but Sathariel held his hand tightly. "We're almost there…"

Another step…another…

"You can open your eyes now."

Eddie did, and couldn't resist the urge to immediately look up.

There was nothing there, just the stairwell shading off into darkness.

Nearby, a brick archway led into a storeroom; the warm light illuminating the stairs came from there. Sathariel stepped into the doorway and uttered a tiny gasp. When Eddie joined her, he saw why:

A large room with crumbling earthen walls was lined with jack-o'-lanterns—hundreds of them. They were on the floor, perched on ancient wooden barrels and trunks, stacked on top of each other, all candlelit from within.

"Wow," Eddie said, taking it in, "I guess Azazel really likes Halloween, huh?"

Sathariel nodded. "And that can't be good."

They stepped into the room, and now Eddie also saw other things: Braziers, a case stuffed with rolled scrolls, a small box with amulets and charms draped over its open sides. Ornamented swords, glass and ceramic vials, even a broom…surely everything a magician would need was here.

"Have you brought me a sacrifice, dear Sathariel?"

They spun to see a figure behind them, and Eddie couldn't imagine where he'd come from. Azazel was tall, with golden skin and hair, the almond-shaped eyes of a large and languid cat, and full, wide mouth. Eddie was surprised by a pang of jealousy—Azazel exuded rich, experienced sensuality, and he'd called Sathariel "dear."

Sathariel, however, eyed him coolly. "Haven't I already given up enough for you?"

Azazel offered a moue of disappointment. "Oh, you're not still blaming me, are you? As I recall, *I'm* the one who just spent four thousand years chained in a lightless hole while the rest of you roamed free, enjoying more..." he ran his exquisite eyes slowly over Eddie, "...earthly pleasures."

"Eddie's here with me now because I can't leave him alone—seems Satan's got something big planned for tomorrow, he's turned loose a psychotic who's coming for Eddie, and you may know something about all this."

Azazel sighed, and fell into an antique gilt-and-velvet chair, the only piece of furniture in the store room. "I hope you're more fun with *him*," he said, waving at Eddie. "Very well, then: Yes, I have given our mutual friend a little something to liven up this year's holiday happening. It was, after all, part of the conditions of my release."

Sathariel frowned. "'Conditions'...?"

"Oh, yes—I'm surprised you didn't figure this one out on your own. Satan guided poor Kasdaya's lunacy. Releasing me was not the mad darling's own idea."

"And what is the nature of this spell that you've provided?"

Azazel leaned back and draped one chino-clad leg over a chair-arm. "It wouldn't be any fun if I told you that, would it?"

In an eye-blink Sathariel was on him, bent over, knife point held a half-inch below one of his sun-colored eyes. "It'll be much less fun if you *don't.*"

Azazel looked at the knife—and sneered. "Now it's threats? What are you going do to—cut me up? Stop sleeping with me?"

"How about I tell the Order of Light where you are and let them take you back to your nice, black pit?"

Fear flickered across Azazel's face, but was swiftly replaced by arrogant assurance. "You can't stop it, but it might be amusing to watch you try. I copied out a spell for him that will open a path on Halloween night from Hell to Earth."

Sathariel dropped the knife tip slightly, considering. "A path..."

He chuckled, watching her face—which displayed sudden, horrified realization. "He's going to bring all of Hell over, isn't he?"

"Oh yes, he is. The same rules will apply—they won't be able to touch any of the humans, and they'll be returned to Hell at sunrise...but can you imagine how much havoc a hundred million demons running loose will create? The human reaction should be utterly intoxicating. I simply adore Halloween, don't you?"

Sathariel staggered back as Eddie joined her, whispering, "I'm sorry, I don't understand—"

"On Halloween, Satan won't be coming to earth alone—this year he'll have all of his demons with him. There are millions of them, Eddie, causing panic and fear..."

Eddie paled. "Oh, fuck...what do we do?"

Sathariel turned back to Azazel. "Where will this happen?"

"Here, darling. It's why I came here."

Eddie blurted out, "West Hollywood." Sathariel looked at him as he added, "It's home to one of the biggest Halloween celebrations in the world. Half-a-million people come to it every year."

"Oh, I can see why you like him, Sath—he's cute *and* smart." Azazel rose and strolled to one of the cases. "It'll happen right in the center of everything. It's all perfect, isn't it?"

Azazel reached up to a shelf, grabbed a vial, drank the contents in a quick gulp, and vanished.

Eddie blinked in shock. "He..."

Sathariel turned to go. "He may even still be here, but if he is we won't get anything else out of him. Let's go." They started to leave, but Sathariel paused as she caught sight of a short sword in a jeweled gold scabbard. She picked it up, pulled the blade forth, and examined the intricate writing etched into the metal.

"What's that?" Eddie asked.

"A sword made for demon killing. It might come in handy." She hefted it up and called out, "Thanks for the gift, old friend."

As they left the hundreds of flickering pumpkins behind and ascended the ominously sagging stairs, Eddie with his eyes tightly closed, he thought he made out a sound behind them, faint and echoing as if from some far distance, but nonetheless distinct:

Laughter.

CHAPTER 11
Los Angeles, October 30th, 2014

Martin Boyer crouched in the bushes outside the dormitory, where he'd been for the last two hours. He was close to giving up when his luck changed:

A young couple strolled up to the outer, locked door of the building. College kids in costumes—her a princess, him a pirate—laughing, nervous after a first date, holding hands. Martin couldn't hear what they said to each other as they hesitated on the walk near the entrance, but he saw when they exchanged an awkward kiss and then parted, both looking down shyly.

His stomach curdled with both envy and disgust.

The girl ran a card-key through a slot by the door, it opened, she turned and waved a last time, then the door closed behind her.

The boy returned the wave, and stood forlornly for another few seconds. He was cute, young—couldn't have been more than a sophomore, probably an eighteen-year-old freshman—blonde and slender.

He was perfect.

He was Donny Jason, the boy who'd been the king of Martin's high school—football team captain, valedictorian, handsome enough to have his pick of any girl in the school. Donny Jason, who'd come up to Martin in an empty school hallway one day after class, surrounded by three of his teammates, and told Martin to stop eyeing Heather O'Brien "because being ogled by fucking geeks like you totally freaks her out." Donny Jason, who'd beaten up Martin a week later while his friends cheered. Donny Jason, who'd wound up as the CEO of a modestly successful chain of auto supply stores, a happily married man with a trophy wife and three lovely children.

As Donny Jason/nameless blonde boy in a pirate costume finally turned and walked away from the campus dorm, Martin forced himself to wait. It was hard, so hard, especially when he felt the heft of the gun in his hand, but he had to let the boy get far enough away to where the shot would go unnoticed, or at least unnoticed for long enough to allow Martin to escape.

After all, this wasn't a suicide mission. He had more important things to see to after this.

So he waited until the boy was fifty feet away, then he pushed out of hiding and followed, moving as quietly as possible.

The boy set off across the darkened campus, and Martin guessed he was heading for the student parking structure on the far side of the classroom buildings.

This was going to be easy.

He fell into a soft lope behind the boy. This late at night, the campus was deserted; he saw no other walkers nearby. Martin increased his speed to close the gap between them; he wasn't good enough to pull off a lethal shot at a distance yet. He'd need to be nearer, point blank range—

The boy abruptly stopped and turned around. "Hey, man, what the hell—why you following me?"

Martin whipped the pistol up and fired before the boy could react.

But the boy had rattled him, his aim was thrown off, and he hit the boy in his right shoulder. The boy started to run, shouting for help.

Martin pulled the trigger again.

This shot was better. It caught the boy in the middle of the back, and he went down.

Martin jogged up, used one foot to roll the boy over onto his back. He was alive, but his breathing was rapid and shallow, a small trickle of blood ran from the lower corner of his mouth. He stared up at Martin in perplexity. "Why...why'd you...?"

The boy shuddered, blood spurted from his mouth, and he was dead.

Adrenaline rushed through Martin. Every cell vibrated with life and energy. This was even better than when he'd killed his father. This was pure, uncontaminated by hate or money.

But he saw the flicker of an approaching siren, and knew he'd have to savor his triumph elsewhere. He shoved the gun in a pocket and walked away, fast, but not running, heading for the side street where he'd parked. He kept his head down, his pace steady, and reached his car without incident. He got in and drove home. He'd never driven with such caution, such total awareness. He pulled over once for a speeding ambulance, and thought, *Too late.*

When he reached home, his hands were shaking with such excitement that he dropped his house keys twice. When he finally got the door unlocked, he went straight to the kitchen, put the gun on the table, and downed his first beer. His hands stopped shaking and he wiped clammy sweat from his face.

You can relax now, Martin—you did it.

He looked at the gun, his hands, his legs, feet, making sure no stray spatters of the boy had hit him, but he was clean.

Well done. Now, would you like to try something bigger?

Martin cracked open another beer and nodded.

Great! I'm going to tell you how to build a bomb, then.

"Neat," Martin muttered, as the voice within him gave him instructions.

INTERLUDE WITH THE DEVIL #4
Ireland, October 31, 204 A.D.

"Drink up, my sweet," said Naoise.

Sathariel smiled and downed the cup of mead. She'd never been much for intoxication, but the taste was pleasant enough and it made Naoise happy to watch her drink. She enjoyed anything that made Naoise happy. He was already a handsome man, with his long red braid and chiseled features, but joy brought a special glow to his green eyes that Sathariel found irresistible. She thought him the most extraordinary human she'd ever seen.

They'd met four years ago, when Sathariel had first arrived on the Emerald Isle. She told the Coriondi tribe she found near the coast that she was a healer and had come in search of a rare herb; in reality, she'd followed a prophecy she'd found in the formation of seeds within an apple, a prophecy about the Devil arriving here.

She hadn't found the Devil, but she'd found Naoise, a soldier whose bravery and skill had already brought the Coriondi great fortune; however, he'd lost the use of his left leg in the last battle, and wouldn't be soldiering any more. The attraction had been instant and mutual, and within three months they'd wed. Sathariel hadn't told him her secret, however, and she tried not to imagine how she would explain it in ten, twenty years when he aged and she didn't, or that she was unable to bear him children. At this moment she didn't care.

The harvest had been generous this year, and they'd brought

the cattle in from the fields just as the first frost had crusted over the morning's dew. Tonight's sunset had marked the beginning of Samhain, the Celts' great three-day celebration. They would celebrate the harvest with food, drink, roaring fires in the hearth of their great hall, and tales of the *sidh*, the ethereal mischief-makers who might cross over from the Otherworld on this one night to wreak havoc.

Fergus the Bard had just finished telling them the favorite tale of Nera, the great warrior whose strange adventures on one Samhain led him to encounter a talking corpse and an entrance to a *sidh* barrow, when the door to the hall opened and a man entered.

Most of the hundred or so revelers present were eating or laughing or fondling a maid or congratulating Fergus on how well he'd told the tale, and so the newcomer's arrival went largely unremarked. There was nothing extraordinary about him—he was neither young nor old, comely nor ugly, tall nor short...

But Sathariel froze in disbelief when she saw him. Or, more precisely, when she saw the flaming aura that surrounded him.

Naoise, already drunk and slurring slightly, saw her expression. "Love, what...?" He tried to peer where she was looking, and squinted as he saw the man approaching.

Sathariel abruptly stood with such force that her heavy chair fell back with a loud *thud*. She picked up a carving knife and shouted at the stranger, "How dare you come here?"

Those near her went quiet and turned to look at the man; the silence spread quickly through the entire assemblage, the last few laughs and clatters of eating utensils dying away.

The stranger saw her, stopped thirty feet away, and grinned. "Sathariel! What an unexpected surprise."

"I doubt that," she answered.

Naoise rose slowly, drink and his bad leg making him weave. "You know this man?"

"He's not a man. He's..." she broke off, thinking about the best way to phrase this, "...*sidh*."

A collective gasp went up.

The newcomer laughed, great gales of howling merriment... and as he laughed, he *changed*. The human mask fell away, revealing a goat-horned, hairy-legged demon. There were screams, dropped goblets, warriors who rose and drew swords, but didn't advance.

The Coriondi king, Conchobar, brandished his own blade and called out, "Speak, *sidh*. Why are you here?"

The Devil ceased his laughter and turned his slit pupils on the king. "I come to do you a favor, King Conchobar: I have a message from the Morrigan and Dagda."

Sathariel nearly blurted out a comment—the Morrigan and Dagda were the rulers of the Celts' pantheon of gods, and if they did exist, she knew that Satan would neither have had contact with them nor served as their errand boy—but she held her tongue and waited with all the rest.

"Speak," said Conchobar.

"The next year will see disasters heaped upon this place—drought will follow flood, plague will be born from fire, famine and failure will be the law of the land. One year from now, your Samhain feast will be a pitiful affair—many of you will have already perished, others will have fled, seeking survival elsewhere. Those who remain will forego the feast in favor of rationing the small amount of food left, and even then they may not survive the winter."

Conchobar asked, "Why do you tell us this?"

"To let you know why it shall come to pass: Because you have failed to pay proper Samhain tribute to the gods."

More cries arose. The leader of the Coriondi Druids, Cathbad, rose and addressed the Devil angrily. "How is it possible we have not appeased the gods? We have offered them only an hour ago a black sheep, grain and mead…"

The Devil's face twisted contemptuously. "You call that an offering? Perhaps something fit for a *Roman* god…"

"Then what do you suggest?" asked Conchobar.

"The gods will be generous with you if you are generous with them. If you would prevent the devastation I've described, then you must make them a gift of the finest thing you have to offer: The life of one of your own."

Before any of the others could react, Sathariel strode forward in fury. "Lies! This creature has no office with the gods! This is nothing but a malicious trick."

The Devil directed his answer to everyone but Sathariel. "How can you speak for this tribe, when you're not even a true Coriondi?"

Naoise thundered around the table to join Sathariel. "She is my *wife*, and as fine a woman as any in this room—"

Cathbad asked Sathariel, "How do you know the *sidh* speaks falsely? Have you been acquainted with him before?"

"I have—"

She broke off as she heard the expressions of dismay and surprise from many of the onlookers. Naoise asked her, in a low voice, "How do you know him?"

"I've fought him before. This is what he does: He appears on Samhain and tries to trick the unwary."

The King turned to Cathbad. "Druid, did you read signs in the remains of the black sheep you sacrificed?"

"Aye, lordship. The entrails were clean and clear. They augured good fortune for the next twelvemonth."

The onlookers turned expectantly to their guest, who asked, "Druid, tell me: what omens did you see in the year *before*?"

The Druid's mouth moved, but no answer was forthcoming. Somewhere from inside the hall, an elderly woman's voice called out, "He told us terrible storms, but we had a calm year."

A younger voice added, "Aye, and the year earlier Cathbad claimed peace, but we ended up fighting off the Brigantes."

All eyes turned to Cathbad, who went pale beneath his white cowl. "The gods can be as mischievous as the *sidh*..." he said, his voice trailing off.

The Devil stepped forward, pressing his advantage. "I can offer you information that neither man nor *sidh* would know, that only the gods themselves could provide." He turned to a young man sitting nearby. "You, Conor—shall we talk about how often you've cried over the death of your brother at the hands of the Brigantes?"

The young man, Conor, gaped in amazement; his expression was more than enough to confirm the truth of the *sidh*'s words.

The visitor gestured next at a middle-aged man, his arms scarred, one eye missing. "Sencha, should I tell everyone here what really happened to your father's serving girl, the late Findabair?"

Sencha snarled and rose halfway out of his seat, but hesitated when the *sidh* didn't continue.

Sathariel saw the way this was going, and knew the Devil would win. Soon they'd be cutting the Samhain cake into small pieces, one of which would be marked by charcoal; whoever drew the blackened square from a leather bag would forthwith be marched down to the local bog, where their neck would be slit, a noose tightened around the neck, and finally they'd be drowned in the thick water. The Celts' gods liked things done in threes.

During her time with the Coriondi, she'd come to love them. They could be savage, but also kind; stingy with outsiders, but generous to kin. They worked hard but found joy in small tasks. Even Cathbad, for all his failures as a prognosticator, was a thoughtful judge when disputes arose, and she'd passed many hours in conversation with the Druid.

She knew sacrifice was a part of their beliefs, and she'd always honored that…but to sacrifice for no reason but to appease a Devil they couldn't possibly even recognize…she couldn't let it happen.

She walked to Cathbad and Conchobar, said, "I offer myself for sacrifice."

Those who heard her stopped and stared. Cathbad looked at her closely. "You do understand we will complete the offering tonight, since it will have the most impact on Samhain…"

"Yes. I would be honored."

She glanced at the Devil, who glowered at her; he alone knew who (and what) she was, and he was undoubtedly already trying to think of arguments to be made against her.

But Naoise saved him the trouble, rushing forward and putting himself between Sathariel and Cathbad. "No! She's not one of us; the sacrifice will have more meaning if the chosen is a born Coriondi."

Conchobar asked, "Do you offer yourself in her place, Naoise?"

"Yes," he answered, with no hesitation.

Despair, grief, disbelief crashed down on Sathariel in a black wave. She turned to Naoise, pleading, "No! You don't have to—let me…" She broke off, realizing what a mistake she'd made during their life together. She should have told him, confessed her immortality; he would have accepted it. Instead, she'd foolishly thought that she was somehow sparing him of something. Now he was losing his life to that failure on her part, and she couldn't tell him here, now, with everyone watching.

He took her face in his hands, looking into her eyes. "Never, love. I can't fight for my king anymore, but I can still do this. My only regret will be leaving you."

Cathbad spoke to him quietly. "Are you sure, Naoise? We can draw lots…"

The Devil strode forward, urgently. "The decision's been made."

Naoise ignored the outsider as he addressed Cathbad. "Let's just do it quickly before I change my mind."

Fifteen minutes later, they stood at the edge of the bog, with those from the celebration ringed around them in the night, carrying flickering torches that cast an orange glow on the scene. Naoise knelt by the edge of the bog as Cathbad stood beside him, reciting an invocation from memory; two other Druids waited behind Naoise, one holding the end of a noose that was around his neck, the other bearing a ritual knife.

Sathariel was nearby, wrestling with her thoughts. The last thing Naoise had said to her, as they'd walked with the group out to the bog, had been, "Love, promise me that you won't try to stop this. Let me do this with dignity. Let me die as a warrior, not as one who allows others to carry his burden."

She'd been unable to answer with words, and so had simply nodded.

Now she watched as Cathbad completed the recitation and turned to the other Druids. The man with the noose tightened it; the man with the blade pressed it against Naoise's neck. She looked away—and saw the Devil grinning at her.

In that instant she lost all reason. As Cathbad pushed Naoise's head down into the bog, blood from his slit throat mixing with the filthy water, Sathariel rushed forward. Conchobar saw the movement and reached for her as she pushed past him. "No, he's gone—!"

She didn't heed. Naoise's body tumbled into the bog, and she dove in after.

There was no sight below the surface, but she found his sinking corpse and clung to it, going down with it. She had no need for oxygen, her lungs didn't struggle, her brain didn't send out panic signals. Instead, she found a dull comfort there in the silt beneath the thick liquid, wrapped in the arms of her dead beloved.

She stayed with him for a long time. It was easier to simply be there, with Naoise, a part of the earth and water. But at some point she became aware that the arms she grasped were thin and withered, mummified, and she no longer wanted to stay. By the time she emerged, on another Samhain night (badly frightening a farm boy who was late coming in from the fields, and who would spend the rest of his life talking about the bog demon he'd seen on Hallows' Eve), the Celts were gone and a new religion had arrived in the land now called Eire. It was her religion, but its arrival on these shores left her strangely unmoved.

In time she thought she might come back to life, perhaps even love again…but she knew she would never forget the Devil's grin just before she'd followed Naoise into the bog.

CHAPTER 12
West Hollywood, Halloween, 2014

The day started with Eddie, only half-awake, pulling Sathariel closer beneath the sheets and slurring the words into her ear.

"I love you."

She'd almost dreaded hearing them. She thought of Naoise, who she'd loved; she thought of all the others, who she'd merely enjoyed, believing they were safer that way.

She still wasn't sure how she felt about Eddie; she thought in time she could love him, easily and deeply, but that thought frightened her, especially given that he might not survive tonight.

Last night, Sathariel had called on Magdalena again, this time using only a phone, after Eddie had fallen asleep. She'd told Magdalena everything Azazel had said, and asked what he might have given Satan that would accomplish opening a gateway to Hell. Two hours later, Magdalena had called back with an answer: The Order's magicians had all agreed that it was likely an incantation, to be spoken aloud from a scroll.

"How do I stop it?" Sathariel asked.

The answer was not good: As soon as the portal opened, the scroll would have to be destroyed…*from the far side of the gateway*. The gateway would close immediately.

Meaning, she'd have to step through into Hell, and then choose to remain there.

After that call, she'd returned to the bed to take whatever comfort she could from Eddie's nearness, the tranquility of his sleeping form. She saw how it would end: With her trapped in Hell, an eternal plaything of the Great Enemy, who would no doubt delight in devising an eternity's worth of fresh new torments for her. Perhaps in time she might find a means of escape...which would likeliest be a descent into madness.

What would happen to Eddie? Would Satan's hand-crafted serial killer hunt him for the rest of his days, perhaps similarly capturing him and submitting him to unthinkable tortures? At least Eddie would have the eventual solace of death, with something kinder waiting for him just beyond.

And what about tonight? Azazel's hint about the location of the gateway—*"right in the center of everything"*—suggested the heart of West Hollywood, which the map Eddie googled showed as the intersection of Santa Monica and San Vicente Boulevards...but what if that wasn't right? What if the location was even just a block off, and thousands of demons had poured through the gateway before they reached it? Even though they couldn't touch living humans, the fear they could create in a crowd of half-a-million densely packed into just a few blocks...she could only imagine a body count in the hundreds, maybe thousands, as terrified revelers stampeded over each other and fought to escape. No, they'd have to hope they'd guessed right on the location, and would be able to reach the gateway before the demons poured out en masse.

The last variable was Satan himself. He'd be there, of course, no doubt trying to block her from reaching the gateway. He might even succeed.

She considered asking for help. But from whom? She didn't trust the Order, Azazel was out of the question, and he was the only other Angel she'd seen in centuries. Eddie was the only choice left, and she wasn't sure what was worse—keeping him beside her near a gateway to Hell, or telling him to hide himself away where she couldn't protect him.

These thoughts were tumbling through her head when Eddie awakened in the soft morning light of the last day of October and said, "I love you."

She let him nuzzle against her for a few moments, savoring the last tenderness she might ever experience, before saying, "Eddie, we need to talk about tonight."

He pulled back and peered at her with mock ferocity. "Don't even think about telling me not to come, okay? Because if the Apocalypse is gonna happen, I want to be with you."

"You're getting to know me a little too well," she said, half-smiling.

"Is that 'know' in the Biblical sense?" Eddie said, reaching down to her thigh.

She plucked his hand away. "Seriously for a change: I think I'm going to need your help tonight."

"You know I'm there for you. Want me to beat up the Devil? I'll do it..."

"No, you leave that to me. But I may need you to keep a clear space, give me some room to work."

"I can do that. But you gotta do something for me first..."

This time she didn't push his hand away.

CHAPTER 13
Los Angeles, Halloween Night, 2014

They'd spent the day doing whatever planning they could. Now it was 11:45 p.m., and they were surrounded by 500,000 people.

Costumed celebrants pushed along shoulder-to-shoulder with gawkers holding up cameras. There were evil clowns, astronauts, nuns with sex toys, cartoon princesses with broad shoulders and deep voices, cowboys and construction workers, beautiful scantily-clad young people of various genders, and slasher movie villains. Come to merely observe were frat boys and middle-aged executives, East L.A. families and Bel Air millionaires, urbanites and suburbanites, academics and those who seemed merely baffled.

Sathariel hadn't seen the Devil yet...or least not the *real* Devil, having seen dozens of costumed imitators. They'd walked the boulevards until 11:30, and Sathariel experienced a small pang of envy over the humans who were just here to experience the joy of the festival. It wasn't the first time—she liked autumn and masquerades and pumpkins with flickering candles. She often wished she could enjoy the time of year without planning for the annual hunt and fight.

At 11:30 they'd planted themselves near the intersection of Santa Monica and San Vicente. During the next 15 minutes, Eddie had been propositioned three times, and Sathariel had received one drunken compliment on her costume, which consisted of her normal clothes with Azazel's demon-killing sword in its bejeweled scabbard thrust through her belt. "I don't know exactly what you're supposed to be, sweetheart," a gladiator who reeked of beer had told her, "but I love it!"

As they waited, Eddie leaned closer, so he could be heard over the constant thrum of music and voices and footsteps, and said, "Y'know, I've been thinking about how we were talking about why you have to do this alone, how we were wondering…you know, where The Big Guy is in all this…"

She looked at him, genuinely curious. "Yes…"

"…Well, I was thinking…maybe He knows exactly what He's doing. Maybe you're like his agent, or proxy. He knows He can count on you, so He just leaves you alone to do your thing."

Sathariel thought it over. "Maybe. But if that's the case…one sign would be nice. Just one."

"The world is still here, and there are still good people in it. Maybe that's your sign."

She was about to respond when a box was dropped at her feet. A shoe box, with her name scrawled on the top in black felt pen. She looked up to see who had placed it, but they were ringed by the crowd on all sides, hundreds all moving in different directions.

"Did you see who dropped it?" she asked Eddie.

He shook his head, scanning the crowd before returning his focus to the box.

She bent and picked it up. It was heavy. Whatever it held, it wasn't shoes.

Steeling herself, she lifted the lid.

The first thing she saw was a note. It was scrawled on a piece of lined notebook paper; the writing was jagged and wild. It took her a few seconds to decipher the message:

Hi Sathariel!
Guess what? This is a bomb. It's going to go off exactly two minutes from when you opened the box.
Happy Halloween!

Beneath the note was a crude pipe bomb, made from three eight-inch lengths of steel pipe duct taped together and capped on both ends.

"What is it?" Eddie asked.

"A bomb." Sathariel didn't know much about bombs, but she guessed this might be pretty powerful, maybe even enough to blow through a heavy trash bin or a sewer tunnel. She had no idea how to disarm it or what to do with it.

So she held it and ran.

Her first instinct was to get it as far away from the crowd as possible. She headed south on the first side street she saw, ignoring the curses and cries her flight engendered as she drove through the crowd. She stumbled and staggered, but the sea of revelers thinned out below the main thoroughfare. She leapt over blockades and dodged parked cars, running. How long had it been now? A minute? Ninety seconds?

She'd reached a residential area, and it was as quiet as any place she was likely to find around here, on this night. There were costumed people even here, but they were spread out.

There was still nowhere to put a bomb.

She finally did the only thing left to her: Threw herself onto the asphalt, on top of the bomb. Her body might shield the blast somewhat; of course, if she happened to be right over a water main or gas pipe…

She waited, tensing for the explosion, for white-hot agony…

It didn't come. It must have been two minutes by now. She began to count.

When she reached thirty, she suspected she'd been tricked.

She sat up and pried at one of the heavy caps on the ends of the pipes. It came off, and strips of orange paper spilled out. She made out the words "*Trick or Treat!*" printed on the slips. And then it hit her:

Eddie.

Sathariel leapt to her feet and ran.

CHAPTER 14

Eddie had just lost sight of Sathariel in the mob as she'd fled with the bomb when he felt something round and hard pressed up against the back of his skull.

"That's a gun," said a muffled male voice. "Don't move."

Eddie froze, waiting. Something nudged up against his fingers. "Put that over your head."

He glanced down and saw a large pull-over rubber mask; it portrayed a horned, cartoonish figure with red skin. "The Devil.

Figures." said Eddie.

The gun barrel thumped the back of his head, hard enough to hurt his neck. "Shut up and put it on."

Eddie did. The inside smelled like cheap chemicals. The eye holes gave him only a narrow field of vision, sound was muffled as well.

"Now put your hands behind your back, wrists together."

Eddie did, and he felt duct tape being wound around his wrists. He thought, *Surely somebody will notice.* But then: *Who am I kidding? This is Halloween in West Hollywood. Nobody's going to pay any attention, even if I scream for help.*

"Now," came the voice again, as a hand grabbed his arm roughly and hauled him around, "you're gonna walk in front of me. I'm gonna tell you where to go."

Martin Boyer—that's who this has to be. Sathariel will come back, find me gone, and go looking for me. She'll miss midnight. Eddie stumbled, and was cruelly shoved from behind, although his captor caught him just before he fell. "Just keep walking, Eddie."

He knows my name. It is him.

Eddie began to race through considerations, scenarios, possibilities. Even through the mask he could hear Boyer huffing, so Eddie could probably take him in a fight...but could he take the gun? With a mask over his head and his hands behind his back?

What if he just stopped, refused to go any farther—would Boyer shoot him right there?

Yes, he would.

But he knew that Boyer intended to shoot him anyway. He probably just preferred to do it somewhere else, in a quieter place where he could enjoy it. Or maybe he planned on keeping Eddie alive for a while, like a cat toying with a mouse.

Through the eye holes, he saw they were now away from the festivities and heading toward a large parking structure. If he got into Boyer's car, he knew it would be a one-way trip. He'd have to make his move soon.

He heard keys jingling behind him. The keys clattered to the concrete—Boyer'd dropped them. He was probably nervous. He was bending to pick them up.

This had to be it.

Eddie suddenly threw himself backwards. His legs collided with Boyer, who was crouching to retrieve his keys, and Eddie went down. Before Boyer could react, Eddie pulled both legs back and drove them forward; he was rewarded with the sound of Boyer crying out as he was knocked sideways. Eddie rolled to his knees, clumsy without the use of his hands, and struggled to find Boyer through the mask's eye holes. He caught a glimpse of a man wearing a Batman mask swinging the gun up and he dove to his right. The gun went off, deafening at close range, and Eddie heard it ricochet off asphalt. He lashed out again with his legs, and the gun clattered to the ground several feet away. He saw Boyer scrabbling after it, and he forced himself to his feet, ran, and literally fell on his hunter just as Boyer had reached the gun. Eddie felt something crack beneath him, and Boyer screamed. Boyer reared up and threw Eddie to the side as he rolled onto his back. That was a mistake, as Eddie rebounded, this time using his masked head to butt Boyer's into the hard concrete. The blow left Boyer dazed and Eddie rose, then drew back a foot and kicked Boyer in the head, making sure he was out. The kick tore Boyer's mask away, and Eddie was looking at a pathetic, chubby, middle-aged man who was prematurely bald. "Fuckwad," he said, as he kicked the gun as far away as he could, then ran from the parking lot.

The mask, his taped hands, the fight, had all taxed Eddie's stamina, and he was staggering by the time he reached Santa Monica Boulevard again. He pushed through the onlookers, frantically searching for Sathariel, calling her name even though he knew he was virtually silenced by the mask.

Then he saw it, even through the mask and the crowd: A deep amber glow, coming up through the street, backlighting the shapes in front of him. People were stopped and staring at something, and Eddie drove himself through them, shouldering them out of the way until he could see:

A hole was opening in the street, fiery light pouring out of it. It was the size of a manhole covering, but expanding slowly. The mob had formed around it, looking down, trying to figure out what kind of special effects were being used.

A shiver raced up Eddie's spine when he saw the first clawed hand reach up from below and try to grasp the widening edge of the hole.

He saw a tumult in the audience on the other side of the ring, and then Sathariel pushed through. He ran forward, screaming her name. She heard him, frowned when she saw a man in a devil mask running for her.

"It's me, Eddie, get the mask off!"

She tore the rubber disguise away, then embraced him. He pulled away and spun so she could see his bound wrists. "Martin Boyer tried to kidnap me, but I knocked him out—"

She drew the sword, used it to cut the tape. Eddie tore the shreds away from his skin, then gestured at the hole, now six feet in diameter. They could see leering faces now—awful, yellow-eyed, fanged heads far worse than any Halloween mask—starting to pull themselves up. Eddie stepped in front of her, made her look at him.

"It's time. You fight, I'll keep the rubberneckers away." He kissed her, gently, and said, "You're the only one who can do this. I'll be here when you're done."

CHAPTER 15

Sathariel had never done anything harder in her life than turn away from Eddie then.

She *did* love him. She'd known it as soon as she'd seen him under the ludicrous mask, his clear, sweet aura a beacon in the crowd. Facing an eternity of torment was bad enough; facing it without Eddie was unimaginably worse.

But he was right—she was the only one who could do this.

She grasped the sword tightly, knelt by the edge of the hole, and looked down.

Dozens of demons were climbing up. The way was a steep incline, and they moved slowly, crawling along the rocky slope, holding on by digging their knife-like talons into the wall. They saw her and cried out in delight. They ran forked, glistening tongues over scabbed lips, their slit pupils fixed on her. The hole had stopped growing, and the first two were halfway up and onto the street. She rose, kicked them away, watched with satisfaction as they tumbled back down, taking others with them. Behind her, she heard Eddie shouting, "Everybody, get back—I think a gas main's going! Clear the area!" She heard shrieks, gasps, feet pounding.

She returned her attention to the tunnel, looking down. She

thought she saw where it evened out maybe thirty feet below. That would likely be where she'd find the scroll.

If she could make it that far.

A voice whispered into her ear, "Go on, *jump*."

Startled, she looked back and saw the Devil behind her. He hadn't bothered to affect another form tonight, but stood there in all his natural, saturnine glory. His breath reeked of rot and sulfur, and she flinched away from it.

"I've got so many special evenings planned for just the two of us," he said, running a claw along one of her arms until she pulled it away. "Of course, most of them involve dismembering you, as slowly and painfully as possible…"

Three more demons reached the edge. Whatever she was going to do, she'd have to do it soon.

"They're coming," said the Devil, not hiding the glee in his voice. "Oh, I did so enjoy reading out that invocation down there. This will be a Halloween to remember—"

Sathariel jumped.

CHAPTER 16
Hell, Halloween Night, 2014

She let herself slide down the rough incline, holding the sword as far overhead as possible, feeling her feet removing monsters. When she reached the bottom, her fall was stopped not by rock floor, but by writhing, clawing, snapping demons. She'd landed in a sea of those she'd knocked down, and they were anxious to taste an Angel.

The sword swung in an arc, and Sathariel was astonished by its power—it cleaved through three of the demons as if they were no more than vapor. She whirled the sword, moving with all the speed she could muster. She soon had cleared a circle immediately around her, and was relieved to see that Hell's servants weren't as invulnerable as Heaven's: Severed demon heads and limbs were piled against the walls, not rejoining their bodies to attack again. She strode over the carnage, cutting down more that rushed up to greet her.

She was in a short tunnel that led to a larger chamber. She battled her way there, her skin stinging where a tooth or claw had pierced her before Azazel's blade dispatched the attacker.

She reached the mouth of the tunnel and took in the cavern beyond, glancing around rushing demons. It was a large, roughly round room with openings periodically puncturing the walls, which glowed with their own firelight. In the center of the room was a pillar of brimstone. The scroll was on top of it.

She only had to fight through a never-ending horde of demons constantly pouring in from all the openings to reach the scroll.

It was impossible. But she had to do it.

Sathariel shouted, an incoherent burst of fury and resolve, and leapt forward. They enclosed her instantly. The sword flashed, clearing one step forward, but they were behind her, pulling at her, tearing clothing and flesh; the wounds healed, but not before the pain had nearly, briefly, blinded her. She pushed onward—the scroll was only eight feet from her now…six feet…five feet…

But there were too many. They were pulling her down, each rending of skin or scalp more excruciating. As she fought the ones on the right, the ones on the left chewed through her left arm and cast it aside. It vanished in midair and reformed at her shoulder, but it was increasingly hard for her to focus on the goal.

Four feet…three…two…

The demons made a concerted push to reach the sword; Sathariel knew she would be lost without it, and so she struggled to concentrate, to dredge up that last ounce of reserved strength.

One foot remaining…

It was enough. She reached out and snatched the scroll. In one smooth motion, she tore it in half.

She was nearly deafened by the defeated shrieks of a million tormentors.

They fell on her then, and she let them. She'd won. She was done fighting.

As they dragged her down, she lost herself in endless, black pain.

CHAPTER 17
Los Angeles, November 1st, 2014

"Sathariel…can you hear me? Hey, don't scare me, c'mon…"

She opened her eyes and saw not snarling, hungry demons but Eddie bending over her. Above him, she saw the smoggy, reddish night sky of Los Angeles; she heard not inhuman screams, but laughter and music.

"What…?"

Eddie gasped out an excited, relieved cry and cradled her face in his hands. "I thought you were…well, even though you said you couldn't…"

She sat up, not understanding, not remembering.

Eddie saw her confusion and tried to help. "One minute that gateway thing was here, and the demons were crawling up, and I convinced everyone they were all just actors from a new haunted house called Hell on Earth, and then they were gone and so was the hole, and you were here instead. I guess that means you did it, huh?"

"I guess it—"

She broke off as she caught a glance of a familiar face in the surrounding mob—was that Azazel, hefting the sword he'd just taken back? But then he'd been swallowed by the swirling crowd, and she couldn't be sure it'd been him at all.

She stood, Eddie helping her, and looked around. It was a normal Halloween—or at least as normal as 500,000 happy, drunken, costumed humans could be, and Sathariel abruptly wanted nothing so much as to be one of them.

"So," Eddie said, "maybe my theory was right, and Somebody is looking out for you after all…"

"Maybe. Or maybe Azazel changed his mind and decided to help an old friend."

"Huh? Azazel…?" Eddie looked around, as if expecting the Angel to be standing with them.

Sathariel pulled his head around, kissed him, and linked her arm around his. "I feel like drinking. How about you?"

He smiled, and Sathariel thought it was the most beautiful expression she'd ever seen on a human face.

"If you want to drink, girlfriend, I'm buying."

Arm in arm, they joined the best Halloween party imaginable.

THE LEGEND OF HALLOWEEN JACK

Jack pushed through the costumed thrill-seekers, clutching his prize tightly. It was Halloween and the French Quarter was packed tighter than a fisherman's net drawn up from a feeding frenzy. Costumed revelers drank and shouted and danced. Wild abandon scented the air like musk, creating a nearly-solid wall of human flesh, fabric, feathers, and jewelry.

Jack, by contrast, was dressed in a simple suit with a gambler's hat, and he was anything but merry. His red-rimmed eyes darted side to side, backward glances made him collide with gyrating dancers. There, a peacock; here, a man dressed as a female rock star; next, a giant rabbit complete with whiskers that flashed on and off, green and purple.

He was lost. He'd gotten turned around by the crowds, even though he'd walked these New Orleans streets a hundred times, a thousand times. He tried to peer above the bouncing heads surrounding him, hoping to spot a landmark, *anything* that might help him orient himself, but everything looked the same—three-story structures with elegant wrought-iron or wooden balcony railings draped with garlands and lit from behind by glowing pumpkins.

Planting his feet, Jack stopped in the middle of the mob,

forcing it to part and flow around him. He was buffeted on all sides, and he had to draw his burden up to his body and cradle it there tightly, for fear that it would be plucked or knocked from his grasp and lost forever. It was all he had now. He couldn't afford to lose it, not here, where it would either become part of the crowd or be trampled beneath its unrelenting motion, ground to nothingness by the buoyant but careless hordes.

He reversed his position and felt panic freeze him:

Behind him stood a devil. It was at least seven feet tall, with red skin, white horns, and black satin cape. But then Jack realized this devil was bouncing, and that the oversized head was a mask perched atop its wearer's shoulders. The devil danced past him, as uncaring as all the rest, and Jack's tension eased slightly.

Not yet. He hasn't found me yet.

There might still be a chance, then. A chance for escape. If he could just free himself from this madness, find his way to a long, empty street where he could run, run…

He staggered forward again, letting the bodies propel him along, but he saw no exit, no path out. His energy was waning, vision spinning. He needed time to stop, think, collect himself—

He staggered through an open doorway and found himself in a famous bar; the bar was slightly less crowded than the street, and Jack pushed his way through the front of the bar to the open courtyard, where there were actually a few open chairs. He reached one and shrank against it, trying to make himself as inconspicuous as possible.

If he was found here, he'd be trapped.

But, he reasoned, he was just as likely to be trapped out on the street, with the mad Halloween celebrants. Here, at least, he could sit undisturbed for a few minutes, maybe longer. He could sit and think. Maybe if he thought back, remembered why he was here—on the run, with his prize, fleeing through the orgiastic insanity of a New Orleans Halloween—maybe then he'd find something he'd missed. Something he could use to help him escape.

Something to trick the Devil one last time.

ooooo

Hell had first sought Jack when he'd been sprawled in an alley near a notorious Baton Rouge bar. Jack had slumped in the filth, his last empty bottle of cheap whiskey rolled a few inches from his fingers, and he'd known he was dying. He was only 32, but his liver had endured several lifetimes' worth of hard, cheap liquor, and was now poisoning him in return.

Jack had only two possessions (aside from the empty bottle) to his name: A small amount of money he hadn't yet drunk up, and the Holy Bible that he'd once read to his parish from. It was a large volume, with stiff leather covers and a crucifix emblazoned in gold on the cover, and it had been difficult to carry, but somehow Jack had kept it on his long ride down.

He'd started life as the son of a thief and a whore, who'd kicked him out at 13. He'd fought a hard-scrabble existence on the back streets of Atlanta, where he'd learned how to pick pockets, fence stolen goods, pull off a convincing shell game, and—once he'd put on a few pounds and years—seduce lonely spinsters with money. At 21, he'd had the bad luck of dallying with a lady who turned out to be nearly as dishonest as he was, a fact he didn't discover until her husband appeared in the bedroom doorway. Jack had collected some buckshot in his sprinting ass, and had fled Atlanta for Louisville, where he'd been caught a year later writing bad checks and had done three years in prison. At 25, he'd found his way to a small town near Baton Rouge, where he'd been mistaken for the new preacher they were expecting any day; he'd taken the identity mistake as a gift from God and had settled in as the town's new religious authority. When the real preacher had arrived, Jack had intercepted him, dropped a sedative into his apple cider, and allowed the man of God to awaken in the local bordello, with three prostitutes draped across him. Jack had promised to remain mum on the incident, and the real preacher had left town quietly.

Jack took to preaching like a duck to orange sauce. Turned out he had a natural flair for it, and he enjoyed making flamboyant gestures and shouts that left folks quivering in fear and admiration. He didn't have much religious schooling, but found a bible in his new church and tutored himself quickly.

The vices were harder to disguise.

He married—a fine young lady of 18 named Annabel—and they soon had two young sons, but Jack was starting to grow bored. He was 30 now, and had no desire to spend the rest of his life wearing the moral straitjacket of a good Christian. He started paying secret visits to the town's prostitutes—all under the guise of redeeming their souls, of course—but his visits to the bars weren't so clandestine. He beat Annabel and the boys, and his sermons began to grow increasingly disordered, as did his appearance. As his followers faded away, his façade crumbled, until finally one day, consumed by outrage and alcohol, he hit Annabel a little too hard. It took his befogged mind several moments to realize that she was dead, her blood splattered across his hands and face, and that he would surely pay with his own life when the crime was discovered.

That night he fled. He made no arrangements for his sons other than keeping them out of the bedroom, where their mother lay dead. He took everything of value that he could carry in one case, and left around midnight. Since the nearest city was Baton Rouge, he went there, sought out the section of town so crime-ridden and impoverished that the law avoided it, and settled in to lose himself.

His plan worked...in more ways than one. He was never found, but he gave himself over completely to the pleasures of drink. His health began to diminish, and his money vanished (occasionally replaced by a small gambling win). When his skin started to turn yellow, he knew his liver was failing, and he was almost glad.

It was October 31st when he found himself alone in the alley, his body growing cold around him, his memories trailing off like smoke. He still felt the bulk of the old Bible under his jacket, and it puzzled him.

Out of everything I could have saved...why this thing?

He was almost sorry he wouldn't live to see tomorrow—All Saints Day was a major holiday here in Louisiana. He wished he could have gone to New Orleans, where they made a festival of the day; he'd heard about how families gathered and visited graveyards where loved ones rested so they could clean and decorate the distinctive local tombs that stood above ground, keeping their residents from rotting in the damp soil. He imagined them all afterward, gathering to toast the memories of their ancestors and dancing into the night. It made him melancholy to think that no one would tend to the pauper's grave where he'd be laid to rest soon enough.

Jack had barely finished this thought when he saw a black hole open before him, large enough for a man to pass through—but what came through could barely be called a "man." It was man-sized and man-shaped, but was bent nearly double, as if it had shouldered decades of burdens; its hands almost touched the ground before it.

And it was covered in blood. So much blood that it instantly created a pool where it stood. Jack stepped back from the pool, and was surprised to find he was standing and no longer felt the pain of dying.

He could distinguish little of the thing's features beneath the blood, but it seemed to have a pig-like face, with yellow eyes and a long mouth of jagged teeth.

"It's time, Jack," it said, in a wet snarl.

Somehow Jack knew then who and what this creature was, but he decided immediately he wouldn't make it easy for the son-of-a-bitch. "Time for what?"

"We've waited too long for you. Step through."

It gestured at the darkness, and now Jack saw glimmers within: Fleeting faces extended in mute agony, forms tortured out of proportion. He felt a chill arc through him, and decided then and there he wouldn't share the fate of those pitiable specters.

"So this is a gateway to Hell?"

The demon's laugh sounded like glass crunching a heavy boot. "To be precise, this is *your* gateway to Hell. Each of you are born with your own entrance. Some of you manage to avoid using it. But you, Jack…is there any sin you *didn't* commit?"

"I did my best."

"Indeed you did." The demon gestured at the black portal, its impatience growing. "Let's get this over with."

Jack returned the gesture. "You first."

Smoke erupted from the demon's snout-like nose. "I can make your torment even worse."

"I doubt that. I think you're afraid I won't follow you through."

The yellow eyes widened in outrage. "'Afraid'? Do you think I'd need to be afraid of the likes of *you*?"

Jack shrugged. "You're not so impressive, you know. I'm not the one standing here bleeding, after all."

The demon shook its crimson-covered arms, and Jack flinched as droplets struck his eyes. "You fool! This isn't *my* blood—it's the blood of those I've been tormenting for centuries. And you're about to join them."

Jack tried to keep his tone even; he knew what he had to do, but wasn't sure if it would work. Was he a ghost now, something incorporeal? Could he still touch, still hold? He reached down toward the empty liquor bottle, and was relieved to find that he could retrieve it. "You sure I'm dead? I can pick up this bottle, after all…"

"Oh, I assure you, you're quite dead. You exist in a twilight state until you cross over."

Jack upended the bottle above his open mouth, but nothing came out. "Damn, here I was hoping for one last drink—"

The demon bellowed, flames erupting from between the shards of its teeth, and then…

It turned and stepped through the portal.

It was just reaching back to snatch Jack, but he was faster—he reached beneath his jacket, pulled out the Holy Bible, and tossed it down in the center of the threshold, the gilt crucifix on its cover forming a sanctified barrier. The demon stared at the book for a second, then looked up at Jack. "You don't think that will stop me, do you?"

"I figured it might."

The demon froze, and Jack knew he'd won.

"Pick it up NOW."

Jack just grinned. "Not a prayer in Hell."

"This won't be so amusing when Satan comes for you Himself."

"Maybe, but…if you go to the Boss Man, you're going to have to tell him you failed to bring me in yourself, and I'll bet that won't go well for you."

The demon sagged in realization.

Jack seized on the moment. "But I'm thinking we can strike a compromise: You give me another year, and then you can come and get me."

"Another year?"

Nodding, Jack said, "One more year. That's it. All I want."

The demon considered, then said, "One more year, then. Now pick that thing up."

"I've got your word?"

"Yes, yes."

Jack retrieved the Bible, halfway expecting to be dragged through the void anyway—

And instead he found his eyes opening, his body aching as he came to in the filthy alleyway.

For an instant he wondered if it had all been a dream, but then he saw what he still clutched in one hand: the Bible.

He sat up and stared at the book, astonished and grateful. It had saved his life. Given him a second chance.

He could still beat the Devil.

ooooo

After an hour or so, the bar where Jack had found temporary shelter was crowded, and he jumped from his table when he thought he saw a flash of horns somewhere in the crowd. He headed out a different exit from the one he'd entered through, but the Halloween mob was—if possible—even denser out here.

It was nearing midnight, and with each passing minute the mass anticipation rose. Jack was jostled and pushed, elbowed and spun, as he fought to protect his precious burden. He pushed through the revelers for several blocks until he finally sensed it thinning out slightly.

Suddenly he broke free, and looking around he saw why: He was in the Saint Louis Cemetery, one square block of tombs and vaults incongruously penned in on all sides by regular buildings.

There were a few stragglers like him seeking refuge from the madness in the cemetery, but they clustered around particular graves, lighting candles, speaking softly.

Exhausted, Jack collapsed onto a tomb. He didn't know how much farther or longer he could run tonight. If he was found here, now...

Thinking that, he lowered himself down to the ground and sat there, using the tomb as protection. He realized he was hiding in a necropolis—a miniature city of the dead— and found irony in that thought, considering where he'd come from...and what he was running from...

ooooo

After Jack had escaped from Hell's clutches, he'd made plans:

He'd repent his evil ways. He'd devote himself to God, no sham preacher this time but a true believer, a veritable saint.

His road was paved with good intentions. And the first stop on the road was a bar, to celebrate his good fortune.

When he woke up two days later, hungover, in a prostitute's stained bed, he'd remembered his vow: To give his life over to God, to earn Heaven instead of Hell. But he still had 363 days. Plenty of time.

A month later, he killed another gambler when the man accused him of cheating. That the man had been right didn't matter; Jack carried a small knife in his pocket, and it had found its way into his accuser's chest.

So he fled to New Orleans, where he arrived once again determined to commit himself to the Lord. But this new city turned out to be a treasure trove of sin: Bars, bordellos, casinos…it was almost as if they could be found on every block. And they weren't like the ones in all those smaller places—the liquor was better, the women more beautiful, the stakes higher.

Jack had some talent as a gambler (he was a gifted cheat, in other words), and he began to make money. And with money at his disposal, in this city of better and more beautiful things, he pushed his plan to find religion aside. He still had months.

Six months…four…two…one month…two weeks…three days…

On October 31st, Jack was wrapping up a three-day winning streak in a gambling den illegally hidden behind a restaurant when he looked up to find the Devil before him.

The Devil had chosen to dress like a man for this visit, but Jack knew him immediately—his finely-tailored suit and polished shoes couldn't hide his claws, his red eyes, or the small white horns that sprouted from the top of his head.

"Hello, Jack," he said, as if greeting an old friend.

Jack's stomach clenched in terror. "No, wait—I had a year…"

The Devil laughed. "It's been a year, Jack. Today's October 31st. It's Halloween again."

Jack looked to his gambling mates, but they stared, frozen, and Jack realized he was in that peculiar twilight space again. Behind the Devil, the black void waited.

"So," Jack said, trying to regain his confidence, "you came to get me yourself this time, eh? Not leaving the job to a flunky."

"Not this time, no," the Devil said, speaking to Jack even as his crimson eyes settled on the cards scattered around the felt-covered table.

"You a gambler?"

The Devil took a seat across from Jack, and began gathering the cards. "Please—I practically invented gambling."

Seeing his chance, Jack squinted. "Care to make a little wager today?"

"What'd you have in mind?"

"One hand. Blackjack. If I win, you let me go. You win, I come with you."

The Devil said, "That's not much of a bet for me, Jack—I can take you without playing."

But he was shuffling the cards even as he spoke.

"Afraid you'd lose?"

The Devil looked at Jack once, and Jack nearly shrank back from the millennia of hatred he saw in those eyes. Then the Devil smiled and dealt.

Jack glanced at his two cards, then sat silently for a few seconds. The Devil did the same. They peered at each other across the table. Finally, Jack reached for a bottle of whiskey. He poured himself a shot, then gestured at a glass before the Devil. "Care for a little amber luck?"

"Why not?"

Jack poured, and they both drank. Then Jack said, "I stand."

Without a word, the Devil flipped over his cards.

He had the King and Queen of Spades. "Doesn't look good for you, Jack."

Jack gaped for a second.

The Devil stood.

Distant shrieks echoed from the black hole.

The Devil started to reach for him.

Jack flipped over his cards:

The Ace and Jack of Spades. A perfect blackjack.

The Devil's eyes grew so red hot they were painful to look at. He stuttered for words and came up with nothing, leaving his forked tongue to flick from one side of his mouth to the other.

Jack knew better than to wait around. "Guess it's just my lucky day," he said, scooping up his winnings.

He left before the Devil realized that he'd pulled the cards from his sleeve when he'd poured the drinks.

∞∞∞

That'd been…what, an hour ago? Two? Jack's head was swimming from everything that'd happened tonight.

Somewhere he heard a bell begin to strike twelve, and he knew that midnight had arrived.

And so had the Devil.

There he was, suddenly standing over Jack, casually, as if he'd been there all night. "Well, hello, Jack. Nice to see you again."

Jack drew himself up, drawing his arms in as if afraid to reveal the sleeves he'd used to cheat the Devil. "What do you want? I won. You can't take me."

The Devil stared at Jack in utter astonishment, then burst into howls of laughter that echoed through the New Orleans night like gales shrieking around a house in a thunderstorm. After several seconds he stopped and asked, "If I was going to take you, don't you think I would have done it by now?"

There was a realization picking at the back of Jack's mind, but he pushed it down. "What do you mean?"

"How long ago do you think that card game was?"

Jack's head was spinning. He hadn't even had that much to drink…had he? "It was…tonight…"

"Not quite. It was this night—but two centuries ago."

"No…" But even as he tried to deny it, the truth washed over Jack like a flood breaking through a levee.

It *had* been two hundred years ago. He'd tricked the Devil, and yes, he'd won…but then he'd died a year later anyway, of syphilis, and he'd wandered the earth ever since, confused and lonely, denied entrance into either Heaven or Hell, unseen and forgotten by the living. And his prize, that which he'd cradled so zealously…

He remembered now: That October night when, driven mad by the despair of his situation, he'd found another way into Hell, and had begged the Devil to take him, said that he'd prefer the companionship of demons and souls in torment to his useless, senseless existence, and the Devil had laughed. Oh, how he'd laughed, as he'd thrown a single walnut-sized fiery brimstone out to Jack, a tiny meteor that burned through the side of a ripe pumpkin at Jack's feet and nestled in the pulpy interior, casting an orange glow through the hole it had created. "There's something to light your way. Enjoy your travels," the Devil had said, before shutting the doors of Hell to Jack forever.

And now Jack looked down and realized that he carried no gambler's winnings, no case stuffed with bills or bag bulging with jewels, but that damned pumpkin, still lit by the eternally burning rock within.

"You should feel honored, Jack," the Devil said, gesturing around him, "the living celebrate your story every October."

Jack followed the Devil's gesture, and saw the candle-lit pumpkins on the balconies and porches of the houses facing the cemetery, and he understood at last that he'd been cursed not just to wander aimlessly forever, his way lit by a piece of Hell in an autumn fruit, but that he was celebrated once a year by those who had no idea who he was, or why they'd named their carved pumpkins after him.

"Happy Halloween," the Devil said, before sauntering off, leaving Jack once again alone, his unique torture cemented forever.

ooooo

(I am indebted to William Wells Newell's 1904 article, "The Ignis Fatuus, Its Character and Legendary Origin," for providing a thorough overview of the original "Jack-o'-Lantern" tales, which I have liberally adapted here.)

SEXY PIRATE GIRL

The worst Halloween ever.

Annie was locked in her room on Halloween night, an act she thought must surely be one of the most unfair things in the long and miserable history of unfair things. "Christ, Annie," her father had said as he'd closed the door, his hand already on the knob, "you're fourteen. You're too old for trick or treat now anyway."

In the other room, she could hear her mother and father fighting. That wasn't unusual; they fought most nights. Since she'd abruptly sprouted prominent breasts, the fighting had worsened. Tonight she was glad, because it meant they'd be preoccupied with hurting each other and would ignore her.

She opened her window and gently pried the screen away. Their house was (like all the others in their neighborhood) only one story, but a thick, prickly holly bush grew just outside Annie's window. Her parents hadn't seen her with the hedge trimmers yesterday, when she'd cut away the back part of the shrub.

Annie stepped through the window, let her feet touch the ground, and edged around the holly until she reached the patchy lawn. She pushed the window mostly closed (just in case), and sprinted past the garage. On the sidewalks, costumed kids clutching plastic jack-o'-lanterns already half full of treats were parading by, ignoring Annie's unlit house. Of course her parents wouldn't be handing out candy. They were too busy drinking and blaming each other.

She found the side gate, pushed it open, and stepped through. Just beyond was the grate that opened onto the foundation of the house; she pushed it in, and felt for the plastic bag she'd stored there three days ago.

The one that held her Halloween costume.

Annie loved Halloween; dressing up had always made her feel somehow stronger, more confident. She'd been a comic book heroine, a secret agent, a female ninja, a cat burglar. But this year she wanted something different.

She wanted "Sexy Pirate Girl." Because this year, she had breasts.

A year ago, at a mere thirteen, she'd been a scrawny teen who hadn't yet had her first period. Then the blood had come, and not long after that her mother had taken away her training bra and given her an adult brassiere in a C-cup. It had taken some getting used to—suddenly having flesh in a place that had always been flat—but Annie had soon discovered that she could use this new development to her advantage. Boys, especially, stared at her in ways they never had before, and she *liked* it.

So this year for Halloween, there would be no head-to-toe black leotard, no trench coat or concealing blouse.

Last week, she'd crept off alone, after school, to a seasonal Halloween store. She'd mowed lawns and washed cars and cleaned her parents' bathroom for weeks, she'd filched a few extra bills from her mom's purse and her dad's wallet, she'd saved it all for *this*. She'd seen the costume online, and knew it must be hers, with its low-cut red velvet corset top and flouncy black mini-skirt and naughty thigh-high boots.

She'd paid for it in dollar bills and coins, then taken it home and tried it on once in the bathroom, before her parents got home. She loved the way it barely contained her new curves, the ample expanse of flesh it offered, the wide belt that she hung a cheap plastic scabbard (an extra purchase) from.

She cast aside her t-shirt and jeans, dressing in the dark at the side of the house; she wished she had a mirror, but she'd have to trust that she looked the way she had three days ago. She struggled into the corset top, pulled on the boots, and—lastly—added the belt and scabbard. A few final tugs, a pillow case for pillage, and she was ready.

It didn't matter much to Annie that she would be trick or treating alone; even as a young child, her parents had often been too drunk to accompany her. They'd sometimes foisted her off on neighbors, but usually she'd wandered the dark Halloween nights alone, feeling invincible in her costume, experiencing the offerings of candy as rewards for her self-reliance.

She didn't care if she was fourteen, or if the other kids her age were off at parties or haunted houses or home doling out candy instead of receiving it. She wasn't going to give up that empowerment, that one special night a year when she didn't feel like some barely-tolerated inhuman animal, trapped in the cage her parents dared call a home.

She reached the sidewalk, waited until a tiny vampire count accompanied by a princess and a smiling parent moved past, and turned right, heading for the first house. She barely knew the family who lived there—she thought their name might be Chavez—but they had candlelit pumpkins on the front steps and a grinning paper skeleton taped to the door, so she approached and knocked.

A smiling, black-haired woman in a cheap orange jack-o'-lantern t-shirt answered the door. "Trick or treat," Annie said, holding out her pillow case.

The fortyish woman squinted at her. "Is that Annie from next door?"

"That'd be *Captain* Annie," she answered, trying out what she thought was a swashbuckling accent.

Mrs. Chavez smiled and reached for a candy bowl just inside the door. "Are you out alone tonight, Captain Annie?"

"Aye," she growled.

The woman dropped two fun-sized chocolate bars in Annie's bag. "Well, you be careful…especially dressed like *that*."

She closed the door.

Annie turned away, slightly disturbed. "*Dressed like that?*" That made no sense. Annie looked great. Was Mrs. Chavez just jealous? That had to be it.

Because she knew none of their other neighbors, Annie went unrecognized at the next four houses. In one, a twenty-something girl had grimaced and told her she was too old, but given her a peanut butter cup anyway. In another, a fat man in a running suit had gazed down at her and licked his lips. "Argggh," he murmured, obviously staring into her cleavage.

That response had given Annie a strange, fluttery sensation. She'd taken the offered candy and turned away with a combination of disgust and excitement.

She reached the end of her block and turned the corner; she was stepping into unknown territory now, sailing untested waters. The evening was growing late, and the number of trick or treaters was starting to thin; Annie saw a woman on the other side of the street blow out the candles in her pumpkins, marking an end to her participation in the night's rituals.

Annie was negotiating the stepping stones leading up to a front door lit by orange lights when she heard a voice say, "Their shit sucks."

She looked into the driveway beside the house, and made out a boy, lounging against the side of a parked car. She stopped halfway up the walk and watched as the boy approached her, stepping into the light. He was maybe a year older than her, a bulky blonde in a letterman jacket, and his eyes darted between her face and her chest. "I should know—I live here."

Annie thought the boy looked vaguely familiar; she might have seen him around school, but she couldn't be sure. Up until now, she'd paid little attention to the other kids in her classes; she had few friends, since she knew she could never bring one to her home.

The boy stopped before her, and leveled his gaze on her features long enough for recognition to hit him. "Hey, you go to my school. Annie, right?"

"Right," she admitted, her pirate voice forgotten.

The boy smiled. "I'm Josh. I think we have English together."

Annie shook her head. "We don't." She wasn't sure if he knew he was lying or was just stupid.

He giggled and shrugged. "You're right, we don't. I just said that because...well, I've noticed you, and I didn't want you to think that was weird."

"You've noticed *me*?"

"Sure," Josh said, as his eyes traveled the length of the deep divide between her breasts.

Annie liked the way he was reacting, and she arched her back, pushing herself out even farther. "What've you noticed, exactly?"

Josh's Adam's apple bobbed and he forced himself to look away. "Are you actually out trick or treating?"

For the first time, Annie was embarrassed by that fact. "Well... yeah."

"Aren't you a little old for that? I mean, do you want to do something more fun?"

"Like what?"

Josh started down the driveway, heading for the sidewalk. "Come on," he said, waving at her to follow him.

She took a few steps before hesitating, uncertain. "Where are we going?"

Josh grinned, ran back, took her hand and tugged her down the sidewalk. "Just come on!"

The feel of his hand on hers was new and delicious, and Annie let him lead her down the street. Her pirate boots had slight heels, and it made her wobble as she ran, struggling to keep up with him. They dodged past the few younger children still out with parents until they came to the end of the street, where a brick wall intercepted the asphalt. Annie wondered what was on the other side as they jogged by it for several hundred yards. The brick ended, replaced by a wrought iron gate, and she saw what they'd run past:

A cemetery.

The gates were closed with a length of chain and a padlock, but Josh approached and pushed, and the chain gave just enough to allow someone to enter. "You first," Josh said.

"You mean we're going in there?"

"Yeah. Why—you afraid?"

"No." Annie stepped through the opening.

A second later, Josh followed. "This way," he said, leading her a short distance down the main drive, then out over the grass and between the headstones and monuments.

After a few seconds they came to a crypt, squatting beside a table-sized tomb. The crypt was topped by a sobbing angel, the marble edges limned in yellow-gold from a dim sodium lamp high overhead. "Here," Josh said, as he sat on the edge of the tomb, motioning for Annie to join him.

"Why here?"

He shrugged. "Why not?" He reached out, plucked the pillow case from her hand, and tossed it aside.

Annie had to hop slightly to reach the lip of the tomb, and then she was seated beside Josh. Once she was in place, her right arm brushing his left, he turned to her, his eyes again seeking that shadow just above the rim of her corset. "So, Annie...why are you out alone tonight?"

She shrugged. "I like it. I mean, it's Halloween; we're all somebody else, right?"

"Yeah, I guess. Who are you tonight?"

"Sexy pirate girl. I mean, that's what the costume's called."

Josh reached into a pocket and pulled out a small silver flask. "It's a good name. I'm sorry this isn't rum, but maybe you'll like it anyway."

He held the flask out to her. Annie didn't reach for it. "What is it?"

Josh raised it to his own mouth, took a swallow, and grimaced. "Whiskey." He offered it to her again.

She took it, sniffed it. Her nose seemed to simultaneously open wide and shut down in response. If it was a warning, Annie ignored it; she tilted the flask up and took a huge gulp. It went down like lava and made her gasp, but Josh laughed appreciatively.

"Well, all right, sexy pirate girl."

He waited, watching her, and the liquor hit Annie's stomach like a nuclear blast with a radius that went all the way to her brain; the sense of floating, of being intensified, hit her almost immediately.

"Your face just went all red," Josh said, smiling, as he leaned in.

He kissed her, and Annie froze in disbelief. She'd never been kissed by a boy like this; by a complete stranger. At first the sensation was so alien she was paralyzed, as if she were a machine, a computer, whose circuits had been overloaded and shut down.

Josh broke the contact and pulled back. "Don't you want me to kiss you?"

"Sure, yeah, but...I was just surprised, is all."

He smiled. "Just relax," he said, then held out the flask to her again. She took it, downed another gulp. Josh screwed the cap back on and set it on the cold stone of the tomb before leaning in to plant his lips on hers again.

This time she was prepared, and the feeling of his warmth, of his mouth on hers, was less unexpected. The alcohol made it easy to fall into the kiss, and it seemed to go on forever, charging every part of her with jolts of pleasure. His fingers were in her hair, his lips parted slightly, and Annie forgot everything else, everything that was outside of Josh and the kiss.

When they finally parted, both breathless, he said, "That was more like it."

The whiskey was working its full magic on Annie now, and Josh's face was hard to focus on; she wanted nothing but his kiss again, the lovely feeling of dissolving into him. He moved closer, this time his tongue ran along her lips—

And then his hand was on her shirt, clutching hungrily through the fabric of the corset top. Annie pulled back, confused, the alcohol making it hard to understand what had just happened.

Josh didn't remove his hand from her chest. "Don't you want to?"

"Well...I just...you know..."

Josh took her hand in his. "Baby, c'mon," he said, placing it against the bulging fabric of his jeans, "you're gettin' me all worked up here." He leapt down from the tomb and stood before her, removing any possibility of escape.

An alarm signal sounded somewhere in the back of Annie's mind, but it was muffled by whiskey. She wanted to say "no," to push him aside and walk away, but her tongue was too thick to create speech, and she knew she'd stagger if she tried to use her legs.

She didn't like the look on Josh's face now, the way his smile tilted up at the ends without compassion. She especially didn't like it when he undid his pants button and pulled the zipper down. "C'mon," he repeated, angling forward, his hands on her knees.

"No," she managed, a single breathy word.

"No'?" Josh seemed to consider for an instant...then that feigned concern was gone. "Don't lie—I know you want to fuck me."

He pushed her legs apart.

Annie instinctively tried to close them, but he was strong and she knew where she'd seen him around the school: In the paper, as the football team's star quarterback. He'd thrown long passes and blocked two-hundred-and-fifty-pound linemen with those hands.

"Just relax." His voice was throaty as he clawed at her underwear.

Annie was struggling to shove back away from him when a new voice interrupted: "What the hell's this?"

She looked past Josh's shoulder to see two figures approaching. At first she couldn't make them out, as they walked forward, silhouetted, through the cemetery's shadows; then they stepped into a pool of light cast by the sodium lamp, and Annie saw two boys about Josh's age and size. One wore a black hoodie, the other a half-assed costume consisting of a butcher's apron and a placard reading "USDA INSPECTOR" on a string around his neck.

Josh saw them, and for a moment he was surprised...then he leered. "Yo, dudes—I thought you'd never get here."

The boy in the blood-stained apron thrust a chin at Annie. "So, what's with this bitch?"

"This bitch, Bobby boy, has had a shitload of whiskey and is ready to party."

Annie found her voice. "Fuck you."

Bobby and the other boy howled.

Josh smacked her. Not hard, but enough to shock her into silence. "That's the idea, dumbass." He wrapped his fingers in her panties, and with one pull had them halfway down her hips.

"Wait, hold on..." said the boy in the hoodie, as he brought out a phone and thumbed through the controls until he found the video camera. He pointed it at Josh and Annie. "We need to document this for posterity. Action!"

Bobby was already massaging his own crotch. "Just cut us in for our share of the treats, right?"

"Hey, bro, we're teammates," Josh said.

As he turned to look back at his friend's camera before continuing, Annie reached down to her side, fingers searching for the plastic scabbard attached to the belt. She found the handle of her makeshift dagger, and when Josh turned to her again, bending forward as he tried to rip her panties away and lower himself onto her, she thrust upward and buried eight inches of well-honed blade in his gut.

Josh's body arched and he uttered a small, strained cry. Behind him, his friends guffawed. "Oh man," said the cameraman, his eyes riveted to the image of his spasming friend on the tiny screen, "did you jizz already, you loser?"

While the others laughed, Annie grasped the knife—the one she'd taken from the kitchen cutting block at home and placed in the cheap plastic scabbard—and twisted it, causing Josh to quiver and finally collapse on her, his strength ebbing with his life.

"Oh my fucking god," Bobby said, nearly doubled over, "you are such a retard."

Annie knew she'd have to move quickly, while they were still laughing. She yanked the knife free, feeling hot blood spray against her bare skin, and pushed Josh's dead body aside. Before the other boys had even stopped braying, she'd jumped from the tomb, moving steadily as adrenaline replaced alcohol. She stabbed the one in the hoodie, plunging the knife into his heart. He dropped, dead before he hit the ground.

Bobby took off running.

He was on the football team, too, and for a second Annie feared he might escape…but then he made the classic victim's mistake, risking a look back at his pursuer. In that interim, he tripped over a memorial plaque set into the grass, and fell, sprawling, screaming.

Annie was on him almost instantly. He had just enough time to turn, hold up his hands, and scream, "No, PLEASE—!" before the knife swung down, severing his jugular. Crimson streams fountained into the air and joined the fake blood on the apron, but Annie didn't pull back; she let it wash over her, confirmation of her victory.

The last blood to hit her was burbled up through Bobby's mouth, spattering her in a shotgun spread of droplets. Bobby died, then, and Annie straightened up, still holding the dripping knife, panting.

When she regained her breath, she went back to where the boy in the hoodie had fallen; she raised one pirate boot and ground his phone beneath it, continuing to stomp long after the picture had fizzled out, until it was nothing but electronic rubble. Then she went to Josh, and used his letterman's jacket to wipe the flask clean. Just for good measure, she also ran the felt-covered arm along the granite top of the tomb. She knew she'd probably left some DNA, maybe even a print somewhere, but she wasn't in any databases yet, so it should be all right.

Of course her parents would know when they saw the news tomorrow. They'd figure out the window and put bars over it. They might even make good on their threat to send her away, to "some place where they know how to deal with people like you." She'd probably find herself stuck in a ward with guys who openly jerked off while they stared at her beautiful new breasts.

But, as she wiped the knife clean, returned it to the scabbard, and prepared to head home covered in blood that would barely be noticed on this one night, she didn't care. It had been completely worth it.

The best Halloween ever.

HELL MANOR

August 20th, 4 p.m.

I know how it sounds if I tell you this story starts with screaming and a blonde walking into my office. It sounds like a whole different kind of story than it is.

But that is how it began. With a blood-splattered maniac who screamed, yanked the blade out on a pocket knife, and lunged at me.

I threw myself aside, nearly knocking over the folding chair I'd been occupying for the last two hours. My arms went up as the knife blade slashed the air inches from my face, and I think I shouted something along the lines of, "What the fuck are you doing?"

Stupid fucking kids. Every year we invite students from the local college drama department to audition for Hell Manor, and every year at least one of them has to take it too far. They probably think it's method acting—*I'm trying out for the part of a lunatic in a haunted house, so I'll go really looney.*

This little madman stepped back and lowered his knife-hand; at least he had just enough sense left to look properly abashed. "I'm just...you know...trying to be scary..."

"That's a real knife."

The kid—who couldn't have been more than 18—stared down at the blade, as if trying to comprehend. "Yeah, but…I don't have a fake one, and I thought—"

I'd had enough of this genius. "Yeah, well, the point of a haunted house is to give the customers a scare in a *safe* environment, right? It's like Halloween: The scares are fun because we know they're not real. Real scares—especially those that involve sharp things near faces—aren't fun. Comprende?"

"So does that mean I don't get the job?"

I restrained my urge to bark back, *Damn straight, Sparky*, and instead told him, "We'll call you if we need you. Thank you for your time."

Even though the little bastard had just slashed the air an inch from my head, I felt bad now about how he shuffled off, his dreams of Halloween stardom crushed. But I didn't feel bad enough to risk Hell Manor by hiring some half-assed frat boy who'd do anything to get a scream out of a hot babe.

Okay, I know you're waiting for the blonde, but I should probably introduce myself here. Name's Jack Lichtner, and, with my partner Greg Strassel, I run a haunted attraction called Hell Manor. You've probably been through a haunted house in your neighborhood at Halloween, something local where they get some kids to volunteer and put up some inflatable walls; maybe they've splurged and bought the audio-animatronic figure of Hannibal Lecter that waggles its tongue at the unsuspecting. But if you're a more serious devotee of Halloween—if you hit the big, professional attractions—then you know that Hell Manor ain't your neighbor's yard or the Jaycees. Hell Manor is 50,000 square feet of the most terrifying shit you'll ever see. I've wanted to scare the pants off all of you since I went through the Haunted Mansion at Disneyland when I was six years old. By sixteen, I was making my own stage blood and leaping out of my garage every October 31st. I met Greg when we were both in college and volunteering at a local charity haunt; we were kindred souls, and a year later we rented a space for our first pro haunt. We bought this old warehouse cheap about ten years ago and we've been here ever since, with Greg running most of the business side of things and me overseeing the creative aspects. Yes, haunting is a year-round, full-time job for us; our season might end in November after the last guest goes through on the final night and we wring the ultimate scream out, but by January we're already planning and building and hiring for the next season. We employ artists, designers, carpenters, sculptors, painters, makeup effects guys from Hollywood, pyrotechnics experts, rent-a-cops, musicians, sound effects creators, and more than 150 actors (although in the haunt biz we call 'em "monsters"). Last year *Haunted America Magazine* ranked us number three, right behind The Pennhurst Asylum and The Darkness. We're aiming for number one.

So, now that you know about me and what I do, let's get back to the blonde. The day hadn't been going well even before Norman Bates Junior had taken the stage. I'd seen ten college kids read from last year's "Infernal Asylum" scene, and maybe six of them wouldn't completely embarrass us. One snotty jock I wanted to slap silly had obviously been here on some fraternity dare. A Goth girl had mumbled through the lines, and then asked if she could just stand in a corner and scream. A boy with more piercings than Pinhead had thrown himself around so much that he was exhausted in thirty seconds. The rest could probably be coached and trained into something that would work; a tall, lanky drama student named Nathan would make a decent scarecrow in the outdoor scare zone (which would be a haunted farm theme, complete with its own little maze of hay bales). But none of them had wowed me. And I desperately wanted to be wowed.

Greg was outside, keeping our would-be monsters in line until their turn, having them fill out applications and handing out scenes, then corralling the ones I liked to make sure we had all their info. The auditions were taking place in what remained of part of last year's asylum set—a medical examination room lined with fake tile and blood splotches. The rest of the haunt was still in limbo; the bare beginnings of the first of our three mazes were set up near the entrance, but right now they were still mostly random wall sections.

I pulled out my phone and called Greg to ask how many were left. I love the guy like a brother, but could've killed him when he laughed in my ear.

"Things are going that well, huh?"

"The last kid actually threatened me with a knife."

That at least got him to stop cackling. "What? Should I call the cops?"

273

"No, it's okay—he just wasn't thinking. He left properly chastised." I actually thought the kid might be back in his dorm room flagellating himself about now.

"Well, it's bad news for you, pal—there are still at least 30 more of 'em out here."

I stifled a groan. "Fuck me. Okay, send the next one in."

I put the cell back in a pocket, tried to get comfy in that damn metal folding chair, and shuffled the applications on my clipboard until the next one was on top. It was filled out in a light, spidery writing, and I had to squint to make out the name: "Maeve MacCumhail." I had absolutely no fucking clue about how to pronounce that last name.

I was still trying to puzzle it out when I heard my applicant approaching. I was already thinking maybe this was going to be another Goth chick, or a Wiccan with long black hair and pentagram necklace.

You can imagine my surprise when I saw one of the most exquisite and whitest creatures I've ever laid eyes on.

She was barely five feet tall, and slender, with hair and skin so pale she was almost phosphorescent. She wore a simple knee-length black dress, which made the curls of her white hair stand out even more. I'd already seen three actors today in makeup, costume and wigs, but nothing like this—she looked 100% real. I made a mental note to find out what she was using for a base and where she'd purchased her supplies.

She was stunning, sure, but there was something…well, unnerving about her, too. She was just too poised, too naturally confident, too knowing. She stood before me and gazed at me with eyes the color of Chartreuse on the Rocks, and something about her sent a chill through me—yes, *me*, the veteran haunter. The Master of Mayhem. The Sheik of Shriek.

She waited until I could gather my wits enough to say something. "You must be Maeve—" I looked at the clipboard again, but there was just no way my clumsy tongue was going to get that last name out.

"It's pronounced 'MacCool,'" she said. Her accent was odd, too; vaguely Irish, but not quite like any dialect I'd ever heard. Not that I was an expert.

The more I looked at her, the more I got the crazy idea that her skin and hair color were natural. Maybe she was an albino…?

But she didn't have the reddish hue to the eyes. And she certainly was no local college student looking to make a few extra dollars at Halloween. I couldn't guess her age, but it was hard to picture her sitting in a dark classroom taking notes on a Psychology 101 lecture.

What the hell was she doing *here*, for that matter?

"Are you looking to be a monster, Maeve?"

"Well, actually, I'm hoping you might need a magician."

That was new. "A magician…?"

"Can I give you a demonstration?"

"Please."

She flung one arm out, and a bouquet of black roses appeared in her hand. I had to admit it was startling; I had actually worked with a magician one year to create some new gags for Hell Manor, and I knew what she had weren't the usual obvious, gaudy, collapsible magician's flowers. Maeve threw the bouquet into the air over her head, reached up and clapped her hands together, and the flowers turned into a rain of ebony petals that fluttered to the ground around her while she waited for my response.

It was reasonably impressive…but way too pretty for us. I needed blood. I needed action. I needed terror.

"Okay," I said, "that'd be great at a birthday party for Wednesday Addams, but that's not what we're about here in Hell Manor. Have you got anything more…you know, Halloween? Maybe something with a little gore?"

A smile flickered across her face. I felt another of those little chills of unease.

Maeve reached into a sleeve, and produced a large scarf embroidered with swirling designs. She waved the scarf over her other hand, pulled it back, and revealed that she now held a skull, its polished ivory surface glinting against the deep night of her dress. She clutched the skull by the lower jawbone, raised it above the scarf, and tipped it over; blood streamed from the empty sockets and nose and into the scarf, cupped in Maeve's hand. She finished pouring, and simply removed her hand from the skull, leaving it to rest in mid-air; it floated there, and its eyes started to glow. Then, without warning, she flung the scarf out at me, holding one corner, and…okay, she got me to flinch. I expected to be drenched with sticky fake blood, but there was nothing, just the skull's eyes flashing brightly. Finished, Maeve wrapped the scarf around the skull, as if caging it, and held it at her side.

"Well?" she asked.

I was impressed. Like a magician, I was an expert in misdirection; every good haunter has to be. You have to know how to get them to look one direction, expecting the scare to come from there—while you're actually making it happen from the other direction, behind them or to the side or over them. I thought I knew every trick of the trade, from how to make fake disembowelings to the latest in high-tech hydraulics. But I had no idea how she'd just done that.

And it was cool as fucking hell.

"Can you do that more than once in a night? Does it take long to set up?"

"I can do it as often and as quickly as you like."

I worked it over in my head. This could be something fresh, something even the hardcore haunt fans wouldn't be expecting. Some haunted attractions were remembered for one particular actor (SpookyWorld had had "Mouse Girl," who'd allowed live rats to race over her body nightly, and had become a cult sensation in the process, still talked about years later), and I could imagine forums in five years where posts would be reminiscing about that insane—and totally hot—magician from Hell Manor…

"Can you act?"

Maeve shrugged.

"Did Greg give you a scene outside?"

She flicked one hand, and there were the pages in her fingers.

I couldn't help but grin. I was already falling for her.

"Read the Executioner's lines."

She glanced from me to the pages, then let her arm fall by her side and she fixed me with those amazing green eyes. "You've come here to see death tonight, and death will see you as well. You'll witness an execution, performed live in front of you right here, but don't be surprised if it's not what you expected…"

Her voice was low and clear, her delivery forceful without resorting to the histrionics of the amateurs I'd seen earlier. But here's the weirdest part: She wasn't reading from the pages. I'd written that scene myself, and I knew she was word-for-word accurate. "Stop," I commanded, then asked, "you've read this scene before."

"No," she answered.

"Then how did you already know the lines?"

"I looked them over while I waited outside."

"So you're a magician with a photographic memory?"

She shrugged again.

I was trapped in a vicious mental circle. She scared me. And because she scared me, I had to have her in Hell Manor. And because I knew she'd be my haunt's star, I wanted her...in a lot of ways. And because I was a confirmed bachelor who was more interested in scaring girls than dating them, what I felt for her scared me. And I was back at the top of the circle.

I forced my thoughts back to the present, pretending to occupy myself with the specifics of her application. "And your schedule's clear from late September to mid-November?"

"Yes."

"Okay. We'll be in touch."

"Thank you."

She turned and walked out. It was hard not to run after her.

I put her application in the "HIRE" folder, then told Greg to send in the next one. While I waited, I thought about my newest employee. I wanted to know everything about her—not just how she'd done the trick with the skull and the blood, but where she came from, what else she liked...why she wanted to work for me.

I had a strange premonition that bubbled up in my consciousness like a decayed hand from a pool of hot wax—*she's going to bring trouble*—but I pushed that away with a big smile.

Before I knew it, another kid was standing before me screaming his fool lungs out, and I got back to work.

September 9th, 8:20 P.M.

She murdered someone on the night of our first preview.

Greg had given out free tickets at a local Halloween shop, so we could test out our new scares before we opened to paying audiences. Later on I'd be working in the maze as a monster, but for the preview I wanted to be part of the audience, to gauge their reactions at the ground level, you might say.

I mixed in with a group of mostly late teens and went through Hell Manor with them. The first maze was our basic Hell Manor introduction, setting up the back story of a once-luxury hotel invaded by demons. That maze emptied out to the outdoor "Hell Farm"; we'd converted the large storage space behind the warehouse into a labyrinth of corn bales and barns, crammed full of scarecrows and scary rednecks. From there, the guests who'd had enough could exit, or they could check out our two other mazes. "3D Inferno" was a three-dimensional extravaganza, but we hadn't gone for the usual evil clown motif; instead, our DayGlo colors and outrageously-costumed actors recreated a section of Hell itself, replete with underground caverns, lakes of fire, and devils galore. The final maze was "Hell on Earth," and was a free-for-all—we had everything from the usual asylum to (I fuck with you not) a haunted version of the current cast of *Survivor*.

By the time our test group reached "The Blood Queen" (as we'd dubbed Maeve) near the climax of "Hell on Earth," they were putty. They'd been reduced to flinching, quivering blobs of anxiety, and I couldn't wait to see what effect Maeve would have on them. I'd made her the penultimate scene (it was almost obligatory for haunted attractions to close with the chainsaw-wielding psychopath who would chase the screaming guests out the "Exit" door), so she'd be the last thing they would really remember.

We'd worked through her routine together, and had come up with some great bits, which now included pulling an endless string of intestines from a small box labeled "BUTCHER SHOP," and a zombie assistant who ate his own arm and then re-grew it. I still had no idea how she did her tricks, and I knew better than to ask. As we filed up to her stage, I was probably as anxious as any of the guests, but for different reasons.

We'd built a raised stage for her (about four feet), and had even had an artist paint a proscenium arch for her; it was a thing of beauty, with demon faces and tendrils twined around the edges. The rest of the room was bare floor space, to accommodate the audience.

The beginning of her little presentation was fine—the audience loved the zombie, and one girl audibly belched as he seemingly ate his arm. They were giggling nervously and hiding their eyes, and I was loving every minute of it.

Then Maeve threw out a curve ball by asking for a volunteer. That wasn't part of the script. I felt that little twist of unease, but figured maybe she just wanted someone else to hold a scarf or something.

A boy in a letterman jacket raised his hand, and Maeve gestured him up the stairs at the rear of her platform. The cocky fucker shot his buddies an arched eyebrow, "she's mine" kind of look, then strutted up to join her.

She told him to kneel. He smirked and did. She bent and picked up a sword and held it up for everyone to see.

A sword? We'd never rehearsed anything with a sword. What the hell was she doing?

"This blade is made from the purest silver," she told us, giving the metal a little flick, "and its edge is razor-sharp." She raised it over her head.

The audience gasped. I was right there with them.

The sword made a hissing sound as it descended.

She cut off the kid's head.

The audience went into chaos. One of the kid's friends cried out and ran towards the stage. A girl fell to her knees, sobbing. The others gasped and screamed.

Blood gushed from the neck stump as the body fell to its knees. It didn't fall all the way, but somehow knelt there, as if in awe, or supplication. Crimson stained Maeve's arms, but she paid no mind as she bent to retrieve the head, hoisting it by the hair. She held it out to the audience, gore dangling from the neck…

And the head laughed.

The kid who had rushed the stage froze in the act of clambering up onto it. The girl on her knees went even paler, and I began to worry that she was seriously in trouble. But I couldn't look at her for long, not when the head Maeve clutched in one outstretched arm was now jabbering away, telling his friends that it didn't even hurt, that it even felt kind of *cool*, like he was floating in space or maybe Heaven…

I heard one of the teens behind me vomit, and I almost joined them. This was too much. It just felt *wrong*; it was like being in a hurricane where you could hear the wind roaring and see things whirling around you, but the air felt perfectly still. Or like standing at the bottom of the sea and being able to breathe. I had no doubt that every single one of us watching knew, in some instinctive, irrational way, that we weren't watching a mere trick. This was no sleight-of-hand, no clever stage illusion. No, Maeve had really just killed a boy, and then brought his head back to life.

Almost as if she had heard my thoughts, she frowned, and

the head stopped talking. She lowered it to the body, wrapped her scarf around the neck, and then dramatically pulled it away. After a beat, the eyes blinked, and the kid stood again, looking dazed. The blood had vanished, and the boy was apparently fine. He walked dumbly away, staggered down the steps, and rejoined his friends, who stared in slack-jawed disbelief. I moved ahead of them, having already decided they'd had quite enough for one night. I told Ernie, who played the final, chainsaw-wielding monster, to just stay put as I escorted the traumatized group out.

Once they'd reached the parking lot, I couldn't resist approaching the boy in the letterman's jacket. "Are you okay?" I asked him.

"What?" he said. His eyes looked unfocused.

"Do you know what happened to you in there?"

"I..." He struggled for a few seconds, then just shrugged. "No. It's weird...I can't remember..."

"Do you know Maeve MacCumhail?"

"Who?"

I believed him. I didn't press. His friends grouped around him protectively and led him off.

Maeve was gone by the time I went back inside, but she was there the next night, on time as always. Before I could even open my mouth, she cut me off. "Don't worry, I won't try that again."

"Maeve...how...?"

She reached up, touched a long, light finger to my lips, and the feel of her cool flesh did more to silence me than any admonition. "There are some things 'tis best not to know, love."

I didn't ask again.

Of course I should have fired her right then and there; after all, I'd sent a kid slouching off with his tail between his legs for pulling a goddamn pocket knife. But there was a big difference involved, of course:

I wasn't completely obsessed with the kid.

October 31st, 2:30 P.M.

The Big Day had arrived.

That's actually kind of a misnomer, because Hell Manor had already been running for six weeks by Halloween. But what can I say, I'm a fan of the day, and I always try to toss a little something extra into the October 31st performance. Besides, we had news crews, journalists, and haunt reviewers from all over the world coming tonight.

It was late afternoon, and I was working in my little office at the rear of the warehouse. Well, okay, so maybe I was really just getting an ego rush from reading praise ("Jack Lichtner and Greg Strassel fucking rocked the haunted attraction world with this year's Hell Manor!") on a haunt forum, but I figured I'd earned that. Still, I flipped the computer screen over to work schedules when there was a knock at the door.

"Come in."

The door opened, and our new star—Maeve, "The Blood Queen" herself—stepped in.

As always, when I saw her my stomach did little Jackie Chan flips, and my throat was suddenly dry. "Hey, hi," I said, trying (unsuccessfully) to sound casual. "What's up?"

We'd worked together now for almost two months, and somehow her presence unnerved me more, not less. I'd convinced myself that her preview performance had been a masterful illusion; the kid had obviously been a plant, and she had access to some amazing technology I didn't know about yet. I still knew next to nothing about her—the only interesting thing she'd revealed about herself was that she'd taken the job because she came from "a family of tricksters." That was enough for me.

And yes, I'd broken my cardinal rule of never getting involved with employees and had invited her out after the show at least three times, but she'd always politely declined. Not that I blamed her for that, of course. She was smart enough to follow the "don't date the boss" rule, and the boss wasn't exactly a catch here—just a thirty-something Halloween dork who hadn't been on a date in at least three years.

It occurred to me to wonder if she lived with someone. I once (stalker alert) drove by the address she'd provided on her application...or rather, I tried, because it was in an exclusive gated community I couldn't get near. Either she: 1) was a rich girl rebelling against mommy and daddy; 2) had lied on the application and didn't live there at all; or 3) had a sugar daddy and didn't need what I paid her, but did it just to entertain people.

And entertaining them she was. Hell Manor was having far and away its best year ever, and I knew she was a large part of the reason. Since we'd opened in September, we had drawn both record crowds and brilliant reviews, and The Blood Queen was always singled out. After that disastrous preview, we'd reworked her routine a little; she would wrap up talking about how the gods demanded a blood sacrifice, and she would ask the crowd three times, "Do you want to see a sacrifice?" When she'd worked them up into a frenzy ("YES"!), she'd step back and behind a curtain at the rear of her stage, only to re-appear instantly *behind* the crowd, shrieking and reaching out for them. The final appearance, of course, was a double that I'd hired and outfitted with wig and make-up; if any of the guests had looked at "her" for longer than three seconds, they would have realized it was actually a wiry boy with beard stubble under his greasepaint. But the crowds were too busy trying to hang onto their consciousness and stampeding down the final corridor.

The fact that Maeve had been completely professional in all other regards—always on time, never missed a night—was just icing on the cake. The one odd thing was that she'd asked to be paid cash under the table, but I figured it was some immigration issue. I tried not to wonder about it too much.

Now she was in my office, taking a chair near me (*too* near, really), and for the first time since I'd known her, she was obviously troubled about something.

"It's Samhain," she said, then corrected herself: "Halloween, I mean."

I smiled. "It is." God, I love Halloween. As a kid, I liked it more than Christmas. Nothing could beat dressing up in a costume, going out and demanding candy from all the neighbors... unless it was dressing up in a costume as an adult and getting money from people who were paying to be scared. I had the greatest job in the world.

But she wasn't smiling, and the little flips in my stomach turned into a high-wire act.

"It's a very important night in my...family."

Oh Christ, I thought, *please tell me she's not going to ask for tonight off.* "For me, too," I said. "We've got news crews coming tonight—even two of the networks are going to be here—and they're already lining up outside."

She shifted her position, uncomfortable. "Jack, I...there's something you need to know about me: I left my family under bad circumstances, and I…well, I think they might be coming after me. Tonight."

"Oh." So I'd been right all along about choice #1: poor little rich girl and family black sheep. Still, pissed-off rich people were nothing to laugh at. "Do I need to hire extra security?"

"No. It won't help."

So these rich people were really pissed off. I wondered if she'd done something other than tell the folks she wasn't going to Vassar.

It might sound like I'm being glib, and…I am. Because I really wanted to tell her it would all be okay, that I didn't like seeing her in distress and that I'd take care of it, whatever it was. I wanted to say, *I'll protect you. Stay here and I'll give my life if I need to.* But I was about to discover the irony of being a guy who made his living at fear and who could chicken out as fast as the next idiot when a girl was involved. Instead of saying any of those nice, reassuring things, I said, "What do we do, then?"

"I don't think I should be here tonight. It's not safe. For others, I mean."

I pretended to think about that while I found my balls again, and finally said, "No."

It was nice to see she could be surprised.

"No," I said again, and then I *did* grab my chance to be her hero. "If the situation is that dangerous, then I don't want you facing it alone. I'll bring on extra security. You'll be here, surrounded by crowds and by people who will protect you, who care about you and won't let anything happen to you."

She smiled then, a little sadly, and reached out and stroked my cheek, and right then I didn't give a fuck if her daddy was Godzilla—I'd get the Japanese Army and we'd take the big asshole on. Her fingers were cold, but her touch wasn't, and I would have done anything to hold that moment forever.

"Jack, I…I don't know what to say…"

"Okay, let's talk practicality, then: Do we need to worry about guns? Knives?"

She lowered her hand, and it was like the end of summer. She shook her head and said, "No."

"Good. Then I won't need metal detectors. We've got an agency we use for this stuff. I'll have them send over three extra guys tonight. Big guys. Big fucking hairy ape guys."

She laughed, and I realized it was the first time I'd heard the sound. I wanted to hear it again. Every day, not just on Halloween.

"All right, then. And…they may not even find me. We might be worrying for nothing."

"You will never be nothing."

She leaned in and kissed me then. The world stopped.

It wasn't a long kiss, or a passionate one, but it was enough. When she pulled away I waited a few seconds before opening my eyes, enjoying the rush. I finally looked at her, and she was close, those eyes green as grass under fresh rain. "I'd like to spend all of Samhain with you. After we close tonight."

I pride myself on being discreet, so I won't tell you what sensation *that* suggestion produced in me. I could barely stammer out an answer. "I…yes…I mean, of course."

She left.

I leaned back in my creaking desk chair, stunned, wound up… and nervous. Certainly her closeness, and what she'd promised, was at the top of my thoughts…but I also had to remember that we had fresh new worries. I finally got myself together enough to punch up Greg's number on my cell, and asked my partner to hire three additional security men tonight—one for the front entrance, and two for Maeve's area. I considered getting someone else to work my part in the maze so I could be near her all night, but I'd need to be by the front to give interviews to the news crews and journalists. Besides, as much as I cared about Maeve, I was still first and foremost a haunter, and tonight was Halloween, and I wanted to be in my maze adding a few extra jolts to our shock factor.

She'll be safe, I told myself…even as I wondered if I'd just made the worst mistake of my life.

October 31st, 10:45 p.m.

I took a deep breath, then yanked the hidden door aside and lunged into the hall, shrieking and grabbing at a group of startled teenaged girls. They flinched and shrank and ran past, and I withdrew, pulling the door shut, waiting for the next group. I'm not ashamed to admit that I got a deep satisfaction out of that.

In fact, I was pleased with how the whole night had gone so far. The CNN and ABC news crews had already come and gone, and I'd hammed it up for their cameras, much to the grimacing delight of the reporters. Our entrance line was still long, despite a closing time of midnight. I'd checked in occasionally with Greg, who'd been in touch with the extra security throughout the night, and other than one drunken football player who'd decked a guy in a demon mask, there had been no major problems.

Maybe my hunches had been wrong, after all.

I peered through the eyehole into the corridor; another group was approaching, but they were out of sight. The art of the scare was all in the timing. Greg and I had worked hard on the lay-out of Hell Manor, trying to ensure both a fluid walk-through that could handle large crowds efficiently, and mazes that would frighten even the most jaded haunt fan. We'd roamed the trade shows and websites and journals in search of new scares, we'd invested tens of thousands in the best effects we'd found, and the money we'd spent had already paid off handsomely. Our profits were solid, sure, but we really loved the fan response, and we'd heard nothing but raves. Just our first room alone was being talked about: It was set up like a once-elegant but now-decayed hotel lobby, with a large mirror hanging above a wrecked fire-place. As a group entered, the door closed behind them, and a ghostly figure appeared in the mirror: "The Concierge" told them that Hell Manor had once been the most luxurious resort in the country, but twenty years ago a group of devil worshippers had held an unholy ceremony there and opened a gateway to Hell. Demons, devils, and the damned had spewed forth from that portal, tortured and killed the hotel's guests and staff, and taken up residence. Now they bent their sinister desires towards those who were foolish enough to venture within…at which point the Concierge began to pound on the mirror (which was actu-ally a high-definition plasma screen), the room went dark, there was the sound of shattering glass, and when the lights came up again, the Concierge stood there in the flesh (the actor having stepped through a cleverly disguised hidden door). Any guests who weren't already screaming and running down the far hallway at that point were politely directed to do so by the Concierge. That first long section of the maze was dressed as a corridor filled with eerie portraits, some of which were equipped with glowing eyes, while others were holograms that changed depending on the angle they were viewed from. But one "painting" was actually a hidden door on hinges, and that was my gag. With my face painted in appropriately ghoulish fashion (I've always preferred make-up to a mask), I'd watch and wait for the next group and then spring out. I can tell you it kept those crowds moving.

I was about to take another look into the corridor when my cell phone screamed (yes, *screamed*—I know, it's corny, but I always heard it). I was wearing a tattered, dusty zombie jacket, and the phone was in my pocket. I glanced at the caller ID—Greg—and felt a stab of adrenaline. Backing as far away from the maze wall as I could, I raised the phone to my ear; the eerie music and thunder sound effects of the maze were loud and would block most of the sound, but it still wouldn't do to have the Hell Manor illusion shattered by the sound of mundane conversation from behind the walls.

"Greg?"

I had to plug my other ear to make out Greg's voice through the phone, but my partner's tension was clear. "We've got a problem in the opening scene—we think maybe the plasma screen blew."

"'Blew'? How does a plasma screen blow?"

"Well, whatever. It stopped. I don't know why."

"Shit." I thought for a second, then said, "Okay, RJ knows the lines for the introduction, right?" RJ was the actor who appeared in the room after the blackout.

"Yeah, but…we don't know where RJ is."

"What—?"

I glanced up then—and the rest of my reply froze in my throat when I saw:

An eye, liquid and aqua green, staring through the peep hole at *me*.

I dropped to my knees, thinking that made me harder to see, and whispered into the phone, "I'll call you back." Then I ended the call and shoved the phone back in a pocket.

The eye hadn't followed as I'd dropped, and I hoped I hadn't been seen at all; there was no lighting here, of course, so I shouldn't have been visible at all. I stayed there, not moving, and after a few seconds the eye pulled away.

I got up, waited a few beats, then stepped forward and risked a glance out.

There were three men in the corridor. They were dressed in costumes that I couldn't identify—belted black tunics, leggings, boots.
All three were similar in appearance, with white, even pearlescent
skin, and hair the color of ice. They moved confidently, without
the usual caution of haunt-goers. Hell, they were even laughing
together.

I knew immediately: They had to be Maeve's kin. Looking
at them, I felt the same sense of everything being tilted, being
wrong, that I'd felt when Maeve had cut that boy's head off.

This was bad. And somehow I knew it was about to get a
whole lot worse.

But Hell Manor was my responsibility, and I wasn't about to
hide and hope they'd wreak havoc without noticing me. I waited
until they'd moved past, then opened the door, slowly, moving as
carefully as I could. They were thirty feet ahead, backs to me, just
turning the first corner.

I grabbed my phone and called Greg. "You got that one security guy out there, right?"

"Yeah—he's already in the first room, trying to figure out what
happened. Why?"

"Send him my way. And don't let anybody else in until you
hear from me. I think we've got trouble."

I put the phone away and jogged down the corridor to the
turn.

I knew that maze, of course, knew it like I knew the lines in
my own face, the ones that grew a little deeper after every Halloween. I knew that a few feet past the bend, they'd come on the
next scene: The maze opened on what was supposedly the one-
time hotel manager's office, but the cabinets and furnishings had
been rifled and flung about, torn and bloodstained. Two monsters
hovered over a victim on the manager's desk, poking at his pro-
truding innards as they uttered ridiculous remarks about being
overcharged for their rooms and lost luggage.

The twist in this scene was that we'd hired an incredibly agile
young man named Marty Jablonski to play the torture victim;
Marty could, in a split second, flip up from the desk and rush the
guests, reaching for them with one hand while cradling his (rubber) intestines with the other. The monsters—actually two hulking jocks in top-of-the-line masks, complete with illuminated
eyes—would then grab Marty and haul him back to the desk,

thus re-setting the scene for the next group.

Crouching low, I risked a glance around the corner. Down the hallway, the strange trio had paused to watch. From where I was, I could make out only one man's face—in profile—and I saw a slight, cruel smile there.

"Room service shouldn't have kept us waiting so long!" shouted one of the monsters, who then shoved a clawed finger into the mess on Marty's abdomen. Marty reacted by writhing and shrieking.

"Yeah, we wanted our Bloody Marys!" said the other monster, lifting a rope of segmented gut before adding, "And next time, add more Worcestershire!"

The dumbass kid was adding that line, and I made a mental note to tell him to cut it. He could barely say it through the mask anyway.

The first monster jabbed at Marty again. "And this is supposed to be a five-star hotel? More like five scars—"

That was Marty's cue line. Right on time, he flipped instantly to his feet, screaming in mimicked agony.

The three watchers didn't so much as blink.

Marty staggered forward, and I knew that he was pushing to get a reaction. He clutched his foam rubber guts in one hand, and made supplicating motions with the other, stumbling forward.

One of the men reached out. Before Marty could react, the man had stepped forward and thrust his hand into Marty's abdomen. Marty's face turned into a mask of shock, and I knew he wasn't acting. Nobody was *that* good.

The man pulled his hand out, and the organs he clutched glistened and dripped with a realism that no make-up simulation would ever be able to match.

As Marty crumpled to the floor, the other two observers laughed and clapped their friend on the shoulders in approval, as if they'd just seen the greatest trick in the world.

My two monsters watched uncertainly, and I was right there with them. None of us had a fucking clue about what to do next. Rush them and hope to gain the element of surprise? Turn tail and run for it? Freeze and hope they'd just walk on by? Or just stand there and wait for the inevitable, knowing deep down on some primeval level that we were completely outmatched?

While we all stood there like the proverbial deer in the headlights of a ten-ton semi, the two other white-haired men turned from their red-fingered friend and stepped up to the paralyzed, costumed boys. The man on the left backhanded Monster #1, sending him to crash against a row of ancient, dented filing cabinets on the far side of the room; the one on the right hoisted the last monster into the air with one arm and held him there, while the other two threw out witticisms in a language I couldn't even guess at. Finally, bored, joke over, he ripped the kid's mask off and tossed the 180-lb. quarterback aside like a forgotten rag doll. The boy landed heavily near the desk, which he promptly crawled under. Meanwhile, his attacker donned the mask, while his fellows laughed again.

They either hadn't noticed me or had decided I wasn't worth it, and now they all sauntered out of the room and down the far corridor.

I waited until they were out of sight, then ran up. I could hear the unmasked monster under the desk whimpering, so I knew he was okay. The one who'd been backhanded was just coming to, moaning softly. I ran forward to Marty and knelt by him.

He was dead, his eyes open and fixed in a faraway stare. The blood pooling around him was still warm, and I could feel it seeping into my clothes where my knees touched the floor. I couldn't think straight; a teenaged kid had just died while in my employ. And I could've stopped it, if I'd listened to Maeve, if I'd been thinking with my head instead of my dick.

"Is that real?"

I jumped as the voice sounded behind me—ironic, the haunter startled inside his own creation—then saw the security guard. He was a big guy, well over six feet and muscular; he could've been the center on an NBA team. *Good,* I thought, *at least this guy won't wimp out on me.*

"Yeah, it's real. We've got three guys—"

"With white hair?" But he wasn't looking at me; his eyes were locked on something behind me.

My skin was crawling before I even turned.

They were coming back.

"That's them."

"What've they got—a knife?"

"I didn't see."

He pulled out his gun and motioned at them. "I'm going to need you gentlemen to step out of that corridor and kneel in this room with your hands on top of your heads."

"I'm not sure they speak—" I was about to say "English," but the one in front, the one whose hands were still scarlet-covered, cut me off.

"What an interesting weapon." He had Maeve's accent, making the link between them unquestionable. "We've been away for longer than I'd realized."

I don't know much about guns, but I knew the sound of a hammer being pulled back when I heard it.

"You take one more step, and you'll find out just how interesting this weapon is," the guard said.

The three men stopped, glanced at each other with mock alarm, and then Red Fingers slowly inched his leg forward.

The guard gave the gun a little threatening bounce. "You don't want to do that, sir."

Red Fingers grinned…and completed a single step forward.

The guard fired.

The gunshot sounded like a nuclear explosion in the confined space of the maze. I couldn't quite believe he'd done it, but I was goddamn glad he had.

Until I saw Red *catch* the bullet.

His hands had moved too fast to see, and were hovering in the air near where his right shoulder had been; they were cupped together. He waited for a moment, then threw his hands out towards us, releasing a small moth that fluttered away.

"What the fuck—" I heard the guard say.

"Go," I hissed at him, "get the fuck out of here and tell Greg to close us down and call the cops—"

He didn't listen; he was a big man with a gun, and he wasn't going to take any shit. He fired two more times.

Red's head knocked back once, twice…then he grinned, and there were the two bullets held in his teeth.

"That ain't right…" murmured the guard.

I was about to shove him out of there, get him moving, anything—but before I could, Red spat the two bullets out—

The guard fell dead, one bullet having passed through each eye and out the back of his head.

Red's friends clapped appreciatively. Red performed a small

bow to them.

Then they all turned toward me.

I was dead. This was real, and they were going to kill me, no trick, and all I could hope was that they left the rest of my cast alone and that maybe Maeve would somehow escape...

"You're here for Maeve," was all I could I think to say.

But it worked. For the first time, I saw a small measure of surprise pass among them. "You must be the owner of this fine establishment," said Red.

"Yes. This is my business, and there are a lot of innocent people here who don't deserve to be hurt..."

"They don't?" Red was mocking me now. "After all the victims they've frightened?"

"It's just play. People like to be scared when they know they won't be hurt; they pay for it. We provide a safe environment, and that's why they like it."

"Oh, we like to scare as well. But we're a bit more truthful than you; we know that our tricks can give bad dreams, anxious feelings. We can make someone fearful for the rest of their life."

I motioned at Marty and the guard. "These aren't tricks, and they're not dreaming."

"Are you sure?"

"Look at—" I broke off as I gestured angrily at Marty.

Who was moving.

His fingers fluttered a little tap dance against the blood-soaked concrete floor. Then he sat up, and the motion caused his intestines to spill forward. Uncaring, he rose slowly to his feet; blood gushed forward, slopping out of his torso, down his legs and to the floor, along with more of his insides. But his eyes didn't move; they kept their forever stare, never blinking.

I swallowed down the urge to vomit, but that need was replaced by panic as Marty turned toward me. His jaw hung slack, thick strings of congealing drool dangling from his lower lip. He moved stiffly, like a puppet, as he walked forward.

At me.

Reflex took over. My legs backed up on their own. Before I knew it, I'd stumbled over the kid who'd hit the file cabinets, and I fell. The kid looked up, saw Marty advancing on us, and he screamed. It was a sound I should've known well, but this wasn't a girl screaming to relieve a little tension, or a surprised boy who'd follow with a giggle; this was a scream that told me a human be-ing had just permanently blown a mental fuse.

I was struggling to hang onto my own circuits. Marty reached me and started to bend low, and I'd seen every zombie movie ever made and had nothing to fight back with and figured I was dinner, and God it was going to hurt—

Marty fell over, truly dead. He fell right across my legs, and the terrible warmth and spongy softness of his insides did make me vomit this time.

And they laughed. No, this time…they HOWLED. They slapped themselves and each other. They wiped tears from their eyes.

Before they'd even finished, they turned and walked away, down the corridor into the heart of Hell Manor.

I spat to clear my mouth, said, "Sorry, Marty," as I pushed him roughly away, and got to my feet. I was covered in blood and shaking like I had the world's worst case of stage fright. My immediate instinct, of course, was to get the fuck out of there as fast as I could and never look back, and I confess I was turning to run…when I heard the kid under the desk. He was still cry-ing softly, and murmuring something over and over that sounded like, "Oh man oh Jesus oh man Oh Jesus…"

That brought me back. I had responsibilities. At least two peo-ple were already dead because of me (was it three? Didn't Greg say they had no idea what had happened to RJ, the actor in the opening scene?). And the boy who'd already shrieked himself hoarse at my feet would need years of therapy just to be able to weave a basket.

No more.

The first order of business was to call Greg and tell him to start clearing out the mazes. I pulled out my cell phone, touched the screen—and the phone displayed the pale, sneering features of Mr. Red Fingers.

I hurled it against the wall. It hit and shattered. Okay, so I couldn't call for help. I'd have to do this on my own.

I leaned down to the kid under the desk, kicking myself for being unable to remember his name. "Can you stand?"

He stopped crying, gulped, then nodded and crawled out.

"What's your name?"

"Terry."

I put a hand on his shoulder and gently guided him towards the corridor leading to the front entrance. "I need you to do something for me: Get out of here, find Greg—you know him, right?—and tell him we have to shut down, clear the mazes, and call the cops. Can you do that?"

The kid wiped at his nose and nodded. I gave him a pat and a small shove. "Good. Get going."

He took a step, then turned and looked back at me. "What are you going to do? You can't stop them."

"I know that. But I think I can get ahead of them, and maybe keep anyone else from getting hurt."

Terry looked like he didn't really buy that, but he turned and jogged off without question.

That really was my plan. The next scene was one without any live actors—it was a luggage storage room, with body parts crushed in suitcases, and a trunk rigged to a sensor that would make it shudder when anyone walked by. The three assholes were moving slowly, and I could use shortcuts and move behind walls to reach the next group of actors before they did. We could clear this haunt out before they finished it.

All of the mazes fed into the central open scare zone, which was our haunted farm area. If they got lost in there—which was easy to do, since we'd created a smaller maze with hay bales— then maybe I could even reach Maeve before they did, get her away and to safety...

I know that sounds a little crazy, like she was the last person I should be worried about. She could probably do the same shit these guys could, could probably take whatever they might dish out, just like she'd cut that boy's head off and brought him back to life...but she'd been scared of meeting these kin of hers, and that "could probably take" them stuff wasn't good enough for me. If there was even a chance I could get her away from here, I'd take it.

I ran after the trio.

Or rather, I ran the way they'd gone. Here's where I should explain a little something about how these haunt mazes are laid out: You're normally setting up in a confined area with limited space, but you want to make the maze seem long and winding, so you double it back on itself a lot. This gives you another advantage: One actor can work two hallways without moving; he just pops out in hallway #1, then goes back to his hiding space, turns around, and pops out in hallway #2. One actor, two scares. It's one of my basic rules of maze design.

I knew, of course, where every one of those hidey-holes was, and I knew I could use them to cut through the maze more quickly. The first one coming up was a sliding panel marked "Trash Chute"; we'd put it right across the hall from a door, so while everyone was edging past expecting that door to bang open, we'd get 'em from behind with the trash chute. I tried to remember who I'd put there, and I thought it was a girl named Lizzie. The trash chute opening was small, but I should be able to shimmy through; on the next corridor, Lizzie pushed through clothes hanging on a rack. Hopefully the trio wouldn't have made it that far yet...

I reached the "Trash Chute" panel and knocked lightly. "Lizzie," I called out in a stage whisper. When there was no response, I pushed the chute down, hoping she'd already taken off—

Instead she half fell on me. She was dead, her throat slit from ear to ear, real blood mixing with the fake stuff from her ghoul makeup. I bit back my own scream, and then pushed her aside. Her body hit the floor with a thud, and I heaved myself through the opening. I had to walk a few feet to get to the other side, and I tried to step carefully, but at one point I walked on what I thought was her hand. For some reason I felt bad about stepping on a dead girl's hand.

I reached the clothes rack and cautiously pushed the clothing aside, looking to my left.

I'd gotten lucky: I spotted the three men just where I'd hoped they'd be, checking out the luggage storage. They were engaged and pointing at things. I'd have to risk stepping out and running to the right. The next part of the corridor was mostly dark, so they might not see me at all.

I took a deep breath and ran. I didn't hear anything behind me but our pre-recorded sound effects and music.

The next scene was supposedly the hotel kitchen. This was a big set, with ovens, counters, cabinets, pots, pans, tons of prop body parts, and four actors: Two demon chefs, a devil diner, and a victim being butchered.

My stomach lurched at what I saw: There were still guests— the same group of teenaged girls I'd lunged at...God, was it really only a few minutes ago?

One of the demon chefs ran at me, raising a rubber cleaver before he saw my makeup. "Boss...?"

"Yeah. Listen, we've got a situation." I pitched my voice loud for the next part, trying to reach both my actors and the group of girls. "We need to clear this place NOW. There's some really bad shit going down."

The four actors looked merely puzzled...but the teenagers burst into giggles. "That's good," said one. "Oh, I remember when they did this last year," added another.

I realized I still had my make-up on, so I rubbed a sleeve frantically over my face, hoping that would get the message across. I saw a smear of greasepaint on the jacket, and the girls stopped giggling. "Listen, this is not an act."

The older guy playing the diner was named Aaron, and I remembered that he had some military experience—a tour in Iraq. "Aaron, I need your help. I'm not fucking around here—we've got a crisis situation and we need to get everyone out of here NOW."

Aaron instantly became my new favorite person. He jumped to his feet, tore off his mask, and pointed at one of the chefs. "Sandy, lead these young ladies out of here." Then he turned to me. "I'll take the rear, make sure we don't miss anyone."

"Good man." I pulled him aside and said, in a low voice, "If you see three white-haired creeps coming up behind you, just fucking RUN, okay? These guys are killers."

He frowned, but nodded. "Got it."

I decided right then Aaron was going to get a raise...if I lived long enough to give him one.

I had to assume that no one had gotten the word out to Greg yet, because Hell Manor was still in full swing; I knew he would've at least cut the music and sound effects if he knew just how bad the trouble was.

I edged around Sandy and the others. I wanted to go first, so I could clear out the actors before they jumped out, since I figured we'd all had enough frights tonight. The next section of the maze was set up like a run of hotel rooms; some of the doors were open, showing scenes within; some doors were fake; and behind some hid monsters, ready to spring. The first open room showed three vampire women attacking a man on the bed. Fortunately they all recognized me, and cleared out quick.

The next open room held a spider-creature (a giant puppet) and a screaming victim in a web. I got the actor playing the victim out.

A few feet down was the first door to pop open; as the actor thrust his masked face into mine, snarling, I snarled back. He stopped, perplexed, then heard what I was telling him and ran.

I cleared out two more rooms, then came to the next closed door that I knew concealed a monster.

Nothing happened.

I grabbed the door and yanked it open, hoping I wouldn't find another dead teenager.

It was Red Fingers and his buddies.

I don't know what I did, but whatever it was, they thought it the height of comedy, because they roared. They stepped out into the corridor, and I backed away, speechless.

"There you are," said Red, amiably. "We were afraid we'd missed you."

I had no idea how they'd gotten ahead of me. It was impossible…but then people sometimes said that about shit *I* did.

"So folks actually pay for you to scare them, is that right? I can see why Maeve would be attracted to this."

"Who are you?"

"Oh, of course—she wouldn't have told you that, would she?" His eyes glinted with some secret amusement. "Well, we've been known by many names: The Good Neighbors, The Little People, *Tylweth Teg*, the Tuatha de Danaan, leprechauns, fairies…but the name we use for ourselves is *sidh*."

He pronounced the last word "Shee," but I knew the spelling from the Halloween books I'd read. The *sidh* were the malicious fairies of old Ireland. Forget what you think the word "fairies" means—we're not talking glittery little cuties with wings and pixie haircuts. The real fairies were nasty pranksters who'd show up on Halloween (or Samhain, depending on how far back in time you went) and maybe steal your baby or set a building on fire. You know the word "banshee," right? The ghost woman whose howling always comes right before someone dies? "Banshee" actually means "woman-fairy"—does that tell you how badass the real fairies were? The Irish called them ironic things like "the good neighbors" for fearing of being overheard by nearby hidden fairies and offending them, because an offended fairy was something you did not want.

And now I had three of 'em.

Or was that four? "So Maeve is…"

"One of ours. Royalty, in fact. But she was naughty and ran away last Halloween, when the doors between our worlds opened up. Her father's understandably a bit upset, and we're here to take her home."

"Fine. Then I'll take you to her, but you have to leave the rest of my people unharmed."

That got them guffawing again, then Red said, "What's your name, lad?"

"Jack. What's yours?"

"It's Finn. These two with me are Angus and Cormac." Angus was the one who still wore a demon mask; Cormac nodded once.

Finn went on. "Now that we're all on a nice first name basis, we can tell you how this is going to proceed, Jack: You see, you have no say in the matter. You can make us neither promise nor offer, and we'll find Maeve without your help just as easily as with. Now, because we applaud your skills at trickery, we will allow you to walk away once; but trouble us again, Jack, and I think you'll find that your own skills are nothing compared to ours."

"I think I've already figured that out."

"Good. Now go back the way you came."

I didn't want to, of course. But maybe if I could just get away from them, have a few moments to think…

So I did the good boy thing, turned, and started walking. One step…two…three…

The floor disappeared, and I was falling.

I instinctively reached out and grabbed at something, anything. My fingers hit the edge of something—the hole I'd stepped into, apparently—and I held on for dear life. One quick glance below me confirmed a black void; above me, I could hear the three *sidh* laughing and walking away.

I wasn't in great shape, and my fingers were already slipping. I grunted and grit my teeth and tried to dig in, but the floor was slick concrete with nothing to grab. I was sliding back, back, slipping away, losing…

My grip. One hand lost it completely. The other was almost gone—

Someone grabbed my wrist.

"Hang on—I gotcha—"

There were two strong hands wrapped around my arm now and I was being hauled up, over the edge. My upper body was safe and I rolled away, then looked to see my savior—Aaron.

"There is no bonus in the world big enough for you, Aaron."

He was peering past me at the hole, which was narrow enough to jump over but wide enough to fall into, and it was easy to miss in the dark corridor. "What the hell is *that?*"

"I'll explain later. Where are the others?"

He gestured behind him. "I've got them hidden in that tight little walkway behind the maze."

I got up, trying to regain my composure. "Fantastic. Aaron, can you wait here and make sure nobody else steps into that?"

"You got it, boss."

I walked away a few feet to think. There was an exit out of the central haunted farm scare zone; if I could get to that, I could see what was going on with Greg, then race around to the end of the Hell on Earth haunt and clear it out, get Maeve and all my monsters to safety.

I just had to get out of this maze first.

I went over the layout in my head. There were two main rooms left: A gym, complete with bubbling hot tub full of blood; and our pièce de résistance, a ballroom full of projections, animatronics, and four live actors. The ballroom was big enough to get lost in; even if I wound up in there at the same time they did, my chances were good of avoiding them.

"You're not going after them, right?" Aaron was looking at me with wide eyes.

"No. But they're here for Maeve—'The Blood Queen.' I have to get to her first."

"Boss...!"

I jumped over the hole and ran, mostly to escape Aaron's common sense arguments. Which would include, "You'll die if you do that." And which would probably be right.

The maze took me through a black-and-white room lit by a strobe; the exit from that room took most guests a while to find, but of course I ran right to it and came out into another section, this one decked out with "windows" (that were mostly just recesses in the wall with curtains and fans). There were normally two monsters stationed here, but they were nowhere to be found now;

I hoped that meant they'd gotten away, or were at least smart enough to stay hidden.

I could see the gymnasium ahead. I crouched low, staying in the darkest parts of the hallway as I approached.

They were there.

They were pointing out things, ironically admiring my skills. They seemed to particularly enjoy the skeleton we'd rigged to the treadmill (I can't take credit for that—Greg had figured out a way to keep the treadmill running and make it look like the skeleton's legs were moving with it). They also enjoyed our yoga class—we'd twisted two mannequins into horrible shapes, and then positioned speakers near them so they screamed in agony.

The *sidh* were preoccupied, yes...but we'd opted to light that fucking gym bright, the way those things are always lit in real hotels. If I tried to get past them, there was almost no way they would miss me.

I'd have to wait.

It wasn't long; they soon had enough of our exercise demonstration, and headed out. I waited until they turned the next corner, then I ran up.

There'd been two monsters in the gym, a demonic instructor and a guy in a steam cabinet. They were both gone. As before, I could only hope that meant they gotten to safety.

I ran through the gym, feeling that strong light on me like a laser sight on a shooting gallery target. But I got through without incident, and jogged down to the corner they'd turned just seconds before. I paused there, straining to hear, but all I made out was the Hell Manor soundtrack. I looked around the corner.

They were at the end of the hall, about to step into the ballroom.

This was it. I counted to five, looked around the corner, then stepped into that last section of maze. I crouched low, crawling to the ballroom entrance.

I reached it, and craned my neck to look inside.

There: They were following the usual visitor path, and had paused to observe our ghostly projections.

Good. The ballroom was dark, and we had some special panels called "ghost glass" set up at angles to create the illusion of dancing specters. I could shimmy behind those panels, and it was unlikely they'd see me.

Unlikely...but not impossible.

We only had two monsters in the ballroom: One was a sort of pretty, pathetic ghost who begged men to dance with her; the other was seated among a band of mannequin musicians near the exit, and was that last scare that was calculated to send 'em running out.

The sad ghost girl approached them, asking for a dance. Damn—Aaron or whatever else had caused the others to clear out hadn't gotten this far.

I had to stop myself from shouting "No!", from offering myself up instead...but that would just get us both killed. Instead I crouched down and moved behind a curtain, then watched.

I couldn't hear their exchange—the ballroom, of course, featured an amped-up soundtrack of dour waltz music and hushed conversation—but I saw Finn suddenly grab her and begin spinning her around. I remembered her name then: It was Anastasia, even though her parents were from El Salvador, and she was 18, and this was her first haunt, and she'd had a natural acting talent and beauty that had made us cast her in this scene. Now her face went from distraught to outraged, especially when she saw Finn grinning. Her lips moved, and I knew she was telling him that we had cameras hidden throughout and security was on the way. We didn't have cameras, of course, but it was a standard line our monsters were all told to use in case of serious trouble.

Finn, of course, kept smiling and dancing.

While the attention was on Anastasia and Finn, I wormed my way around the far edge, crawling behind chairs and flats and mannequins. I made it unseen to the band, where I saw my monster, waiting for his chance.

This one I knew: DeManne had been with us from the start, and was one of our best veteran monsters, a pro through and through. I even felt like I could call him a friend; we'd been out for a lot of beers together, and DeManne had given me one of my best ideas for a scare ever, the year we'd done a maze called "Possessed" and he'd figured out how to make a monster baby burst out of a possessed girl's chest. He'd even come up with a way to fill that room with strange smells.

I crept up behind him and got as close as I dared. "DeManne," I whispered.

Of course he nearly leapt out of his chair at hearing someone behind me, but I hissed, "Stay still!"

He did, thank God, then whispered back, "That you, Jack?"

"Yeah. DeManne, listen: Whatever you do, don't move when these guys go by, okay?"

"What's going on?"

"Later. Just promise me that you will *not move*. Got it?"

He nodded slightly. "Yeah, okay, you the boss."

I clapped his shoulder once in acknowledgment, then moved past him. I was almost to the exit.

I paused to look back. Finn and Anastasia had stopped dancing, and I prepared for the worst—

But they walked away from her, while she stood staring, incredulous.

I exhaled in relief and then ducked out of the maze.

I was out in the cool night air now, the haunted farm looming before me. To the left was 3D Inferno; ahead, beyond the farm, was Hell on Earth. To the right, the exit—it was a gate in a section of chain link fence. The nice big green sign shining right above it was about the most beautiful thing I'd ever seen.

I ran to it, laid a hand on the latch—

It wouldn't budge.

That, of course, was impossible. It was just a metal latch that fell around the frame of the fence next to it. It was the easiest thing in the world to flip it up, push the gate open, and walk out. But the thing wouldn't move at fucking all. It was as if it had been welded shut.

Fine. I'd just climb the fucking fence.

I put my fingers into the link, started to pull myself up—and slid down instantly again. It was as if the fence was covered with grease, or ice. There was no way to get hold of it. No way out.

The bastards had sealed us in. They obviously didn't want Maeve escaping before they got her. No wonder everything was still live and there were no police. Greg was probably outside, wondering what the fuck to do.

Okay, so I needed a Plan B. I walked away from the useless exit, thinking furiously. What could I remember from my reference books like *The Halloween Encyclopedia*? What had the old stories said about keeping the *sidh* away? There'd been all kinds of folklore about protection against fairies on Halloween night, since that was the one night a year they could cross over into our realm. I remembered something about not throwing out water on Halloween night, since getting doused might piss visiting *sidh* off; some of it was about how to find or see fairies. But there was one, something about what to put near a baby's crib to keep the fairies away...it was...

Iron.

Right—the Irish would lay something made of iron near a child's bed, or hang it over a doorway...

So I needed iron—

Wait. The guard had shot these guys, and they hadn't so much as flinched. I tried to remember my basic metallurgy: What were bullets made of?

I recalled lines from old movies: "Fill 'em full of lead!"

Right. Bullets were lead. Not iron.

And Maeve...I understood now why she'd made a big deal out of her sword being made from silver. At the time I'd thought she was pulling my leg, but now I knew she'd been right. She wouldn't have been able to handle a blade made of iron.

I still had a chance, then. If I could just get something made of iron. Or steel—steel was mostly iron, so maybe that'd work, too.

If any of it would work. If this wasn't just an old wives' tale. But I was discovering more and more that those same old wives might have been right about a thing or two.

I needed tools—a crowbar, an iron rod, a hammer, a—

Pitchfork. Of course. We had pitchforks for decoration in the haunted farm area. There was one fifteen feet away from me, attached to the scarecrow that guarded the front of the hay maze. I ran over to that sucker, who was mounted about six feet above the ground on a stack of bales, and I yanked him down. I'd used twist-ties to attach the pitchfork, and I had nothing to cut them with. I felt a pang of guilt as I broke the scarecrow's arms, but it was the only way I was going to get that pitchfork free.

And I could hear the *sidh* coming.

I tore at the mannequin's rubber arms, and finally the pitchfork slid loose, taking some scraps of flesh-colored foam with it. I threw the rest of the figure aside, grabbed the fork, and ran into the maze.

Around the first turn was a fake corn field, and I knew my first monster was placed there. As I ran forward, he did his job and leapt out—then stopped, startled, as he saw me standing there.

I knew how I must look, with make-up smeared across my face and a pitchfork in hand. I couldn't remember this guy's name, so I just had to order him. "It's me, Jack, the boss. I want you to run that way and into the 3D Inferno, find something to block the entrance, and don't fucking come out. You got it?"

He swallowed, then said, "What—?"

"Just do it!"

He nodded and ran. I hated to shout at a kid who was at least fifteen years younger than me, but I'd maybe just saved his life.

I backed up into the shadows, tightened my grip on the pitchfork, and tried not to think about how likely it was that this would only get me killed. I could be remembering the metal wrong... what if it was not metal at all, but some type of wood? What if that was just a legend, with no basis in reality? Would they already know I was here, waiting for them, and just not come this way at all?

While I was thinking exactly that, I heard them. They were conversing in that strange language; they were loud, making no attempt to move quietly. Why should they? They thought nothing could harm them. I had to hope that was wrong.

The voices grew nearer...nearer...I tensed...only a few feet away now...

I saw the first one round the corner, and I charged.

The tines of the fork impacted with what felt like flesh, and he—Cormac or Angus, I didn't know which—actually cried in pain and clutched at the pitchfork impaling him. I yanked, and the tines pulled free. He fell.

I was exultant—it'd worked. I had an honest-to-fuck weapon.

The other two appeared and dropped to their knees by their comrade, concerned. They jabbered at each other frantically, and I leapt forward again, jamming the pitchfork down. But it collided with nothing but the dirty asphalt—Angus and Cormac suddenly winked out of existence. I staggered, then righted myself, lifting the pitchfork to face Finn, who stood a short distance away.

"Well played, Jack," he said between clenched teeth. "You've hurt Angus badly, and Cormac's taken him home. But you still have me to deal with."

I didn't waste time with a (not so) witty remark; I just jabbed.

Finn sidestepped and vanished. But a second later I heard his voice echoing from somewhere close by. "So, you're willing to risk your trickery against mine, Jack? The duel's on, then!"

He howled again, and the sound faded off into the night.

I wasn't howling. In fact, if truth be told—I was scared. Scared shitless.

I was a professional trickster who relied on tricks. Misdirection. Sleight-of-hand. Modern technology. He was a mythological trickster who had real magic at his disposal. This guy could make bottomless pits with a wave of his hand.

He could do anything. I had a pitchfork.

Okay, I tried to tell myself, I had other advantages. This was my playground, after all; I knew every inch of it. I knew all the twists and turns, all the places I could hide or attack from. I had a weapon that could hurt him. And I knew what he was after.

I was thinking all this, mind you, as I was moving. I wasn't about to stay in one place too long and let him turn the corn behind me into snakes, or the hay bales into boulders. He'd have to find me first.

I knew he'd gone further into the hay maze, so I backtracked and came out of it. The farm scare zone was big, and the hay was only one part of it. Going around the outer rim of the scare zone would take longer, but I gambled that he was moving slowly. And the hay maze was deliberately designed with misleading paths that went nowhere; if I was really lucky, he'd got lost in a few of those and I'd gain some extra time.

Since most of the haunted farm was a scare zone, we had a lot of monsters roaming there. As I ran past them, I tried to order them all to take shelter in the Hell Manor maze, guessing that Finn would keep going forward and not bother going back the way he'd come. I didn't have time to see if they'd heard me and understood; I had to keep moving.

I also encountered a few knots of guests, still making their way through the scare zone. There wasn't much I could do for them at this point, so I just ducked around them.

Until one of them roared at me and turned into a towering, slavering wolf-thing.

Yeah, okay—I was so startled I fell right on my ass—this thing was a good twelve feet tall, and so broad it blocked out all the lights. But I never lost my grip on the pitchfork, and I held it up, gesturing with it in what I hoped was a threatening manner. The wolf-thing roared louder, but didn't come any nearer. I got to my feet and thrust the pitchfork up.

The thing vanished. I got a peripheral flash of Finn running back into the hay maze.

The guests had all screamed and fled, and for a second I really did think it was a pity that I couldn't figure out a way to re-create that effect with projections and animatronics. Then I was jogging again, hoping that little episode hadn't meant that Finn was way ahead of me.

As I dodged around the rusted equipment we'd found free or cheap and filled our scare zone with, I thought about something Finn had said, about dueling with trickery.

My main goal was to keep him from reaching the "Hell on Earth" maze before I did, so how could I do that?

It hit me: I could rearrange the farm maze. It would be simple enough to move a stack of hay bales, lead him to believe he'd reached a dead end and had to retrace his steps. I knew just where to do it, too: I was running along the exterior of the maze, and a few feet ahead of me it took a sharp turn just before reaching the exit. From where I was, I just had to move three, maybe six bales…

I spotted the corner I was looking for. There would be no way to find out if Finn was right on the other side of me or not. I'd have to take my chances.

The bales here were stacked three high, and I used the pitchfork to pull down the top one. It fell beside me, and I pulled out the middle one. Now I could risk a look into the maze:

No sign of Finn. But one of my monsters was staring at me in shock.

"Mr. Lichtner…?"

"Help me move these bales. We've got to block off the way out."

"Why are we doing that?"

I could've throttled the kid. I was surprised he hadn't been standing there texting. "We've got a problem. Just do it!"

He looked like a whipped puppy, but helped me reposition the bales.

I heard Finn coming. He was reciting nursery rhymes: "Jack be nimble, Jack be quick, Jack will soon be quite, quite sick!"

He was close. I hissed to the kid, "Get out of this maze and hide somewhere."

He started to open his mouth to question, then must have seen the look on my face. He ran.

I backed away, ready to run myself, if Finn realized my deception and just busted through the bales.

"Where are you, Jackie boy?" We were no more than ten feet apart now. I held my breath and waited.

"I'll find you soon enough..."

He turned around and went back.

I held in a sigh, waited a few extra seconds to be sure, then headed for "Hell on Earth," hoping it wasn't about to live up to its name for a whole new reason.

I reached the entrance and was about to step in when I heard a sound behind me. I turned, and saw—

The hay maze was on fire. The nine-foot tall walls were filling the night sky with flame; it was as if the whole thing had caught at once. Smoke swirled, the air was charged with the smell of burning straw and the whoosh of the flames.

The bales nearest to me collapsed, and Finn strode confidently through the fire, right at me, teeth bared.

Fuck.

I ran into "Hell on Earth." I had no ideas left, except to get away.

The opening of this area was a recreation of a catacomb; I ran past coffins, some upright, filled with mannequins; two held monsters, who made a sort of half-hearted effort to grab at me, confused by my speed. "Get back in the coffins and don't move," I yelled as I shot past them.

This maze was less dependent on narrow, twisting corridors and set up with an emphasis on large rooms that led directly from one to the next. The catacomb ended and I was in a sewer tunnel with giant animatronic rats springing from trash cans. I leapt over them and ran into a boiler room. This was a great set because it really *wasn't* a set—it was an actual boiler room we found in the back of the warehouse, and we'd used it every year, since it had plenty of places for monsters and animatronics to hide. I paused there to catch my breath and looked back; there was no sign of Finn yet, but I knew he was coming.

"What the hell...?"

I jumped at a voice right behind me, and then realized I'd just been startled by one of my own monsters. This one I knew—

another long-timer who was basically doing a Freddy Krueger this year, complete with slouch hat and knife fingers. His name was, ironically, Jason. He was a good guy, and I could probably trust him to do something for me…I just didn't know what that would be.

"What's with the pitchfork? Is that real?"

I'd forgotten I was still carrying it. It was time to remember again.

"Yeah, it is. Jason, we've got trouble, and it's headed this way."

"Oh. Shit. So…what do you need me to do?"

It hit me, then. I knew what I had to do. I didn't know if it would work, but it was our best—and maybe only—chance.

"Okay, I want you to go through the rest of the maze and get everybody—customers and monsters both—assembled in the room where Maeve's working."

"You got it." He asked no more questions; he just ripped off his mask and hat, and took off.

I heard Finn approaching now; the bastard was howling as he came, like some mad dog.

He was cocky, arrogant…maybe I could use that.

I took off out of the boiler room. The next room was decked out with tables and chairs, and a banner strung overhead read "WELCOME MANIACS LODGE 666." Normally there would have been three monsters in here, wearing little red fezzes on top of their "Doll Face" and "Hannibal" and "Michael Myers" masks, and lifting glasses full of fake blood as they ran after new victims. Jason, however, was doing his job and had gotten them out already, so there was nothing left but piles of body parts and fake cleavers everywhere.

But what I was looking for was the next room.

We called it "the Meat Locker," and it was a big space we'd packed with bodies and carcasses wrapped in plastic and hung from overhead. They were so close together you had to literally push your way through them, and it was impossible to see more than a few inches ahead in any direction.

Unless you dropped down to the floor, however; then you could see the feet of everyone in the room.

I made my way quickly to the middle of the room and moved off to one side, then lowered myself, holding the pitchfork ready in one hand.

I waited.

It wasn't long. Twenty seconds, thirty at most.

"Where are you, Jackie? Olly-olly-oxen-free..."

He came into the room, and the foam rubber corpses started swinging. I saw his booted feet moving forward; if he kept going straight, he'd pass right by me, close enough to reach out and touch.

Or stab.

I knew I couldn't kill him from this angle, but maybe I could slow him down, hurt him enough to seriously fuck up his thinking.

"I can smell you, Jack...nothing quite so intoxicating as the fear of another trickster."

Closer...two feet away now...the bodies almost directly overhead moving back and forth, spinning and banging against each other...I took a deep breath and tightened my grip...

Two of the bodies right over my head were suddenly pushed apart, and there was Finn, looking right down at me.

"Hello—"

He broke off as I jabbed the pitchfork into one foot. Then he *screamed*.

I'm sure they heard that all the way back at the entrance to the first maze. He screamed, and he clutched at the pitchfork handle, and I threw it at him as I jumped up. The wooden shaft hit him in the face before he could get it, and in that moment I ran past him, leaving the pitchfork embedded in his foot. I ran, and he screamed words that I can guess were the worst curses from his native tongue.

The next room was our version of *Survivor*, where we had several monsters in designer track suits in a jungle setting fighting for pieces of the contestant they'd just thrown off the island. The monsters were gone, leaving nothing but the fake palm trees with the giant spiders and snakes, and the remains they'd been arguing over.

I wasn't far from Maeve's room now. I dodged through the lunatic asylum we'd recycled from last year, the hospital scene, the alien laboratory...and all the time I still heard Finn screaming, although the sound was receding. He wasn't following me yet.

Good—I *had* bought myself a little time, then.

When I reached Maeve's area, I couldn't hear him anymore.

There she was on the little stage we'd made for her, levitating the skull with the glowing eyes. I saw her, and my heart danced. She was safe…and if my plan worked, she'd stay that way.

My other monsters were there, along with a knot of nervous customers; they were nervous because the monsters—most of whom had discarded their masks and props—were nervous. But the room was packed, which I needed if I was going to make this work.

Maeve saw me, and for a moment she hesitated. In that space I ran up to the stage and whispered to her, "Finn's on his way, but whatever you do, *don't stop*."

She froze, afraid; obviously she knew the name "Finn." "Maeve!" My voice called her attention back. "It'll be okay," I told her.

Although I knew it wouldn't. At least not for all of us.

But she nodded then, and went back to her routine.

I pushed through the crowd until I reached the black muslin where I knew Andrew, the actor who played Maeve's double, waited. He gaped when he saw me, and his eyes nearly popped out of his head when I hissed, "Andrew, give me your costume."

"What?"

"*Now.*"

He moved quickly. As he pulled off the dress and wig, I tore off my jacket and pants. Fortunately, I was slender like Andrew and was able to pull the dress over my head as he handed it to me.

I could hear Finn screaming. He couldn't have been far.

Andrew heard it, and he looked out into the room. "What was that?"

"Never mind. Help me with the wig."

He adjusted it for me.

Finn was almost to the room.

"Get out of here now," I whispered to him.

Even though he was wearing nothing but shorts and a tank top, he did. I pulled myself back into the alcove. I was yanking the muslin into place as Finn entered.

He must have stopped screaming when he saw Maeve. I heard her stumble on a line, and prayed that she wouldn't panic and run, or call out to me.

She didn't. Just that one stumble, then she was back on track. Talk about a pro.

At that exact moment, I knew I loved her. And I needed to know that, considering what I was about to do.

I didn't risk a peek, but I could imagine Finn, still in pain, mesmerized by her, just standing there watching until he remembered again why he was here, what he had to do…

Maeve knew that, too, because she cut a couple of tricks and moved right to the end of her routine.

I took a deep breath and listened hard.

"The pagan gods demand more than simple prayer," she intoned, "they must have blood. Do you want a blood sacrifice?"

Line number one.

The crowd was large but hushed, too anxious to really get into the routine. But Maeve wasn't about to let them off the hook. She put real power into it as she asked again, "Do you want a blood sacrifice?"

Line number two.

About half the crowd shouted back "Yes" this time.

My heart was hammering.

"Do you want a blood sacrifice?"

Line number three.

Now her audience was hooked. "YES!" they shouted. I gave her the one beat I knew it took her to step back and through the curtain—

And I jumped out.

The crowd, properly primed, screamed and scattered.

Finn didn't. He leapt forward and wrapped his arms around me.

Light vanished. Gravity vanished. Time stopped. Something was ripped from me.

I'd won.

October 31st forever

It was a while before I could see. When my eyes focused and my brain started processing again, I saw green everywhere. It felt like I was in a soft bed, but looked like I was outside in a forest.

I was definitely surrounded by trees, tall ones, with sunlight just barely leaking in through the top branches, throwing the ground into deep green shadow. And these trees were *old*, their huge, scarred trunks covered in moss.

As I sat up, I saw I was apparently supported on a bed of leaves and flowers. When I stood, it collapsed, providing a soft carpet to walk on.

I felt comfortably warm, although where the heat came from I couldn't imagine.

Then I noticed the faces.

They were everywhere. Some were in the trees—boles in thick bark were actually noses, holes and cracks were mouths. Others watched from between trees, and all I could see of them were glowing eyes that tracked me as I moved.

This forest was literally alive, and obviously nowhere on Earth…my Earth, that is.

This could only be the world of the *sidh*.

"Welcome to my father's palace, Jack." I turned and saw Finn walking forward. He stopped a few feet away and sat; instantly a chair formed beneath him. He was dressed differently now, in matching green, and his injured foot was wrapped in some sort of poultice. He was smiling at me, but it was a different expression, without the malicious intent I'd seen there before. It was the kind of smile you'd expect from an old friend.

"You beat me with that last move. I salute you, Jack."

"This is…"

"Your fairy tales call it 'the Otherworld,' although Arthur knew it as Avalon. Of course, it wasn't my intent to bring *you* here, but since I did…you are our honored guest. You'll find it quite pleasurable here, Jack."

I heard something in the distance then, some sort of animal sound that set my teeth on edge and belied Finn's trustworthiness. Finn heard it, too; he cocked his head, listening.

"What was that?"

He returned his attention to me. "The *sidh* world is home to many things, not all of which are quite so friendly. There are shapeshifters here, ghosts, pookas, the Samhanach…but you'll learn about all that later. In the meantime, you're perfectly safe in the palace."

"But I don't see a palace."

"Oh, well—we can fix that, until you get used to it." He gestured, and walls formed around me. They were stone, and exquisite tapestries depicting the *sidh* in various settings—a great battlefield, a celebration—were draped at intervals. There were comfortable furnishings, and a large hearth with a cozy fire. Small faces carved into the mantelpiece watched me.

"You see, Jack? You can have whatever you want here."

"What I want is to go home."

"Ah." Authentic regret crossed Finn's features. "*That* is the one thing you cannot have. Surely you must have known that, and considered it before you risked yourself."

He was right. I *did* remember the very oldest stories, the ones that went back to the ancient Celts, the ones about mortal heroes who crossed into the *sidh* world only to discover they could never return.

I was one of those heroes now.

"Then Maeve..."

Finn did laugh now, and a little of that former viciousness was back. "Yes, Maeve. Your ruse was quite successful, Jack; by the time we'd discovered your trick, Samhain had ended and the portal was closed. Maeve's father has decided he won't pursue her anymore. If she so badly wants to live in the mortal realm, she's now welcome to it."

Good. My sacrifice had been worth it, then. Maeve was free.

Finn must have known what I was thinking though, because he walked toward me, then clapped me on the shoulder. "Jack, Jack, Jack...you still haven't figured it out yet, have you?"

I hadn't, because I didn't know what he was talking about. I just kept my mouth shut and waited for him to tell me.

"You still don't know who won the duel of deception."

I looked at the wry turn of his lips, thought for a moment...

And I knew.

Fuck. Of course. What an idiot I'd been.

"I'm sorry, Jack."

I believed him, because we'd both been had—

By Maeve.

Of course she'd never felt anything for me. She'd used me to elude her pursuers.

I'd like to spend all of Samhain with you. What a lie. Had I even really loved her, or had that been nothing but some sort of magic spell she'd cast on me?

And the worst part of all was that my biggest regret about being here, in this world that I could never leave, was that she wasn't here with me.

"Happy fucking Halloween," I whispered bitterly. I hadn't meant it for Finn, but he answered anyway.

"It's always Halloween here. You should like that part of it. In fact, I think you'll come to love it here."

Maybe I will, in time.

But right now I feel like a ten-year-old who's just gotten home on Halloween night only to discover that their trick or treat bag had a hole in it and they've got nothing. I'm the tween who always looks the wrong way in the haunted house and who screams every fucking time another monster jumps out. I'm every sucker who'd ever been scammed by the blonde in a bad movie.

And when I see her again, I'm going to tell her exactly how I feel.

THE MAZE

Three seventeen-year-old boys and one girl stood at the front of the dilapidated farmhouse, eyeing the hand-lettered sign that read: "CORN MAZE—$5—ENTER THROUGH BACK."

"This looks a lot more like the 'trick' side of 'trick or treat,'" said Dozelle, shifting his jersey-clad bulk from one foot to the other.

Adam ran a tattooed hand through his long blonde hair, blown about by the late October breeze. "Yeah, Doze is right. This just looks lame, Sean. I hear that haunted house out by the mall will scare the shit out of you. They've got these guys made up as zombies who eat real raw meat—it's just totally fucked up."

Smirking, Ashley said, "You're the fucked up one, if you believe those stories."

Sean eyed the surroundings, silently debating. He was genuinely curious about elderly Miss Mackenzie, who owned the house and a couple of acres of farmland behind it. When a local blogger had reviewed her maze, he'd said that Miss Mackenzie had avoided using any of the usual agri-entertainment companies that specialized in creating corn mazes and had used her own methods of cutting the design, although she wouldn't divulge her "trade secrets." She was rumored to be into some strange stuff, and Sean, who'd recently developed an obsession with folklore, wanted to see the "bizarro Halloween shit" hinted at in the article.

And, although he'd never admit it to his friends, he missed trick or treat. He'd loved Halloween as a kid—the candy, the costumes, the rich feeling of being out in the night disguised as someone else, someone more powerful than Sean Andrews. He wanted to find a special Halloween experience to fill that hole. He was the only one of the quartet in costume—old moth-eaten army fatigues he'd found in the attic—because he hoped to crash some parties later in the evening, since he hadn't actually been invited to any.

Dozelle made a dismissive gesture. "Let's go."

Sean was about to try to convince his friends to stay when Ashley stepped in for him. "C'mon, we can do this and still do the haunted house by the mall." She gave Sean a slight smile, and relief flooded through him.

Adam shrugged. "What-fucking-ever. Let's just get it over with."

Sean led the way around the ramshackle house, its peeling sides badly in need of paint, the roof creaking two stories overhead. As they passed beneath an open window, he got a whiff of something musky and pungent, some sort of herb he couldn't name.

"Look at this shit," Dozelle said, standing above a little pyramid of flat stones surmounted with a small animal skull.

"Eww," Ashley said. "Is that a cat skull on top?"

"That's fucking weird," Adam said.

Sean joined them, grinning. "See? This might be good after all."

The driveway took them behind the house, where a shallow backyard opened onto a wide vista of tall corn, the stalks fading from green to gold. An old woman sat in a folding chair beside an entrance into the corn. She had a cigar box and a small stack of cards in her lap. She sat in silence as they approached, but her eyes—clear, green, strangely youthful—locked on Sean, making him uncomfortable.

"One, please," Ashley said, thrusting a five-dollar-bill at the woman. Dozelle and Adam also held out cash. Sean fumbled in his wallet, counting out ones, still sensing her gaze on him.

Ashley took a card from the woman and said, "We read about this place in the paper. You're Miss Mackenzie, right?"

The old woman squinted up at Ashley, giving Sean a chance to look her over. He realized she wasn't really that old—she might have been no more than sixty. Her face held few lines, her hands were steady, but her long silver hair made her look older. She wore a simple white polo shirt and baggy chinos, but the heavy gold necklace around her throat was unusual—it was a solid band of gold, not a chain, and had no decoration. "Is that a torque?" Sean asked.

The woman smiled at him. "So it is. Not many folks know that."

He heard Dozelle and Adam snickering, but ignored them. "I like history. In fact, I just read a book about Halloween, and it talked about the ancient Celts. That's where I read about torques."

"You're a smart boy," she said. "So you know what tonight is really all about, then."

After a second of thought, Sean answered, "The night when the border between our world and the next is at its thinnest, and the *sidh* could come through, right?" He hoped he'd pronounced *sidh* correctly—"shee."

Evidently he had, because the old woman nodded. "Or so the Celts believed." She laughed, a sound that was strangely unnerving.

Sean passed his money to her, anxious to be out of her presence. She hesitated before taking it, then said, "You'll be my last guests this year, looks like."

Sean realized the sun was about to dip below the horizon, leaving the muddy paths between the corn stalks already deep in shadow. "Are we too late? Will we need flashlights or something?"

"Shouldn't take you that long in there. It'll still be light enough to see."

Sean took the card she offered, saw it was a little hand-drawn and Xeroxed map of the maze. "Well, okay, then. Let's get lost."

Dozelle and Adam were already well into the maze as Ashley and Sean approached the entrance. Ashley leaned into Sean and whispered, "What are the *sidh*?"

"Evil fairies that the ancient Celts believed would come out on Samhain—their Halloween night."

Ashley said, "How do you know that?"

"I was just reading this book about the history of Halloween, and about how it goes all the way back to the Celts."

They were on the verge of stepping into the maze when Sean heard the old woman call after him, "Thank you for your sacrifice."

Again, Ashley leaned in to ask, softly, "What did *that* mean?"

"Bad joke about my army costume, I guess." Something nagged at the back of Sean's consciousness, however, and it took him a few seconds to pin it down. *Halloween...history...Samhain...* "That's weird..."

Ashley asked, "What is?"

"That crack about sacrifice. Sometimes the Celts sacrificed humans on Samhain."

Ashley mimicked gagging before saying, "Nice."

"Actually, it was supposed to be a great honor to be chosen for the sacrifice."

Stopping at the entrance to the maze, Ashley asked, "You mean they just went *willingly*? That's crazy."

"It is, but...yeah, I don't get it, either." And he didn't; in fact, he'd rolled it around in his head for a while, and just couldn't see how anyone could accept such a useless death. Even if you believed in all the old gods and that sacrificial deaths would appease them, why would you offer *yourself*? It didn't make sense.

Adam and Dozelle were already at the first turn in the maze, peering down at the maps, shoving each other, snickering. They vanished around the turn, leaving Sean and Ashley to catch up. "I love the smell in here," Ashley said.

Sean inhaled deeply and nodded. The smell of corn husks mixed with yesterday's rain and fertilized earth. The corn, still mostly green this far into the season, was tall and thick, obscuring their view in all directions except the three-foot-wide path before and behind them. The sky was the blue of autumn, so deep it almost hurt to look at.

"This way," Ashley said, tugging at his arm as they reached the turn.

Adam and Dozelle were thirty feet ahead, standing at a fork, comparing it to the map. "Which way?" Adam asked.

"Shit, man, I don't know."

Adam considered and then said, "Left." They wandered off that way.

Ashley and Sean reached the branching pathways. Ashley looked the map, said, "I'm pretty sure it's to the right here."

Sean looked at his own map and agreed. "Let's go right, then."

"What about Doze and Adam?"

"They'll figure it out. C'mon."

They veered to the right. On the map, the design looked like a series of branching spirals—not the usual farm scene or logo of most corn mazes. "I wonder if this design means something," Sean said.

Ashley paused, her head cocked. "You know what's weird? I can't hear Doze and Adam at all."

Sean stopped to listen. "I don't hear anything outside of us. I guess the corn is like the ultimate sound baffle or something."

"I guess."

Ashley continued on ahead of him, and Sean found himself looking at her back—or, more specifically, at her ass. She hadn't exactly worn a costume for the evening, but she'd dressed differently from her usual school outfits of black jeans and band t-shirts; instead, she wore leggings and a low-cut blouse. He wondered if she'd dressed that way for him. He hoped so. She looked *good*, and he hoped that at some point tonight they might leave Doze and Adam and head off on their own. He'd known Ashley since they'd both been twelve, but he'd only recently noticed how much better she looked than all the other girls. He thought she might feel the same about him; maybe on Halloween, dressed as a brave soldier from some long-gone war, he'd have enough courage to find out.

Ashley turned a corner, and stopped abruptly, uttering a little cry. Sean looked past her. "What...?"

Then he saw what had caused her to react: Ahead of them was a pumpkin-headed scarecrow, hung on lengths of wood so it stood slightly above the corn. The eyes of the jack-o'-lantern glowed red, the flaps of the old jacket flapped slightly in the evening breeze, and Sean laughed at the surprise.

Beside him, Ashley said, "Didn't expect to meet up with *this* guy."

Sean looked past the scarecrow, saw the path continue on the other side. "Guess we go around him."

"Yeah..."

He went first. There wasn't much space between the scarecrow and the corn, forcing Sean to turn sideways to get by, and he wondered how on earth Dozelle—who was a quarterback for the school's football team—would get past. He looked up overhead at the scarecrow as he wormed his way under it, and he had the unsettling notion that it had moved, especially the arms. He half-way expected to feel its twig-fingered hand on his shoulder, holding him, pulling him back…then it was behind him, hanging, unmoving in the last rays of the sun. Ashley joined him, giggling. "Yep, now it's getting good."

Sean had an urge to reach for her. Just her hand; no one would know. She stood close to him, it would be so easy…but then she turned away, heading off into the maze again, and Sean had the unreasonable thought that he'd lost that chance forever.

The path took several wide sweeping curves, moving along the outside of the map, spiraling in. The sun fell below the unseen horizon, and Ashley had to squint to read the map. "Okay, at the next fork we should go left."

"You're the navigator. Wonder what happened to Doze and Adam…"

"Wanna bet that they end up calling us and begging to get them out?"

Sean smirked. The comment made him think about his own phone, and he pulled it out of his pocket to take a photo. "Hey, how about a selfie?"

Ashley leaned in next to him. "Do it."

He held the camera out, smiled. The app clicked. He checked the photo, said, "Oh, it's good—I don't look like a total idiot. Want a copy?"

"Sure."

He tried to punch in Ashley's number, but the phone had no signal. He moved it around, walked a few feet back and forward, but nothing. "That's strange—I can't get a signal in here."

Ashley pulled out her phone, thumbed icons on the screen. "I can't either." She shrugged then, putting the phone back in her purse. "I guess Doze and Adam are on their own. Good luck, dumbasses."

They continued on, moving in a tightening arc to the left. At one point Sean pushed some of the corn leaves out of the way and felt moisture on his fingertips. He used the light from his phone to look and saw dark red on his fingers, even smeared on the cuff of his army jacket. "What the fuck…"

Ashley looked at him. "What?"

"There's blood…" He showed her his fingers.

"Are you sure it's real?"

Sean rubbed his fingers together. He'd once mixed some fake blood for a zombie Halloween costume, and the stuff had been thick and sticky; this didn't feel like that at all. He sniffed it, got a hint of copper. "No, but…I don't think it's fake. Maybe an animal…"

They kept going, until they reached a sharp turn, where Ashley slipped. Sean jumped forward to catch her, and his own feet encountered a treacherous slickness. Looking down, he saw that the ground glistened in the dim light. He turned his phone light on, saw they stood in a huge scarlet pool. The smell hit him then, thick and metallic, turning his stomach. "Holy shit…"

Ashley looked pale in the phone's glow. "Fuck."

Sean waved in the direction they'd come. "We're not going through there. Let's go back the way we came, just get out of here."

"Yeah. What about Doze and Adam?"

"If we go back, we should be able to find them along the way. Then we all just get the fuck out of here, okay?"

"Good plan."

Sean turned and took the lead, moving back the way they'd come. But something was wrong—this wasn't the long curves they'd traversed before; now they walked along a series of short straightaways with sharp angled turns. He finally paused at an intersection and held the map up to the phone's light. "We took a wrong turn somewhere."

Ashley peered over his shoulder. "That doesn't look right at all. Sean…what if the map's *deliberately* wrong?"

Sean looked at Ashley's face, her eyes worried, and he didn't hold back on taking her hand. "It can't be that big. If worse comes to worse, we'll just push through the stalks in a straight line until we get out." But Sean felt the lie in that even as the words left his mouth—he knew the stalks were stronger than he was.

For a second, everything whirled into a delirious joy as Ashley squeezed his hand. "Let's just make sure we don't get separated, okay?"

He tried to smile reassuringly. "Okay."

They walked to the right, made another turn, another…and found themselves back at the pool of blood, but now on the other side. "How did we get here?" Ashley asked.

"I don't know, but let's just keep going. It's getting darker."

Sean led the way through the gloom. At one point he turned a corner and stumbled on something. He looked down, perplexed, used his phone to reveal the object—and gasped at what he saw:

An arm, severed just above the elbow, the edges ragged as if it had been torn, not sawed or hacked off.

Ashley saw it and uttered a choked scream. She clutched at Sean and said, "That's fake, right?"

It didn't look fake to Sean. It smelled real, it looked real… and then he realized: the skin on the arm was dark brown, the muscles thick…

"No. I think…it's Dozelle's."

"Oh my God." He felt Ashley's body start to tremble and wasn't so sure that his own wasn't doing the same. He was abruptly sorry that his army costume hadn't come with any weapons, not even a knife or a nightstick. Ashley hadn't brought a purse. They had nothing.

He heard it then: something in the corn, moving. A *lot* of somethings, rather, creating a leafy susurration that raised the hairs on Sean's neck.

"What *is* that?" Ashley's eyes were wide as they darted around, seeking the source of the sound.

"I don't know, but let's keep going."

Holding Ashley's hand like a life rope, Sean led the way down the path between the stalks. They turned a corner and saw the flicker of flames coming from somewhere ahead; they slowed down, tiptoeing, Sean's head stretched out. They came to an open area in the corn where a number of the paths converged, and it took Sean a few moments to comprehend what he saw there.

Torches were set around a cleared ring about fifty feet across. In the middle of the circle was a 55-gallon drum; a man's body was draped over the lip of the drum, the head and shoulders inside. Sean saw that the big corpse was missing one arm, and he knew instantly. "Dozelle."

Beside him, Ashley clamped a hand over her mouth in shock. Sean looked around warily, but saw nothing, so he stepped forward. He didn't dare touch the body, but as he neared it he saw a noose dangling down the back, knotted around the neck, and a huge swath of blood staining the side of the drum. Firelight glinted off liquid in the drum, but he couldn't see Dozelle's head, since it was submerged. He couldn't tell what had killed Dozelle—the water, blood loss, or the noose. Then he remembered something from the book he'd read, about how the Celts had used three forms of death in their sacrifices. "This is a ritual killing."

"It looks like the work of a maniac," Ashley said, her voice quivering.

Sean saw she was right—aside from the torn-off arm, Dozelle's body was covered with cuts, scratches…*bite marks.*

Sean tightened his grip on Ashley's wrist. "Let's go."

"Which way?" They stopped, eyeing the number of paths leading out of the circle. There were a half-dozen.

Ashley examined the map by the light of her cell phone, then lowered both. "None of this is on the map. This whole thing is a trap." She crumpled up the useless card and tossed it to the ground.

Sean pushed aside the pang of terror that arced through him. "Okay…okay, we're on our own. We can do this." He examined the paths; after a few seconds, he pointed to the opening second from the left. "That way."

"Why?" Ashley made no indication that she intended to move.

"Because I think we need to veer to the left to get out of here, but the far left path is too obvious."

He held his hand out to Ashley. After a few seconds, she gulped. "Okay." She accepted his hand, gripping it tightly, even painfully, and they set off on the chosen route.

The path curved slowly, but it also grew tighter, the wall of corn closer—and the sounds just behind it louder. They ignored several turn-offs and intersecting paths to continue on the main one. As they reached the point where the leaves began to brush their heads and shoulders, Ashley tugged on Sean's hand, forcing him to stop. "I don't wanna do this."

Sean looked at her, desperate. "Do you want to go back, try one of the other ways?"

She shook badly; the noise in the corn now sounded like a chorus of voices whispering in a language never spoken by human tongues. "No, but…"

"Then we have to go on, Ashley. We have to try." He held her eyes with his, hoping he looked stronger than he felt. After a few seconds, she nodded. They began walking again, crouching to avoid as much of the corn as possible. They'd gone maybe a hundred feet when Sean yelped and pulled back, colliding with Ashley. "What?" she asked.

He held up his hand to one ear, pulled it away, saw blood on his fingers. "Something bit me."

Ashley was next, staggering into him with a yelp. "Something touched me on the leg."

Now they heard laughter, small but distinct.

"C'mon!" Sean began running down the narrow path, shielding his face with one hand, holding onto Ashley with the other. He felt tiny mouths and claws reaching for him, finding him, tearing his skin, he heard the laughter and the rush of movement…but he saw nothing.

The path suddenly opened before them again, into a long rectangle, and they pulled up short when they saw the thing at the far end: It was a scarecrow, like the one they'd already seen, but this one was made of flesh. Human flesh.

It was Adam. He was clearly dead, his arms tied crucifixion-style to a cross bar, legs wrapped around the central vertical stake. His face had been painted like a jack-o'-lantern's, with dark holes for the features…then Sean realized those black places weren't paint, but chunks carved out of Adam's face. Blood had pooled around the base of the stake where it was jammed into the ground, telling Sean that Adam had been killed very recently.

Behind Adam was the far end of the space. There was an opening there, leading to another path through the corn…and there was light at the end of that path.

Sean began pulling Ashley toward the opening, but she resisted. He looked back at her, and she asked, "What are you doing, Sean?"

"Behind him—there's an opening in the corn and I can see light there. I think it's the exit."

Ashley looked past him, then gave him a quick nod. He wanted to kiss her then, like the hero in a movie would…but he didn't feel much like a hero, and he didn't think Ashley wanted to be kissed within a few yards of the mutilated body of their friend. Besides, they needed to keep moving.

Sean and Ashley hugged the outside of the rectangle as much

as possible, but they would have to pass close to the corpse to reach the opening. Sean tried to push the corn back, to give them as much leeway as possible, but he still felt Adam's blood drip on his shoulder, into his hair, and he fought back the urge to vomit.

At last he was in the opening, moving, pulling Ashley along—and then her hand was yanked from his grip.

He turned, almost expecting to see Adam alive, grabbing her, leering—but what held Ashley had never been human, or even truly alive. Sean could only see outlines in the gloom, faint glowing figures. Dozens of them, *hundreds*, none taller than a foot. They were humanoid in shape but winged, and they held the shrieking girl suspended in mid-air. As Sean watched, paralyzed, they began to tear pieces of her away, and he knew they'd also done this to Dozelle and Adam. Ashley twisted and bucked and screamed in agony, her blood spraying out, adding more definition to the ephemeral shapes that held her...

The *sidh*. The words appeared in Sean's mind, on the surface absurd, but nonetheless true, and he knew that his recognition of them was something buried deep in his very cells, an instinct as basic as eating or breathing. They'd always been there, waiting for October 31st, waiting for veils to drop and gates to open...

When they tore off Ashley's head, Sean's paralysis snapped and he ran. He stumbled down the path, arms flailing, screaming, his only thought that he had to *get away, get away GET AWAY*—

In front of him, not far, stood Miss Mackenzie's house, lights glowing in the windows like beacons, and knew he was almost there, out of this nightmare, free—

His legs went out from under him and he went down.

Looking up, Sean saw why he'd been allowed to make it this far, and why he would never leave this maze: A massive shape stood before the house now, blocking any escape. The shape was at least thirty feet tall, broad, with a great horned head that hid part of the indigo sky. Like the *sidh*, it was indistinct but gaining more form with each passing second. Sean glimpsed something else through it, something on the ground: Miss Mackenzie, dressed now in a white robe, kneeling in supplication.

He understood, then.

"*Thank you for your sacrifice.*" That had been no flippant response to his costume. A sacrifice had been made tonight—Dozelle and Adam and Ashley had already been given to the *sidh*

325

and this horned god. Now Sean would be the final offering, the last one made to an ancient god on a modern Halloween night. Would this open the gateway forever? Or was there a chance Miss Mackenzie was trying to shut something that had already opened?

Sean couldn't rise; he would run no more. His life belonged now to the deity before him. He would be taken by it and joined to its sacred matter. Whatever forces Miss Mackenzie had set in motion by arranging the deaths of his friends would be finally concluded by him. He would become the central character in the single most important story in mankind's history.

In the desire to merge with godflesh, he finally understood the real nature of sacrifice.

He prostrated himself and waited for what was to come.

THE ENCHANTED FOREST

He stood at the rusting metal gate, heart hammering as he stared into the dark woods beyond. A black cat perched on one of the gate's stone columns, its green eyes glittering with mischief. In a small clearing between the gate and the trees, headstones circled a small fire like campers listening to a ghost story. Beyond the mossy and cracked grave, the path that led from the gate into the forest was limned in moonlight, pouring down in a blue cascade between the tall, black-barked trees.

Connor forced himself to examine the surroundings and think. The gate, the cemetery, the forest…something about it was familiar…the forest…

The Enchanted Forest.

The name burst into his consciousness with the force of a physical blow. He staggered back, refiguring, grasping at memories that rushed through his misfiring mind. *The Enchanted Forest*…the beginning…he knew this place…no, he'd *created* this place, he was this place and it was him…

Drawn now by familiarity that lurked just out of his reach, teasing, Connor leaned forward on his cane and pushed open the gate. The hinges protested, but the cat remained undisturbed, causing Connor to suspect that it wasn't entirely real; but when he poked it with a finger, its fur was soft and its head turned to eye him. He suppressed a shiver as he moved past it. The answers he needed lay farther along the path, deeper in the woods. He hobbled warily past the graves, half-expecting some terrible surprise, a jack-in-the-box specter or paralyzing shriek, but there was nothing.

He knew the real scares waited ahead.

In the meantime, as he made his way along the narrow trail, his cane thumping against hard-packed earth, he tried to remember more about this place. About the day. About the beginning...

ooooo

"Dad, have you been taking your pills?"

Connor looked up at his son, Jeff, whose handsome brow (*When had he gotten that big?*) was furrowed in concern. Beside Jeff stood Terry, the diminutive Guatemalan caregiver.

"Hell yes, I've been taking my damn pills."

Jeff gestured at Terry, who stood by, impassive. "Terry says she hasn't seen you take them."

"Of course she hasn't. That's because I take them before she gets here in the morning."

Connor wasn't about to confess that he had been opening the little compartments of the huge pill container that Terry made up for him once a week, taking out his morning handful, and flushing them down the toilet. He was sure the pills were making him groggy and tired, and did nothing for him otherwise. But when he'd tried to argue that in the past—with Jeff, with Terry, with doctors and nurses—they'd all told him, *Oh no, Mr. Carson, you must take your pills, and you can't miss a single day.*

Bullshit.

"Dad, did you hear me?"

Connor looked up sharply. He didn't want to admit that he hadn't. "I heard you."

"So what day is this?"

Connor tried to gather his thoughts. What day was it? He didn't know, and he didn't care. Days hadn't meant much to him since Margie had died. *Nothing* meant much anymore, even his art. It had taken him a while after she'd gone to realize that everything he'd done—the work at the amusement park, the designs, the paintings—had all been for her. Without her, there was no reason to do it. "What damn difference does it make?"

Jeff tried a smile. "It's Halloween, and I've got a surprise for you."

Halloween…God, he and Margie used to love Halloween. They'd hold grand parties, costume affairs for all of their friends from Merry Mountain, and some years even the great man, George Merry himself, would turn up, elaborately costumed as a knight or a cartoon Napoleon. "Halloween…"

Jeff's smile broadened. "Right. The surprise isn't ready yet, but give us another few hours." Jeff and Terry exchanged a conspiratorial look.

"Just don't throw me a party. I haven't had much interest in parties since your mother passed away in May."

The smile on Jeff's face crumpled. "Dad…Mom's been gone for three years. Are you *sure* you've been taking your pills?"

Three years…? Had it really been three years since the cancer had taken Margie, since Connor had picked up a paint brush?

"I'm fine," he lied.

∞∞∞

Connor pushed into the woods, his way lit not just by the moon's rays but by mysterious glimmerings from behind the trees. Animal voices—bird caws, more distant mournful howls—sounded around him, and Connor felt a shiver that left him both fearful and strangely happy.

At least I know I'm still alive.

He rounded a slight turn in the path, and found himself surrounded by dozens of glowing red eyes. Things were hidden in the branches, in the trunks, small night things that peered out at him curiously, sometimes blinking.

I've been here before. If I'm right, around the next turn I'll see bubble-sized glowing things bobbing overhead, I'll hear tiny voices laughing…

He turned the corner, and was unsurprised to find himself facing an aisle between the trees filled with multi-colored lights floating just out of reach. He approached the first one and saw a humanoid figure, smaller than his fist, with iridescent wings.

Connor nodded and felt a deep sense of homecoming. "The Enchanted Forest," he murmured as he let the sense of familiarity fill him.

ooooo

"I want to call it 'The Enchanted Forest,'" George Merry had said on that day in 1968.

Connor Carson, the latest hire into the design staff for Merry Mountain, tried to stay focused on the boss's words, but he was confused—he had the odd sensation of being two places at once. Part of him whispered, *This is a memory*, but another part was living it now, and he went along with that part.

"Think you're up for the job, Connor?"

Connor nodded vigorously. "Oh, yes, sir, Mr. Merry! If we can't make this the best walk-through attraction ever, I'll eat a dancing skeleton."

Merry chuckled. "That's what I like to hear. Now go draw me some good scares."

ooooo

Connor was staring into the golden eyes of a huge wolf. Its head had pushed out from between the branches next to him, bringing him back to this place, and now he was breathing hard. The wolf's head was as big as an elephant's, its lips were pulled back in a snarl, its mouth filled with lethal white teeth each as big as a knife blade.

The wolf...how did I forget about the wolf?

The head abruptly withdrew, vanishing back into the shadows behind the trees. Connor's breathing slowed, and he pushed on, trying to remember what came next...

ooooo

Connor was hungry. He was surprised to see it was after 1 p.m. Where had the day gone?

"Terry...?"

His caregiver appeared, unfailingly cheerful. "What you need,

330

Mr. Connor?"

"Food."

"We have some lunch."

Connor saw he was in his bedroom, and he let Terry help him up out of bed, positioning his hand on his cane. "I hate this goddamn thing."

Terry giggled. "Oh, no no, Mr. Connor, you can't hate the cane."

"I do. I hate the way it squeaks on the tile. I hate the stupid rubber tip on the end. But most of all, I hate having to use it."

Terry gave his arm a reassuring pat. "I know. I know. C'mon, I get Jeff and Patrick in here and we all have some nice tuna sandwiches, okay?"

"Jeff and Patrick are here...? What are they doing?"

"Something in the front yard—decorating for Halloween."

That's right—today is Halloween. "Terry, did I ever tell you that George Merry himself once told me he thought The Enchanted Forest was the greatest contribution to Halloween since trick or treat?"

Terry smiled. "You did tell me that, Mr. Connor. Many, many people love your Enchanted Forest."

Just then, they passed out of the hallway into the living room and Connor saw—for the millionth time—the huge framed poster for The Enchanted Forest. He'd designed that poster himself for the attraction's opening in 1972. Silk-screened in Day-Glo colors, the art showed a little girl clutching her father's hand tightly as both pulled back, their shoulders tensed, from a gigantic wolf's head thrust out from between menacing dark trees. The bright violet type set against the dark blue background of the overhead sky read: "The Enchanted Forest Now Scaring at Merry Mountain." Connor remembered how opening day for the new attraction had broken the park's attendance records, how he and George had stood outside the exit of The Enchanted Forest, disguised in low hats and sunglasses, watching families exhaling and laughing. George had clapped one hand on Connor's shoulder and said, "They love it. Good job, Connor. Good job."

George had walked away, but Margie—who had stood quietly just behind the two men—had stepped forward, taken Connor's hand, and kissed his cheek.

It had been the best day of Connor's life.

ooooo

He couldn't remember what came after the wolf.

Connor stood a few feet from the next twist in the path, leaning heavily on his cane, afraid. The wolf had startled him. What if something even more frightening waited just ahead?

He didn't want to go forward. Should he turn around, go back the way he'd come? But the wolf was behind him, and he didn't relish facing it again. Besides…what if someone was waiting for him outside? How would it look if he'd been unable to complete the trip through his own creation?

He had to go on.

Taking a deep breath, he moved forward, cautiously placing the cane with each stop—it wouldn't do to fall here. It might be days before he was found, alone in this haunted place.

He turned the corner. The route ahead wasn't immediately visible—it narrowed and twisted—but he saw flickers of orange light, heard a low voice muttering.

What IS that?

Connor moved around the last group of trees blocking his vision and saw a clearing, with a house at the back and a figure near the path. The structure was an oversized gingerbread house, with walls and roof made of huge brown slabs of cookie, trimmed in white icing, a smoking chimney was built from red sugar plums, the windows were spun sugar, the trim gum drops and jelly beans. The figure was a wizened crone in a black hooded cape, stirring a huge bubbling cauldron as she softly recited a spell. The clearing was surrounded by a low fence made of candy canes and red licorice cross-beams. Near the witch, the black cat from the entrance sat atop a post, looking at Connor.

Connor was paralyzed with fear, unable to take his eyes from the witch. She was a fairy tale figure, certainly, but from where he stood she seemed completely real, so real he could almost feel evil rolling off her in waves. What if she looked up and saw him? The path was only a few feet from her—surely there was no way to move past her without being discovered. And how had the cat moved from the front without him seeing it? Had it run through the forest, a secret trail only it knew about?

Then awareness started to return, and he relaxed: *Of course— how could I have forgotten about the Witch? She became the most famous character in all of Merry Mountain. Even now, in the 21st century, haunters and designers call her the most realistic audio-animatronic character ever.*

But even with the return of his memories—weeks spent over his drafting board, getting every crease in her face and gnarled knuckle just right—Connor was uneasy. For one thing, he could smell the rank odor of whatever she was brewing up in the cauldron, he could feel the heat radiating from the cook-fire…wasn't the fire fake, just a few shreds of fabric and crinkles of foil cleverly lit from below to create the illusion of flames?

He shouldn't be feeling any heat from it. And that smell, like—

"…Eye of newt and tongue of frog, a tick from the tail of a diseased dog…" the Witch muttered, as she used a long branch (a broomstick?) to stir the cauldron.

The words, something about the words…a memory of a writer handing Connor a script, a new draft of the Witch's words…

Connor knew that some part of this wasn't real, but which part? Was the Witch nothing but the amazing robot the Merry Mountain technicians had created? Was the cat that watched him even now with a malicious glint in its emerald eyes nothing but gears and metal framework? Or were they not even *that* real, concocted from his memories?

There was only one way to find out.

Connor took a deep breath and moved forward.

"…A mirror's shard and a skin scarred, a potion made for a dear price paid…" The Witch moved slowly, bent over the cauldron, stirring, muttering, stirring, muttering…

And then she looked up at Connor.

He froze, staring back, nerveless, immobilized. There was nothing mechanical about her eyes—hazel green, flecked with red, moist and set in fleshy folds beneath tufted brows. Her mouth twisted up into a grin, and she said, "You haven't taken your pills, have you?"

The absurdity of the question jolted Connor. He looked down, confused—

When he looked back up, the Witch had become Jeff, leaning forward over the kitchen table. His partner, Patrick, sat beside him, chewing a sandwich. The smell of tuna hit Connor, and he saw he held a forgotten half-sandwich in one hand, tuna salad spilling out of the sides onto the plate. "I...what?"

Jeff glanced back at Patrick, who set his sandwich down, concerned. "Connor," Patrick said, "you aren't taking your pills in the morning, are you?" Behind Patrick, Terry stood, arms crossed, frowning.

"Look, the goddamn things make me groggy, okay? Yes, I stopped taking them. What's the big deal?"

"Dad, you can't just go cold turkey off some of these medications. That's why you've been so confused lately."

Connor started to utter a denial, but he couldn't do it—he *had* been confused. He felt like a kid busted for underage drinking.

"Look," Jeff said, his tone conciliatory, "I'll make a deal with you: if you take the pills today, we'll get the doctor on the phone on Monday and see if we can't swap them out for something that'll make you less groggy, how about that?" Terry stood now with the white and tan and yellow pills in a napkin and a glass of water.

With all of their eyes on him, he felt the weight of obligation. Silently, Connor reached out, took the pills and water, and downed the handful in a single gulp. "There," he said, rattling the table as he slammed the empty glass down.

Patrick smiled. "Connor, we're just concerned about you. And you know how much we'd love to see you paint again."

Connor shook his head. "That won't happen. Not without Margie."

Jeff patted his father's hand. "Maybe...just think about it." Jeff glanced at Patrick, and they both rose. "We've got a little bit more work out front, so why don't you rest until we're done."

"Fine."

The two younger men rose and headed back out, and Connor let Terry help him to his feet. "I don't want to go back to the bedroom, Terry. I'll stay out here."

"Okay, Mr. Connor." She led him to his favorite couch, the one surrounded by art he'd done for both George Merry and himself. Once he was comfortable, he found himself staring at an oil painting he'd done for Margie ten years ago, one that showed a group of trick or treaters at a door, surrounded by glowing jack-o'-lanterns and holding up their treat bags and buckets. Margie had loved Halloween and she'd loved that painting.

No, no more. Not without her.

He closed his eyes and slept.

ooooo

It was dusk when he awoke. Jeff and Patrick were standing over him, both covered in dust and paint. "Dad," Jeff was calling softly. "Dad…"

Connor looked up, awakened from a dream that had left him agitated although he couldn't remember what it had been about. "What?"

"The surprise is finished. Come out front."

Connor groaned as he rose from the couch, knees protesting. Shuffling with the cane, he followed them out the front door and down the walk. He saw children running on the sidewalks, shrieking and swinging orange plastic pumpkins, and it took him a moment to remember:

Today was Halloween.

"Don't look back at the garage yet," Patrick said, trying to walk between Connor and the house. Connor saw tree branches and cables and wires, and he had to admit he was curious. Jeff had vanished, but he called out, "Don't turn around until I tell you to!"

Connor waved over his shoulder. "Okay, okay…"

Across the street, other houses were just setting out lit jack-o'-lanterns and turning on lights and fog machines. From somewhere down the block, Connor heard amplified sound effects—shrieks and moans and jangling chains—and he felt the ghost of his Halloween excitement stir. How he'd loved this day as a child—the freedom, the night, the imagined power—and later, as an adult, he'd understood that the holiday spoke to him on some deep, primordial level. It whispered into his ear with a voice as crackling and rough as tree leaves crunched underfoot, *The seasons change, and death happens, and you can't stop it so you might as well celebrate it.* He'd answered that voice with his own creativity and George Merry's urging, and The Enchanted Forest had been the result.

Connor was still gazing out on the street, drinking in the

335

lit pumpkins and costumed revelers, when he heard an electric buzz behind him, and a glow lit the street. "Turn around, Dad," his son called from behind him.

He turned—and was dumbstruck.

The entrance to The Enchanted Forest now covered his driveway. There was the old iron gate set into the stone pillars; there was the winking black cat perched at one side. Where his front lawn usually was, tombstones circled a reasonably believable fake fire; the interior of the garage had been filled with faux trees and lit artfully from overhead to suggest a full moon lighting a receding path.

Jeff had been bent over an extension cord, having plugged in the lights. He approached his father and Patrick now, smiling tentatively. "What do you think?"

Connor asked, "This is what you were working on all day...?"

"Yep." Jeff put an arm around Patrick. "We've been working on parts of it for the last six months. This is the first time we've set it all up. I think it came together pretty well."

Connor listened, and heard the sounds: crickets, owls hooting, wind in leaves. "You even got the audio..."

Jeff answered, "We called your old friends in the Merry Sound Department, and they got us the original tapes."

Connor took a few steps forward, drinking it all in. "Is it all here?"

Patrick cried, "Oh, gods, no!"

Jeff added, "We couldn't afford to do all of it, but...well, follow the path. I think you'll be surprised by what we *did* manage to pull off."

Without another word, Connor moved forward, and fell into The Enchanted Forest.

ooooo

The path moved on past the Witch, and for an instant Connor glimpsed something else behind her—a normal sliding glass door. Some part of his mind recognized his house, realized that the path had actually wound down the side of his home and into his back yard...but this was The Enchanted Forest, *his* world.

After the Witch came the Pumpkin Village. Sure enough, he

turned a corner, and there were dozens of pumpkins all around him, stacked on bales of hay, held under the arms of scarecrows, perched in the crooks of tree branches. He knew this was too small to be the Pumpkin Village from the real Enchanted Forest at Merry Mountain—that had *hundreds* of jack-o'-lanterns, not dozens—but some of the pumpkins were animated, singing in chorus. Connor remembered writing some of those lyrics, and as he listened he began to sing along:

Pumpkins glare in the midnight dark,
Watch out for the branches or they'll leave a mark!
The Halloween moon's full and the trees are stark,
Here in The Enchanted Forest.

The pumpkin nearest to him screwed up its face into a toothy grin and a wink, and Connor didn't care whether it was real or not, in the past or present. If this was all just some episode of withdrawal-induced dementia, at least it had become a happy one.

Then he remembered what came next, and his happiness snuffed out like a tired candle at the end of Halloween night.

The storm.

The Merry Fantaseers (for such had the designers and engineers of Merry Mountain come to be known) had spent years on the storm. They'd perfected ways to project overhead images of rushing clouds and lightning flashes; they'd figured out how to mimic water in trees, and strong winds, and thunderous sounds. The experience had been so realistic that guests had tried to flee into the trees for shelter, and they'd had to create a waist-high fence to keep them confined to the path. Some laughed when they reached the other side, checked themselves over, and realized they were completely dry.

But tonight, Connor knew something was different; he heard the winds ahead, felt an icy chill rushing down the path, and he knew *this* storm wouldn't be so tame. He was seized by an almost irrational fear of facing it. He remembered this wasn't the real Enchanted Forest, but an elaborate Halloween haunt; he was in his own backyard...wasn't he?

"Jeff...Patrick?" he called out, but his voice sounded weak and hoarse, and no one heard. He couldn't see anything beyond the trees and the pumpkins, only the path leading ahead, into the storm.

Fine, Connor thought. He would swallow back his dread, walk through whatever came, illusion or harsh reality. He would reach the other side and this would all be over.

He set off along the trail, leaving the leering pumpkins behind. The temperature dropped, leaving the old man to shiver. He tried to move faster, but the cane was hard to handle on the dirt. The path grew even smaller, the trees pressing closer, and he saw the faces in the trunks, twisted wooden faces, full of scorn and menace. Were some of the faces moving? He wasn't sure, but the idea terrified him.

The path widened and he was in the storm.

Winds buffeted him, forcing him to lean into them. Thunder was deafening, lightning blinding. He heard voices around him, carried on the air currents, screeching and howling; there were hints of spirits in the air, barely-glimpsed shapes tearing along with the wind. The rain seemed quite real, causing the ground to slicken. The cane slid and Connor went down; he caught himself, though, and wound up on all fours.

He gave in at that point. He puts his hands over his ears, squeezed his eyes shut, and screamed.

When he finally ran out of breath, before he could draw in more air to continue screaming, silence descended. Connor moved his hands from his ears, waiting...but the quiet held. He was no longer shivering, the rain had stopped, and when he opened his eyes, he saw something unexpected before him.

There was a small figure now crouched in the center of the opening a few yards away; a boy, maybe eight years old, bent over something, his back to Connor, his hands moving.

Connor's breath caught as he searched his memory: what was this? He couldn't remember it being part of the storm, or any other scene in The Enchanted Forest. At Merry Mountain, the storm had spilled out into the Dance of the Dead, the attraction's grand finale: an open meadow where glowing blue phantoms waltzed to music played by a skeletal band. But this, this kneeling apparition...was it something his son had added? Or was it some bit he'd forgotten, the memory misplaced along with so many others?

Would it be the most frightening thing he'd ever seen? Would it leave him scarred in some way?

He found his cane, painfully got to his feet and inched

forward, cautiously, trying to give the figure as wide a berth as possible, never taking his eyes from it. He heard a small sound—high-pitched, musical—and realized the small figure was humming, something familiar…

It was *Monster Mash*. It'd been Connor's favorite song as a child. He'd had a 45 rpm record of it he'd played every Halloween, while he…

Connor suddenly knew.

He no longer walked with fear, but with burgeoning joy. As he rounded the kneeling boy, he saw what he'd realized would be there: a grinning jack-o'-lantern, its face still only half-finished. The boy had a tiny pocket-knife which he used to saw through the thick orange flesh, up and down as he created the toothy smile. If he saw Connor, he didn't react.

He *was* Connor. Connor stood over him, watching, recalling…

The joy he'd felt every October, when the plans he'd set up all year long came to fruition. Plans for costumes, for pumpkins, for yard decorations. Plans that had given him his first taste of artistic satisfaction, that had paved the way for a life spent pursuing dreams. A successful life, and for the most part a happy life, until…

The boy looked up and he *did* see Connor. He stopped working on the jack-o'-lantern for a moment, screwed his small face into a squint, and said, "You should never have stopped. *She* didn't want you to."

The boy vanished. Connor saw, clearly now, his house behind the single layer of cardboard trees that Jeff and Patrick had set up, the speakers tucked in among the trunks, the floor fans half-hidden by mossy netting. He pushed past the forest, opened the rear sliding doors, went into the house, and looked at the framed paintings on the walls.

My God, I've wasted three years. Margie would've kicked me in the pants.

"Did you like it, Dad?"

Connor looked up to see Jeff and Patrick standing in the front entry way, eyeing him uncertainly.

He gave them back a smile. "I can't believe how much of it I'd forgotten. You did it real justice."

Jeff's face lit up, while Patrick hugged him with one arm.

"Tomorrow," Connor said, "I'm going to have Terry drive me

down to the art store. But tonight…"

Connor marched past them, his gait so strong he barely needed the cane. He picked up a bowl of candy ready for trick or treaters, and marched out the front door. He wasn't sure why he felt so good; maybe his medications had kicked back in, or maybe it was seeing even this reduced version of The Enchanted Forest.

As he made his way down to the beginning of The Enchanted Forest, a black cat ran past his feet. On any other day, Connor might have made a joke about it being bad luck, but tonight it felt like magic, *good* magic.

"Happy Halloween," he called after the cat.

ABOUT THE STORIES

"Pumpkin Rex" – This was written for a wonderful fellow named Peter Schwotzer, who used to review books for the online version of *Famous Monsters*, and who I'm flattered to say was a fan of my work from early on. Peter ran his own website called "Literary Mayhem," for which he occasionally bought fiction from authors he liked. He asked me if I'd consider writing a Halloween story for him, and of course I agreed. At the time (2012), I'd just finished writing *Trick or Treat: A History of Halloween*, and I'd been intrigued by uncovering the popularity of Halloween raves in (of all places!) South Africa, so I decided to write a story about a boy visiting an American version. Raves—with the thumping music and mass of people and various intoxicants—feel ritualistic to me, so I knew the story would have a theme of ritual and transformation. Since the pumpkin has been the holiday's favorite icon for about a century now, the choice of the new Halloween king's identity was obvious.

"The Devil Came to Mamie's on Hallowe'en" – I wrote this story because my partner Ricky had (in 2009) developed an obsession with early female blues singers, so I was surrounded by the music of Ma Rainey, Bessie Smith, Victoria Spivey, and others.

Ricky was also reading a lot about these remarkable women, telling me anecdotes about their struggles, and I was moved by the tremendous amount of obstacles they had to overcome to achieve success (to say nothing of the obstacles they endured even *after* they'd succeeded). I'd been intrigued by the nature of some of the American folklore surrounding Halloween—very different in character from, say, Scottish or Irish, frequently both more macabre (the boiling of the cat, for example) and more humorous (the name "Jacky-ma-Lantern"), and I started to see how these two interests—the great women blues artists and Halloween in the American South—could come together. I added some additional research (what the bordello would have been like), and I was pleased when *Cemetery Dance* purchased the tale. I hope I've done the brilliant women of the blues justice here.

The Samhanach – When I was researching *The Halloween Encyclopedia*, I came across exactly one reference to a Halloween bogie called the Samhanach, in an obscure nineteenth-century folklore book. Here's the complete entry from the Encyclopedia: "A Scottish name for the dreadful bogies that were abroad on Hallowe'en, stealing babies and committing other monstrous crimes." The entry cross-references "bogies," where we read (in part) this description: "Malicious spirits found around British bogs (hence the name), which often take the form of either a demonic ram, a ghostly white cow or horse, or a monstrous hound with glowing eyes." The name quite obviously derives from "Samhain," the name of the Celtic New Year celebration that was Halloween's great-grandma, so "Samhanach" also speaks to ancient pagan practices.

Any horror writer is going to read all that and instantly conjure stories. The name itself is strange and compelling, lending itself immediately to a title. I ran with the idea that this thing would steal babies (or, in the case of my story, a young child who—yes, I know—is technically not a baby), but rather than have my bogie transform into animals, I extended its shapeshifting powers into human form. I had the absurdly ambitious notion of using this piece to explore the entire history of Halloween, so I added the family curse and gave the protagonist Scottish ancestry. When I started plotting out *The Samhanach*, I wasn't sure whether it would be a short story, a novella, or a novel, but I wasn't worried—I knew it would find its own length.

I tried to incorporate as many Halloween traditions, both recent and not-recent, as I could, which is why the story is packed with trick or treating, parties, pumpkin carving, and pranks. I also wanted the climax to take place in what I think of as the deep hole of human consciousness that these dark legends spring from. When Merran, the heroine, crosses the border at the conclusion, is she going into the Celts' "Otherworld," which they believed could be entered on Samhain, or is she descending into her own subconscious? I'm fine with whatever you choose to make the story.

Oh, and I'm sorry, but no—I *don't* know how to pronounce "Samhanach."

"Finding Ulalume" – When Nancy Kilpatrick invited me to submit to a Poe-themed anthology (*nEvermore!: Tales of Murder, Mystery, and the Macabre*) she was co-editing with Caro Soles, the choice of material was easy: Poe's poem "Ulalume" is both wonderfully macabre (with lines repeatedly referencing "the ghoul-haunted woodland of Weir") and the only time horror's greatest practitioner offers up what might be a reference to Halloween (he refers to October and "this night of all nights in the year"). As with "Tam Lin," I thought it would be an interesting challenge to transcribe the poem's events to modern times. Since the poem references demons, ghouls, and the tomb of a dead lover, I chose to bring the horror into the 21st-century with more literal depictions of ghouls and a haunted tomb. I also wanted to capture a bit of Poe's style without creating a total pastiche, so I hope in the end this is recognizably a Lisa Morton story.

"Alive-Oh" – This one was originally written for an anthology themed around mutations (although it ended up making its debut in Jeani Rector's marvelous online magazine *The Horror Zine*). I wanted to see if I could run with the mutation theme in a Halloween setting, and apparently I was still stuck on haunted attractions (!), so this story came out of that strange confluence. It was particularly inspired by some blog post I'd read at a haunted attractions website (sorry, I've forgotten which one) about how the author did road trips every Halloween season to visit as many haunted attractions as he could. This same author seemed to be somewhat blasé about most of what he saw, so I started thinking about what it would take to shake up a guy like this.

Summer's End – This novella was done mainly because I wanted to work with editor Norman Rubenstein, whose work I had long admired (and it turned out he felt the same way about me). When he took on an editorial gig at JournalStone and suggested we do a novella together, I leapt at the chance. I had just read an article about a previously-unknown Celtic history that had been found in a tomb, and I was quite taken with the story. What if that history was about Samhain (which we really know very little about)? What if they called in a contemporary Halloween history expert who ended up seeing this work and realizing that it up-ended everything we think we know about Samhain and Druidic practices?

Originally I was going to write this from the viewpoint of a fictitious Halloween expert; because I wanted it to be someone who had studied this for years, the expert would be middle-aged. Because I like female protagonists (who I believe are under-represented in horror fiction), it would be a woman...you probably see by now where I'm going with this. Yes, at some point I realized, *Wait—this is me.* I started imagining writing this piece with myself as the protagonist, and because that thought made me deeply uncomfortable (how much of myself was I willing to expose? Would this seem wildly self-indulgent? Was it just crazy?), I knew I had to do it. I tried to make it as honest a portrayal of me as possible, right down to using my real-life partner, my apartment, my cat, and my own works as a Halloween historian, but I still thought of this Lisa Morton first and foremost as a character in a story, so inevitably there are aspects of her that are most definitely not me.

One amusing anecdote about the editing process involved the scene in which the story's Lisa is possessed by an ancient Celtic deity. The novella is written in first person point-of-view, so this had to be written in the same voice but filtered through the experience of divine possession. I wanted to get a swirling, trance-like quality to the writing, so I wrote a lengthy passage with no punctuation. Needless to say, this drove poor Norman nuts. I got phone calls and e-mails that would beg for things like, "Just let me put one period here!" And I'd say no. In the end, Norman let it stand (although I think I did compromise a little by ending the non-punctuation section a little sooner than in my first draft).

I have sort of mixed feelings about this one now. It got some very generous blurbs from authors I had tremendous admiration for (Gary A. Braunbeck and Ray Garton), and it garnered me my first stand-alone review from *Publishers' Weekly* (my short stories had been mentioned a number of times in their reviews of anthologies), but it was a mixed review that stung a little. I now think of *Summer's End* as "the crazy book."

"Tam Lane" – When Jonathan Maberry asked me if I'd like to submit a story to his forthcoming anthology *Out of Tune*—an anthology in which each story would relate to a classic ballad—I went straight to "Tam Lane." "Tam Lane" (usually spelled "Tam Lin," and I'm no longer sure why I went with this variant spelling) is *the* Halloween ballad, with versions being recorded as early as 1729, although the ballad probably predates that by many centuries. It's a romantic and spooky long poem about a human girl, Janet, who falls in love with the young hero, a handsome nobleman kidnapped by the Fairy Queen. After Janet becomes pregnant with Tam's baby, she vows to rescue him from the fairies, a feat that can only be accomplished on Halloween night.

I'm not the first to modernize "Tam Lin," certainly (there's even a 1971 film that sets the story in the Swinging Sixties), but I was curious to know if I could make the tale work in a contemporary Los Angeles setting. The building that most of the story occurs in is the old Herald-Examiner building in downtown L.A., designed by Julia Morgan, the same architect who did Hearst Castle. I once wrote an awful movie that was shot there (it's a frequent filming location), and I got to spend the day roaming the huge and largely-unused building. The third and fourth floors were mostly empty; even though the rooms there had long ago been stripped of their décor and furnishings, the sense of faded opulence was still palpable. I loved the dust motes in the air, the strange things left in some of the offices (a single chair in one, a pile of papers in another). It wasn't hard to imagine this place being haunted by spectacular ghosts, so when it came time to write my modern "Tam Lin," it was easy to set it in Morgan's still-spectacular structure.

"The Halloween Collector" – This story was written for a site called halloweenforevermore.com that sells some lovely modern Halloween collectibles (like wax warmers). In case you didn't know, Halloween collectibles are incredibly hot nowadays, with both vintage and contemporary items much in demand by collectors (myself, I collect vintage Halloween postcards—in part because they make such excellent illustrations for non-fiction Halloween books!—and the metal and wood noisemakers that were once an integral part of any trick or treater's arsenal). I thought it would be fun to write something about Halloween collectors, hence this short-short.

The Devil's Birthday – This novella turned out to be one of the fastest things I've ever written. In 2014, Roy Robbins was in the process of (sadly) shutting down his Bad Moon Books press, but he decided he'd wanted to put out one last Halloween novella, so he asked me to write it just weeks before it would have to go to press. Because Roy is both a good friend and a man I credit with giving my career a huge boost (he published my first novella, *The Lucid Dreaming*, which went on to win a Bram Stoker Award and made it much easier for me to sell fiction), I said yes.

I wanted to make this novella a special gift for Roy, who was giving up publishing to become a pastor. Roy and I have had some interesting conversations about his religious convictions, and I wanted to honor that despite being a lifelong non-believer myself. I also wanted to deal with the way Christians often (mistakenly) dismiss the holiday as being somehow diabolical, calling it "The Devil's Birthday" (I discuss this mistake at length in *Trick or Treat: A History of Halloween*, but suffice to say that it's all based on the terrible error of a dilettante eighteenth-century historian).

Years ago I wrote a horror screenplay about fallen angels, so—with not much time to spare, after all—I cribbed from the research I'd done for that script, pulling out my fallen angel folklore. Sathariel is indeed one of the 200 fallen angels named in *The Book of Enoch* (if you ever want to read something genuinely insane, check that thing out), although the angels are typically described as either male or androgynous. I thought Roy would like a story about a fallen angel trying to redeem herself in God's eyes, but I also made her someone who likes sensual pleasures and struggles to find balance between her quest for redemption and her enjoyment of fleshly ways. While writing this, I was also aware that it could be read as a paranormal romance—something I've never been at all interested in writing—but I don't care how someone categorizes my work as long as they enjoy it.

"The Legend of Halloween Jack" – When my friends at Cemetery Dance asked me if I'd like to write something for a new line of e-book shorts they were doing, I decided to create my own version of the legendary trickster Jack, who loaned his name to the Halloween jack-o'-lantern.

New Orleans is one of my favorite cities, and somehow the rich culture and history of Nola aligned perfectly with the American version of Jack's story that I wanted to tell.

Amusingly, last year I co-edited (with Ellen Datlow) an anthology of Halloween stories called *Haunted Nights*, and I'd say that re-tellings of Jack's story may have been the most common theme among submissions we received. We ended up taking two "Jack" stories ("Wick's End" by Joanna Parypinski and "Jack" by Pat Cadigan) for that book, so if you like Jack stories (and who doesn't?), I humbly suggest checking out those two very fine pieces.

"Sexy Pirate Girl" – This was written for *October Dreams 2*, a sequel to Cemetery Dance's seminal 2000 Halloween anthology. When I was invited into the book, I had just finished giving a round of interviews about the popularity of "sexy" costumes at Halloween. They'd been much in the news recently (in 2013, Walmart had marketed a black lace "Naughty Leopard" costume to toddlers—yes, *toddlers*—but had caved to consumer outrage and pulled it), and as a Halloween expert I was fielding multiple requests to comment. I'm frankly not sure how I feel about the overall "sexy" costume thing—on the one hand I think women should be free to express their sexuality in a playful way, but on the other hand I don't think it's good that it's nearly impossible now to buy a woman's Halloween costume that *isn't* "sexy." So, I knew I wanted to write something about "sexy" Halloween costumes, and about the way these things are increasingly marketed to consumers who may be too young to wear them, and dammit, I wanted the story to be *angry*. "Sexy Pirate Girl" was the result.

Hell Manor – After doing *The Samhanach* with Roy Robbins and his press, Bad Moon Books, Roy asked if I'd like to do another Halloween novella for him. *The Samhanach* had been a great experience all 'round, so I immediately agreed. I knew I wanted to write about the biggest of the modern Halloween traditions—the haunted attraction—but I wanted to avoid as much as possible the idea that the haunted house itself was real, since I'd read so many stories around that theme that it had almost become cliché (even by 2012). I decided that instead my haunted attraction would have otherworldly invaders whose malicious pranks would contrast with the harmless illusions presented in the haunted house.

Okay, here's a confession: I would *love* to design a haunted attraction (big surprise, right?). I've studied them at length for my various books, I've talked to maze designers and actors who have performed in them and fans who go to dozens of them every year, and I'm convinced I could design a pretty cool one. One of the things I would employ that I don't see done often in these places is the use of stage magic or sleight-of-hand. When I was in my teens I was a junior magician who did a lot of birthday parties and competitions (I was, frankly, only so-so), so I have some rudimentary knowledge of magic and know that there are some really nice tricks that could easily be incorporated into haunted attractions. That's why my hero, Jack, is also incorporating magic into his haunted attractions.

Hell Manor also should be considered a companion to *The Samhanach*, since it concludes with Jack taking up residence in the same Otherworld that Merran entered in the earlier piece.

"The Maze" – In 2015 I was approached by a lovely fellow named Mark Parker; Mark was putting together a Halloween-themed anthology and asked me if I might submit something. I don't mind admitting that by this point I was starting to feel like I was running out of topics for Halloween fiction! I'd covered Samhain, trick or treat, haunted attractions, raves, Jack-o'-the-Lantern, and even the "sexy" costume craze. Because I'm not interested in repeating myself, I had to ask: what was left?

I'd been plotting a new Halloween novella for a while—something that would extend the holiday into a post-apocalyptic setting—and I saw an opportunity to make "The Maze" a prequel to this longer work. I realized I hadn't written about corn mazes yet, which have been around Halloween for decades but have only recently burgeoned in popularity with the rise of "agri-tainment," or agriculturally-themed entertainment for families (yes, this is really a thing, including both corn mazes and pumpkin patches). Corn mazes always feel somehow mystical to me, so I decided to use one as the device that begins the supernatural apocalypse I'd tackle later in the novella.

The novella, by the way, still has yet to be written.

"The Enchanted Forest" – When Mark Parker called again to solicit a story for *Dark Hallows II*, I said yes because I'd enjoyed working with him on the first book, and then realized I had no idea what to write about. After cogitating for a while, I came up with the idea of writing something loosely based on the great grand-ghost of all Halloween haunted houses: Disneyland's Haunted Mansion. I'd once had the opportunity to spend time with the legendary Disney Imagineer Marc Davis, who'd been one of the two principal designers of the Haunted Mansion, and I wanted to weave elements of him in with what I've dealt with at home for the last few years—my mother's progressive dementia. I'd been with my mother as she'd endured some especially terrifying bouts of hallucinatory dementia (believing, for example, that there were people living in the front entryway closet of the house we share), and I began to imagine that confusion combined with the extraordinary gifts of a design genius like Marc Davis. "The Enchanted Forest" is the result.

By the way, the reason I made my amusement park attraction a walk-through display is a little tip of the hat to the history of the Haunted Mansion, which was originally designed as a walk-through attraction.

Lisa Morton is a screenwriter, author of non-fiction books, award-winning prose writer, and Halloween expert whose work was described by the American Library Association's Readers' Advisory Guide to Horror as "consistently dark, unsettling, and frightening." Her work—which includes three nonfiction books on Halloween, four novels, and more than 130 short stories—has been translated into eight languages and received six Bram Stoker Awards®, a Black Quill Award, and the Halloween Book Festival Grand Prize. She co-edited (with Ellen Datlow) the anthology *Haunted Nights*, which received a starred review in Publishers Weekly; other recent releases include *Ghosts: A Haunted History* and *Cemetery Dance Select: Lisa Morton*. Lisa lives in the San Fernando Valley and online at www.lisamorton.com.